AS
LONG
AS THE
LEMON TREES
GROW

AS
LONG
AS THE
LEMON TREES
GROW

ZOULFA KATOUH

LITTLE, BROWN AND COMPANY
New York   Boston

Little, Brown and Company
Hachette Book Group
1290 Avenue of the Americas, New York, NY 10104
Visit us at LBYR.com

First Edition: September 2022

Little, Brown and Company is a division of Hachette Book Group, Inc. The Little, Brown name and logo are trademarks of Hachette Book Group, Inc.

The publisher is not responsible for websites (or their content) that are not owned by the publisher.

Library of Congress Cataloging-in-Publication Data
Names: Katouh, Zoulfa, author.
Title: As long as the lemon trees grow / Zoulfa Katouh.
Description: First edition. | New York ; Boston : Little, Brown and Company, 2022. | Audience: Ages 14 & up. | Summary: Eighteen-year-old Salama Kassab, a pharmacy student volunteering at the hospital in Homs, is desperate to find passage on a refugee boat for herself and her pregnant best friend, but first she must learn to see the events around her for what they are—not a war, but a revolution.
Identifiers: LCCN 2021051288 | ISBN 9780316351379 (hardcover) | ISBN 9780316351614 (ebook)
Subjects: CYAC: Fear—Fiction. | Survival—Fiction. | Hospitals— Fiction. | Syria—History—Civil War, 2011—Fiction. | LCGFT: Novels.
Classification: LCC PZ7.1.K3727 As 2022 | DDC [Fic]—dc23
LC record available at https://lccn.loc.gov/2021051288

ISBNs: 978-0-316-35137-9 (hardcover), 978-0-316-35161-4 (ebook)

Printed in the United States of America

LSC-C

Printing 1, 2022

*To Hayao Miyazaki, who founded
my imagination*

*To Ali Al-Tantawi, who
revolutionized my imagination*

*And to all the Syrians who loved, lost,
lived, and died for Syria.
We will come back home one day.*

كُلُّ لَيْمونَةٍ سَتُنْجِبُ طِفْلاً   وَمُحالٌ أَنْ يَنْتَهِيَ الْلَيْمونُ

نِزار قَبَّاني

Every lemon will bring forth a child and
the lemons will never die out

—Nizar Qabbani

THREE SHRIVELED LEMONS AND A PLASTIC BAG OF pita bread that's more dry than moldy sit next to one another.

That's all this supermarket has to offer.

I stare with tired eyes before picking them up, my bones aching with every movement. I stroll around the dusty, empty aisles once more, hoping maybe I missed something. But all I'm met with is a strong sense of nostalgia. The days when my brother and I would rush into this supermarket after school and fill our arms with bags of chips and gummy bears. This makes me think of Mama and the way she would shake her head, trying not to smile at her red-faced, starry-eyed children trying their best to hide the spoils of war in their backpacks. She'd brush our hair—

I shake my head.

Stop.

When the aisles prove to be truly empty, I trudge to the counter to pay for the lemons and bread with Baba's savings.

From whatever he was able to withdraw before that fateful day. The owner, a bald old man in his sixties, gives me a sympathetic smile before returning my change.

Outside the supermarket a desolate picture greets me. I don't recoil, used to the horror, but it amplifies the anguish in my heart.

Cracked road, the asphalt reduced to rubble. Gray buildings hollowed and decaying as the elements try to finish what the military's bombs started. Utter and absolute destruction.

The sun has been slowly melting away the remains of winter, but the cold is still here. Spring, the symbol of new life, does not extend to worn-out Syria. Least of all my city, Homs. Misery reigns strong in the dead, heavy branches and rubble, thwarted only by the hope in people's hearts.

The sun hangs low in the sky, beginning the process of bidding us farewell, the colors slowly changing from orange to a heavy blue.

I murmur, "Daisies. Daisies. Daisies. Sweet-smelling daisies."

Several men stand outside the supermarket, their faces gaunt and marked with malnourishment but their eyes sparkling with light. When I pass by, I hear bits of their conversation, but I don't linger. I know what they're talking about. It's what everyone has been talking about for the past nine months.

I walk quickly, not wanting to listen. I know that the military siege inflicted on us is a death sentence. That our food supplies are diminishing and we're starving. I know the hospital is about to reach a point any day now at which medications will become a myth. I know this because I performed surgeries without anesthesia today: People are dying from hemorrhages and infections and there's no way for me to help them. And I know we'll all succumb to a fate worse than death if the Free Syrian Army isn't able to stop the military's advances on Old Homs.

As I head home, the breeze turns cold and I pull my hijab tight around my neck. I'm acutely aware of the dried spots of blood that have managed to creep under my lab coat's sleeves. For every life I can't save during my shift, one more drop of blood becomes a part of me. No matter how many times I wash my hands, our martyrs' blood seeps beneath my skin, into my cells. By now it's probably encoded in my DNA.

And today, the echo of the oscillating saw from the amputation Dr. Ziad made me stand in for is stuck in my mind on a loop.

For seventeen years, Homs raised me and cultivated my dreams: Graduate from university with a high GPA, secure a great position at the Zaytouna Hospital as their pharmacist, and finally be able to travel outside of Syria and see the world.

But only one of those dreams has come true. And not in the way I thought it would.

A year ago, after the Arab Spring sparked across the region, Syria grabbed the hope awakening in the masses and called for freedom. The dictatorship responded by unleashing hell.

With the military deliberately targeting doctors, they became as scarce as laughter. But even without doctors, the bombs didn't stop, and with the Zaytouna Hospital standing on its last legs, they needed every helping hand they could get. Even the custodial staff were promoted to nurses. Having spent one year at pharmacy school, I was the equivalent of a seasoned doctor, and after their last pharmacist was buried under the rubble of his home, there was no other choice.

It didn't matter that I was eighteen years old. It didn't matter that my medical experience was confined to the words in my textbooks. All of that was remedied as the first body was laid out before me to be stitched up. Death is an excellent teacher.

In the last six months, I have participated in more surgeries than I can count and closed more eyes than I ever thought I would.

This *wasn't* supposed to be my life.

The rest of the way back home reminds me of the black-and-white pictures my history textbooks showed of Germany and London after World War II. Flattened homes spilling their interior wood and concrete like a perforated intestine. The smell of trees burned to ash.

The cold air bites through my lab coat's worn-out material, and the harsh touch of it makes me shiver. I murmur, "Feverfew. They look like daisies. Treats fevers and arthritis. Feverfew. Feverfew. Feverfew."

I finally catch sight of my home and my chest expands. It's not the one I once shared with my family; it's the one Layla gave me after a bomb fell on my own. Without her, I'd be out on the streets.

Layla's place—our place, I guess—is a one-story house stacked right beside others just like it. All of them bearing bullet holes that decorate the walls like deadly art. All of them quiet, sad, and lonely. Our neighborhood is one of the last where homes are still mostly intact. In other neighborhoods, people sleep under broken roofs or on the streets.

The lock is rusty and creaks when I twist the key and call out, "I'm home!"

"In here!" Layla calls back.

We came into this world together when our mothers shared the same hospital room. She's my best friend, my rock, and because she fell in love with my brother, Hamza, my sister-in-law.

And now, with everything that's happened, my responsibility and the only family I have left in the world.

When Layla first saw this house, she was immediately infatuated with its quaint aesthetic, so Hamza bought it for her on the spot. Two bedrooms were perfect for a newlywed couple to make their own. She painted branches of green vines from the bottom of one of the walls all the way to the top, etched purple lavender blossoms on another, and covered the floors in thick Arabian rugs I had helped her buy from Souq Al-Hamidiyah. She painted the kitchen white to contrast with shelves made from walnut wood, which she filled with different assortments of mugs she designed. The kitchen overlooks the living room, where, back in the day, her art supplies cluttered every nook and cranny. Papers smudged by her colored fingertips strewn across the floor, paint from her paintbox dripping from brushes. Many times I would come over only to find her sprawled under her easel, auburn hair fanned out and staring at the ceiling, mouthing lyrics to a popular old Arabic song.

The house was the embodiment of Layla's soul.

But it's not that anymore. Layla's home has lost its spark, the colors completely faded, leaving a sunken gray shade in their wake. It's a husk of a home.

I make my way to the kitchen to find her lying back on the daisy-printed couch in the living room and put the bag of pita bread on the counter. As soon as I see her, my exhaustion disappears. "I'm heating up the soup. Do you want some?"

"No, I'm good," she answers. Her voice, unlike mine, is strong with the promise of life. It's a warm blanket cocooning me in sweet memories. "How did the boat thing go?"

Crap. I pretend to busy myself with pouring the watered-down lentil soup into the saucepan and lighting the ignition needle on the portable gas stove. "You sure you don't want some?"

Layla sits up, her seven-months-pregnant belly stretching the navy-blue dress she's wearing. "Tell me how it went, Salama."

I glue my eyes to the brown soup, listening to the hissing flames. Since not long after I moved in, Layla has been nagging me to talk to Am at the hospital. She's heard the stories of Syrians finding safety in Germany. So have I. Some of my own patients have been able to secure passage across the Mediterranean Sea via Am. How he finds the boats I have no idea. But with money, anything is possible.

"Salama."

I sigh, sticking a finger in the soup and finding it just about warm. But my poor stomach rumbles, not caring if it's truly hot, so I remove it from the stove and sit beside her on the couch.

Layla looks at me patiently, her eyebrows raised. Her ocean-blue eyes are impossibly huge, nearly taking over her face. She's always looked like autumn incarnate, with her golden-red palette of auburn hair, scattered freckles, and pale complexion. Even now, with all the pain, she still looks magical. But I see the way her elbows stick out oddly and how her once-full cheeks have narrowed.

"I didn't ask him," I finally say, eating a spoonful of soup and bracing myself for her groan.

And she delivers. "Why? We have some money—"

"Yeah, money we need to survive when we get there. We don't know how much he'll ask for, and besides, the stories . . ."

She shakes her head, strands of hair falling over her cheek. "Okay, yes. Some people aren't . . . reaching land, but there are more who are! Salama, we *need* to make a decision. We need to leave! You know, before I start breastfeeding."

She isn't finished, her breaths becoming labored. "And don't you *dare* suggest I go without you! Either you and I get on a boat together or neither of us does. I won't be in God knows where, scared out of my mind and alone, not knowing if you're dead or alive. There's no way in *hell* that's happening! And we can't walk to Turkey—you told me that yourself." She points at her swollen stomach. "Not to mention, with border guards and snipers scattered all over like ants, we'd be shot as soon as we stepped out of the Free Syrian Army's area. We have *one* option. How many times do I have to repeat this?"

I cough. The soup slides thickly down my throat, landing like stones in my stomach. She's right. She's in her third trimester; neither she nor I can walk four hundred miles to safety, dodging death the whole way.

I set the saucepan on the pine coffee table in front of us and stare at my hands. The crisscross slashes of scars covering them are the marks death left when he tried to take my life. Some are faint, silvery, while a few are more ragged, the new flesh still looking raw despite the fact that they've healed. They're a reminder to work faster, to push through the exhaustion and save one more life.

I move to pull my sleeves over them, but Layla's hand covers one of mine gently and I look up at her. "I know why you're not asking him, and it's not the money."

My hand twitches under hers.

Hamza's voice whispers in my mind, tinged with worry. *Salama, promise me. Promise.*

I shake my head, trying to dissolve his voice, and take a deep breath. "Layla, I'm the only pharmacist left in three neighborhoods. If I leave, who will help them? The crying children. The sniper victims. The wounded men."

She clutches her dress tightly. "I know. But I'm *not* sacrificing you."

I open my mouth to say something but stop when she winces, squeezing her eyes shut.

"Is the baby kicking?" I immediately ask, inching closer. Even though I try not to let the worry escape, it does. With the siege, prenatal vitamins are scarce and checkups are limited.

"A bit," she admits.

"Does it hurt?"

"No. Just uncomfortable."

"Is there anything I can do?"

She shakes her head. "I'm fine."

"Okay, I can hear you lying a mile away. Turn around," I say, and she laughs before doing so.

I work through the stress knots in her shoulders until I feel the tension draining away from her. She's barely got any fat under her skin, and every time my fingers connect with her acromion and scapula, I shudder. This . . . this is wrong. She *shouldn't* be here.

"You can stop now," Layla says after a few minutes. She flashes me a grateful smile. "Thank you."

I try to return it. "It's the pharmacist in me, you know. The need to take care of you is in my bones."

"I know."

I bend down and put my hands on her stomach, feeling the baby push back a bit.

"I love you, baby, but you have to stop hurting your mama. She needs to sleep," I coo.

Layla's smile deepens and she pats my cheek. "You're too adorable for your own good, Salama. One of these days someone will snatch you up and take you far away from me."

"*Marriage?* In this economy?" I say and snort, thinking of the last time Mama told me we were having an auntie and her son over for coffee. Funny enough, they never made it. The uprising happened that same day. But I remember being giddy about that visit. At the prospect of falling in love. Looking back now, it feels as if I'm watching a different girl, one who wears my face and speaks with my voice.

Layla's brows furrow. "It could happen. Don't be so pessimistic."

I laugh at her affronted expression. "Whatever you want."

That part of Layla hasn't changed. Back then, when I called her to tell her about the visit, she was at my doorstep within fifteen minutes, sporting a huge bag filled with clothes and makeup and squealing her head off.

"You're wearing this!" she had announced after pulling me to my room, rolling out her azure-blue kaftan. It was a rich fabric that glided smoothly over my arms. The hemline was stitched in gold, as was the belt at the waist, where it flowed from the sides like a waterfall. The color reminded me of the sea made from rain in Spirited Away. *Magical, that is.*

"Pair that up with a blue eyeliner, and you'll have him begging you to see him again." She winked and I chuckled. "You look absolutely gorgeous in blue eyeliner!"

"Oh, I know that." I waggled my eyebrows. "Perks of being brown."

"Whereas I look like a bruised corpse!" She wiped imaginary tears from her eyes, her wedding ring sparkling.

"Stop being dramatic, Layla," I laughed.

Her smile turned devilish; her blue eyes glowed. "You're right. Hamza likes it. A lot."

I immediately clamped my hands over my ears. "Ew, no! I don't need to know anything about that."

Guffawing, she pulled at my arms, trying to make me more uncomfortable, but she couldn't string two words together coherently. Not with my mortified expression making her fall into a fit of giggles.

The sound of Layla sighing snaps me out of my daydream.

"Life is more than just survival, Salama," she says.

"I know that," I reply. Our teasing mood has vanished.

She gives me a pointed look. "Do you really? Because I see the way you act. You're just focusing on the hospital, on working, on me. But you're not *actually* living. You're not thinking about why this revolution is happening. It's as if you don't *want* to think about it at all." She pauses, holding my stare, and my mouth dries. "It's as if you don't care, Salama. But I know you do. You know this revolution is about getting our lives back. It's not about survival. It's about us fighting. If you can't fight here, you won't anywhere else. Not even if you changed your mind and we made it to Germany."

I stand and gesture at the forlorn, peeling paint on the walls. At nothing. "Fight *what*? We'll be lucky if the worst that happens to us here is death, and you know that. Either we'll get arrested by the military or a bomb will kill us. There's nothing to fight for because we *can't* fight. No one's helping us! I volunteer at the hospital because I can't *stand* seeing people die. But that's *it*."

Layla looks at me but there's no annoyance in her eyes. Only compassion. "We fight while we're still here, Salama, because this is our country. This is the land of your father, and his father before him. Your history is embedded in this soil. No country in the world will love you as yours does."

Tears sting my eyes. Her words echo from the history books we read at school. Love for our country is in our bone marrow. It's in our national anthem, which we sang every morning from our first day in school. The words were just words then. But now, after all of this, they have become our reality.

Our spirits are defiant, and our history is glorious.

And our martyrs' souls are formidable guardians.

I avoid Layla's gaze. I don't want a guilt trip. I've had enough of that already.

"I've lost enough in this war," I say bitterly.

Her voice is firm. "It's not a war, Salama. It's a revolution."

"Whatever."

And with that, I walk back to my bedroom, closing the door behind me so I can breathe. All I care about—all I have left in the world—is Layla and the hospital. I'm not a monster. There are people suffering and I *can* help. It's the reason I wanted to be a pharmacist. But I refuse to think about *why* they end up in the hospital. Why all of this is happening. The *why* took away Mama. I remember her fingers, cold against mine. It took Baba and Hamza to God knows where. I don't want to dwell on the past. I don't want to cry about how I'm going to end my teen years with nothing more than lost hope and nightmare-filled sleep. I want to survive.

I want my family. I just want my family back.

Even *if* what Layla says is the truth.

I change into the only pajamas I have left. A black cotton sweater and pants. Decent enough if I ever need to make an escape into the night. In the bathroom, I ignore my wasted reflection and dry brown hair falling past my shoulders and open the water tap out of habit. Nothing. The neighborhood hasn't had water or electricity in weeks. It used to come in bursts but has stopped altogether with the siege. Luckily it rained last week, so Layla and I put out buckets to collect the water. I use a small handful for ablution and pray.

The sun's feeble rays have vanished from my room's scratched floorboards, and the dark cloak of the night takes over Homs. My teeth chatter for a bit with anticipation before I clamp my lips shut, swallowing thickly. Whatever control I exude during the day falters when the sun sets.

I sit on my bed, close my eyes, and take deep breaths. I need to clear my mind. I need to focus on something other than the fear and pain that have taken root in my soul.

"Sweet alyssum. Sweet as its name," I murmur, praying for my nerves not to fail me. "White petals. Used for pain relief. Also for colds, abdominal cramps, and coughs. Sweet. *Sweet.*"

It works. My lungs begin distributing the oxygen evenly to my blood, and I open my eyes and watch the thicket of gray clouds outside my window. The glass is chipped at the sides from when Layla's home took the impact of a nearby bomb, and the frame is splintered. When I moved in, I had to wash blood from the pane.

Despite the window being locked, a chill sweeps the room, and I shiver, knowing what's about to happen. The horror I see isn't just confined to the hospital. My terror has mutated in my mind, bestowed with a life and a voice that never fail to show up each night.

"How long are you going to sit there without talking to me?" The deep voice comes from beside the windowsill, sending gooseflesh all over my neck.

His voice reminds me of the freezing water I splash over myself when I come home drenched in the martyrs' blood. It's stones weighing on my chest, sinking me to the earth below. It's heavy as a humid day and deafening as the bombs the military throws on us. It's what our hospital is built on, and the wordless sounds we make.

I turn toward him slowly. "What do you want now?"

Khawf looks at me. His suit is crisp and clean. It troubles me, though, the specks of red lining his shoulders. They've been there since we met, and I still haven't gotten used to them. But I don't like looking at his eyes either—icy blue. With his midnight-black hair, he doesn't look human, which I suppose is the point. He looks as close to human as he can try to be.

"You know what I want," his voice ripples, and I shiver.

2

I LOST EVERYTHING LAST JULY.

All in the span of one week.

Back then I lay on a hospital bed, silent tears stinging the cuts on my face, my left thigh aching from the fall, and my bruised ribs protesting painfully every time I breathed. My hands were wrapped in such heavy gauze, they looked like mittens. Shrapnel had dug holes into my hands; the blood burst out like a fountain. But all of that was manageable.

The only serious injury was at the back of my head. The force of the explosion had me flying back, and concrete met the base of my skull, marking me for life. Dr. Ziad stitched me up. It was the first time I met him. He told me I was lucky to escape with only a scar. I think he was trying to take my mind off the fact that Mama hadn't been as lucky. That the bomb snatched her away from me and I'd never be able to hug her again.

Later that day, when Khawf appeared and told me his name, it took a bit for me to realize I was the only one seeing him. At first I thought the drugs were giving me visions—that he would disappear when the morphine did. But he stayed by my side, whispering horrible things while I cried for Mama. Even when the pain subsided, and my ribs healed, and my hands scarred, he didn't leave. And once that conviction settled in, panic followed soon after.

He was a hallucination who had come to stay. One who, every night for the past seven months, has cruelly plucked on my fears, breathing life into them.

There is no other explanation. Boiling him down to scientific facts is the only way I'm able to face him.

"Whatever makes you feel better." He smiles wickedly.

I rub the scar at the back of my head, feeling the callous ridges against my fingers. "Daisies," I whisper. "Daisies, daisies."

Khawf brushes his hair out of his eyes and takes a pack of cigarettes out of his breast pocket. The carton is red, always the same shade as the spots on his shoulders. He plucks one long tube and presses it between his lips before lighting it. The nub blazes, eating away at the edges, and he takes a long drag.

"I want to know why you didn't talk to Am," he says. "Didn't you promise yesterday you would? Like you've been promising me every night?" His voice is low, but there's no mistaking the threat poisoning each word.

That's how it started with him: a snide remark here and there, nudging my thoughts toward leaving Syria, until one day he decided I should ask Am for a boat. And he hasn't stopped demanding I do so. Sometimes I wonder how my brain could conjure someone like him.

A drop of cold sweat trickles down my neck. "Yes," I manage to answer.

He taps the cigarette and ash falls to the floor, disappearing just as it should hit the ground. "What happened?"

A five-year-old girl with curly brown hair died from a sniper shot to the heart while I saved her older brother from sepsis. I am *needed*. "I—I couldn't."

His eyes narrow. "You couldn't," he repeats dryly. "So I take it you want to be crushed under this house. Alive and broken and bleeding. No one coming to save you because how could they? Muscles as atrophied by malnourishment as yours are can barely lift bodies, let alone concrete. Or maybe you want to be arrested. Taken to where your Baba and Hamza are. Raped and tortured for answers you don't have. Have the military dangle death as a reward and not a punishment. Is this what you want, Salama?"

My bones shiver. "No."

He blows out one last trail of smoke before grinding the cigarette under the heel of his oxford shoe. Then he crosses the threshold and stands in front of me. I raise my head to look at him. His eyes are as cold as the Orontes River in December.

"Then *couldn't* isn't going to cut it," he says. "You promised you would ask Am for a boat today. And three times he passed by and you *didn't*." His lips pull into a thin line, a muscle working in his jaw. "Or do you want me to go back on my deal?"

"No!" I shout. *"No."*

One snap of his fingers and he could completely alter my reality, unleashing hallucination upon hallucination, showing everyone that the exterior I've put up is nothing more than brittle twigs against a strong wind. Dr. Ziad wouldn't let me work at the hospital anymore. Not when I could be a danger to the patients. I need the hospital. I need it to forget my pain. To keep my hands busy so my mind doesn't scream itself hoarse. *To save lives.*

Worse, I'd be piling more worries and anxieties on Layla, affecting her health and the baby's. *No.* I'll endure it all for her. I'll drown in my tears and offer my soul to him if I can keep Layla safe in the knowledge I'm all right.

And so, Khawf has promised to keep to himself during the day and confine the terrors he shows me to the night. Far away from anyone else's eyes.

An unkind smile tilts his lips upward. "This is your last chance, Salama, and I swear to you, if you don't ask him tomorrow, I will tear your world apart."

Anger awakens between the heartbeats of fear. My subconscious may have me under its thumb, but it's *my* subconscious.

"It's not that easy, Khawf," I hiss, shaking away the look on the boy's face when he held his little sister in his arms, her body small. So *small.* "Am might not have a boat. And even if he does, the price will be so high we won't be able to pay it. So then the *only* way out would be to walk to Turkey. Making us a perfect target for the military. That is, *if* Layla survives the walking!"

His eyebrows quirk up in amusement. "Why are you choosing to ignore the promise you made to Hamza about getting Layla out? Your conflicted feelings about the hospital are causing chaos in your heart. Point is, you made promises and you're backing out. All of this babbling is nothing more than excuses to keep your guilt at bay. What price wouldn't you pay for Layla's safety?"

I look away and dig my hands into my pockets, sinking into the mattress.

"This memory"—he straightens, smirking—"should solidify your decision."

Before I can scream, he snaps his fingers.

The rich smell of mint and cinnamon stewing in a broth of yogurt and meat invades my nose and I'm overwhelmed with nostalgia. I hesitate for a second before opening my eyes. When I do, I'm no longer in my musty room but back home. *My* home.

The kitchen is exactly how I remember it. The marble walls alternate between beige and cedar brown, where hanging frames show Arabic calligraphy and painted golden lemons. The storage space beneath the counters holds our saucepans and pots, neatly stacked. A white satin cloth embroidered with lilies drapes over the kitchen table. Around the table stand four wooden chairs, and on top of it, orchids sprout out of a crystal vase. Blue orchids I bought for a visit that was supposed to happen later that day—today. I always bought blue orchids when we had a social gathering.

I finally turn to my left, where Mama stands beside me, her eyes on the shish barak, stirring the pot with a wooden spoon. All the while her lips moving in prayer.

"Keep them safe," she whispers. "Keep my men safe. Bring them back to me alive and well today. Protect them from those who wish them harm."

I'm rooted to the spot, my heart tearing in two.

She's beside me.

A few silent tears trickle down my cheeks, and the need to throw myself into her arms overwhelms me. I want my mama. I want her to soothe away my sadness and kiss me while calling me ya omri and te'eburenee. *My life* and *bury me.*

Instead, I gently poke her arm. She glances up with bloodshot eyes, distracted, before a tired smile appears on her lips, and I can see how this war has drastically changed her. Her face, which never seemed to age beyond thirty-five, is weary with nerves, and the roots of her umber-brown hair are gray. She never let her roots go gray, always the picture of prim and proper. Her bones poke out sharply, and dark shadows tint under her eyes, where they never existed before.

"Te'eburenee, we'll be okay. Insha'Allah," she whispers, wrapping one arm around my shoulders and squeezing me to her. *Bury me before I bury you.*

I did.

"Yes, Mama," I manage to choke out, melting into her touch.

"*Aw*, Saloomeh," Hamza calls as he walks in with Baba from the living room, and I nearly cry out. They're here. Hamza's honey-colored eyes are full of life and mirror Baba's. They're both wearing coats with the Syrian Revolution flag hanging over one shoulder. One twist and it could be a noose. "Are you seriously going to cry?"

I don't ask Hamza where Layla is because I know she's back at their home, waiting for him. But he won't be returning to her today.

"Hamza, don't tease your sister," Baba says, walking over to Mama. She immediately engulfs him in a hug, and he wraps his arms around her, murmuring something in her ear.

I can't bear to see this, so I turn away.

"You're leaving now?" I ask Hamza, my voice breaking, and I have to tilt my chin up to look at him. I haven't done that in seven months.

He smiles softly. "The protest is happening after the prayer, so we need to get there early."

I bite back the urge to wail. He had just turned twenty-two, freshly graduated from medical school, and had applied for a residency at Zaytouna Hospital. He didn't know he was going to be a father. Would that have stopped him from joining the protests?

"D-don't go," I stammer. Maybe this hallucination can end well. Maybe I can change things. "Please, you and Baba. Don't go today!"

He grins. "You say that every single time."

I grab his arm tightly, my eyes memorizing his faint scruff, the dimple in one cheek that appears when he smiles. This is the last memory I have of my brother. With time, memories distort, and I know I'll forget his exact features. I'll forget Baba's brown hair, streaked with gray, and the gentle twinkle in his eyes. I'll forget how Hamza is at least two heads taller and that he and I share the same shade of brown hair. I'll forget the dimples in Mama's cheeks and her smile, which lights up the world. Our family photos are buried under the rubble of this building, and I'll never get them back.

"Ew. Salama, why are you being weird?" he says, and then shakes his head when he sees the tears in my eyes. He adds kindly, "I promise you we'll come back."

My lungs constrict. I know what he's going to say next. I have replayed this conversation in my mind on a loop until the words scramble together.

"But if I don't . . ." He takes a deep breath, turning serious. "Salama, if I don't . . . then you take care of Layla. You make sure she and Mama are okay. You make sure you three stay alive and safe."

I swallow hard. "I already promised you that."

When the people flooded the streets during the very first protest, Hamza immediately took me aside and made me vow exactly that. He was always intuitive. Smart beyond his years. He always sensed when I was down, even if I didn't say anything. His heart, as soft as a cloud, reached out to everyone around him. He knew that Mama, despite her terror, would need to be dragged out of Syria kicking and screaming, that Layla would scoff if he asked her to run away, leaving him behind. But I would make sure they both stayed alive. I would put my family's safety above everything. Whoever was left of it.

"Promise me again," he says fiercely. "I can't go out there in good conscience without knowing for sure. I need to hear those words." The honey in his eyes burns like fire.

"I promise," I manage to whisper. Two words were never heavier.

Now he's supposed to ruffle my hair before walking out with Baba, never to come back.

But he doesn't.

His hands grip my shoulders. "Did you?"

I falter. "What?"

The fire rages in his gaze. "After the military took me and Baba, did you get Mama out? Did you save Layla? Or did you throw their lives away?"

My bones rattle.

"Salama, did you lie to me?" Agony drips from his expression.

I back away, pressing my hands to my chest.

"Did you let Mama die?" he asks, his voice louder.

Mama and Baba stand beside him, blood trickling down the right side of Mama's face. It falls to the ceramic floor she polished every single day. Each drop feels like a knife to the heart.

"I'm sorry," I plead. "Please. Forgive me!"

"Sorry?" Baba says, his brows furrowed. "You let your mother die. You're letting Layla die. For what?"

"Mama might forgive you," Hamza says. "But I won't. If Layla suffers because of your choices, Salama, I will never forgive you."

I collapse to the floor, weeping. "I'm sorry. I'm sorry."

"Not enough," they all say in unison.

The floor shakes underneath me, and vines twist around my ankles, pulling me beneath the tiles. My kitchen and home crumble, and I fall into the black abyss, screaming. My back hits a slab of stone, and I struggle to take in a breath. When I open my eyes, smoke from a building on fire covers the pale blue sky above.

Oxygen becomes scarce in my lungs and I cough, shakily getting up onto my feet. Before me stands the seven-story building I called home. The balcony on the sixth floor has laundry drying outside and the one under it has the Syrian Revolution flag hanging proudly from the balusters. It ruffles in the wind, looking as if it'll fly away. But Hamza had knotted it tight on each side to make sure it stayed put. After he and Baba were arrested, Mama couldn't bear to take it down.

The air around me is very still. I know where I am without needing to ask. Khawf has dragged me a week into the future to one of the worst days of my life.

Mama.

"No," I groan. "No."

"You can't save her." Khawf stands a few feet from me. "She's already dead."

My building is fifteen steps away. I can make it. I can save her.

"Mama!" I scream, running toward her. "Get out! Get out! The planes are coming!"

But it's too late; they're faster than my voice, and the bombs don't care that there are innocent people inside. The high-pitched sound rings against my ears as they smash the building to bloodied fragments. The aftershock doesn't blow me away. It razes the building to the ground, and I'm standing over Mama's mutilated body. She wasn't wearing her hijab; her brown hair is gray with debris, her head bent at a wrong angle. And blood. There's so much blood staining my bare feet, my stomach heaves at the sharp metallic smell.

I cry, falling to my knees, and clutch her body, drawing her closer to my living one. My hands shake uncontrollably as I try to brush away the hair plastered to her cheeks, but I only smear her with her blood. Flecks of it land in my mouth. "*Mama!* Oh God, not again! *Not again!*"

Her eyes gloss over, staring right back at me.

"Why didn't you save me?" Mama whispers, her eyes vacant. "Why?"

"I'm sorry," I sob. "Please, please forgive me!"

I drip tears on her still face, my lips pleading with her to come back, and I hug her. Even with all the blood drenching us both, she still smells the same.

"She's gone, Salama," Khawf says from behind me. "Look, there you are over there."

I glance toward where he's pointing. Between the rubble and smoky haze of the bomb, there's past me. Her cheeks are still full, her eyes beginning to come to terms with a pain that will become her constant companion. She's only seventeen and has barely glimpsed what true horror means. She coughs, her clothes and hijab torn, trying to crawl toward Mama's corpse before her muscles give way, and she falls to the ground, unconscious.

Anger and sadness intertwine through my heart, latching to my deteriorating bones.

"That's enough," I pant, pressing Mama closer. "Take me back."

Khawf crouches beside me, wiping a drop of blood from my cheek, and smiles. The rubble doesn't come near him; his clothes are untouched. Yet the red spots on his jacket's shoulders have grown, and I don't know if I'm seeing things, but they seem to be leaking down his lapels.

He snaps his fingers and I'm back on my bed, all traces of soot and blood gone. I blink, staring at my chapped, scarred hands, unsettled by the sudden disappearance of Mama from my embrace. The tears on my face, still wet, are the only proof of what I went through.

Khawf takes a deep breath, satisfaction etched on every line of his pale face, and retreats to the window.

"That will be Layla if you continue to be obstinate." He takes out another cigarette. "You've already broken half of your promise. Do you want Layla's death to be your undoing?"

My body betrays me, shaking all over, and I clutch my ragged blankets to hide it.

He blows out a cloud of dark gray smoke that falls to the tattered floor in wisps before vanishing. "Every day more of your patients pass away. Each one of them is another regret in your heart. Staying here will destroy you even if Layla survives."

"Go away," I whimper, hating my brain for doing this to me.

"I don't like being treated as a fool, Salama," he murmurs. "Give me what I want and I might leave you alone."

My tongue is dry, and the half-moon scars on my palms, the result of my own nails, begin to hurt. Instead of answering him, I turn away, my brain banging against my skull. My eyes fall on the closed drawer of the nightstand beside the bed, where I keep my hidden stash of Panadol pills. I've been collecting them since July in preparation for Layla's labor, and for one brief second I consider taking one. But decide against it. I don't know if we'll have access to medicine wherever we'll be.

"Jasmine. Jasmine. Jasmine...," I murmur over and over until I swear I can smell them like I used to when Mama took me in her arms.

3

THE NEXT MORNING, I KISS LAYLA ON THE CHEEK
and head to work. We never know if we'll see each other
again. Every moment is a goodbye.

"Talk to Am." Her smile is warm, and I remember
Hamza.

I nod, unable to say anything, and slip out the door,
locking it behind me.

The hospital is a fifteen-minute walk from Layla's house.
It was a perk Hamza was looking forward to, seeing as he
wouldn't need to drive: a young doctor training at his neighborhood's hospital. From the moment he was able to read,
at three years old, Mama and Baba recognized that their son
was a genius. He enrolled in school early, breezed through
middle school and high school, and had his pick of universi-
ties. He chose the one in Homs to be close to our family. But
I knew it was really so he'd be close to Layla and begin his
life with her.

Now I've taken the job that was supposed to be his.

One that's way out of my field. Pharmacists prescribe medications—they don't perform surgeries. I was supposed to graduate and be that. Or a researcher. I'm not a surgeon. I wasn't made to cut into bodies, stitch wounds, and amputate limbs, but I made myself become that person.

The Homs surrounding me when I step out feels like something from the history books. The carnage in front of me has been seen in so many cities throughout the years. The same story but a different location. I'm sure the martyrs' ghosts roam the abandoned homes and streets, their fingers running across the flags of the revolution painted on the walls. The living sit outside on plastic chairs, wrapped in coats and scarves. Today there are children playing with whatever they've been able to pull from the wreckage. An old woman yells at them to be careful of the carpets made from glass shards. When she sees my lab coat, she grins, a few teeth missing.

"Allah ma'ek!" *May God be with you.*

I smile shakily and nod.

The hospital isn't immune to the dictatorship's disease, and the outside walls, discolored in washed-out yellow and red, show it. The dirt underneath my old sneakers is marred with blood of the wounded carried in day after day.

The doors are nearly always open, and today is no different. It's bustling as usual, the groans and cries of the wounded echoing over the walls.

Surgery equipment and medications are at an all-time low, and I can see the effect of it on the sunken faces lying on the beds all around me. Lately I've begun using saline and telling the patients it's an anesthetic, hoping they believe it enough that it'll work as a placebo. I remember the articles I read about placebos during my first year at university that mentioned their success. Back when I would be tucked in the corner of the steps outside the lecture building with my thermos full of zhoorat tea, going over the notes I'd made in class. I would lose a few hours immersed in my studying until Layla would appear at dusk and flick my nose to get my attention.

Despite all our lacking resources, our hospital fares far better under the Free Syrian Army's jurisdiction than ones in the regions controlled by the military.

We've heard stories of those captured by the military. The patients in the hospitals are dying not from the injuries they sustained during the protests but from what is inflicted on them inside the hospital. While we suffer from the siege, injured demonstrators there are blindfolded and tortured, their ankles chained to the beds. Doctors and nurses sometimes join in.

Here in our hospital, the beds are stacked one beside the other, with families surrounding the patients, so I have to squeeze between them to ask the patient how they're feeling. Dr. Ziad hurries toward me, carefully stepping through the countless bodies of patients draped across the floor; those are all alone in this world with no families. Not even a bed. His salt-and-pepper hair is disheveled, the wrinkles around his brown eyes more pronounced. He took the job as head surgeon after the last one died in a raid. Before that he was an endocrinology doctor with hours he set himself, slowly easing into retirement. When the unrest started, he immediately sent his entire family to Lebanon, and the hospital became his home. Just as I was forced to become a surgeon, so was he.

"Incoming. Reports of a bomb hitting Al-Ghouta. Twenty casualties. The seventeen injured are being brought here," he says. As head surgeon, he's connected to the Free Syrian Army, which supplies him with any information they get that could help us save more lives.

My heart expands for one second with relief. That's on the opposite side of my neighborhood. A half-hour car ride. Layla is safe. And then it shrivels up. Bombs mean anything could come through these doors. Intestines out and looped inside themselves, burns, severed limbs . . .

I wait by the entrance with Dr. Ziad, who's whispering verses of the Quran that talk about serenity and God's mercy. It calms the cold sweat trickling down my neck. Any minute now, the doors will slam open.

Any minute.

Khawf appears beside the windows in front of me. His suit gleams despite the hospital's broken light, and his hair is swept back, not one strand out of place. He's grinning at me. Khawf loves the hospital. He knows that my fear of Layla's becoming the next mangled body I bury will wither my resolve to stay. That eventually I'll want to leave Syria.

We hear the screams before the doors open, giving us a split second to ready ourselves. But no matter how many times I see it, no amount of warning can prepare me for the sight of a human struggling for breath. This is not normal, and it *never* will be.

"Salama, get to the children first," Dr. Ziad says sharply, already running toward the patients. "Nour, you make sure none of them bleed out. Mahmoud, don't let them run out of bandages. Use the bedsheets if you must. Go!"

Five victims are transported on stretchers while the rest are carried by volunteers from the scene. There's a huge crowd gathering around them, everyone screaming and shouting. Dr. Ziad continues yelling orders to the rest of the staff, and once again I'm grateful for his calm in the face of these atrocities. He's the one who grounds us. The reason we're able to save lives.

Khawf stands tall, watching the chaos unfold with a satisfied smile, and begins to hum a tune, one that ricochets over the din: "How Sweet Is Freedom," the protestors' anthem. But I don't have time to tell him off. Death doesn't wait for anyone.

For me, bandaging patients, trying to heal them, comes with more challenges than just keeping them alive. Sometimes they see me and demand an older, more experienced doctor. At first I used to flinch, try to stop my trembling, and stutter an explanation of how all the doctors are busy. That I'm just as capable. But now, if anybody tries to cost me precious seconds, I just tell them *This or death*. That helps them reach their decision pretty quickly.

Working here has hardened and softened my heart in ways I never guessed it would.

As I'm bandaging my fifth patient, I spot someone looking frantic, carrying a little girl in his arms. He doesn't look much older than I am. Late teens. The girl's head has lolled to the side, and blood drips from her shirt onto the floor. My eyes follow the boy, watching the hospital's flickering light bounce off his messy, tawny curls. He looks familiar. But before I can try and place him, Dr. Ziad calls me to help him with another patient. This survivor's ulna is fractured, tearing through his arm. The sight of bone jutting from skin makes the acid in my stomach rise to my throat, burning. I swallow it down, feeling its descent as it melts my gastric mucosa instead. And I set to work on returning the bone to where it belongs.

While I rest after three back-to-back surgeries, I spot Am passing. I have to talk to him. Today. And I feel Khawf's gaze drill into the back of my head, his threat echoing in my brain.

I will tear your world apart.

He's adamant about my leaving Syria and would do anything to make that happen. In all the months I've known him, I've never understood his desperation. But today, a whisper echoes in my brain. A result of my conversation with Layla.

What's the harm in asking? You're only getting information. Just to know how much it costs. Do it for her.

"Am," I blurt out, and he stops, turning toward me.

"Yes?" he says, surprised. He's younger than he looks, but with everything going on, it's no surprise that a man in his late thirties would begin to gray.

"I—uh . . . I was wondering about—" I stutter and chastise myself. I should have thought of what to say.

"You want a boat, Salama?" he says, cutting to the chase, and my face becomes hot.

I clutch at my ruined lab coat, wrinkling the rough fabric. He thinks I'm a coward. Of all the people to ask him for a way out, it's me. The last and only pharmacist in three neighborhoods.

"Do you?" he repeats, raising his eyebrows.

Hamza's anxious expression flashes in my mind. "Yes."

He turns to the side, checking if anyone is within earshot before saying, "All right. Meet me in the main hallway in ten minutes."

I can spare a few minutes before Dr. Ziad or Nour come looking for me. Dr. Ziad always insists I take a break. But still my palms break out in a sweat. A whole lot can happen in ten minutes. A sudden respiratory failure, cardiac arrest, another patient vomiting blood and bile. *Anything.* But I promised Hamza. Layla is my sister, my only family. She's pregnant with my brother's child. One he didn't know of and will never meet. And I need to *at least* know if we can afford it. I don't want to test Khawf's limits either. If he makes good on his threat, today could be my last day working at the hospital.

"Daylilies," I whisper as I walk to the main hall, training my eyes on the muddied floors. "Relax muscle spasms and cramps. Can cure arsenic poison. Daylilies. *Daylilies . . .*"

The main hall is filled with patients, and I understand why Am chose this place. It's free publicity to anyone within earshot. They'd know who Am is, what he does, and what he's promising them: a chance to live.

Am comes around to the hospital every day to look for people who might take him up on his offer. Payment in the form of a lifetime's savings to sail away on a boat to another continent that many of us have only read about in books. Everyone at the hospital knows Am, even Dr. Ziad, who strongly believes more people should stay in Syria. Though he'd never stop anyone who chose to leave, seeing as he sent his own family away. As long as Am doesn't get in the way of saving patients' lives, he's free to spread his agenda. And Am does just that. He stays away from all the doctors, focusing on the patients. He makes sure everyone knows about the successful passages by showing people pictures of those who finally reached European shores. No one would be willing to risk drowning without the assurance that this *has* worked. At some point. But then, perhaps, even without evidence a sliver of a chance at survival is better than living at the mercy of genocide.

No one takes to a rickety boat on the sea if there is another choice.

Among the tired faces Khawf's sticks out, with his gleaming eyes and a knowing smirk.

Maybe the reason he's willing to break me in order to get me on a boat can be explained in a scientific manner: He's a defense mechanism my brain has provided, trying to ensure my survival by any means necessary. But still my stomach gnaws with apprehension at what horrors await me at his hands.

Within ten minutes, Am finds me in the main hallway. He wades his way through the sea of bodies until he reaches me by a half-broken window that's covered with a flimsy sheet.

My nervous system is going haywire, zapping electric impulses all through my body that I can't seem to calm down, no matter what methods I use. My paranoia over Dr. Ziad making an unexpected appearance is high, and I dig my hands into my pockets to hide their trembling. I don't think I'd be able to go on with this conversation if he were to see me. I'm turning my back on my people.

"So, how many are you?" Am asks, and I snap back toward him.

"Two," I say. My voice sounds distant.

He studies me for a second. "That's your whole family?"

Chips crack from my heart, falling through my rib cage. "Yes."

He nods, but his expression is impassive. It's not out of the ordinary now to be a family of one.

"I'll drive you to Tartus," he says as if he's discussing the weather. "The boat usually sails from there. About a day and a half through the Mediterranean Sea and you reach Italy. A bus will be waiting for you there to take you to Germany. The most important thing is to get to Italy."

My heart flutters with every word he says. And despite his dry tone, I can see the journey unfold in front of me. The boat rocking gently over the blue sea, the water lapping against shores that promise safety. Layla, turning to me, an honest laugh escaping her lips that: *We're safe.* Yearning rips through my stomach.

A baby cries, shattering my daydream, and the patients' moans of pain are suddenly deafening against my ears. *No. No.* How can I think of my safety when I vowed to heal the sick?

But Layla's pregnant, and I *promised* Hamza. Layla would never leave without me, and I can't have her stranded alone in Europe when she barely speaks English, let alone German or Italian. Being a pregnant girl and all alone would make her easy prey. Monsters aren't confined to Syria.

Indecision is a poison germinating in my blood vessels.

I clear my throat. "How much does it cost?"

He thinks this over. "Four thousand dollars. And there's a line."

I blink. "What?"

"I deal in dollars. Liras are weak. Four thousand dollars. Two thousand each."

Blood drains from my face and my mouth is dry. That's more than we have. Baba was able to withdraw six thousand dollars in the beginning, but most of the money has gone as the price of food has increased. We barely have three thousand left.

He notes the change in my expression and snorts. "Did you think getting to Europe would be cheap? Did you think it would be easy? We're talking about smuggling two entire people to a different continent. Not to mention bribing all the soldiers on our way there."

I've lost feeling in my legs. "You . . . you don't understand. The other person, she's my sister-in-law. She's seven months pregnant. If she gives . . . The money will be needed for her to survive. I don't have enough. *Please.*"

He considers me for a minute. "Four thousand dollars and I'll let you jump the waiting line. That's as far as my courtesy will extend. Don't take too long to think about it. The boat doesn't wait for anyone."

And with that, he walks away, leaving me rooted to the ground while Khawf stares after him with narrowed eyes. I wonder what my brain will do with this obstacle.

4

WHEN DR ZIAD FINDS ME, I'M ON THE FLOOR IN the corner of one of the recovery rooms, clutching my knees as I rock back and forth, shaking and crying, trying to soothe myself. Two little girls lay motionless before me, bullet holes ripped through their throats. Military snipers take to the roofs at the borders between the military's posts and the Free Syrian Army's protected zones. The girls look about seven, clothes torn, knees scraped.

The snipers' victims are always the innocents who can't fight back. Children, the elderly, pregnant women. The Free Syrian Army informed Dr. Ziad that, early on, the military would target them for sport. Even Layla had a very near miss in October; now she's not allowed to leave the house. Ever. Not without me.

Dr. Ziad crouches beside me, his kind face weathered with pain.

"Salama," he says gently. "Look at me."

I tear my eyes away from the small faces with purple,

bruised lips to meet his eyes. I press my hands to my own lips, begging them to stop trembling.

"Salama, we talked about this. You can't work yourself to this point. You have to take care of *you*. If you're drained and in pain, you won't be able to help anyone. No one should have to handle this horror. Especially someone as young as you are." His glance softens. "You've lost more than anyone ever should. Don't confine yourself to the hospital. Go home."

My hands fall to my lap as I process what he's saying. Over these past seven months, he's become a father figure to me. I know one of his daughters is my age and that he sees her in me. I also know he'd never ask of her what he expects of me every day. To drench my hands in the blood of innocents and push it back into their bodies. Witness the horror and still come back the next day. And a small part of me, a very small one, begrudges him for it. Though he tries his best to take care of my health, not letting me exceed my limits.

I clear my throat. "There are still more patients—"

"Your life is just as important as theirs," he interrupts, his voice leaving no room for negotiation. "Your. Life. Is. *Just*. As. Important."

I close my eyes, trying to hold on to his words, trying to believe them; but each time I try to catch the letters, they vanish from my grasp.

Nevertheless, I stand on unsteady legs as Dr. Ziad throws a white sheet over the bodies.

Layla doesn't say anything for a long time after I slump down on the couch.

With my eyes closed, I relay my conversation with Am, my voice cracking when I tell her the price. I hate him. Innocent lives don't matter when he can fill his pockets from our suffering. No one wants to escape more than people who have been broken down to the core. They're looking for a lifeline, no matter how brittle it may be.

"Say something," I beg, and open my eyes when she stays quiet. She stares at the coffee table in front of her. She's thinking of a plan. And then she grimaces.

"I have nothing to say." Her brows are furrowed. "Unless . . ."

"Unless?"

"We could sell our gold?" She twirls a strand of hair around her finger. The late-afternoon sun filtering through the stained windows pools in the middle of the living room, turning the Arabian rug under us into something ethereal. I watch the way the light dances around my shadow between the forest-green plants sewn into the material. If I focus on it, I can pretend whatever exists outside the yellow halo is all right—is safe.

Sell our gold.

Gold is passed on through our families. Deep beneath its glittering surface, it holds our history and stories in its thick braided strands.

When I went back to my demolished building after the bombing, I wasn't able to find anything that belonged to me. The granite ensured it. My gold is still under there, buried, but Layla's is here. Gold that Hamza gave her as part of her dowry.

"Who would buy it?" I ask.

Layla shrugs. "Maybe Am would accept it instead of money."

I've never heard of anyone buying their way with gold, and we're surely not the first ones to think of it. And anyway, I'm not willing to part with Layla's—my family's—gold like that. Not to someone as crooked as Am.

"He didn't say money *or* gold." I pick at the threads spilling out of the couch. "If he wanted gold, he'd say it."

Layla watches me while I continue to poke at the strands.

"So you don't want to try and ask him?" she finally says.

"I'll . . . haggle with him."

She bites her lip before bursting out laughing. "*Haggle with him?*" she repeats. "What do you think this is? Souq Al-Hamidiyah?"

I point at the mahogany frame that houses a canvas Layla painted. It's a painting I've always loved looking at. Dark blue skies mingling with the gray sea at the horizon. I have no idea how Layla was able to capture it so clearly, as if it were a photograph; the water sometimes feels like it's about to drip out of the frame's edges, soaking the rug. The clouds are congealed and huddled together, moments before a storm.

"Who convinced that man to let you buy the frame for half price?" I fold my arms. "That gorgeously made frame? Was it you?"

Layla smiles. "No, it was you."

"Yes, it was. So . . . I'll haggle with him."

But I don't say the rest of what I'm thinking. That I'm only humoring her. That I'm torn between my duty to my brother and to the hospital, the ropes holding me on each side both fraying at the edges. And I don't know which will give before the other.

Though something in her gaze makes me suspect she knows all of that.

"You talk about Germany as if it's the land where all our dreams will come true." My eyes catch back on the painting. It looks so real. "We don't speak the language. We can barely speak English as it is, and we have no family there. We'll be stranded in the middle of nowhere, and there are many who would try and take advantage of us. Refugees are being swindled out of everything they own, you know that. Not to mention kidnapped."

Once, a lifetime ago, I wanted to live a year in Europe. Another in the States. Canada. Japan. Planting seeds in all the continents. I wanted to do my master's degree in herbology and collect plants and medicinal flowers from all over the world. I wanted the places I visited to remember that Salama Kassab walked through them. I wanted to take these experiences and write children's books with pages etched in magic and words that whisked the reader away to other realms.

"What about you?" I had asked Layla one day. "Where do you want to go?"

We were in the countryside at my grandparents' estate the summer after we finished high school. University life was just two months away. The apricots were ripe and we had spent the whole morning filling a dozen baskets of them to eat and to give to our neighbors.

We were taking a break, lying on our backs over the picnic blanket and watching the clouds. The sun was hidden behind them, her rays turning the sky into an azure blue. A butterfly flapped her wings and a bumblebee buried herself into a daisy. It was a quiet day, a good day where hopes and dreams would be traded. Where sweet childhood memories would be revisited.

Layla breathed in deeply, taking in the apricot scent. "I want to paint Norway."

"Like the whole country?" I laughed.

She turned to me and raised her hand to flick my nose. I squealed and covered it.

"You're not funny." She rolled her eyes, but a smile played on her lips.

"I'm hilarious," I said and turned to my side. My hijab slipped a bit and my bangs peeked out. It was all right because we were hidden away from any passerby's eyes. I shrugged it off a bit, and my pony-tail fell to the side.

Layla sat up and looked around. Spotting no one, she gathered my ponytail behind my back and slipped off the hair tie.

"I have seen all shades of blue except the one in Norway," she said quietly. Her voice carried over the breeze. "I've only seen it on Google, and it was breathtaking. I want to see the real thing. I want to paint every shade and have an art exhibition. Something called Blue from Every Angle. I don't know."

I turned around. "That sounds so beautiful, Layla. Very Studio Ghibli."

She smiled and began braiding my hair. Something she did whenever I was stressed. "I have dreams that will take me away from here."

In her glance, I could see the question—would I be okay if she *left? She and I had been joined at the hip ever since we were born. She was as close as a sister to me. With her being an only child and me an only daughter, we'd forged that relationship on our own.*

"Salama!" we heard Hamza call from the distance. "Layla! Yalla, lunch is ready."

Layla's eyes sparkled at the sound of his voice, and she jumped up and ran toward him. He caught her by the waist and they nearly fell down.

I stood up. Watching them, I felt as if I were standing on the other side of a door I couldn't walk through.

Layla's brows furrowed. "What's wrong?"

I realized my expression had been forlorn and quickly cleared it away with a smile. "Nothing."

How childish my worries were back then. How innocent were our dreams.

Now, a pregnant, starved girl sits before me, her eyes too large for her face, while my stomach rattles about like an empty drum.

"Salama," Layla says, and I look at her, snapping out of my daydream. "Today was full of sadness, wasn't it?"

I pick at my sleeve. "Every day is."

She shakes her head slightly and pats her lap. "Lay your head."

And I do.

Layla's fingers sink into my hair and she starts making small braids. My hijab lies discarded somewhere beside the sofa, and I sigh with relief at her gentle touch. Her pregnant belly cushions my head, and I feel the baby kicking against her stomach. Only fabric, layers of skin, and placental fluid separate it from the terrors of this world.

"Don't focus on the darkness and sadness," she says, and I glance up at her. She smiles warmly. "If you do, you won't see the light even if it's staring you in the face."

"What are you talking about?" I mumble.

"I'm saying what's happening now, as horrible as it is, isn't the end of the world. Change is difficult, and it's different depending on what needs to be changed. Look, I'll even science it up for you. If a cancer has spread, wouldn't whatever needs to be done to remove it be different than for something like a wart?"

A smile threatens my lips. "Since when do you know medical stuff?"

Her eyes twinkle. "As an artist, I'm a student of life. Humor me, Salama."

"Well," I say slowly. "With cancer, we need to perform surgery to take out the tumor, but it's a tricky process. Chances of survival. Cutting into healthy tissue. It's a lot to consider."

"And a wart?"

I shrug. "Just treat it with salicylic acid."

"And when that cancer surgery is successful, when the patient has fought for their life, wouldn't their life be improved?"

I nod.

"Don't you think the Syrian dictatorship is more like a cancer that has been growing in Syria's body for decades, and the surgery, despite the risks, is better than submitting to the cancer? With something so deeply entrenched in our roots, change doesn't come easy. It has a heavy price."

I don't say anything.

"There is light, Salama," she continues. "Despite the agony, we are *free* for the first time in over fifty years."

Her fingers feel heavy in my hair.

"You're talking as if you want to stay," I say.

She looks at me meaningfully. Like she knows exactly what I'm hiding in my heart. "The fight isn't just in Syria, Salama. It's everywhere. Like I told you, fighting starts here. Not in Germany or anywhere else."

She chooses her words carefully, and each one squirms through my auditory canal, echoing over my eardrum, right through the nerve cells to my brain. They settle there like little seeds planted between the cells.

"How come you're not as bitter as I am?" I joke weakly, but it comes out flat and rings truer than I'd like.

When Hamza was arrested, Layla went through two major changes. For the first five weeks she was inconsolable. Sobbing until her throat went hoarse, not eating or showering. Then, suddenly, she was back to her old self. Calm and loving with a smile that could power the entirety of Homs.

"First off, we can't all be perfect," she says, and I finally smile. Satisfied, she continues, "Because I see the love you have for me. I see your sacrifice and your kindness. I focus on the hope rather than counting my losses. I have love in my heart because of you. Because of all the help you gave me when . . . when they took him away."

A tear blooms in the corner of her eye, slides down her cheek, and I catch it before it reaches her chin. She lost her parents when the bombs started falling. And then, in the middle of mourning her family, in the span of one week, we lost Mama, Baba, and Hamza. Worst of all, we still don't know whether Hamza and Baba are alive.

I'd like to believe they've died. And I know Layla would too. Death is a far more merciful end than living every day in agony.

"If only everyone in the world were like you," I murmur.

She lets loose a shaky laugh, and I take her hand to grip it firmly. But a thunderous noise outside makes us jump. Whatever warmth we were feeling evaporates, and the air is cold again. Layla squeezes my hand, her eyes closed. I pray with her that it's nothing. *Please God, let it be nothing. Let it not be a raid! Please!*

My heart lodges in my throat for several beats, but when no screams pierce the night, Layla relaxes her grip.

"I think it's just rain," she whispers, trying to hide the fear from her voice.

"Better grab the buckets, then." I get up from the sofa as another thunderclap shakes the night. My head spins a bit, missing the safety Layla's lap offered.

"And don't forget to pray. Prayers are answered when rain falls," she reminds me.

The wind blows past me when I open the veranda door to place the buckets outside. It cools my skin's hot flush, and my heart begins to migrate back to its proper place in my chest. I inhale as much of the fallen clouds as I can. They're gray and dense, hopefully bringing protection against the warplanes that could shatter our lives.

After that, I help Layla get ready for bed. She doesn't sleep in her room anymore. Too much reminds her of

Hamza. I haven't even stepped in there since the day I moved in. I don't want to see my brother's clothes hanging from the closet, his favorite watch on the nightstand, and the photograph of his laughing face as he kissed Layla's cheek during their wedding.

So Layla sleeps on the sofa. I fill it with pillows and blankets. Her eyes are misty, her expression faraway. I know that look. She's in the past, and I don't want to jolt her out of her daydream. Even though the memories ache, it's the only way we get to see our loved ones—replaying their words to us, letting our imaginations magnify or soften their voices however we please. Layla moves purely on muscle memory and then lies back against the pillows.

Finally, her eyes clear and she looks at me. "Salama," she says as if she didn't know I've been there the whole time.

"Do you need water? Panadol? We can spare some now that you're in your third trimester," I say.

"No thank you. The baby's being very polite today."

"She's being considerate of her mama's feelings."

"She?" Layla says softly. Her expression lightens.

I nod. "It's a girl. I can feel it."

"Really?" Layla rolls her eyes good-naturedly. "And is that a part of your medical detection skills?"

"When you've been in the business as long as I have, you get a sixth sense about these kinds of things." I wink. "Trust me, I'm a pharmacist."

She smiles. "With my life. And my baby's."

"Too much responsibility!" I pretend to crumble, and she laughs. "Thought of any names?"

"Well, when Hamza and I used to discuss names for any

future babies, he always thought of boys' names. Always wanted a boy. He told me that he would be too soft if our first-born was a girl. That he wouldn't be able to deny her anything."

"Oh, we both know Hamza would become a literal carpet for his daughter to step on."

"Which is why we need to leave," she whispers. "We can't let her be born here. If it were just you and me, Salama, I wouldn't leave my husband. But . . . it's his child. It's my *baby*."

My breath hitches and I ball my hands into fists.

Lavender has antiseptic and anti-inflammatory properties. Purple petals. Can be used for insomnia. Lavender. Lavender. Lav—

"You—you were telling me names?" I choke out, and her gaze drops between us.

"Yeah," she says after a minute. "If it's a boy, Malik, and if it's a girl—"

"Salama," I interrupt.

"How did you know?" she gasps.

I snap back in disbelief. "Um, what? I was joking."

"I'm *seriously* going to name her Salama if she's a girl!"

"And why wouldn't you? Salama is a great name," I answer with a goofy smile.

She laughs. "I agree."

I scoot over and whisper against her stomach. "You'd best be a girl. I love you, little Saloomeh."

The pain in Layla's eyes has mostly vanished, but traces still linger. Enough for the guilt to dig its thorns into my heart. I take a deep breath and exhale.

"Good night." I smooth her hair back and tighten the blanket around her.

49

She squeezes my hand in reply.

As she succumbs to her dreams, I finally let my fear show, the words she said to me repeating on a loop in my mind.

With my life. And my baby's.

5

"WHAT ARE YOU GOING TO DO?" KHAWF ASKS FROM the dark corner, and I jump and press a hand to my heart.

"What?"

He steps out, the shadows melting off him, eyes glinting. "What are you doing about Am?"

"I don't know."

"That means you'll do nothing."

"It means I don't know." I swallow down my anxiety. "Leave me alone."

He chews his cheek, examining me from head to toe, and I press my legs to my chest in an effort to become smaller.

"I did what you wanted," I say. "I asked Am. Is it my fault that the price is so high?"

He doesn't answer me, simply takes out a cigarette and tucks it between his lips. His smoking mannerisms remind me of my grandfather. When asked a question, Jedo—may his soul rest in peace—wouldn't answer until he took that drag of smoke. But Jedo had a gentle smile and such a proud way of looking at me, and there's nothing like that about Khawf. Nothing.

"No, it's not. But it seems like you've given up. Didn't you tell Layla you'll haggle with him?"

I shrug.

His eyes bore into mine. "While your apparent enthusiasm is admirable," he sneers, "it's not enough. You *need* to get that boat."

"I'm at my limit here. What do you want, Khawf?" I say wearily.

A plume of silver smoke obscures him from my view.

"Why, your safety, of course." He grins. "Don't you believe I'm some sort of a defense mechanism?"

I manage a pathetic snort.

He stands in front of me and I instinctively jerk back. "Salama, you should know better by now. Unlike you, I don't tire, I don't feel pain, and I won't stop until I get what I want. Fighting me, fighting your *mind*"—he twirls his fingers and my pulse races as pitch darkness envelops us until nothing is visible but his icy-blue eyes and the flash of his white teeth—"you won't win."

I can't see anything. Can't hear the faint voices of the protests outside. Nothing exists but Khawf and me in this black hole. He extends his hand to my chin and I flinch, but he doesn't touch me. Yet his power over me is so great that I look up, shivering and frozen in place.

"I am infinite, and you are not," he whispers. He trails a finger I don't feel along the hollow of my throat, but my teeth still chatter as if I can sense the blade of his fingernail. "Find a way to get that boat."

The morning sun bleeds over my shivering body. I get dressed, trying to ignore the weight of Khawf's presence on my life. My stomach rumbles with hunger; my limbs ache. But none of my pain matters as long as I can save lives today. If I can make up for my shortcomings. For all the lives that I couldn't save yesterday.

The year I spent in pharmacy school didn't prepare me for any of this. Even if I had graduated, it wouldn't have made a difference. I was never supposed to do the work I do now. My first-year classes were mostly theoretical, and my lab courses were about mixing simple formulations, laying the foundation to build on in the coming years.

My first day at the hospital was akin to being dropped with no swimming lessons into the deep end. I taught myself how to swim, to kick my legs and stay afloat before the heavy weight of the waves dragged me down.

At noon, catastrophe strikes in the form of shrapnel raining on a nearby elementary school. On children.

When they are wheeled in, the world slows down. My legs are rooted in the sticky blood staining my sneakers. I'm standing in the middle of the carnage, watching the moments between life and death unfold in front of me. My eyes catch every tear falling and every soul rising to meet its Creator.

I see a child crying for his mother, who is nowhere to be seen.

I see a tight-lipped boy no older than ten, face as white as a sheet, with a large slice of metal stuck in his right arm. He grimaces in pain but doesn't let out a sound, not wanting to scare his little sister, who's holding his other hand and crying te'eburnee.

I see doctors, the last few in Homs, shaking their heads at small, limp, frail bodies and moving to the next.

I see little girls with legs twisted into unnatural positions. Their eyes carry the full meaning of what's about to happen. Amputation.

I wish we were being broadcast live on every channel and smartphone in the world so everyone could see what they're allowing to happen to children.

A little boy starts singing with glazed eyes, staring into the ceiling. He's shirtless, and his black hair is thin. His chest heaves with each breath; he's struggling to fill his lungs. I can see his ribs, count each one of them. He sings one of the many freedom songs made by the rebels. His young voice is quiet but strong. It carries over the chaos and embeds itself within the hospital walls. If these walls could speak, imagine what they would say. I walk toward him in a trance, guided only by the tune of his singing. There's no one beside him. Neither his legs nor his arms are severed. There's no blood coming out of his mouth or dripping from his head. He's not a priority. And yet . . . I clasp his hands in mine. They're as cold as ice. His little coat must be back at the school, buried under the rubble.

"Are you hurt?" I ask through silent tears.

He doesn't stop singing, but his voice is lower. I check his pulse; it's slow and unnatural. I don't see any wounds.

"Are you *hurt?*" I ask again, urgently. At this rate, his heart will stop.

He turns toward me. "My name is Ahmad. I'm six years old. Can you help me find my mama?" he says quietly. His eyes, deep blue, are sunk so far into his skull, I'm scared they'll vanish.

He's in shock. I take off my lab coat, put it around him. I warm his hands in mine and kiss them.

"Yes, habibi. I will find your mama. Can you tell me if you're in pain?"

"I feel funny."

"Where?"

"My head. I feel . . . sleepy"—he coughs roughly—"and my chest . . . I don't know."

Internal bleeding.

I yell for Dr. Ziad. The doctor hurries to my side and checks Ahmad's pulse. Ahmad tells him he's thirsty while Dr. Ziad inspects his head. Extreme thirst can only mean one thing. With a deep sigh, he shakes his head.

"What does that mean?" I demand. "Are you giving up on him?"

"Salama, we don't have a neurosurgeon. No one here knows how to operate on internal bleeding in the brain." His tone is grave, full of regret.

"What? So, we're just going to let him . . . ?" I hiss but can't get the horrible word out. I don't want Ahmad to hear it.

Dr. Ziad wipes back Ahmad's hair from his forehead. There are droplets of sweat coating it. I swallow the bile in my throat.

"Are you in pain, son?" he asks.

Ahmad shakes his head.

"Adrenaline and shock. He doesn't need morphine. We can't do anything except make his last moments better."

"I'm going to do a blood transfusion." I turn around to where we stack the equipment. As an O-negative, I'm a universal donor. We have a manual device Dr. Ziad made to donate blood to the patients because the transfusion machines don't always work. Not with the electricity shortage. "I can give him my blood. I'll give him——"

"It won't help," he says in a pained tone.

"Dr. Ziad——" He holds up a hand, interrupting me.

"Salama, it won't. If I could give my life so this boy would be safe and well and healthy, I would. But I can't. I can't help him. But I can help the little girl whose intestines are all over the floor. We can't save everyone."

He leaves before I can yell.

"Auntie——" Ahmad begins softly, stopping to gasp for breath.

"Yes, habibi?" I turn around and clasp his hands back into mine. *If you live, I'll take care of you*, I vow. *Just live. Please. Just live.*

"Am I going to die?" he asks, and I see no fear. *Do all six-year-olds know what death is? Or is it only children of war?* My hands shake.

"Are you scared of death?" I reply instead.

"I——" He coughs, and a hint of red drips from his lips. *My God.* "I don't know. Baba's dead. Mama said he's in Heaven. Will I go to Heaven too?"

I shudder in a breath. "Yes, you will. You'll see your baba there."

He smiles gently.

"Alhamdulillah," he whispers. "What can I do in Heaven, Auntie?"

How can a child have so much composure in the face of death?

I swallow my tears, drowning inwardly. "You will play all day. There are games and food and candy and toys and everything you could ever want."

"Can I talk to God too?"

I'm taken aback by his question. "Of. . . of course you can, ya omri."

"Good."

We sit silently for a few minutes, and I listen as his lungs struggle. Already his eyes are losing focus, his breaths becoming shallower by the second.

I pray for his soul and recite Quran verses in a whisper.

"Auntie—don't cry—when I go to Heaven—I'll tell God—everything," he chokes out. I look up, and his face has gone still. His eyes are glassy, and it looks like little stars are caught in his blue irises.

I DON'T MOVE FROM AHMAD'S BODY FOR A LONG time. I don't even let go of his hands. Pressing them to my lips, I try to will life into him again. The background noises are muted in my ears. All I hear, stuck on repeat like a broken cassette: *I will tell God everything.*

Gooseflesh erupts on my neck, and I'm chilled to the bone. I half expect God's wrath to strike down.

A hand taps on my back. I ignore it. I don't even hear what the person is saying.

"Hey!" The tapping increases and borders on annoying. I'm grieving a boy I never knew, but who I let down.

"What?" I snap, turning around.

It's a boy. My age or older. He's panting and shaking. His hands can't keep steady; they're running over his face and tawny curls; his green eyes are wild. He looks familiar and it takes me a second to realize it's the boy from yesterday, who was carrying a little girl in his arms.

"Please . . . *please!* You have to help me." He jumps over his words, shoulders trembling.

His tone jerks me back to reality. Ahmad may have died, but the living are still here. I push my grief down into the dark edges of my mind. I'll deal with it later.

I jump to my feet. "Yes? What happened?"

"My sister—*please*—she came in yesterday because of the bomb—there was shrapnel in her stomach—it was taken out—we took her home—hospital said there's no space—they said she'd be okay—please—*just*—" he stammers, unable to keep up with the pace of his words from pure terror.

I snap my fingers in front of him. "Hey! I need you to calm down. Deep breaths, right now."

He stops himself and tries to breathe but it's pitiful. He can't keep it in long enough.

"My sister," he begins in a forced calm tone. A vein pounds in his throat. "Last night, she got this fever, and it hasn't broken all day. Even when I gave her Panadol. It's bad. Really bad. She's vomited three times, and I can't carry her here. Every time I try to move her, she screams in pain. Please . . . you *have* to help me."

I immediately know what it is. Reluctantly, I take my lab coat off little Ahmad's body. I don't even get to say goodbye.

I look around to see if any of the doctors might be able to help, but each of them seems to be caught up with their own patients. I have to do this by myself. When I started here a few months ago, I saw how Dr. Ziad goes above and beyond for his patients, which made me want to do the same.

Despite his objections. Because I know the consequences if I don't do just that. I learned how to take out shrapnel, sew gaping wounds, and attempt to stop death all by myself. I became a surgeon by force. Removed enough bullets to melt down the steel and build a car. Grabbing the emergency surgical bag, I motion for the boy to lead.

"Where do you live?" I ask as we hurry through the chilly afternoon.

His eyes are trained to the skies and tops of buildings; he's looking for snipers and planes. "Just a few roads ahead. Doctor, why is she in pain? Do you know?"

I hesitate for a few seconds before replying. "I think there's probably a piece of shrapnel inside her wound."

He mumbles a curse word.

"I'm sorry."

He shakes his head. "No. With the hospital overstretched like this, I understand how it could happen. At least it's one piece."

I *hope* it's one.

"How old is she?"

"Nine."

Dammit. Likely starved and highly vulnerable to infection.

"We have to hurry."

He picks up the pace, and I follow him through the old alleys of our torn-up city. A few people are out, either deep in conversation or waiting in line at the bakery.

"I'm Kenan," he says suddenly, and I turn toward him, distracted.

"What?"

"Kenan," he repeats, and manages a small smile.

"Salama," I say. His name feels familiar, like I heard it in a dream once.

But before I can try unraveling that faint thread of recognition, he stops. In front of us is a building. Or what's left of it. Like every building around, it's been affected by the many stray shells and gunshots. The paint is chipped and peeling off, layer by layer. It's five stories high and must have been brown once.

Kenan opens the building's front door slowly and gives me a tentative look. I frown, not understanding. His whole demeanor changes. Like he's ashamed. We walk up the concrete stairs, which are chipped at the edges, until we reach the second floor. Their door is wooden and old and opens up to the living room, which looks as if a small bomb exploded right in the middle. Broken furniture, deteriorating walls, and dusty ripped rugs. On the other side, I'm taken aback by the state of the balcony. It's more than half destroyed; chunks of it have clearly fallen down to the streets below. A huge hole allows for gusts of the winter wind to freeze those inside. Standing close to the edge would put you in danger of falling over.

He calls out and one of his siblings, I guess, hurries to him. He's young, banging on the door of his teenage years. There's a big hole in the side of his shirt, and his jeans hang loosely on him.

I can hear their sister moaning from where she's lying on the floor in the living room. I need to work fast. Kenan sinks to his knees beside her and asks if she's okay, whispering encouragements and love. The younger boy stands beside the doorway, fidgeting with his hands and throwing nervous glances to the little girl.

"Lama, this is the doctor. She's going to help you."

The little girl gasps for air before nodding. Her whole face is twisted with pain. I sit beside her.

"Lama, honey. I want to help you, but you have to help me first. All right?"

She nods again.

"Did they give her blood at the hospital yesterday?" I ask Kenan, taking out the tools I need.

"Yes," he breathes. "One of the doctors donated. O-negative maybe?"

I nod and unbutton her shirt. Her skin is translucent, and her ribs are sticking out like Ahmad's were. I can't have tears blurring my sight so I command myself not to cry. Kenan holds her hand and keeps on talking, trying to distract her from her agony. She yelps in pain when I take off her sweat-soaked shirt. I press a palm to her hot forehead.

"Lama, where's the pain coming from?"

"My—my stomach," she gasps, sweat trickling down her cheek.

I cut her bandages as carefully as I can and say, "I'm going to press my hand on your stomach, and when the pain is too much, tell me."

She nods. Kenan watches my every movement with tear-filled eyes. I'm astonished at my own composure. The moment I touch her abdomen, she screams.

Shit.

I apply pressure, and she screams even louder.

Daisies. Daisies. Daisies, I recite to myself, steadying my hand.

"What are you doing?" Kenan says hoarsely.

"I need to find out where the shrapnel is."

Lama continues to scream, but I can't stop. I must feel the edge of a metallic object pushing against my hand.

"You're hurting her!" he yells.

I silence him with a look I learned from Mama. "You think I want to do this? I need to find out where it is!"

He goes quiet, but I can see the fire raging in his eyes.

"She has bruising and stitches everywhere. I can't make out which the shrapnel is responsible for. That is *why* I'm doing this."

He nods, his face white as a sheet.

"Lama, you need to tell me when the pain is worse, okay? You're so brave, and I know you're going to be strong now too. All right?"

She squeezes out a few more tears before nodding again.

"Good girl."

I press gently, making a line down her stomach. She grits her teeth and doesn't scream anymore, but her breaths come out in short bursts until I reach just below her belly button.

"Here!" she shrieks.

I immediately stop. I felt its edge before she told me.

"Good job, Lama." I breathe in, trying to make my tone lighter. "You're amazing. Now all that's left is to get the shrapnel out."

"Do it," Kenan says.

"I just—" I swallow the acid in my mouth and look at him. "It's going to be a bit difficult."

"Why?"

I shake my head. *How do I say this?*

"I need—"

"You need to cut into her stomach, and there's no anesthesia."

"Yes," I whisper.

Kenan runs his hand through his hair and over his face, torn.

"I need to do this right now. Before the shrapnel moves and ends up God knows where."

His breathing shatters.

"Do it. We have no choice. Just do it." His tone is as pained as his sister's.

"Get her something to bite on."

He takes off his belt.

"Lama, I'm so sorry. I know you're in pain, but you can do this. I'm here. Your brothers are here."

She starts crying.

"Bite on the belt," I tell her.

This isn't what I ever envisioned myself doing. I was supposed to be a pharmacist. I wasn't supposed to cut into children's stomachs in their homes.

My hands shake as I take out the disinfectant and a scalpel. Until now, every time I've operated alone has been at the hospital, with Dr. Ziad always somewhere nearby in case I messed up. It's reassuring to know he's there.

But here, if I slip, if I cut a vein or cause even more internal bleeding, she will die. And I'll have murdered her.

I shut my eyes tightly, try to regulate my breathing and think of the daisies.

"Hey," I hear Kenan saying. "Are you okay?"

I immediately open my eyes.

"Yes," I say, and I'm proud that my voice doesn't break. All the times I've needed to keep a cool head at the hospital are paying off. His eyes go soft, and I think he can read the fear I'm frantically trying to hide. I ignore the quick flash of hesitance darting across his expression.

I look at Lama, who's staring up at the ceiling with tears glistening in her eyes. Her lips quiver where she bites on the belt. She's too young for this.

God, please guide my hand, and let me save this poor girl.

I disinfect her stomach and the scalpel and look at Kenan. This is going to hurt him far more than it'll hurt her.

"Hold her hand," I instruct him.

He nods, white-faced. I press the cool metal against her stomach, and she winces.

"Lama, look only at me," her brother says.

I take a deep breath and move the scalpel down in a small cut. It doesn't stop Lama from howling. She tries to push me away, kicking her legs all the while, but Kenan holds her down.

"Lama, please, I need you to stay still!" I say, working as fast as I can.

Blood spurts out of the wound I made, and I dig in two fingers to feel for the shrapnel. She sobs, begging me to stop. I feel like a monster. But there's no time for me to be delicate. The tip of my finger brushes against a pointy edge.

"Found it!" I yell and clamp on it. It's lodged in a shallow area, away from her large intestine, and I nearly keel over with relief. Despite that, I pray hard it isn't causing any internal bleeding. I pull out slowly. This was a close one. Carefully, I make sure there is no more debris sticking around before stitching her wound up. Every puncture through her skin sends a fresh wave of pain for her, Kenan, and me. The suture is ugly and will definitely leave a scar, but she's alive and that's all that matters. I press around her stomach, making sure there's nothing else.

"I'm done." Panting hard, as if I'd run a marathon, I start gently wrapping her with a set of fresh bandages.

Kenan's face sags with relief. He kisses her forehead, smoothing away her sweat-soaked hair.

"You did amazing, Lama. I'm *so* proud of you. You're so brave." Their tears mix together. She smiles weakly, her eyes drooping with exhaustion.

But my work is still not done. I get up to wash her blood off my hands only to remember that the water is cut off.

"Here," I hear Kenan say from behind me. He holds a big bucket of water, which they probably use to drink and cook.

I shake my head. "I can't do that. You need this water. I'll wipe them back at the hospital."

"Don't be silly. Come here and wash the blood off you. We have buckets of water."

No one has buckets of water.

But I take it from him. The water runs over my scars like little streams washing away the blood.

"Did the hospital give you any antibiotics?" I dry my hands on my yellowed lab coat.

"Yes." He takes them out of his pocket and hands them to me. Cephalexin, 250 milligrams.

"Give her two tablets every twelve hours for seven days."

He hurries over to her and makes her swallow two of them. She complains that her sides still hurt but takes the pills. Their brother emerges from behind the door and sits beside her, trying to make her as comfortable as possible. He sniffs, rubbing his red eyes, and she smiles slightly before closing her own. Her fatigue is so palpable I feel it on my own skin.

I look at my watch. It's nearing six p.m. I have to get back to Layla.

Kenan walks back over to me.

"Thank you so much, Doctor. I don't know what else to say."

I wave off his appreciation. "It's not a big deal. Just doing my job. And I'm a pharmacist."

"I guess this isn't in your job description," he says, looking at me with awe. Adrenaline shoots through my system once again and I look away. There's life in his eyes. Something I'm not used to seeing outside of Layla's. "And you're young."

I fiddle with my fingers. "Not that much younger than you."

He shakes his head. "I didn't mean it in a bad way. I think it's amazing that you can do all of this."

I shrug one shoulder. "Circumstances."

"Yeah," he says, and his gaze lingers on me for a few seconds before he looks away. His cheeks turn pink.

I clear my throat and gesture toward Lama. "Now, your sister won't be able to eat anything for a while. That's where fluids will play a role. Let her drink as much as she can. Soup, water, juice . . . anything really. Fruits too. If there are any."

He's nodding at every word I'm saying, storing them in

his head. I can see him try and work out where he'll be able to get all these things. They aren't starving by choice. I don't ask where his parents are. If they're not here, then it's not a mystery what happened to them.

"I'll be at the hospital if you need anything. When she can move a bit, bring her there so we can see what more we can do."

"Thank you."

I hoist the surgical bag over my shoulder. "Again, no problem."

He walks with me downstairs. "I'll take you back to the hospital."

"No, it's fine. I'm going home anyway. Your sister needs you more."

He looks torn between wanting to be chivalrous and staying for his sister.

"It's fine," I repeat more firmly.

"Let me at least see you out," he says, and I nod.

We walk together, going down the stairs in silence. At the front door, I turn toward him and he smiles.

"Thank you again," he says.

"You're welcome," I reply, and step over the threshold.

"Take—" But his voice is drowned out when shots rip through the air. I whirl in fright to see his eyes widening, and immediately he grabs my arm and pulls me inside.

"Hey!" I protest, wrenching myself out of his grip, but he doesn't notice, instead slamming the door shut.

He holds a finger to his lips and presses his ear against the metal frame. I wait with bated breath, praying it's not

what I think it is. Hope shrivels away when more shots follow and our worst suspicions are confirmed.

"It's not safe," he finally says.

"Obviously. I need to go." I move to the side, but he
blocks the space.

"It's probably the military clashing with the protestors.
You need to stay indoors until it's over. They'll have snipers
all over the buildings."

Even though this is expected to happen at any time, I start
to panic. Layla's alone. I can't leave her like that the whole night.

"I have to go. Layla needs me," I echo again.

"Who's Layla?"

"My friend. She's my sister-in-law, too, and seven
months pregnant. I can't leave her."

"How are you going to be any help to her if you're dead
or captured?" he says forcefully, forming a body shield
against the door.

Goddammit.

"Can't you call her?"

"We have phones, but we don't use them. I'm too scared
the military will track them and know she's alone."

He hesitates for a few seconds, then takes out an old
Nokia. "This is like a burner phone. It's only used to call
people. You can use it."

"How the hell did you get one?"

"Do you want to ask questions, or do you want to call
her?" He hands it to me and heads back upstairs.

Kenan pauses halfway up and then says, "Don't run into
death."

I nod, and he disappears.

I dial her number, my heart beating loudly as the beeps go by. She doesn't pick up, and I nearly faint from terror. Three more times. No answer.

Khawf materializes in front of me, and the uneasiness opens the blackest hole in my heart.

"What's happening?" I gasp.

"Imagine if she's in labor right now," he says.

The earth shakes under me.

"These are the choices you make every day, Salama." He stands closer, regarding me with pity. "You're gambling with Layla's life. Not to mention the life of her unborn child. Your *niece*. Which is more important? The patients or Layla and her baby?"

I hear my bones cracking under the weight of his words. I remember Layla's anguish when Hamza was taken. How she spent weeks screaming and clutching her stomach, wishing to die, her torment overflowing like a flood, threatening to drown her.

I imagine what Hamza would say to me if I let any harm come to Layla.

If she died because of me.

1

I OPEN THE FRONT DOOR OF KENAN'S APARTMENT and walk in like a possessed body. This doesn't feel right. I need to be with Layla.

"How's your sister-in-law?" Kenan asks, coming out from the kitchen.

"She didn't pick up the phone." I swallow hard.

"Keep it," he says, reading my fear. "And try again."

"Thank you," I whisper.

He nods and I stand by the wall, trying to soothe my agitated nerves. The afternoon's hazy orange glow begins to dwindle, and it drags the harsh cold breeze inside Kenan's half-destroyed apartment. I shiver, pressing my lab coat tighter to me. Kenan notices and, with his brother's help, hangs a gray wool blanket from either side of the hole, trying to minimize the frigid air's reach.

"Thank you," I murmur, and he smiles at me, shaking his head.

He goes into one of the rooms, lugs out an old mattress,

and hauls it across the floor. His brother casts me shy glances, his cheeks hollow and his wrists bony. He looks a bit like Kenan, though his eyes are a lighter shade of green and his hair a darker shade of brown. Two characteristics he shares with his sister.

"So, we put the mattress beside Lama. I thought you'd feel more comfortable not being alone tonight." Then Kenan says quickly, as if trying to get the words out as fast as he can: "If you want, you can have any of these rooms. Yusuf and I will be awake the whole night. But if you need anything or just—"

"You're right," I interrupt. "She's still feverish, and I want to make sure she'll be fine. I won't be able to sleep either. Your brother should, though. It doesn't make sense for the whole house to stay awake."

He doesn't argue with me and whispers something to Yusuf, brushing his hair back. Yusuf barely reaches Kenan's chin, and he looks up at his older brother adoringly before slipping inside his room.

I'm glad someone will be sleeping, because I don't know if I'll be able to this far away from Layla. I wander to the mattress and sit beside Lama, checking her temperature. She's still a bit too warm for my liking, but I'm hoping the antibiotics will bring her back. I wipe her brow with a wet cloth, remembering how Mama used to do it for me when I was sick. Her gentle fingers, her encouraging words when I downed a glass of squeezed lemons.

"*Bravo, te'eburenee,*" she used to say, her cool palm on my sweat-slicked forehead. "*I'm so proud of you. Yalla, drink it all. Kill all those germs.*"

I squeeze my eyes shut. *No. I'm not going there.*

"How is she?" Kenan asks, sitting down on Lama's other side.

I manage a smile. "Despite the fever, her breathing is better. I'm optimistic."

"Alhamdulillah."

He hands me a halloumi sandwich, and I'm surprised. Bread and cheese don't come easy. I notice he doesn't have one.

"You're our guest," he says, and I can't help but wonder what this'll cost them.

"I can't take this. Give it to your brother."

"No, he already has one. If you don't eat it, I'll throw it away, and then no one will. So please, don't fight me on this."

It would sound like an empty threat coming from anyone else, but he doesn't look like he's joking around. His eyes are obstinate, holding no room for negotiation.

I let out a sigh and break it in half, holding out the bigger one. "Take it."

He shakes his head.

"If you don't take it, I will throw it away right now, and no one will eat it."

He laughs and takes it.

"That wasn't too hard, was it?"

"I'm pretty sure my parents' souls are glaring at me from Heaven right now for accepting. But I was outwitted." He laughs again. His glance falls to my hands, to my scars, just for a second. My stomach goes hollow and I pull my sleeves over them. The action doesn't go unnoticed, but he doesn't say anything.

"One has to be smart in these times," I say, trying to enforce a casual tone to my voice.

Dusk has turned the sky into a deep pink flecked across the blue. After we finish our food, he calls his brother and we pray together. Kenan begins reciting verses from the Quran in a beautiful melodic tone. I feel hypnotized by each word, drinking in their meaning, feeling them bring peace and serenity to every cell in my body, washing away the sorrows. I can't remember the last time I was so at peace, nearly empty of worry.

After prayer, I check on Lama. No change.

Kenan brings out a few candles, lights them up, and thanks to the blanket covering the hole in the wall, they don't go out. I excuse myself to go to the washroom to freshen up and try to call Layla again, with no success.

She's fine, I repeat to myself as I massage my scalp and splash water on my face to calm down.

When I go back into the living room, Kenan is beside his sister, and I take the opposite side of the mattress. A laptop is on the ground near him with the screen turned off.

"When will we know if she'll be totally okay?" he asks, dabbing her forehead with a cloth.

"Cephalexin takes about ten to twenty-four hours to reach a steady concentration in the blood. Tomorrow, insh'Allah, she'll be all right."

He looks at me. "You sure do know a lot about medications."

I shrug. "It's my job."

"Yeah, but you know the timings and stuff by heart without hesitation. That's got to be an advanced level."

"It is." I feel myself coloring up and avert my eyes to the window beside us, focusing on the blue morphing to black. It finally dawns on me that I'm spending the night at a boy's house. Under extraordinary circumstances, yes, but it's still happening. My hands become clammy, and I try not to imagine Layla's eyes widening at this juicy piece of information. The most scandalous thing anyone I know has done was when Hamza kissed Layla's hand after their Al-Fatiha. And they weren't even formally engaged. It was a pre-engagement party. I teased Hamza about it endlessly until he flicked my nose, red in the face.

And now here I am, sitting on the living room floor with a boy mere feet away from me.

"You still remember all this information even after graduating?" Kenan asks suddenly, and I glance up, registering the tone he's using. He's trying to distract himself and, in turn, me, from the awkwardness of this situation.

I clear my throat, and the voices go quiet in my mind.

"I didn't graduate. I had just begun my second year when—you know." I don't tell him I stopped going when protests broke out at our university and the military arrested dozens of my classmates. I don't know him well enough.

"I finished my second year last year. Bachelor's in computer science. I had dreams of becoming an animator. Everything was going perfectly," he muses, nodding his chin toward the laptop. "Ironically, with all that's happened, I have so many stories to tell. To be animated into movies."

"You mean like the Hayao Miyazaki ones?"

"Exactly like that," he says, stunned. "You know him?"

"I'm *obsessed* with his movies."

He straightens up, eyes shining with excitement. "Me too! Studio Ghibli is my goal. That place is where ideas and imaginations run wild. They weave stories like magic there."

His enthusiasm stirs something in my heart. "That sounds beautiful," I murmur.

He closes his eyes, smiling. "A silver lining."

There's an honest joy in his voice, but for the first time tonight, I can see his real face behind the fragments he's had to glue back together over and over again. He looks broken, and my heart hurts for him. But he also feels *so* familiar.

I shake my head and ask him bluntly, "Have we ever met?"

His eyes snap open, surprised.

"How do you mean?" he replies slowly.

"It may be nothing." I play with the hem of my sweater. "But I think I've seen you before. Not around the hospital but . . . somewhere else."

My voice trails the last words like a question. He bites his lip, and I can't read the look on his face. The eagerness has dissolved into something else. Confusion? Incredulity? Pity? I don't know.

Suddenly Khawf appears by the front door and slowly glides closer. Sweat breaks out at the back of my neck.

"I . . . um . . ." Kenan clears his throat, scratching the floor with his hand. "We've never met."

Huh.

"Must be in my head, I guess," I say, playing it off as a common mistake and trying not to let Khawf's presence unnerve me. "You must look like someone I know or treated."

He nods, but it's plain as day: There's something more going on.

"What's your last name?" I ask loudly, and he jumps from his spot. In a way, everyone knows everyone in Homs by their family names. My grandmother could recite a person's entire family history if they told her their last name. She'd know who their grandfather was, what their aunt studied at university, which other families they were related to. She'd name it all, dissecting the line like a scientist analyzing a cell under a microscope.

This is a specialty shared by *all* Syrians.

He smiles. "Aljendi."

That's a well-known family name that many share. I rack my brain, trying to remember if Mama ever mentioned an Aljendi, and come up blank.

Khawf narrows his eyes and impatiently brushes down his suit before taking out a cigarette. Khawf doesn't care where we are. There's nothing else for me to do except ignore him, focusing on Kenan and Lama and praying he doesn't torment me. I can't question my grip on reality with Kenan and his sister right here. I can't lose myself tonight.

"Your sister was amazing today," I begin. Khawf raises his eyebrows. "I haven't met many nine-year-olds who could have gone through that and still been able to smile at their brothers."

"Yeah, she's a tough one." He gently caresses her hair to the side. "Always has been. I think she hates herself for screaming so much, which shows you how much pain she was in."

I feel guilty. "I'm sorry."

"I wasn't trying to blame you! It must have been hard on you too."

"Ask him again. Where do you know him from?" Khawf interjects, blowing out silver smoke.

I continue ignoring him.

"Do it, and I won't bother you again tonight."

Please go away, I beg in my mind.

"Are you really satisfied with that stutter of a reply? Any fool would know he's hiding something. What if it's bad? What if it's something that could harm you?"

I shoot him a furious look. He doesn't seem abashed in the slightest.

"You're here, all alone, for the whole night. And even if Layla knew where you were, how much help do you think a pregnant girl would be? All you have is your scalpel." He straightens, eyeing Kenan up and down. "And judging by his physique, even though you're both starving, he could overpower you in five seconds. Three, if you don't resist."

The back of my neck breaks out in sweat. Why does he do this to me? Wedge every doubt and dread in my brain until all I can think about is what he's saying.

Kenan Aljendi. His name sounds so familiar. Where have I heard it before?

"He knows you," Khawf presses on. "He recognized you. That gives him the upper hand. I bet he already knew your name. He didn't ask you about *your* last name."

Shit, he has a point.

I clear my throat. The rational part of my brain knows Kenan won't harm me, but the other part is annoyed he's hiding something.

"Kenan. I'm sorry, but I feel like we really have met." I leave no room for negotiation in my tone.

The candlelight flickers across his clouded eyes.

"I told you we haven't," he insists.

I stare at him, my gaze turning colder by the second. "I'm pretty sure we have."

He sighs loudly and stands. My body instantly goes into defense mode, but the surgical bag is a bit far away for me to grab a scalpel from. Even if I were to stand, he'd still be much taller than me, and I hate that. I should have listened to my gut and walked home, snipers and all.

Calm down!

"I'm not lying, Salama, when I say we haven't met." He turns around to look at me. Khawf enjoys this immensely, glancing from me to Kenan and back to me.

"Then?" I feel vulnerable from my place on the floor.

"We haven't met because we never got the chance to."

You know what? I'm going to stand too.

"Can you please stop talking in code?"

He looks at me pointedly. "We were supposed to meet for coffee about a year ago."

Coffee.

Friday.

Layla's blue kaftan.

"Oh my God," I breathe, putting the pieces from over one year ago together. "You were—"

"I was, but life changed."

"You were going to come to my house for that marriage talk thing!" I finally splutter out.

Khawf gasps and claps his hands.

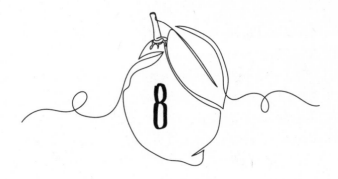

8

KENAN STARES AT ME, HIS CHEEKS AND EARS GROW-
ing redder, and I stare right back, remembering Mama and
how the beginning of the end began.

The day before my world came crashing down around
me, I was on my phone scrolling through my Facebook
feed. I'd just paused *Princess Mononoke* on my laptop—Layla
had tagged me in a makeup tutorial video—when Mama
walked in.

"Salama," she said.

I looked up, my hair falling over my eyes. I pushed it back.

*Her smile was tentative, and she brushed her fingers along the
devil's ivy leaves cascading from my bookshelf to the floor. Layla had
gifted me the plant when I was accepted into pharmacy school, and I
named her Urjuwan. The name was ironic, seeing as it meant purple,
while my devil's ivy's leaves were the darkest shade of green. Still, it
is a name I love. The way the U, R, J, and W all come together to
create a melodic word that sounds the most Arabic. Urjuwan looked
pretty beside the jars of herbs and flowers and the two scrapbooks I*

had made containing all the information I had gathered on medicinal flowers and herbs over many years, with dried petals glued to the heavy pages and captions scribbled on the side. Drawings by Layla when I needed a hand. I was so proud of those scrapbooks, I even showed them to my professor, who praised me in front of the whole class. That was the day I decided to specialize in pharmacology.

Mama sat beside me on the bed. "They're coming tomorrow."

I'm sure she didn't think this day would arrive so soon. Especially since Hamza and Layla had gotten married not even a year ago.

"At three p.m. after Friday prayer," I said in the voice of someone reciting the history of concrete. "I know."

She chewed her cheek, and in the light where the sun fell on her face, she looked younger. Enough to be mistaken as my twin.

"Why are you anxious?" I laughed. "I thought that was supposed to be my job."

She sighed. Even though I shared her facial features and the color and softness of her russet-brown hair, our eyes were where the similarities ended. While mine were a mix of hazel and brown, like the bark of our lemon trees, her eyes were deep blue, the color of the sky during twilight. And now they were filled with warmth for me.

"Well, you're not acting anxious," she said indignantly. "So, I'm doing it for the both of us." After a small pause, she said, "Maybe we should postpone."

"Why?" I had seen his picture on Facebook, and I liked what I saw. I wanted to see if his personality matched his cute face.

"After——" She stopped, took a breath, and continued in a low voice. "I'm not sure if the unrest in Dara'a won't affect us here in Homs."

The unrest she was talking about was the government's

kidnapping of fourteen boys—all in their early teens. They were tortured, their fingernails ripped off, and then sent back to their families—all because they'd scribbled "It's your turn, Doctor" on a wall after the success of the revolutions in Egypt, Tunisia, and Libya. By "Doctor" they meant the president, Bashar al-Assad, who was an ophthalmologist. The irony of a man who was drenched in innocent blood taking a vow to do no harm was not lost on me.

I bit my lip, looking away. No one had spoken about it in university, but I could feel the tension in the air and in the streets. Something had changed. I saw it in the way Baba and Hamza talked at the dinner table.

"Dara'a is miles away from here," I said quietly. "And . . . I don't know."

"It doesn't matter." Mama grasped my hands in hers and squeezed. "If we show even a small amount of resistance, then . . . I can't let them take my babies away."

"Mama, relax," I said, wincing a bit when her hold got tight. "I'm not going anywhere."

"Yes you are," she said with a sad smile. "If it works out with Kenan tomorrow, my baby girl is going to get married."

I stared at my devil's ivy, admiring the veins jutting through the leaves, the intricate details. "Is it really bad there are protests in Dara'a? Who would want to live under the thumb of a government like this? You've always told me how Jedee and his brother were taken away and you never saw them again."

Mama was the one who winced this time, but by the time I turned toward her, there was nothing but serenity on her face.

"Yes, they took my father and uncle." Her twilight eyes went wet. "They dragged Baba away in front of my sisters and my mother and me. I was only ten, but I'll never forget that day. I remember hoping he died. Can you believe that?" She stopped, eyes going wide, but I didn't feel any surprise.

I knew that for fifty years we had lived in fear, trusting no one with the rebellious thoughts in our minds. The government had taken everything from us, stripped away our freedom, and committed genocide in Hama. They'd tried to smother our spirits, tried to torture the fear into us, but we'd survived. The government was an open wound, hemorrhaging our resources for their own gain with their greed and bribery, and yet we persisted. We held our heads high and planted lemon trees in acts of defiance, praying that when they came for us, it'd be a bullet to the head. Because that was far more merciful than what awaited in the bowels of their prison system.

She took a deep breath. "Of course I want justice for my family, Salama. But I can't lose you or your brother. Not to mention your father and Layla. You four are my world."

Her eyes glazed over.

"So, um, knafeh?" I said meekly, trying to draw her back to me.

She blinked. "Ah, yes. Knafeh. I got you all the ingredients you'll need."

"I'll make it as soon as I'm done with this." I smiled. "Why knafeh, though?"

Mama's lips hid a secret. "Because you're so good at it and I believe in fate."

"What's that supposed to mean?"

She got up and pressed a kiss to my forehead. "Nothing, hayati. I love you."

"Love you too."

Kenan runs a hand over his hair, and my eyes snap back to him, my heart beating painfully against my rib cage.

"I'm right, are—aren't I?" I stutter, feeling hot in my

thin sweater and lab coat. Kenan looks away, cracking his knuckles. "The marriage proposal. The one our mothers set up!"

He grimaces and glances back at me. "When you put it like that, it doesn't sound very romantic."

The air feels knocked out of me, and I sink back onto the mattress, hugging my legs. Oh, Layla is going to have a field day with this! I'm hiding in the house of the boy I might have married.

Might.

What a word. It holds infinite possibilities of a life that could have been. So many options stacked one on top of the other, like cards waiting for a player to pick and choose. To try their luck. I see fragments of a life where *might* happened. Our souls fit together perfectly from our first conversation. The rest of our visits bloom. I count down the seconds until we say *I do*. We buy a beautiful house in the country, dance in the dusk, travel the world, raise a family, discover new ways to fall for each other every single day. I become a renowned pharmacologist, and he becomes a famous animator. We live a long life together, partners in crime, until our souls meet their Creator.

But that is not reality.

Our future is bleak. A half-destroyed apartment, with his little sister fighting for her life. Our life is the stabs of hunger, frozen limbs, orphaned siblings, bloodied hands, old shrapnel, fear of tomorrow, silent tears, and fresh wounds. Our future has been ripped from our hands.

Somewhere far away, I hear freedom's familiar tune. Or maybe it's Khawf humming it to himself.

Kenan fiddles with his fingers. "I didn't want to tell you because I didn't know if you'd remember." He blows out a puff of air. "How creepy would I have sounded if I'd said, 'Hey, our mothers set us up on a social visit about our future marriage. That's where you know me from'?"

I rub my eyes and laugh to myself silently. He must feel self-conscious and gawky, which is helping a lot.

"It's fine. I get it." I grin.

He eyes me warily. "Why are you smiling?"

"Because it's the last thing I would have thought of." I keep giggling until it's grown into full-blown laughter. His smile grows wider until his laugh joins mine. Every time we look at each other, we double up with mirth. The Arab proverb has never been truer: The worst of outcomes is what is most hilarious.

Khawf smokes his cigarette and retreats to a corner of the room, seemingly satisfied with the result.

We settle down, chuckling quietly.

"Well, that is one hell of an icebreaker," I say.

"If I'd known this would happen, I would have come clean sooner."

Suddenly Lama wakes up, choking out "water," and the mood instantly changes. Kenan jumps to his feet and fetches a jug. I wipe her brow again and am pleased when I find she has continued to sweat.

"She sweated through her whole shirt." I smile.

"And that's good?" he asks with a raised eyebrow, helping her drink.

"It's excellent. Lama, drink some more water, please." She obliges. "This is a good sign. It means her body is healing. You can see her breath is steady, and there's no pus around the wounds. Alhamdulillah. She's making progress. Keep her warm and make her drink a lot of water."

Kenan's eyes brim with tears again. He clearly thought he was going to lose her and had steeled himself to accept the fact she might not open her eyes.

As Lama settles back to sleep, I wrap another blanket around her.

He stares at his sister's face, taking her small hand in his, engulfing it completely. When he speaks, it's dreamlike.

"She's the youngest in the family. We were all so happy when she was born. Two boys are a handful, and then this angel came into the world. I remember the sound of Baba crying with joy when the nurse told him she was a girl. She was so spoiled. A butterfly touching her skin was a catastrophe. We never let any harm come to her. How could we call ourselves her brothers then? Her protectors? And now . . . her body is hurt by hatred." His voice breaks, frustrated and angry. "I failed. I couldn't protect her. Yusuf hasn't even spoken since my parents died, and he flinches at the slightest sound. She and I were the ones who were able to keep it together. Not letting the cracks show. But . . . they're finally making her suffer. I promised Baba I'd protect them with my life and . . . I've let him down."

With shaking hands, he tucks the blanket around her more securely. I think of Baba and Hamza. And Layla.

Please be okay, Layla, I pray. *Please.*

"What do you do during the day?" I ask, trying to change a horrible subject to one less horrible by a fraction.

"For money? I have family in Germany. They send some whenever they can."

I fiddle with my fingers. "The hospital doesn't pay, but it's something to help the people. Although who knows if I'm staying long en—"

I immediately stop talking, and Kenan looks up, his brows furrowed. It's easy for him to piece it together from the mortification on my face. I press my hands against my chest, reciting *daisies, daisies, daisies*. I can't believe I let that slip. This *must* be the lack of sleep and today's horror catching up with me.

"You're going to leave?" he asks.

I ponder for a minute. "I don't know."

He looks confused. "You don't know?"

I chew my tongue. "Wouldn't *you* leave, given the chance?"

He has two very malnourished siblings under his care as reasons to leave, so what's stopping him? The hospital is the only thing holding me back.

"No," he says without hesitation, looking me straight in the eye.

"What—what about Yusuf and Lama?"

He inhales sharply and glances at Lama. Her face is scrunched with pain, her mouth parted as she breathes. Strands of hair are plastered to her forehead, and Kenan brushes them away, his fingers shaking. "I'd—I'd probably send my siblings alone if it were safe for them, but it's not. Yusuf is thirteen. She's nine. They . . . they can't make it on their own."

I stare at him. "Then why don't *you* leave with them?"

The sadness disappears from his eyes, replaced with a ferocious intensity. "This is my country. If I run away—if I don't defend it, then who will?"

I can't believe the words I'm hearing.

"Kenan," I begin slowly, and I don't know if it's the wavering candlelight, but his cheeks look flushed. "We're talking about your siblings' lives."

He swallows hard. "And I'm talking about my country. About the freedom I'm so rightly owed. I'm talking about burying Mama and Baba and telling Lama they'll never come back home. How—" His voice breaks. "How do I leave that? When for the first time in my whole life I'm breathing free Syrian air?"

How can he be so obstinate? I want to shake him.

"I don't get it. How is your staying here helping this *war*? Is it just by *breathing free Syrian air*?"

Kenan frowns at my word choice, but he doesn't comment on it. He takes in a deep breath and says, "I record the protests."

I lose all feeling in my knees and my stomach plummets. "You . . . you what?" I whisper.

He shudders and his hold tightens on Lama's hand. "It's why I can't leave. I'm showing the people—the world—what's *happening* here." He nods to his laptop. "I upload the videos on YouTube when the electricity is back."

My nails drag nervously against the floor. "Why are you telling me this? You do realize if you were found out, you'd be worse than dead? If the Free Syrian Army fails to defend us from the military, you'll be arrested."

Kenan laughs, but it's a hollow sound. "Salama, they're arresting people for no reason. They'll torture me for answers I don't have, knowing full well I don't have them. And I'm not the only one who's recording. There are so many of us protesting in our own way. In Daraya, one man, Ghiath Matar, gives out roses to the army soldiers. He fights guns with flowers. And I know in my heart they see that as a threat. Any form of protest, peaceful or not, is a threat to the dictatorship. So it doesn't matter to them if I record or not. I live in a place the Free Syrian Army protects. We're all in the same danger, because we're all in Old Homs. I'm complicit just by existing here. If I'm guilty either way, I might as well protest." He looks at my hands, and I cover them again with my sleeves. He's too far away for me to read the flash of emotion searing in his eyes. But it looks like pain.

My mouth is dry, and I stare at him. I don't believe he's that indifferent to the threat of being arrested. My gaze slips to the side, to the bedroom's doorway, and I see Yusuf's eyes peeking out beneath his messy hair. He's a thirteen-year-old boy; he's supposed to be on the brink of leaving behind the innocent wonder he enjoyed in his childhood as adolescence shapes his mind and stretches his limbs. But I don't see that in him. I see a frightened boy regressing into a child. Desperate to return to a time that was safe. Back when his parents were alive and his greatest worry was whether he'd be allowed to watch an extra hour of cartoons. His eyes are huge and full of tears. He fully understands the choices his brother is making. And the consequences.

I see Layla in him. I see her fear every time I evade the topic of fleeing.

Oh God. Oh God! If anything were to happen to me, she'd be destroyed. She'd be worse than dead.

My hands shake, and I cover my face, commanding myself to take a deep breath. Is this how I sound to her? So stubborn I can't see the way my actions are devastating those around me? Honorable as they may be, it doesn't lessen their destruction.

I have to leave. I have to take Layla and leave, or she won't survive this. Not the pregnancy, but me. She won't survive my death. And I won't survive hers.

If Layla died, my last family member—*my sister*—I would become a husk of a person. We came too close back in October. What would I do if she was gone? Khawf's low chuckle draws my eyes to him, and he shakes his head, smiling humorously.

"Now you see," he says.

I bang a fist against my forehead, cursing myself at my stupidity and naivety. Khawf was right. What price wouldn't I pay for Layla's safety?

I have to leave.

The decision blooms an ache inside my heart and the backs of my eyes burn with tears that refuse to fall. *How* did I not see it? I look up once again to see Khawf standing behind Kenan, leaning against the wall, wearing a satisfied grin.

He winks. "Now all that's left is to grovel to Am."

My head feels dizzy.

He straightens up, dusting off his glossy suit jacket. "And true to my word, I'll leave you alone now. But I'll see you later."

When I blink, he's gone.

My gaze falls, and Kenan is staring at me uncertainly, twiddling his fingers.

"Uh, Salama," he says, treating each word as if it were a delicate vase he was holding in his hands. "Is everything all right?"

I start. Not at the words but at his tone. "Yes," I answer a bit too fast. "Why?"

He scratches the back of his head. "I don't know. You were looking behind me as if the devil himself were standing there, and I'm too scared to turn around and check myself."

His voice comes out easy, his lips turned into a tentative, joking smile.

I smile back but it feels forced. "I'm great, thank you." It's the best I can do right now.

Kenan's confusion settles in, and I realize I must have been silent for a while. And my smiling right after such a long silence must be nothing short of unnerving.

I clear my throat. "Although I disagree with you. On staying here, that is."

He considers me for a second before saying, "Aren't you a pharmacist at the hospital bandaging the wounded who *are* protesting?"

"That has nothing to do with anything. I'm upholding my Hippocratic oath. You're putting yourself *and* your siblings in the crossfire."

He shrugs. "I guess I love Syria so much that the consequences don't matter."

Something snaps inside me. "And by telling you to leave, *I* don't?"

He becomes alarmed. "No! No, that isn't what I meant

at all! I . . . Salama, this is my *home*. For my entire life—my whole nineteen years—I've known no other. I'd be cutting out my heart by leaving. This land is me and I am her. My history, my ancestors, my family. We're all *here*."

His fierce resolution reminds me of Hamza and the spirited speeches he'd give when he came back from the protests with Baba. He would have definitely liked Kenan. The thought makes my stomach constrict.

I shake my head, focusing on the promise I made Hamza. Focusing on Layla's happiness when I tell her I was wrong and I'm sorry. That I'll save her and myself. Even though I know Kenan is right.

When I leave, it won't be easy. It's going to shred my heart to ribbons and all the pieces will be scattered along Syria's shore, with the cries of my people haunting me till the day I die.

I WAKE UP WITH A JOLT, AND MY HANDS FLY TO MY hijab. It had gotten tangled and nearly fallen off during the night. I hold a hand against my head, trying to remember what's going on. Kenan woke me up for Fajr prayer, and then I instantly fell back asleep.

"Ugh," I groan, rubbing my forehead and quickly adjusting my hijab.

I notice Lama's little body shifting beside me. I hurriedly crawl over to her and let out a sigh of relief when I touch her cheeks. She's not as feverish anymore. Kenan walks out of the kitchen with two mugs of hot tea and hands one to me. His hair is ruffled, sticking up from all sides, courtesy of sleep. The sight of the pink blush on his cheeks and his starry eyes makes me feel flustered.

My God, I spent the night here. In his apartment.

"Good morning," he says.

"Thank you." I accept the tea gratefully. "Lama is more than fine, alhamdulillah."

It's hot and I take a sip. *Mint tea. Yum, Layla loves mint tea. Layla.*

I choke on my tea, and Kenan looks up, worried. "What's wrong?"

"I'm fine," I gasp, my eyes smarting from the tea scalding my tongue. "I forgot about Layla. I need to leave. What time is it? I need to get to the hospital. My God, how long was I asleep? It doesn't matter. I need to go back to Layla! Keep an eye on your sister, okay? She's fine, but make her take the antibiotics. Thank you for the tea."

I gulp it down in one swig, grimacing as it burns, and jump to my feet.

"Kenan, what time is it?" I say, distracted, when I catch a glimpse of myself in the mirror. *God, I look horrible.* I grab my lab coat, hurry over to the destroyed balcony, and peer outside. Kenan has taken down the blanket to let the breeze in, and the fresh air is what I need for my overheated body.

"Is it safe?" I put on my lab coat. "Are there snipers? I'm worried about Layla. She *better* be okay. Kenan, what time is it? I have a shift at the hospital." I snap my fingers behind my back to get his attention while watching the roads outside. They're half empty and it seems no one is trying to hide on the rooftops.

I realize Kenan hasn't said anything for quite some time. Turning around, I see him sipping his own tea, watching my outburst with an amused look.

"Why aren't you answering me?" I demand. He takes another sip and puts his mug on the floor.

"Didn't give me a chance there with your monologizing. It was too entertaining to stop." He grins.

"Glad you're enjoying this." I glare. He doesn't look fazed at all.

"Are you always like this?"

"*This?*" I repeat, raising an eyebrow.

"Panicky with a hint of control freak?"

"Most days."

"That's good," he says, still grinning, and I don't know if he's being sarcastic or not. He doesn't sound sarcastic. Anyway, I don't have time to analyze his tone or features.

"Okay. I need to go *now*. Are there snipers outside?" I pull my bag tighter on my shoulder. I hate that I feel self-conscious about how I look, with my chapped lips and wrinkled hijab.

"How should I know?" he says. "They always change their timing. The FSA pushes them back sometimes."

I sigh. I'm going to have to wing this.

"All right, I'll manage," I say half-heartedly and move toward the door.

He holds up an arm against the doorway. "Where do you think you're going?"

"*Um*, home?"

"You honestly think I'd let you walk alone? When there could be snipers?"

"Do you have a secret invisible airplane I can take?"

"Ha. I'm coming with you," he says, putting on his jacket.

"No you're not. Your sister needs you."

"I'm sorry, are you my mother?" he argues. "I make my own decisions, thank you very much. Let's go."

"You can't——" I begin, shaking my hands for emphasis.

"Yusuf can take care of things until I'm back. He's not incompetent."

He doesn't give me a chance to answer before he's out the door.

Dammit! Now I have to worry about his life and whether his soul will be on my conscience.

Yusuf is out of his room, glancing shyly at me before sitting next to Lama.

"Take care of her, okay? And yourself," I say. He nods, and I ignore the pang in my stomach at the sight of his tattered shirt and narrow frame.

Kenan has to leave, I decide, *before these children bury their brother too.*

I peek outside, equally pleased and scared to see the sun shining down on us. On one hand, it provides warmth against the last traces of winter, while on the other, it provides perfect conditions for snipers.

There are a few men standing in front of Kenan's building, holding chipped mugs of tea, deep in discussion, while a couple of children zoom about, shouting excitedly. I even hear a few laughs and clutch that shred of innocence that's still alive and fighting, tucking it safely in my heart.

Loose gravel crunches under our shoes as we make our way to my home. We pass by a run-down bakery still operating. A long line is outside, people warming their hands and pulling tightly on their coats. They wait patiently, although there's an edginess in their eyes, all worrying the bread will run out and they'll have to return to their families empty-handed.

With each step we take, I come to terms with the decision I made last night. Enveloped in the darkness and illuminated by feeble candlelight, it was easy to make. It was a secret I was able to whisper to myself. But now in the blazing sunlight that lays my soul bare, it feels like a permanent stain of shame.

I glance at Kenan's tall form. Not even the baggy jacket can hide the sharp edges of his elbows or his bony hands. He's not supposed to look like this. He and his siblings should be healthy and safe and happy. He should be working on his Japanese and trying to get into Studio Ghibli.

He can't stay here.

"Are you really staying in Homs?" I whisper. "Are you really going to die here?"

He stops walking and turns around to look at me with surprise.

"I'm not planning on getting killed," he says slowly.

I shake my head. "At the rate you're going, with your ambitions and dangerous thoughts, that *will* be how your story ends. Would your parents be okay with that? If you were taken away and your siblings were left alone to suffer and mourn for you? What about the promise you made to your father?"

He stares at me, a deep sadness settling on his expression.

"I was the only girl in my family," I say. "An older brother, Hamza. He was my world. My best friend. My everything. He and Baba were at a protest, and they couldn't get away when the military swooped in. A week later, Mama died when a bomb fell on our building."

"Salama," he says. His tone is soft, almost frightened of what I'm about to say.

But I continue. "I lost my family and you still have yours. I see it every day at the hospital: People would sell their souls for another minute with their loved ones. I would."

The backs of my eyes burn, but I stop myself from breaking down.

Daisies. Daisies. Sweet-smelling daisies.

"I tried to visit them in prison. But I wasn't allowed to see them. I was about to be arrested myself, and it was a miracle they let me walk free. They warned me not to come back."

He takes in a shuddering breath and I quickly brush away the tear falling down my cheek.

I remember it all, the stench of oxidized blood, the faint screams echoing against my ears. It was a few weeks before the siege on Old Homs happened. The prison isn't in Old Homs, and I was able to walk into the detention facility with trembling limbs. The wound on the back of my head was in the early scarring stages and Khawf was beginning to plague my nights. Layla hadn't the slightest idea of what I was doing because she was bedridden with grief, her eyes vacant, tears streaming down her cheeks like two rivers.

"Salama Kassab," the military man said, leaning heavily back in his chair and skimming through a coffee-stained list. I hoped it was coffee.

"Yes." I gripped the edges of the old leather couch where the stuffing was coming out, all wrinkly and moldy yellow.

He grunted, staring at the list through his silver sunglasses. I couldn't see his eyes, and it unnerved me.

"Your father and brother have stirred up quite the trouble," he said smoothly, but I sensed the danger lurking under his tone.

"Please," I whispered, heart hammering. "Please, they're all I have. My mother di—my father suffers from hypertension. He needs his medication, and my brother . . ." I cut myself off. I couldn't tell them about Layla. They'd use her to punish him.

"Do you know how many times I hear the same sob story?" he said in an exasperated voice. "Please let my mother out, she didn't know what she was doing. Please let my son out, he's the only one I have in this world. Please let my daughter out, she didn't realize how great an offense this is. Please let my husband out, he's old and frail." He slammed the list on the table, and I flinched. "No. No I will not let them out. They broke the law. They disturbed the peace with these notions."

A pained shriek reached my ears. I squeezed my eyes shut before opening them to stare at the man who held the fate of my loved ones in his grasp. I hated him.

"I've never been to a protest, and I never will. I swear. So please, for me, let them out. They won't do anything like this again. I promise." My voice took on a pleading tone, and I began to hate myself too. To grovel to our murderers and torturers. The government had long since promised the consequences if we were to rebel. Everything we had feared for fifty years was coming true.

The man smiled, all yellow teeth, and got up heavily from his seat.

"Little girl." He stood in front of me, and I dug my nails into my hands, wincing. The wounds were just budding into scars. "You better leave before you join them."

"I'm sorry," Kenan whispers, and his voice awakens me from the nightmare replaying in my mind.

"Don't be sorry for me." I swallow hard. "*You* still have your siblings. If you're staying, then don't throw your life away."

His shoulders constrict. And I understand why he's doing what he's doing. God, I do. But not like this. Not when I felt Lama's blood running between my fingers like a spring and heard him tell me about her courageous heart. Not when I know Yusuf can't talk anymore because of the trauma. They need help that isn't in Homs. They both need to be allowed to be children.

But it's clear from the flickering flames in his eyes and the suppressed agony in his words: He knows that a desolate future awaits him if he doesn't leave. He's not a fool. But his heart overflows with so much love for his country he's willing to let it drown him and his loved ones. The thing is, hearing stories about the ocean's rage is different from being caught in the middle of the angry waves.

"What do you record exactly, Kenan?" I ask, and he looks surprised by the question.

"Uh, the protests, like I told you. The revolution songs."

"And deaths?"

He grimaces. "When the gunshots go off, I stop and run."

I consider him for a second before nodding and make to walk past him, an incoherent thought wakening in my brain, but he clears his throat.

"My mom's Hamwi," he says in a quiet voice.

I stop.

"She survived the Hama massacre," he continues, and I turn to look at him. "When the military stormed her city and laid waste for a whole month, she survived. She was seven years old, and she watched her nine-year-old brother get shot in the head. She saw his brain splatter everywhere. She starved with her family. They ate once every three days. I've lost family even before I was born, Salama. Injustice is all I've ever known." He pauses, his chest heaves once, and when he looks at me, there's absolute determination in his eyes. I nearly shiver from the intensity of it. "This is why I protest. Why I record. Why I should stay. All those years before the revolution started. Didn't you lose family to the dictatorship too, Salama?"

He knows the answer. No Syrian family has evaded the dictatorship's cruelty. We both lost family in the Hama massacre before we were born, but Kenan's loss steeled his resolve from when he was a child. It grew with him. Shaped him. Unlike me. I ignored the loss until it became my reality.

A knot forms in my throat and it's difficult to swallow without bursting into tears, so instead I walk toward my house. After a second, he follows.

We're getting closer, which makes me more anxious. I need to touch Layla to know she's alive and well. I need to make sure the baby didn't decide to throw a wrench in our plans and come early.

We stay silent the rest of the way, lost in our worries and thoughts. When my home comes into view, I let out a small breath of relief. My neighborhood is quiet, and Kenan and I are the only ones on the streets. Everything looks as normal as can be, the faded blue front door still in one piece. I take out my keys, fumble desperately at the lock.

Kenan leans against the wall. "I'll wait outside."

"What! Get in before someone shoots you!" I usher him inside and close the door quickly.

The house is quiet. No light filters from the living room's drawn windows. Shadows dance against the hallway walls and somehow it feels colder inside the house than outside it.

"Stay here," I mutter. He nods and turns toward the front door in case Layla makes a sudden appearance hijab-less.

I call out loudly, "Layla, I'm home!"

She doesn't answer. A knot twists in my stomach.

"She might be sleeping?" Kenan suggests, still facing the door.

"Maybe."

I check the living room where she usually sleeps, but it's empty and disturbingly cold, no sun rays seeping through the curtains. The rug under the couch is dark, the whorls akin to gray clouds swirling before a storm. The kitchen overlooking it is also muted, like someone watered down the colors. The uneasiness grows like vines, wrapping around my skeletal system.

"*Layla*," I repeat and head down the hallway, my sneakers thudding softly against the carpet.

Shadows envelop my footsteps, and my heart is in my throat, fluttering like a baby bird. Her bedroom door is fastened shut, and I trail my fingers along the surface before deciding to check my room first.

When I creak open my door, all the while begging God for her to *please be there*, I almost fall to the floor with relief.

Layla is sprawled on my covers, hugging my pillow to her chest. Her eyes are closed, her lips moving in silent prayer.

"Layla!" I cry out, and her eyes burst open, a choked sound escaping her throat.

"Salama!" she gasps. She jumps from the bed.

We collide into each other, my arms shaking as I hold her close, her hair in my mouth. But I don't care. She's alive and pregnant. Very much pregnant, her stomach bumping me.

She leans back, grabs my shoulders, and shakes me. "Where *were* you?" she demands.

"A patient couldn't be moved from their home, so I had to go there and operate. Then a fight broke out between the FSA and the military, and I couldn't leave," I say, breathless.

Her eyes are rimmed red, her cheeks blotchy, but she takes in a deep breath. "Okay."

"The patient's brother brought me home. He's, uh, he's here," I say, trying to be casual.

She glances over my shoulder. "Here? As in, in our home?"

I nod.

Realization slowly dawns on her and scandalous shock is in every word. "Oh my God, Salama. Did you spend the night at a boy's house?"

I shove her shoulder playfully and she giggles.

"Stop it," I mutter. "I was nearly sick with worry. Why didn't you answer when I called?"

She looks at me pointedly. "You know I don't answer unknown numbers."

I drag a hand across my face, sighing. "Fine. Fine. Alhamdulillah you're okay. That's all that matters."

"I am."

"I have to tell Kenan you're fine. You can say hello if you want."

She gives me an exasperated look and points at herself. The flyaway, fiery hair, the watery eyes, and the wrinkled clothes. "Say hello looking like this? No thank you, I'd rather stay here."

I shake my head, smiling.

Kenan still has his back to me when I walk out. My eyes trail over his broad shoulders and the casual way his hands are in his pockets as he rocks back and forth on the heels of his boots. I stop and for one minute allow myself to imagine our *might* life in this dusty hallway. That I'm living my very own Studio Ghibli movie. That in this universe he and I have our own inside jokes, and my ring finger wears the golden band he gave me. Those thoughts make my cheeks burn, but I don't care. I am owed this. I'm owed at least my imagination.

"Kenan," I call. "You can turn around. Layla isn't coming out."

He does so slowly, his gaze still glued to the carpet.

"Is she okay?" he asks, finally meeting my eyes.

I nod.

His stare darts over the hallway as he takes in the shabbiness. He says nothing, and I detect sadness in his expression.

"Are you sure she's fine?" he asks again. "I can go get you something. Like . . . bread or milk if they have it at the grocery."

I shake my head. "Thank you. We're fine. She's doing good."

He exhales. "All right. I guess . . . this is goodbye."

I chew on my tongue, feeling a bit crestfallen at that word. How I hate it. *Goodbye.*

"Right," I say instead.

He nods at me before opening the door and looks back one more time. "Thank you, Salama, for everything. You've not only saved Lama's life but you've saved mine and Yusuf's too."

He smiles, green eyes bright and warm.

For now, I think.

He slips through the door and the incoherent thought that's been forming in the back of my mind finally makes its way to my mouth.

"Kenan!" I shout. He stops a few feet away.

"Yes?" he asks, and I swear I can hear hope.

I walk toward him, rubbing my arms. I can save him and his siblings. I know I can.

"Record at the hospital," I say when I'm close enough that I can see the two freckles on his neck.

He looks taken aback. "What?"

"Come to the hospital and record the injured. You say you want to help, right? Show the world what's happening? Well, nothing screams injustice more than that. The protests are usually at night. And because it's dark, the visibility isn't that good. But at the hospital, you'd . . . It'll be more impactful." My voice trails off into a quiet whisper.

His eyes soften at my words and he stares at me for a long minute before saying, "Why?"

"Why?" I echo.

"You've made it clear you think what I'm doing is

dangerous. Why do you want me doing more of that, closer to you?"

I crack my knuckles, looking for a way to drain the anxiety building in my blood.

Because when you see the people who are dying. When you see the mutilated children and you hear them crying with fear and pain. Maybe then you'll know how lucky you are that you are okay. That you can leave.

Instead, I fix him with a cool stare. "My thinking it's dangerous has nothing to do with the fact that I love my country and I don't want to see more people murdered."

His ears turn red and he covers his face with one hand. "I—I'm sorry. I didn't—"

I shake my head. "It's fine. I know you didn't mean it like that. Look, I'm not forcing you. Do you want to do this?"

His arm falls, and I'm met once again with his brilliant green eyes. "Yes," he says. I feel a shiver run up and down my back. "Yes, I want to."

I let out a relieved breath. "Good. We have to ask Dr. Ziad's permission, but I doubt he'll mind. He's all for this war."

"Revolution, Salama," Kenan says. His smile is sad. "It's a revolution."

I purse my lips. "Be at the hospital tomorrow at nine."

As I walk back inside, I see Layla standing right in front of the door with the biggest grin I've ever seen on her.

"Kenan, huh?" She wiggles her eyebrows and I groan. "You sounded awfully cozy there. I was this close to opening the door and marching over there myself to see what was happening."

I push past her, heat claiming my cheeks, but she's fast, grabbing my arm and turning me around.

"Why are you blushing?" she asks.

"I'm not," I stutter.

She narrows her eyes. "Do you know him?"

"Yes?"

"Oh my God, if you're going to drag out your answers, I will hit you on your head," she says with a fierce look.

"Fine! I—we—he was the one who was supposed to come with his mother last year for the marriage talk thing." I say it in a rush like I'm tearing off a Band-Aid.

Silence. Then . . .

"Ohmygosh!"

There's no way to get a sentence in when Layla starts gushing. Everything I thought she would say and everything I didn't yet think of bursts right out. Kenan and I are meant to be. This is fate. This is true love. I'm going to be happy. I will get married. We will be a power couple. She'll be the lovable aunt our children will adore. This is great. Our children will grow up together. We will survive. Her chatter follows me from the kitchen to my room where I change into a fresh sweater and back into my lab coat—because I'm already late for my hospital shift—and I head to the front door again.

"Layla, that sounds nice and everything," I finally say when she stops to breathe. "But we have bigger things to worry about."

I take a deep breath, steeling myself for the words that will be my undoing. "I've decided we're going to leave. I'm going to talk to Am and I'm going to find a way to pay for that boat."

Layla stops short, her mouth dropping open. "What— what changed your mind?" she whispers.

I scratch at a stain on my sleeve. "Reality set in."

Layla reaches out, grabs me by the shoulders, and hugs me tightly. "I know how hard this decision is for you. But you're not doing anything wrong, okay?"

I say nothing, just breathing in her daisy scent.

"Say it," she says fiercely. "Say you're not doing anything wrong by leaving."

I let out a choked laugh. "I'm . . . not doing anything wrong by leaving."

She pulls away and brushes my cheeks. "Good."

Before I walk out, she grabs my hand and I look at her.

"Salama," she says, smiling. And with the sunlight pouring from the cracked door caressing her face, she looks like she did in the old days. Rosy cheeks and ocean-blue eyes sparkling with life. "It doesn't hurt for you to think about your future. We don't have to stop living because we might die. Anyone might die at any given moment, anywhere in the world. We're not an exception. We just see death more regularly than they do."

I think about Kenan and that *might* life. Saturday nights marathoning Ghibli movies. Collecting potted plants and flowers so our apartment is always filled with life. Having Layla and Baby Salama over for dinner and doting on my

niece. Hamza and Kenan bonding over something like soc-
cer or video games.

I clear my throat rather loudly. "Yeah, I'll see you
tonight, Layla."

The smile she gives me mirrors Kenan's in its melancholy.

10

"NO," AM SAYS, AND ACID POOLS IN MY STOMACH. "No exceptions."

We're standing in the main hallway again and my hands are sticky with the blood of the woman I helped twenty minutes ago. The wound she had sustained to her head burst open, the stitches not holding tight, and she went faint with blood loss. All the while I was mending the wound, I was preparing what I would say to Am, but he cut me off as soon as I opened my mouth.

"I don't do charity, Salama," he says, eyes hard. "Everyone who wants my services has problems. You're not the only one. I've had a father with three children and an ill wife ask. I said no to him and I'll say no to you as well."

My jaw clenches and I dig my nails into my palms. I hate him and the way he's profiting from our terror. I know I can use Layla's gold to bargain with him, but my tongue is heavy with pride. I've finally made the horrible decision to leave my patients behind and honor Hamza's wishes, only to be stopped by Am's greed.

He bites at a nail. "Nothing to say?"

I have to tread carefully. Layla and I cannot survive on pride alone. If I offend him, he might not get me a boat, even if I offer him all the gold in the world. Just to spite me.

"I'll find a way to get you the money," I say in a forced-polite voice. "But I ask you to reconsider. Layla and I are young, and we don't speak German. We've never left Syria. You and I are kin. We're Syrians."

Am doesn't say anything, but there's a different shimmer behind his eyes. He looks as if he's impressed with me. Finally, he grunts. "If only we could all live on chivalry. Find the money or there's no boat."

And with that, he walks away.

When mixed together, disappointment and terror form a bitter pill whose effects are long-lasting. Its taste stays in my mouth the entire day and strengthens when I go home, bone weary, and see Layla's crestfallen face as I tell her what Am said. She doesn't ask why I didn't offer up her gold, and I'm grateful. She just tucks me in bed and brushes back my hair.

"It's okay," she whispers. "We'll be okay."

I stare at the ceiling, feeling a hollowness in my chest. Like my heart doesn't exist there anymore and I'm surviving on whatever fragments latched to my ribs.

As soon as I allowed myself to think about leaving, seedlings of hope grew in my brain, taking over my imagination. Not a *might* life, but a *real* life with Layla and an apartment in Germany. It's cramped but that's okay. We heal and fill it with laughter and Baby Salama's drawings. And one day, I find the will to pen the magical stories I have long buried deep in my mind. She and I, we make a home from what's left of our family.

Layla stays with me until the dusk turns to night.

"I'll be right here if you need anything, okay?" she says, and I nod.

When she closes the door behind her, eerie silence claims her wake, and my stupid imagination picks up where it left off. Only this time, Kenan is there in our apartment. And so are his siblings. We're happy and safe and well fed. And for a minute, the night's darkness doesn't seem that bleak.

That is until someone chuckles from the corner. I refuse to look.

"If I could summarize your life in one word, Salama . . ." I hear the hiss of his lighter. A deep inhale. An exhale. "It would be *irony*."

"Screw you," I croak.

I sense Khawf sitting beside me, but still I don't turn to him, hoping he'll go away. My bones are made from steel and I'm busy trying to collect the pieces of my heart to sew them back together for tomorrow's inevitable hell. I'm painfully aware of the hidden stash of Panadol in the drawer and I have to fight myself to not take one. Or three. Not even Layla takes one when she has a headache. We're saving them for a rainy day.

I can breathe through this.

"I have to say," Khawf continues. "I'm pretty proud of

your progress. But let's take it up a notch. You will tell Am tomorrow you'll give him all your gold. Hell, you'll also give him this house if he wants it. Not that he'd profit from it. But still."

I stay quiet and find myself yearning for last night, when Khawf stayed away. Yearning to talk to Kenan again and see that blaze of life burning in his eyes.

"No," Khawf says curtly. "That boy is nothing but trouble. With your soft heart, his patriotic notions will easily dissuade you from leaving. I have worked too long and too hard for him to change your mind. You're—"

"Leaving, I know," I snap, finally looking at him.

His gaze flicks over me with displeasure but I don't care. "Stay away from Kenan."

"Don't worry, my promise to Hamza comes first," I say. "You better pray that Am accepts the gold."

Khawf grins, his incisors sharp. "Oh, I trust you'll do everything you can to convince him." He flexes his fingers, the cigarette dancing from one digit to the other, and the shadows on the walls and ceiling begin to change form. Gaping mouths and hollow eyes stare at me. Pained shrieks follow soon after, so I clamp my hands over my ears and squeeze my eyes shut.

"You do know what Hamza would say, don't you?" Khawf's voice cuts. "How he'd want you to leave. How he'd beg you."

"Salama," Hamza's voice murmurs in my ears. It sounds bruised. "Salama, you promised, remember? You would save Layla. And yourself. You'd make up for letting Mama die. You wouldn't go back on your word, right?"

The backs of my eyes burn and I roll over to press the pillow over my head. "Please, *stop*."

A silence takes over the room, and for a minute I believe he has. But when I open my eyes, Hamza stands in front of my bed.

There's an open wound on his forehead. His hazel eyes are narrowed with displeasure and there's a mottle of bruises across his cheeks. He's wearing the clothes I last saw him in, but they're ripped, muddied, and bloody.

"*No*," I whimper. This is not him. This is Khawf.

But deep down in my heart, I know it *is* him. Even if what is before me is an apparition, Hamza must be suffering right now. That is, if he's not dead.

"Salama, if they catch Layla, do you know what they'll do to her?" he whispers, and a pained sound escapes from my lips. "If they catch you? You and Layla would *never* be allowed to die. Salama, you *have* to leave. Think of Baba. Think of me."

My tears feel like acid on my skin, dripping onto my pillow. "Hamza, *please*, I said I will."

He shakes his head. "Then why didn't you give Am what he wanted? Salama, survival is everything."

"I will," I say. "I promise I will."

When I blink, Hamza has disappeared and Khawf's voice looms over the quiet once more. "Remember your brother every time Kenan's words make you doubt your decision."

"Bloodroot," I chant. "White petals. Yellow center. Secretes a red fluid. Effective in low doses for respiratory diseases. Bloodroot. Bloodroot. Bloodroot."

"If that boy changes your mind, Salama," Khawf continues, "I'll make it so that you don't even remember what flowers are."

114

11

THE NEXT DAY DR. ZIAD RUSHES TO ME AS SOON AS I walk in. He's wearing a smile I haven't seen in a long time.

"Salama!" he exclaims. "We got a medication shipment. Panadol. Ciprofloxacin. Azithromycin. Even morphine!"

My mouth drops open, my heart lifting until it's soaring through the clouds. If life were normal, it would have been part of my daily duties to update Dr. Ziad on the medication restock. Dispensing, counseling, and inventory would be my domain. Restocking would be boring at best. Not cause for celebration. *"How?"*

"The FSA was able to smuggle it," Dr. Ziad says. He runs a hand through his hair, and there's a certain hopeful energy coming off him. "We put the boxes in the medication stockroom for you."

I beam. "I'm on it." The hospital is brighter today. The patients' faces, though still tired and pained, show some degree of happiness. Or maybe that's just my imagination.

Before I race off, Dr. Ziad holds out an arm. "You left

the hospital a bit suddenly yesterday. Is everything okay? Are you eating well? Sleeping? Do you need anything?"

"I'm all right," I say. And in this moment, surrounded by patients, it doesn't feel like a lie. For now, I'm all right. I'm just all right.

If he doesn't believe me, he doesn't show it.

To distract him, I tell him about Lama and how the surgery went well. His face brightens and he praises my quick thinking.

"Well done," he says, smiling.

I skip to the stockroom, my steps lighter than before, forgetting all about the nightmares that dragged me down last night. Today is a good day. It *will* be a good day insh'Allah.

The cardboard boxes are wrinkled, the corners squished, but when I open them, the medications are all intact. They're cool to the touch, and I hug a whole bottle of children's acetaminophen syrup to my chest. We'll be able to soothe their fevers.

"I heard we got a restock," a voice says from the doorway, and I turn around to see Nour. Her round face shines with delight. Nour was part of the custodial staff for three years before she was promptly promoted to a nurse when the first martyrs were wheeled into the hospital. It was from Nour that I first learned how to stitch wounds, fashion makeshift bandages, and drain fluid out of patients' lungs. Her nerves are made from steel, and her heart is softer than feathers.

I wave a flucloxacillin box. "You heard right!"

She ululates and I laugh. The joy sounds strange against my ears, but I welcome it.

"I have to check on a patient but I needed to see this

miracle myself." She smiles. "If you need any help, look for me."

"I will."

She leaves. I stack the empty shelves for a while, then look up at the clock. It reads 10:13 a.m.

Kenan.

I told him to be here at nine, but he still hasn't shown up. To dispel some of the anxiety I'm feeling, I decide to take a quick spin around the hospital. Maybe he's here but can't find me. I casually go from room to room but can't find him anywhere, so I return to the stockroom. Worry reclaims its place in me and I try not to think of all the reasons he's not here. His sister is still recovering and she probably needed him. I send a quick prayer for her health to be restored. Maybe I can pass by their apartment with a Panadol strip after my shift. A part of me—a foolish, hopeful part that has somehow survived everything—is happy I'd get to see Kenan again.

I shake my head. This is not the time for my selfish thoughts of a *might* life and a tall boy with warm, vivid green eyes.

"Good morning," Kenan says from behind me, and I nearly jump out of my skin.

My heart pounds like thunder. I turn around slowly, giving myself time to look calm and collected before he can read all the thoughts written on my face.

The morning chill has coaxed him into wearing a jacket over his old sweater. He leans on the doorframe, arms folded across his chest. His hair is tousled, the ends curling around his ears, and his face is flushed with the cold. An old Canon camera hangs at his side, smudged white at the edges and a bit chipped.

"Good morning," I answer, commanding my voice to stay calm and not too eager. "You're late. Is everything okay? How's Lama?"

He smiles and butterflies flutter in my stomach. "Yes, thank you for asking. Lama's fever broke, alhamdulillah. Yusuf is doing well too, now that she is. They slept in this morning, and I couldn't leave before they woke up."

I fiddle with the antibiotics box in my hands. "Well, I'm glad you're all good."

"We are." He stares at me for a few seconds and I feel the touch of it everywhere.

In our *might* life where he and I are promised to each other, he'd be standing in front of me now, holding up two fresh halloumi mana'eesh, the melted cheese on the warm bread seeping through the paper wrapping, while supporting two cups of zhoorat tea, the mint leaves filling the air with their freshness. A quick breakfast before we both go on with our day. He'd joke with me and tell me about the dream he had last night. And before he left, he wouldn't kiss my hand or my cheek because we're not officially engaged, but he'd give me a smile that feels like he had.

I wonder if he's thinking that.

He clears his throat. "So, uh, where's the doctor whose permission I need?"

I blink. "Right."

I put down the antibiotics and motion for him to follow me. He falls into step as we walk back through the hallways to the main atrium, where Dr. Ziad usually is in the morning.

"Okay, listen," I begin, taking a deep breath, and he glances at me. "I know it was my idea for you to do this, but it doesn't come without risks. We live in dangerous times and you don't know how this might affect you."

He frowns. "As in someone snitches?"

I nod. "Everyone here—as far as I know—shares your ideals, but those could just be words. So if you don't want to do this, it's—"

"I want to," he interrupts. "I've thought about it long and hard. And I told you, it doesn't matter to the military if you're recording or not. If you're healing people or not. We'll all be tor—we'll all face the same fate. And you're putting yourself in the same danger as I am."

I shudder. He's right. As a pharmacist I'd face exactly what Hamza faced. Dr. Ziad would probably have it the worst of us, seeing as he's the head surgeon.

"So, might as well go down fighting," Kenan finishes. "I won't let them own my fears."

His words strike a chord with me and I quickly look away so he doesn't catch my expression.

I won't let them own my fears.

When we find him, Dr. Ziad is beside a man whose arms and legs are heavily wrapped with bandages and whose left eye is swollen shut. He's lying on a bed, alone, staring vacantly ahead. We wait until Dr. Ziad is finished checking up on him.

When he turns toward us, he's smiling sadly.

"Uh, Dr. Ziad, do you have a moment?" I ask, trying not to look at the injured man.

He glances from me to Kenan. "Sure." He nods and leads us into what functions as his office and an extra room for high-risk patients. There are two patient beds propped against the wall; Dr. Ziad's desk is cluttered with stray papers. Light filters in from the yellow-tinted window.

"Something I can help with?" he asks after closing the door.

I catch hold of the ends of my hijab. "Dr. Ziad, this is Kenan. The boy whose sister needed my help."

"How is she?" Dr. Ziad asks Kenan.

"Good, alhamdulillah. Thanks to Salama's effort. She's brilliant." He smiles at me, and my internal temperature rises a few degrees.

"We're very lucky to have her," the doctor agrees.

"That's very kind of both of you to say," I murmur, feeling self-conscious. Then, in a louder voice, I continue, "Doctor, Kenan here"—I look at him and he nods—"he records the protests, and I was wondering if he could also record the patients coming in, to document their stories so the whole world can see what's happening."

"And I'd like your permission, sir," Kenan says.

Dr. Ziad looks interested and he scratches his chin, thinking. The wrinkles around his eyes are more pronounced, the crow's feet digging deeper.

"You have my permission," he says. "If you're doing individual stories, you'll need their approval first. But if a large bombing happens and they bring in the victims, show it all."

Kenan grins as he shakes Dr. Ziad's hand, thanking him.

Dr. Ziad bids us goodbye before leaving to complete his rounds.

"I like him." Kenan stares after Dr. Ziad admiringly.

"He's a superhero." There's no word to describe Dr. Ziad other than that. "Yalla. Let me show you around the hospital."

Kenan's eyes light up with an equal amount of sadness and happiness, and the effect of it plays on my silly notions of hope. On that *might* life. He listens intently to every word I say as I explain the different departments and how we divide the patients based on the severity of their cases. I tell him about the more common cases we have. Sometimes the shock of seeing bloodied bodies, especially the children shot by snipers, is enough to make me break down. I don't tell him about the many times that has happened. How often I've had to rush out of the hospital and vomit.

We pass the maternity ward on our way back to the main hall.

"This is where the pregnant women stay. We can't use any sedatives on them because we wouldn't have enough for surgeries. We've lost—some didn't make it. The worst is when the mother dies but the baby lives. The babies are there." I point toward the other room adjacent to the hall.

He grimaces in sympathy and turns around, sees the babies inside.

"They're in incubators?"

"Yes. I—*um*—I don't like coming here. Seeing them so small and defenseless, it's too much. Some were pulled out of their mothers' wombs and need the incubators to survive. Others are a few months old and sick."

"What happens when they get better?"

I grimace. "The lucky ones have family. The others either stay here until an orphanage can take them . . ." I shudder. "I don't want to bury babies."

My heart races.

Lotus. Pinkish leaves. Stabilizes blood pressure. Heals inflammations. Lotus. Lotus. Lotus.

When he doesn't say anything, I glance at him. His eyes are still glued to the metal boxes, the ones keeping the babies alive, and a flicker of emotion passes across his face. He grits his teeth, and a vein flexes on his neck.

"You feel helpless, Salama. But I . . ." His tone is quiet but livid. "No one deserves this. Here babies are starving, while in cities like Damascus people are throwing away their leftover lunch because they're full."

I can feel him shaking without touching him. I don't spare much thought for the people in Damascus, where a few protests were quickly squashed under the boot of the government and people returned to their "normal" lives. If Damascus should ever fall from the dictatorship's clutches, its grip would vanish from all of Syria. Damascus is the capital. Every decision made there has effects that ripple all over the country. She is their stronghold. Victories for our ancestors throughout history are embedded in her soil. But she belongs to the people who are laying down their lives to free her.

It amazes me how there's only a two-and-a-half-hour drive between Homs and Damascus. In one city, people are being pulled from the ruins of bombed-out buildings, and in the other, people sit in cafés drinking coffee and laughing.

I try not to think about that. I have distant family there. As do most people in Homs. In the end, we're all somewhat related.

"There's no use being angry about that," I say sadly. "We all have different paths to walk. For what it's worth, at least we're doing the right thing."

He taps his fist against his forehead a few times. "You see the military beating people up in the streets, dragging them away, and murdering them, and you see your kid siblings trying to warm themselves at night, and you think it can't get any worse. But this, Salama, this is where hope dies. The fact they don't know what's going on because *how could they?* They're babies. They're just babies."

I remember Ahmad, the way his body was hollowed out like a shell. His labored breaths and the vast calm in his eyes as he accepted death. He was also just a baby.

Kenan's not done either. "Salama, that's not even the worst part. How can you guarantee the bombs won't hit the hospital? How—"

"Don't," I whisper. He faces me and catches the terror on my face. "Don't say it."

He shudders, nodding.

This time, we're both thinking the same horrible thoughts.

That our days at the hospital are numbered. That it's only the Free Syrian Army in Old Homs who are defending us against the military. We are surrounded from all corners and the sky. Any day now the military could drop a bomb and obliterate this flimsy shelter of ours to fragments. That if, God forbid, Layla gives birth here with no hospital, her chances of survival would be almost nonexistent. That is, if everything else doesn't get her first.

My eyes dart all over, searching for Khawf, waiting for him to threaten me or magnify the fears as a punishment for not finding Am first thing this morning. But he isn't here. Kenan follows my gaze, his sadness changing to confusion.

"What are you looking for?"

"No one," I answer rather too quickly.

"No one?" he repeats, and I chastise myself.

"Nothing," I amend. "I mean nothing." Before he can say anything, I continue, "I have to go. You know where the patients are."

He opens his mouth, reconsiders, and then nods.

I turn away from his bewildered expression, walking fast. I don't go back to the stockroom but head toward the main atrium to search for Am. It's the same as I left it, patients strewn all over, surrounded by what's left of their families. Those without anyone break my heart the most. I scan the gaunt faces but Am is nowhere to be found.

I sigh, rubbing my arms, and think about checking the other rooms, when muffled voices leak through the closed entrance doors. Gooseflesh erupts all over my skin and my body stands on alert.

The doors burst open and an avalanche of people swarms in, blood soaking their clothes and dripping to the floor. Limp bodies are being carried in rescuers' arms; shouting and yells clang against the ceiling. I know they're victims from a sniper attack when I see no dismembered limbs but blood fountaining out.

And they're all children.

From the crowd, Am runs in, carrying a bleeding little girl in his arms. His face is torn with anguish and fear.

"My daughter!" he yells to anyone who will listen. "Help me!"

Khawf stands beside me now and presses a finger I don't feel to my forehead. A horrible thought comes to life.

"Do it," he says, and Layla's tearstained face flashes in my mind.

12

MY LEGS MOVE ON THEIR OWN, MAKING A BEELINE toward Am, who's still yelling for help. The scarcity of the medical staff plays in my favor. He's pressing a dirty shirt against the girl's neck with one hand, but the blood is soaking through the material and onto the child's yellow shirt. I need to act fast before I lose her.

"Follow me," I call, and his eyes focus on me. We run between the sprawled screaming patients, finally finding an old operating table.

"Put her down slowly." I sound so emotionless I almost don't recognize my voice.

Quickly, I rip out gauze and press it against the gaping wound on her neck while checking for a pulse. It's there, but weak. The bullet must have missed her artery by millimeters. I can do this. I can save her. I've done it before.

But my arms don't move, the horrid idea in my mind keeping me still. I look around to see if Kenan is near, if he's taping, but I don't see him. If I play this out right, no one will notice.

"What are you doing?" Am demands, practically hissing, when I keep on pressing on his daughter's neck. "Save her!"

"Give me a boat," I say in the same emotionless voice.

"What?"

"Give me a boat or . . . or I remove my hands." I can't believe the words coming out of my mouth.

His eyes widen and his eyebrows are in danger of disappearing into his hairline. His limbs shake with anger, and he advances on me but I don't flinch.

"You—" His face contorts with fury and turns purple. "How *dare* you? You call yourself a pharmacist? You would let her die?"

It's getting hard to hear over the sound of my heart galloping. "You're wasting her breath being angry. She doesn't have long."

I'm bluffing. I know that, but he doesn't. I need to risk her life a heartbeat longer more to save Layla's and her baby's. *My* niece. To keep my promise.

His daughter jerks under my hands, about to reach her limit. My eyes fly to Am and then to the people all around, but no one gives us a second look, each engrossed in their own world.

"Fine!" he yells, tears pricking his eyes. "Fine! Please save her."

I can feel Khawf's satisfied smile on the back of my hijab. Immediately, I start working, thanking God this is my thousandth neck suture so I'm able to make it quick and without wasting a huge amount of blood.

Am strokes back her hair. "I'm here, Samar. Don't worry. You're going to be fine."

Nour walks past me and I yell for her to bring me the makeshift blood-donating device.

"Finish her stitches," I tell her when she gives it to me, and she takes over.

I inject the fine needle into my vein while the other goes inside Samar's. My skin is translucent enough for the veins to appear without poking around and so is hers. I watch my blood crawl through the thin tube all the way into Samar and pray it's enough to heal her. To make up for the ugly thing I did. And the ugly thing I'm about to do.

"All done," Nour says, wiping her hands on her lab coat. "She'll live, insh'Allah."

"Thank you," I say, but she doesn't hear me, already off to help another doctor.

My head begins to feel dizzy, so I take out the needle before I collapse. I've learned the hard way when enough is enough.

I turn to stare at Am, who's watching me curiously. His dislike for me is still there, but there's something else. Gratitude. Even though he's trying his best to hide it.

My mouth feels dry, but I force myself to speak. "You will get a boat for Layla and me. And it's not going to be four thousand dollars."

He barks out a harsh laugh. "What makes you think I'll keep my word? You've already saved her life. Unless you're thinking of slashing her throat. But then again, it wouldn't surprise me after what you did. What do you think Dr. Ziad would say if he knew about this?"

My chest hurts at the thought. I shove Am's insults down

into the darkest corners of my heart. I'll be a coward if it means Layla makes it out alive.

I nod to the stitches on his daughter's neck. Her black hair is matted, sticking to the blood on her forehead. "You need medications."

He lets out an incredulous laugh. "And you'll only give them to me when I secure you a boat."

"We'll be providing you with enough antibiotics to keep the infection away, but there's only so much Panadol we'll be able to give. Everyone around here needs it. I can give you more than the hospital will. And believe me, Samar will need them. That pain will not disappear easily."

I'd have to sacrifice the two Panadol boxes I've been saving for Layla and me. But as long as we get to Germany, it doesn't matter. Nothing matters.

His jaw tightens, his expression still sour. "You can't just have two free seats. Money is needed for the journey there. I've told you we need to bribe every guard on the tens of borders from here to Tartus."

I take a minute to think about it. He's right. The road is scattered with borders where the soldiers stationed there can drag anyone away.

I stick my chin out. "I'll give you a gold necklace along with a thousand dollars. The necklace is worth about a thousand dollars. Will that work?"

I was with Mama when we bought it as part of Layla's dowry.

He purses his lips, mulling it over. "Yes."

On the bed, Samar's breaths wheeze out slowly, and I check her heartbeat to find it returning to normal.

"My blood runs through her veins now," I say in a low voice. Nausea is tight and heavy on my tongue. A side effect of giving my blood. "I'm a part of her. You owe me."

He sits down heavily on the plastic chair and takes Samar's tiny hand in his rough one. "Be here tomorrow at nine a.m. with the money and gold." He pauses and looks at me, half disbelieving. "I shouldn't have underestimated you, Salama. You're more vicious than you look."

I press my hand over the puncture in the crevice of my elbow. "No one knows about this."

"Obviously."

"Stay here. I'll go get you the antibiotics."

He laughs humorlessly. "I'm not leaving my daughter, Salama. Not when her life is in your hands."

I walk away, quickly wiping the tears forming in my eyes, and press my shaking hands to my chest.

What did I do?

Before going back to get the medications, I wash my hands. I scrub until the red isn't from blood but from rawness as my skin protests with discomfort.

Then, alone in the tiny stockroom, I clutch my stomach and sink to the ground. My trembling doesn't stop, and the tears, spurred by my mountain-sized guilt, blur my vision. What would Mama say? Hamza? My brother, who was going to be a resident at this hospital?

I used a little girl's life as collateral. I risked her life.

"You did what you had to do," Khawf says behind me. "And it worked. Hamza would understand. And even if he didn't, these are dangerous times. You need to live."

"Samar could have died." I hiccup. "I was going to have an innocent girl's murder on my conscience."

"But she *didn't*," Khawf points out. "She's alive, and you have your boat. Now get up, wipe your nose, and give Am his antibiotics for today. This is all for Layla, remember?"

Layla. Would she understand? Or would she be filled with horror? I can never tell her.

Khawf taps his foot. "You *have* to leave. If word of this gets out, what do you think Dr. Ziad would do? Your reputation will be sullied."

When I hand Am the antibiotic pills, he shakes his head at me like he still can't believe what happened. Neither can I. I feel like a spectator hovering outside my body, watching my muscles move on their own.

I scurry back to my stockroom, passing by Dr. Ziad, who smiles, and my shame deepens. I shouldn't be allowed here. I *shouldn't* be trusted with people's lives.

Alone in the refuge of the musty stockroom, I sob quietly as I stack the rest of the medications.

"Daisies . . . Da—daisies . . . sweet . . . sweet smelling—" My voice breaks and tears drip on the floor beside my feet as a horrible realization dawns on me.

I may escape from Syria. My feet could touch European shores, the waves of the sea lapping against my shivering legs and the salt air coating my lips. I would be safer.

But I won't have survived.

13

WHEN I FINISH MY SHIFT, I FIND KENAN STANDING beside the front door, fiddling with his camera with a concentrated look on his face. I stop in my tracks to admire it: an expression that isn't lined with worry or pain or shame. One that reminds me of late spring afternoons. Something about the way he stands there so casually in his wool sweater creates that aching feeling in my stomach for the *might* life that was robbed from me. From us.

In that life, I'd train here and he'd be waiting for me on the steps of the hospital, doodling in his sketchbook. He'd treat me to booza at Al-Halabi Desserts and tell me about the quaint Japanese town he wants us to move to. He'd teach me a few Japanese characters, chuckling at my awkward pronunciation. But he'd be patient until I said them right, beaming proudly at me. He'd quiz me on my next pharmacology exam. But we'd quickly get distracted, falling into another conversation. I'd tell him about the stories I have in my mind that are inspired by Studio Ghibli. That I, too, find little bits of magic in our world and amplify them in my stories.

"Hey," I say, and he jumps, but smiles when he sees me. "Is something wrong? Do you need anything?"

"No, I'm okay. Are you done with your shift?"

"Yes?"

"Good." He straightens and I have to tilt my head back a bit to look him in the eyes. "I'm taking you home."

Oh my God.

"You don't have to do that."

He shakes his head. "It's fine."

"You don't have to keep paying me back for saving Lama. Taking me home means you're spending more time outside. As a target."

My palms start sweating with the way he's staring at me. It's as if he's tuned everyone out and I'm the only one here.

"Salama." My heart skips a beat when he pronounces my name. All soft and warm. "I want to do this."

Well, if he wants to, the foolish part whispers to me, *then let him.*

"Unless I'm bothering you," he says hastily, his face stricken with panic. "I'm sorry, I didn't even realize—"

I shake my head quickly. "No, you're not. I promise."

He smiles hesitantly and every worry flies out of my head.

We walk side by side, our footsteps echoing over the gravel, the sounds magnified against my ears. The rustling of dead leaves, a sad bird's cries atop the bare branches, and the faint arguing of people standing outside their houses. I can hear each breath he takes, and my heartbeat is deafening against my eardrums.

I glance at my hands and see splotches of red pigmenting my skin. Red like Samar's blood. I bite back a shriek because I'm sure I washed my hands. I spent ten minutes doing it. When I look again, the red is gone, but the sounds all around me are still screaming: *murderer*.

"*Salama.*" Kenan's voice cuts through the shrieks and I stop, gasping in a sharp breath.

I take in my surroundings, and realize I'm sitting on the ground with Kenan standing in front of me. His expression is fearful in the crease between his eyes.

For me, I realize.

"Salama, are you all right?" He crouches beside me. "Are you hurt?"

I don't trust my voice, so I shake my head. He's eye level with me and so close I can smell the faint scent of lemons on him. Or maybe I'm hallucinating that too.

"Then what is it?"

I look around, searching for Khawf, and I find him a few steps behind Kenan. His smirk is sharp, satisfied with today's proceedings. I close my eyes, willing him away. His presence is an anchor on my chest, sinking me deeper and deeper, a reminder of what I've done. Of everything I've lost and will ever lose.

A few shattered buildings line the quiet road. It's only a few minutes away from my home, and right now Kenan and I are the only ones here, kneeling beside the wreckage.

But Khawf is still *here*, and I can't think of anything but what I've done. Blood drains from my body and quickly I say, "Tell me something good."

Kenan draws back a bit, the confusion settling deeper. "Wha—"

"Kenan, please," I plead and tear my eyes back to him. *"Please."*

He looks over at where I was staring, but he can't see Khawf. I stare at Kenan, studying his features, and murmur under my breath, *"Daisies. Sweet-smelling daisies. White petals. Yellow centers."*

Kenan's cheeks are hollow. It's a sign of malnourishment, but I'm sure that even if he were a healthy weight, those cheekbones would look like they could cut me if I touched them. He glances back at me and I can see him fighting with himself not to ask the million questions teetering on his tongue.

Finally, he takes a deep breath and says, "My favorite Studio Ghibli movie is *Castle in the Sky*. It made me see the world differently. There is so much magic in it, Salama. A boy with a dream to see a floating island. A girl who's the last of her people. How both these children are able to save the world from a power-hungry man's evil ambitions. It has robots and a magical amulet and one of the best ending theme songs ever."

He laughs quietly, lost in his own words. My breath slows and I listen to what he's saying. I don't remember when I last watched *Castle in the Sky*, but I can still see it playing out so clearly in my mind.

"There's this scene," Kenan continues, "where Pazu and

Sheeta are standing atop the airship and it's night. Even animated, the sky is . . . endless. And they talk about their fears and how a series of unfortunate events made them meet. I was only ten years old when I first watched it, but that scene hit me like no other. This was a story about kids the same age I was, who were scared but still doing the right thing. It made me want to be brave too. Made me want to tell my own stories. Create my own worlds. And I thought maybe—one day—I'd have my own adventure and meet my Sheeta."

He's been staring at me the whole time but I don't think he's seeing me. His eyes have taken on a dreamlike sheen, and I'm entranced by the peace his words have painted on his expression.

The world around us has gone silent, the breeze the only sound swishing between us. And just like that, my panic subsides and I wish we could stay here, sitting on the ground forever, surrounded by the sanctuary his words have created.

But then his gaze sharpens, and when he finally sees me, his cheeks are as pink as carnations. He's paler than I am and not very good at hiding his expressions.

He clears his throat and the spell is broken. "Are—was that something good?"

I nod and hold on to this moment, tucking it in my heart to revisit when the sadness comes back.

He smiles. "All right."

We stand and continue walking. I'm thankful he doesn't ask what happened, but it doesn't feel right to stay silent.

"Did you get what you need?" I nod toward his camera.

"Oh yes. I recorded the sniper victims, and there was

one family who didn't want their faces blurred. They want the truth to be blazing."

My stomach feels hollow. He *did* record the sniper victims. I thought I made sure to check if he was in my vicinity, but then again, I was running on adrenaline and nerves and could have easily not seen him.

"Oh," I say casually. "What kind of shots did you take?"

He shakes his head. "I was interviewing a family in another room when the sniper victims came in. By the time I got there, I couldn't move through the sea of bodies and I didn't want to be in anyone's way. The closest to me was Dr. Ziad, so I recorded him and his patient."

My chest expands with relief, but guilt sours every breath I take.

"But I saw you save that girl's life," he says in awe. "I looked up and saw you stitching her neck. The bullet went straight through, right?"

I try not to falter. "Yes."

My home is around the next corner, ten feet away.

"You saved her father's life by saving hers," he says, thankfully not catching on to the shame I'm trying to erase from my expression. But there's something in his tone that makes me glance at him, and when I do, he looks almost terrified. It vanishes as our eyes meet and he smiles his kind smile. "You're amazing."

The compliment tastes like cyanide in my mouth, and I swallow the tears. God, I don't deserve this. I don't deserve his kindness or his dreams.

"We're here," he says, and my blue door comes into view.

I take out my keys, hands shaking a bit.

"Hey, listen," he says, and I look up at him, quickly blanking my face. "I remember you mentioning Layla is seven months pregnant, right?"

"Yes," I say slowly.

He runs a hand through his hair, looking suddenly bashful. "I know we met yesterday. But I'd like to believe in an alternate universe, where this"—he gestures between us—"would have worked out spectacularly. If there's anything you or she need, please tell me."

My eyelashes flutter.

When I don't say anything, he continues, more flustered than ever, "Especially because, you know, there could be snipers or something, and Layla shouldn't be getting groceries in her condition. And neither should you—"

"Thank you," I interrupt, and he lets out a relieved sigh. "But Layla doesn't leave the house anyway."

He frowns. "Is she all right?"

I nod, fidgeting with the keys. "We had a close call with a sniper last October. Layla was on her way back from the supermarket. Actually, just over there—" I point to the end of the dusty road where a huge electrical pole stands broken in half, the metallic skin of it gleaming in the afternoon light. Rusted blood coats the pavement under it. "Snipers started shooting. She wasn't the only one there. Three women and one man died that day. Layla and one other child were the only survivors. She hid under a stray chunk of debris until it was safe." I take a deep breath. The terror I felt that day when I heard there was a military sniper in our neighborhood was unparalleled.

I had run back home, not a care in the world for my safety. All I could hear was Hamza's plea replaying in my brain like a broken cassette. His voice beseeching me to save his wife. I arrived to find the aftermath of blood trickling down the streets between the glass shards and rubble. The martyrs had been carried away to the grave-yard. Only a soul-crushing silence was left, as if the essence of this corner in Old Homs were shell-shocked. My legs could barely propel me to the front door before I flung it open.

And Layla was there, sitting on the floor with her back to the peeled wallpapered wall, sobbing. Her face was tear-stained, small cuts on her forehead and arms. When I hugged her, she smelled of rubble, smoke, and blood, but it didn't matter. She was alive.

"You're alive," I choked through my cries, pressing her closer. "You're alive."

It was from that day on that Layla became adamant about leaving Syria.

"Oh my God," Kenan whispers. "That is . . . I can't begin to imagine."

"Yes," I reply and tighten my hold on the keys until it starts to hurt. "You *can* imagine, Kenan. That time it was Layla, and it was only by God's mercy that she walked away unharmed. Today, tomorrow, in two weeks, it could be Lama or Yusuf. But they might not be so lucky."

Kenan looks stricken but I don't push him anymore. I hope the sniper victims, the family he talked to, and now my own story will slowly begin to crack through his resolve. These newfound feelings of fear need time to grow from vague, chaotic forms into solid thoughts and decision-making. All I can do is try to spell out those thoughts for him.

"I think," I say in a loud, clear voice, and he straightens up. "I think your adventure doesn't have to end here."

His eyes soften and I see gold circling his irises. For

another moment, we stare at each other, and I finally realize that this boy with the old sweater and the disheveled brown hair who wears his heart on his sleeve is beautiful. Standing in the middle of this ravaged, torn city, he is beautiful and *real*.

I wonder what he's thinking. If he's continuing the sentence that I'm too shy to say. *That he could find his Sheeta.* Somehow his smile tells me he is.

"I'll see you tomorrow, then?" he asks, his voice warm, like a cup of zhoorat tea. There's no pink coloring his cheeks now, only a vast calm like we're not on borrowed time but have eternity stretching in front of us.

"Yes, definitely," I reply, smiling.

14

"So Am, out of the *kindness* of his heart, agreed to one thousand dollars and a gold necklace?" Layla leans against my doorway with her arms folded. "For the both of us? Like a 'buy one get one free' kind of deal?"

I shrug. "What can I say? I told him about your swollen feet and how you're starving. You're an excellent bargaining chip."

"So he knows I'm pregnant?" she says, still staring suspiciously. "Shouldn't that cost more or something?"

"Yes, he knows," I reply. "And no he didn't say anything about a pregnancy costing more. And I'm not going to be dumb about this, Layla. I'm giving him five hundred dollars tomorrow and the other half plus the gold necklace when we're at the boat."

She blows out a puff of air. Her hair slips from its bun, auburn wisps falling to her shoulders. Her freckles are nearly invisible in the dying sunlight of my room. "I don't know, Salama. I'm worried. I mean, we know the stories about the refugees on boats. We know they get scammed and they dr—drown. You know there are sharks in the Mediterranean, right? This feels like a trap."

I chew my tongue. "It's not."

"How can you be so sure? You, the most paranoid person I know."

I sit on my bed, putting on my warmest socks. The cold evening has already seeped through the cracks in our walls and into our bones. "I've seen proof of the survivors. He has photos and videos of them in Europe. It's not a scam. If everyone were dying then no one would be taking the boats."

That's not true and I know it, but I'd rather Layla believe the lie.

"I still don't like it," she says stoutly.

"Neither do I, Layla, but we need to leave," I repeat weakly. Because if we don't, then what I did today was for nothing. I shattered my Hippocratic oath. Muddied my moral compass and snapped its arrow. Samar's and Ahmad's faces flash in my mind. I can't stand seeing another broken child. The scars on my hands begin to tingle and I rub them. This is all just in my mind. I know it. The guilt is manifesting into a phantom pain.

"I want to leave," I add quietly. Low enough for Layla to pretend she doesn't hear me. But she does. She takes my hands in hers. Her touch is soft, and the pain vanishes.

"I can't save them," I continue to whisper, staring at our joined hands. In my room, I feel safe spilling my thoughts. There's no one to judge me. Only my sister is here. "I couldn't save a little boy. I couldn't . . ." I shudder in a breath, pushing down a sob. "Everyone is dying. Nothing I do works. My brain hurts. I haven't slept well in over a year. I feel like I'm screaming into an abyss that just swallows everything up. Soon enough it will swallow me too."

I look up and Layla lets go of my hands to brush my hair back. She shakes her head, smiling gently. "It won't swallow you."

I give her a watery smile. "You have more faith in me than I do. Layla, I miss doing nothing. The days when I would just lie in bed watching movies. Or when we'd talk on the phone for hours. Remember those?"

She nods. "The dictatorship aged us all even before the revolution started. But now I feel like I'm about ninety years old."

"Wish I felt ninety. I *look* about a thousand," I scoff.

Layla gives me a pointed look. "No you don't."

I shrug and fiddle with my sleeves. "So which necklace do you want to give him? I'm thinking the one with the bow in the middle."

Her nose wrinkles. "I don't care about the necklace. Choose whichever you want. Nothing is worth more than you and Baby Salama."

Her tone drips with sadness. I don't like it. I want to bring back some of the easiness we're owed; an escape from the ever-creeping melancholy. So I say, "Kenan walked me home today."

She gasps. "*What?* And you didn't lead with that!"

Bingo.

She holds my face in her hands, forcing me to look up.

"Kenan," she says solemnly, staring me in the eyes, and my face instantly becomes hot.

143

"Ha!" she exclaims. "You like him!"

I wrench away from her grasp. "*Excuse you?* I have never in my *life*—wow, you—like you even *know*—shut up!"

She falls on my bed, grinning. "Look at your face! It's a ripe tomato."

"It's not," I retort, running to the mirror all the same. I look petrified but not in an *I'm-about-to-die* way.

"I've never seen you so nervous." She laughs, letting her hair fall from her scrunchie completely and running a hand through it. "Even at university with that cute guy from dentistry."

I groan and flop onto the bed beside her. She looks down at me with a twinkle in her eyes.

"No, wait, I remember his name. Sami." She taps a finger against her chin. "He liked you." She rests her head against her palm. "And you quite liked him. But not like this, young Salama. No, your heart was waiting for Kenan, wasn't it?"

I hug my pillow over my head, and she laughs.

"Embrace the feelings," she sings.

"Even if I had them," I say, my voice muffled against the pillow, "nothing would happen. He wants to stay here. I want to leave."

I feel Layla getting up and peek under the pillow at her. She doesn't look troubled at all. Instead, there's a knowing look on her face.

"A lot can happen between now and when we leave." She twirls around the room. "A lot of *what if*s and *maybe*s and *might*s."

She stops and clutches a hand over her heart. The dusk throws shades of orange and pink on her and she looks ethereal in the soft glow. Like she has one foot in the after-life and one foot here.

"Feelings give you hope, Salama." She smiles. "Don't you think we could use a bit of that now?"

I nod.

"So." Her blue eyes are luminous. "Do you like him?"

I play with the hem of my sweater. "The circumstances aren't exactly screaming romance, Layla!"

She flicks my nose.

"*Ow!* What did you do that for?"

"What did I say?" she demands. "I said, feelings give you hope. There's nothing wrong with finding comfort amid what's happening, Salama."

I rub my nose. "Say I did like him. Our choices are limited. Where would we go, Layla? Stroll around the destroyed market? Or maybe go outside Old Homs, dodge bullets to the Orontes River, and have a picnic by its bank? Plus, we don't have a chaperone! My parents and Hamza aren't here."

She bites her lip before laughing. *"Chaperone!"*

"What?" I say indignantly.

She wipes her eyes, still chuckling. "Nothing. You're so cute." She sits beside me, tucking her feet under her, and says, "Tell me more about him."

I fidget under her gaze. "He's . . . honest. With every-thing. His thoughts, his expressions. He's kind. It's a rare kindness, Layla. I'm sure he still dreams. Maybe he's the only one in this whole city who still dreams at night. And when he looks at me, I feel . . . I feel like I'm being seen, and there is . . . there is a tiny bit of hope."

She grins and links her hand through mine. "That right

there," she whispers. "I want you to hold on to that. No matter what happens, you remember that this world is more than the agony it contains. We *can* have happiness, Salama. Maybe it doesn't come in a cookie-cutter format, but we will take the fragments and we will rebuild it."

My bruised heart twinges.

"Salama," she continues, and her hold tightens. "You deserve to be happy. You deserve to be happy *here*. Because if you won't try it in Syria, then you won't try in Germany. Getting to Europe won't solve your problems."

I pause. I've never thought of this before.

"Promise me you'll look for the joy." She smiles sadly. "The memories are sweeter that way."

In her words lie the coping mechanism she's been using ever since Hamza was taken. That she met the love of her life when they were children and had a lifetime with him. That the memories of him are what's keeping her upright or else she'd have collapsed in on herself from the pain.

"I . . . I promise," I say, the words heavy on my tongue.

When the sun sets, I tuck Layla in on her couch, securing the blanket firmly around her so the cold doesn't bite. She drifts off to sleep after a couple of minutes, smiling at me, and my hands drop to her bulging belly. My niece is on the other side and, if I concentrate hard enough, I can imagine her pressing her tiny palms against the placenta right under mine. Now that Layla is in her third trimester, Baby Salama's brain and neuron development are in full effect, but no doubt, being as malnourished and underweight as

Layla is, her kidneys *will* be affected. Baby Salama wouldn't survive a harsh winter in Homs. I curse myself silently for three months of doubting whether or not we should leave. How could I have been so selfish?

No.

How did we come to this?

Layla snores softly, and I mourn silently. Even though I'm here, she's alone. It's as if it were yesterday: Layla and Hamza coming back from their honeymoon, their eyes glowing like the Ramadan lanterns.

Layla rested her head against Hamza's shoulder where they sat on the balcony in our home. His face went a deep shade of pink but he looked pleased with himself.

I was in the living room watching the intimate secrets traded between them that only my daisies in their pots were able to hear.

Layla caught my eye and waved me over, her auburn hair falling across her shoulders. Hamza immediately brushed it back so he could stare at her.

"You two looked deep in conversation," I said, smiling and step-ping out onto the balcony. The warm morning breeze was a welcome after months of winter. "Didn't want to bother you."

They shook their heads in unison.

"Bother us?" Layla laughed and pulled me to her. "My sister is never a bother."

"Tell me about the Dead Sea, then," I said, wedging myself between them. Hamza gave me an exasperated look. He scooted to the end but kept holding Layla's hand, their fingers intertwining right in front of me.

"Very salty," Layla declared instantly.

"Itchy. Burned a bit too," Hamza said, and Layla laughed.

"Yes, someone stayed too long in the water."

"I was floating! In water! Without any effort! Of course I had to stay."

"Everyone was staring at us because Hamza was acting as if he'd never seen the sea before," Layla whispered in my ear. "I had to pretend I didn't know him. It was so embarrassing."

I laughed and Hamza rolled his eyes.

"If you're going to act like this at my art exhibitions," Layla said loudly, "you're not invited."

Hamza raised her hand to his lips, brushing a kiss over her knuckles, and I stared at him incredulously. I was sitting right there, but he had eyes only for Layla.

"I'll be much worse, my love," he said softly. "If you think I'm going to be anything but incredibly proud and very loudly showing you off to everyone, then think again."

Layla blushed, but she was beaming.

"Oh, Salama." She shook her head. "What am I going to do with him."

I sigh and walk into my room, pushing that starry-eyed girl who didn't survive from my mind. Mourning her doesn't help me. It won't feed me and it won't get me out of Syria.

Khawf is already leaning against the window in my room, smoking. His head is turned away from me and I ignore him, kneeling in front of the dresser to pull open the last drawer. Tucked underneath the old clothes in the far right corner is Layla's gold and the rest of the money we have. I take out five hundred dollars and choose one necklace, putting it aside. Hamza gifted it to her the day of their Al-Fatiha. It's a thick, intricate rope and feels heavy in my hands. A lump forms in my throat, and I tuck the necklace back in before the tears spill.

"You did good today," Khawf murmurs, and he blows out a cloud of smoke. "It went far better than I thought it would. You have no more reason to stay here and let your blood-soaked hands heal the sick."

I clutch at my ears, shaking my head, and focus on Layla's words to me. Hope. Finding love and happiness beyond the misery.

Khawf rolls his eyes. "If it gets you on that boat, you can believe in unicorns for all I care, but come on, Salama, *hope*? Let's be realistic." He curls his finger, beckoning me toward him, and I oblige. "Look outside."

The city is painted black under a gray huddled sky. The moon's light is trapped behind the clotted clouds, just as we're trapped in Old Homs, unable to pass through. The buildings in front of my window are ghosts, no flames flickering from any of them. If I close my eyes and let my hearing take over, I can catch the muffled voices of people protesting neighborhoods away. They've never stopped, not for a single night, and with the uprising's anniversary a month away, their spirits are only growing stronger.

"Tonight you might not die from the airplanes," Khawf says, standing right next to me. "The skies are thick with clouds."

"Lilacs." I take a deep breath. *"Lilacs. Lilacs. Lilacs."*

"Salama," he continues, but he isn't looking at me, rather staring at the same horizon I am. "What happiness can you find in this wasteland? Hm? There's *nothing* for you here. Your family is gone. And Kenan will only bring you heartache if you continue to develop feelings for him. He won't leave. There's no happiness to scavenge from the wreckage. But Germany holds possibility and"—he finally looks at me, and his eyes remind me of frozen lakes in winter—"it's better than staying here. Layla alive is better. And being away will dull your remorse for what you did to Samar. This place is nothing but reminders of your failures and the inevitability of your death."

I fiddle with my fingers. "But Layla said—"

"Layla?" he repeats, then flicks his cigarette; and it disintegrates before hitting the window's glass. "Let me show you *Layla*."

He snaps his fingers and my grief-stricken city disappears from in front of the window, replaced by a memory. For a second I'm taken aback, because this isn't the memory I expected. It isn't riddled with pain, but one very near to my heart.

Layla and Hamza's wedding.

It's as if I'm watching a movie, but it doesn't stop me from pressing my hands against the cold glass.

It's held outside at my grandparents' farmhouse, between the gardens under the lemon trees. We have the place covered in fairy lights and music is blaring from the speakers. The female guests are scattered all over, talking between themselves or cheering for Layla as she dances in the middle of the dance floor.

Layla's face bears no agony. She sways in her off-white, princess-cut dress that flutters with every movement she makes. Her laugh, true and full, reaches my ears and fills me with warmth. Life colors her exquisitely. Her long auburn hair is in soft curls cascading down her back, with the white roses and baby's breath I picked out for her woven between the tresses.

Mama stands beside her in a sparkling purple abaya, waving her arms joyously, and I push harder against the glass, needing it to disappear. Needing to run to Mama and throw myself into her arms. Needing to turn back time. Khawf has never shown me Mama like this before. Healthy and alive.

"*Mama*," I choke out.

"*This* is Layla's happiness, Salama," Khawf says beside me.

Suddenly the women all rush to wrap their hijabs around themselves as the prerecorded DJ announces Hamza's arrival. I stifle a whimper at the sight of my brother, who's smiling bashfully as he walks up to Layla. His gaze only on her, his eyes shining like the stars in the sky. When he reaches her, they embrace despite her dress's full skirt, and Layla's flustered giggles echo against the window's glass.

Baba, dressed in his finest suit, laces his fingers with Mama's, and my knees weaken with longing. I want to hold them all so badly, I cry out.

My eyes wander all over, drinking in this memory like a parched man in a desert. Mama's graceful way of twirling her hands when she speaks, Baba's gray-peppered hair, which he keeps pushing back, Hamza rocking back and forth with Layla clutching his arm to keep him steady. My eyes finally fall on a woman who's perfectly manicured from head to toe. A bit of her dark brown hair peeks out from the top of her hijab against her forehead. Her face is beautiful, with soft wrinkles around her eyes. She's wearing a forest-green abaya that matches her eyes. Hazel green. I gasp. I

151

know those eyes. I *have* seen those eyes before. On a tall boy with messy chestnut-brown hair.

Is this how it all started? At a wedding? How very Syrian. I nearly smile at the thought.

"Salama," Khawf says, trying to draw my gaze to him, but I refuse to let go of this beautiful illusion and be faced with his unforgiving stare. "*Salama*, you can't live in the past. I'm reminding you what true happiness was. *This* doesn't exist anymore. *This* isn't something you'll find here."

"No," I growl, holding on to what Layla told me. Life here is more than the horror. "*No.*"

He sighs and snaps his fingers again. The wedding slowly dissipates, molecule by molecule, shifting into a terrible memory. One I never want to revisit for as long as I live.

My heart feels like it's been wrenched from my thoracic cavity and I moan in pain.

Layla, sprawled against the hallway of our home in July. Her mustard-yellow dress bleached of its vibrant color and crumpled uncomfortably around her body. Her ocean-blue eyes are vacant. Tears streak two lines down her cheeks and her hands are trembling, but she doesn't do anything about it.

This was the day Hamza was taken.

She sat there for three days, not eating, barely breathing, and never responding to me when I tried to talk to her. Her hair clung weakly to the sides of her cheeks, thin and brittle like straw. She sat there and cried silently until her eyes were swollen and red, and by the end of the third day, suffering from mild dehydration and shock, she turned to the side and vomited. Later we realized it could have also been due to morning sickness.

And in front of me in the dimly lit hallway sits that Layla, a hollowed shell of a girl. A broken doll. Nearer to death than life. The familiar sickening feeling of helplessness takes hold and I scratch the window's glass with frustration.

"*That*"—Khawf taps a long finger against the glass—"is what you have in Homs. It was a miracle that Layla pulled out of her depression."

I bite my fingernail.

He doesn't wait for my reply. "I think Layla realized you're her last family, aside from the baby. She decided to pick herself up and be strong for her family. Just until you're all safe. She knew succumbing to the pain would hurt you, so she bottled it up."

"She's fine now," I say through gritted teeth.

Khawf rolls his eyes. "The Layla you know now *isn't* fine, Salama. She's shoving down all her suffering. Layla will wither away until she's in Europe. Whether the both of you are happy there or not *doesn't matter*. You'll be *alive* and you'll have fulfilled your promise to Hamza."

His words crawl over my skin, dissolving through the pores, and I face him, slowly comprehending his existence. I think I've always known he's here to ensure my survival, but now I can see it. He isn't promising me happiness or closure. Germany is not the answer to a life of guaranteed joy. It's not home. But it's safety. And that's what Layla and I need now.

He snaps his fingers one last time. Old Homs gazes back

at me with her haunting eyes. The air is heavy with dead souls and the weight of my sin.

"Leaving means you leave behind what you did here," Khawf whispers. My heart is in my throat. "For the rest of your life, you'll never achieve peace of mind with what you did to Samar. It'll eat you from the inside like a cancer. It's already started. At least in Germany, you'll be miles away from the reminders. At this point, Salama, all you can hope for is survival. Not happiness."

15

"DO YOU EVER STOP STUDYING?" SHAHED ASKED, AND
I looked up from the Medical Terminology *textbook I was reading.*

*It was a week before my first-term university exams and Shahed,
Rawan, Layla, and I had decided to visit a café downtown after
classes. The streets were bustling with people. The tables outside and
inside the restaurants were crowded with families enjoying an early
dinner of every Syrian dish imaginable. Kibbeh barbecued on coal,
lamb chops skewered to perfection, tabbouleh, wara'a enab, freshly
squeezed oranges picked from the countryside. There were a few pass-
ersby who looked like they were hard on their luck. Tattered clothes
and gaunt faces, their hands outstretched, begging. But most people
walked by without glancing at them.*

*We were craving sweets and we all ordered two dishes each.
Every inch of our table was covered in dessert. I ordered a booza and
rez bhaleeb. The booza had to be eaten fast as the ice cream was
beginning to melt despite the cool breeze. The latter, the sweetest rice
pudding with orange blossom water drizzled on top, was the perfect
conclusion to a long day at university. High school had always been*

demanding, but it was the equivalent of learning the alphabet compared to my first year in pharmacy. The difference was astounding and yet all that separated them was a summer vacation.

"Seriously, stop studying!" Rawan joined in, shaking her spoon at me. "Enjoy the weather. The food."

I frowned. "I can't. I have an exam Monday morning and if I don't know the difference between an ulna and a humerus, I'm failing."

"I'll break your ulna and humerus," Shahed muttered.

I crossed my arms. "Scientific names for body parts are difficult! I will fail!"

"You're so dramatic, drama queen." Layla rolled her eyes. She picked up the chilled lemonade, her diamond ring glittering. "You always say that and then end up getting the highest grade."

"Yeah, everyone stopped believing you by the time we were twelve," Rawan said. Then she imitated my voice: "Oh my God. The exam was so difficult. I couldn't answer anything. I have no idea if I'm going to pass or not——"

I bit back a grin. "That's so not how I s——"

"It totally is," Shahed said through a mouthful of her halawet eljebn. "And then you pass and get certificates of honor while we sit here contemplating your murder."

I closed my textbook and dropped it onto the table rather forcefully, and the glass bowls jumped. I also startled a few people sitting around us. In particular, one boy with messy chestnut-brown hair. He looked up, blinking. I blushed at the commotion I'd caused, and our eyes met before I hastily looked away.

Those were the greenest eyes I've ever seen in my life.

"Fine," I said. "I'm not studying."

I spent the rest of that afternoon trying not to look over at the

*boy with the greenest eyes, who was busy on his laptop. He was alone
and there was a large plate with four servings of knafeh on the table.
I did a double take, amazed that someone would be able to eat all of
that and not fall into a sugar coma.*

*I tried commanding my brain not to look, but my traitorous eyes
refused to listen and I caught snapshots of him in the milliseconds
my gaze would stray toward him. He looked my age. Maybe a year
older. Cute. I wanted to push back the hair falling over his eyes so he
could see his laptop screen better.*

*On the seventh glance, he suddenly raised his head and looked
directly at me, our eyes locking for the second time. My cheeks burned
and, in that moment, a lifetime was born. There was a delicate look in
his eyes, a curious interest in the way his lips curved upward, and I——*

I wake up with a jolt, gulping in air. My hair is plastered
to my neck with sweat, and my eyelids feel heavy with leftover tears. I shiver when I get out of bed, the cool morning
air freezing my bones.

Was that a dream or a memory? I shake my head, unable to
find the energy to make out the truth. I don't have the time.
I get dressed and don't eat the stale bread Layla passes me
but stuff it in my bag along with the five hundred dollars.

When I get to the hospital, Am's in the same clothes
as yesterday, his back hunched as he sits beside his sleeping
daughter. The main atrium still nurses the wounded from
yesterday's sniper attack. The stench of festering lesions and
rusted blood reeks but I don't gag. Not anymore.

"Am," I say shortly, avoiding looking at Samar.

He turns. There are shadows under his eyes and he's
in need of a shave. He looks as if he's aged ten years, and I
ignore the guilt burning behind my eyes.

"How is she?" I croak.

He fixes me with a hard look. "Better. She can't move her neck yet, but she's going home today. Not enough beds here."

"I . . . I see. She has to hold on for a bit until we can remove the sutures."

"I know. Did you bring everything?"

I look around but I don't spot Dr. Ziad or Kenan, so I take out the wad of bills and quickly pass it to him. His gaze creases with concentration as he counts, and then it turns ugly.

"What are you playing at here, Salama?" he says with a hiss. "This is only five hundred dollars. And where's the gold? Are you tricking me?"

I straighten my back, digging my hands in my pockets. "No. I'll give you the rest when you take us to the boat."

He stares at me for a second before barking out a laugh. A few heads turn our way, and I clutch my stomach to curb my panic. They look away, each too engrossed in their own worries to care about a laughing man.

"I keep underestimating you. All right, there's a boat coming in a month. It's a standard route, one taken many times. Through the Mediterranean to Syracuse, where a bus will drive you to Munich. You'll be setting sail near Tartus. I'll drive you there myself."

It all sounds simple enough, though it's far from that. Tartus, which overlooks the Mediterranean, was once an hour away from Homs. But that was without the new borders and the military swarming the route like poisonous ants. Now it takes hours. All I know about Syracuse is that it's on Italy's coast and that Munich is a city in Germany. I have no idea how far they are from each other.

"How will we get to Tartus with all the checkpoints?" I ask, hoping my voice doesn't betray the terror behind it.

He shrugs. "Don't worry about the military. That's where the money comes in. I've never been detained before."

A headache, the result of the never-ending stress, originates in the center of my brain, producing a dull throb. This journey feels impossible. Germany and Italy feel impossible. As of now, they're just words I've read in books and heard on the news. I can't even picture them in my mind.

I clear my throat. "Why does the boat need four weeks? Isn't there one sooner? Layla will be in her eighth month."

He clicks his tongue. "It's returning in a few days, but it'll take some time before it reaches port here. The men will need to make sure everything is working well. Besides, you're not the only one who'll be sailing on it. I'll know more within a week or so. These things take time."

Helpless. I feel helpless and shackled to events I can't control. Ones that determine Layla's fate.

The hospital's doors slide open, and I stand on alert, ready to witness another lifeless body, but it's only Kenan. His eyes are sparkling and he's wearing a different sweater under the worn-out brown jacket. His camera swings at his side. My heart catches at the sight of him.

I know I could easily love him. In a *might* life with the fantasies I orchestrated for myself, it would be so easy to fall for his lopsided smile and passionate dreams. I think about Layla's words. I wonder if it's worth finding happiness in Homs before I leave. Or if that happiness will lead to heartbreak and losing someone I might want to share my life with.

Layla can preach about a rosy world, but Khawf and his cynicism are the reality.

When Kenan's eyes fall on me, he smiles, his whole face brightening like the sun on a spring day, and my heart speeds up.

"Wait a minute," I tell Am absently.

"What about my Panadol?" he protests.

"I'll get it for you. One minute," I say, not taking my eyes off Kenan as I hurry over to him.

His smile deepens when I'm in front of him, and my heart won't calm down.

"We need to talk," I say breathlessly.

His expression turns serious at my anxious tone, and he follows me to an empty corner on the other side of the atrium. He maintains a respectable distance from me, but not so far that I wouldn't be able to whisper.

I cut to the chase. "There's a way for you and your siblings to leave Syria."

He blinks, taken aback, and his brows furrow.

"I'm . . . I'm leaving," I say.

Two words are enough to shatter whatever flimsy illusion we'd built between us.

"Oh" is all he says.

One syllable in a broken voice is all it takes for the hope to shrivel in my soul. Khawf was right. There's no happiness here.

He examines his boots, unease written in his expression, but I know he's not judging me. He knows the terror. He lives it every day.

I bite my cheek. "A boat will leave in a month for Italy. I

can negotiate three seats for you and your siblings. You don't have to kill yourself for this cause."

He swallows hard once. Twice. A vein pulses on his neck, and an array of emotions flit across his face. Sadness, hurt, guilt, relief.

Finally he says, "I know this is asking a lot, but I'd feel a lot better sending my siblings alone if you're there with them. You wouldn't have to do anything, just make sure they get to Italy. My uncle can meet them there."

"Kenan, listen—"

He shakes his head. "Salama, please. Please don't ask me to leave. I have to show the world what's happening."

His words are certain but his face has settled on one emotion. Fear. The toll of yesterday's massacre has clearly done more damage to his resolve than the whole year combined. He's grasping at straws, choosing to deliberately turn away from the horrific truth that'll cost him more than his life. Conflict creates a storm in his irises, and I think I can read the dark truth at its epicenter. He wants to leave but the guilt is what's holding him back. His duty to his country. I remember my hallucination of a broken Hamza and wonder when it'll become Kenan's reality.

Over his shoulder, I see Am staring at me, interested, and I snap back to Kenan. His shoulders are hunched, and I see the same misery I feel reflected in him.

"I'll keep my promise to Baba like that," he mumbles, and it seems it's more directed to himself than me.

I take a deep breath. "I don't know who told you that leaving is the cowardly thing to do, but it's not. Saving yourself from people who want to murder you *isn't* cowardly."

He shakes his head. "It all comes down to one truth, Salama. This land is my home. I don't have another one. Leaving is a death in itself."

I ball my hands into fists. I've already died. I died the day Baba and Hamza were taken. I died the day Mama was murdered. I die every single day that I can't save a patient, and I died yesterday when I held a little girl's life hostage. Maybe in Germany some piece of me can be revived.

"The boat costs one thousand dollars per person," I say. "Well, usually it's two thousand, but I can bargain. Can you afford that?"

"Yes," he immediately replies.

I nod. "You have a month, Kenan," I say in a low voice. "If you don't change your mind, I'll make sure your siblings get to Italy, but know that I'm one girl and the road is dangerous. I can't guarantee anyone's safety."

With that, I turn on my heel, catching one last glimpse of his shocked face before I go to the stockroom and fetch Am's Panadol strip from my bag.

"Two extra seats," I tell him.

Am frowns. "What?"

"I need two extra seats. Two thousand dollars."

He lets out a short laugh. "No. That wasn't part of the deal."

"It is now," I snap. "They're children. They won't be taking up much space."

He stares at me stonily and I return it.

I fold my arms. "The gold necklace is worth more now. Probably at least three people. You're also getting an extra two thousand dollars. Not to mention the Panadol. I think you're profiting *very well* from me."

His mouth curls into a sneer. "Fine. But I swear to God, Salama, if you don't hold up your end of the bargain, I will make you watch the boat leave while the military drags your sister away."

My grip tightens on my lab coat. I don't doubt his threat for a second and I want to claw at his face for daring to bring Layla into this. Instead, I try to answer in a steady tone, "I know."

"Good. Tell your friend to bring half of the money tomorrow."

Only hours later, a bomb filled with shrapnel hits an apartment building and the victims are carted into the hospital in fragments. The floors soon become slick with blood and the fresh metallic smell overtakes the stale air.

I work steadily, picking out the pieces of debris wedged between flesh and bone. I bandage and soothe. I close milky-white eyes with shaking fingers, and I murmur prayers for the martyrs' souls. I work until my limbs protest with exhaustion and then I work even harder. Anything to shut out what I did yesterday. Each person laid out in front of me is Samar and each one I don't save is Ahmad.

I don't feel the time passing. Not until my brachii muscles scream and I let my scalpel clatter to the medical basin. It clangs loudly, spraying flecks of blood over my lab coat. My arms shake and my neck feels stiff. When I look up, my eyes cross and I sway a bit.

163

"Whoa!" I hear someone exclaim, and a hand grabs my arm before I collapse on the floor.

I see two Kenans wavering above me. Their hair sticks up from all sides, a sheen of sweat glistening on their foreheads and worry coating their eyes.

"Salama?" they ask, their voice distant and echoey. "Oh my God."

I blink and Kenan's one face refocuses. He's near, so near. He looks up, searching the atrium for help, and I'm suddenly aware he's half supporting me, one hand on my back. My feet find the ground, and it gives me the boost I need to push myself up and away from him. The lingering heat of his fingers is still pressed against my back, burning through the fabric into my skin.

"I'm sorry." He raises his hands, embarrassed and pink. "You were falling and I—"

"It's fine," I say, my voice raspy and throat rough. From misuse, from tightening its muscles the whole day, I don't know. I look around and all I see is red and gray, figures slumped over one another and the miasma of despair clinging to the air. My head feels light from the lack of food and exhaustion, and I sway once again.

"*Salama!*" Kenan extends an arm and I hold on to it, my stomach twisting. I'm choking on the blood my hands are soaked in and I turn around to wash it away. My clothes stick to me like a second skin, and I need my brain to stop shouting at me.

"I need—" I say, then stop, feeling like I'm about to vomit.

He nods, quickly steering me away through the patients

and flinging the front doors open. I'm confronted with the late winter wind, freezing the sweat on my face.

I'm supporting myself on his arm, gripping him tightly, trying to breathe through my nose and focus on anything but the gnawing sound of amputated bones.

Peonies. Fragrant flowers. A tonic from the petals can be used as a muscle relaxant. Peonies. Peonies. Peonies.

My legs still can't carry me and I almost trip, but Kenan's arm slips under mine, hauling me upward so my cheek is pressed against his jacket. The material is soft with wear and I take in his scent. Lemons. I have no idea how, but he smells like the freshest of lemons and it's a comfort against the panic raging through me.

I've never been held close by a boy before, certainly not one I might actually like. Not someone to whom, in a *might* life, I would be married by now. I glance up at him. He's staring straight ahead. A faint, light brown scruff dusts his jaw and cheeks, and I have this sudden urge to touch it. The thought shocks me, stabilizes me. I press a quivering hand against my chest.

Oh, it would be so easy to fall in love, I think wistfully. *So easy.*

He glances down. "Are you okay?"

My breath hitches in my throat. I try desperately to gather at anything scientific to explain the act of falling in love. How long does it stay in the body incubating before I begin to show symptoms? Is it chronic or fleeting? Are the circumstances with the war a factor in speeding up the process?

Will my heart even care that I'll be parted from him within a month?

"Salama?" he asks again when I haven't said anything in a minute.

"Y-yes," I whisper.

He studies my features, and my synapses fire neurotransmitter after neurotransmitter. He analyzes my expression, and some emotion sears through his eyes.

I catch it before it disappears and fold it into my heart to replay later when I'm alone.

He sets me down on the cracked steps of the hospital's gates overlooking the main road. There are a few scattered twigs on the cracked pavement. We're far away from the front doors so we can't hear the voices of those inside. He sits beside me, leaving a few inches between us, and rubs his hands together as if trying to get rid of the cold. His fingers are long, delicate. Like an artist's fingers. I stare at them and imagine that *might* life: We'd be sitting right here, huddled in thick scarves and coats. He'd lace his fingers through mine and I'd marvel at how much bigger his hand is. He'd kiss my knuckles and I'd feel like I was floating on a cloud.

"I'm sorry," he says again, biting his lower lip. "I know I shouldn't have touched you. I—we're not promised to each other, and—I—" He messes his hair, looking guilty, and drags a hand down his face. "I don't want you to think I'm taking advantage or anything. Salama, I'm not—"

"Stop talking," I say, and he falls silent, cheeks still red with remorse. "I'm not upset."

My teeth chatter and I pull the edges of my sweater's sleeves over my frozen hands and hug my lab coat firmly to me.

"May I give you my jacket?" he asks, and I stare at him.

He seems shocked by his question, but he's determined.

I nod.

He shakes it off and looks slimmer without it.

No. Starved.

He drapes it over my shoulders, and I sink into the body heat still clinging to its insides. Lemons. It puts a damper on the regret, quieting the screams of those I couldn't save, and blurs the image of Samar bleeding on the hospital bed.

I pull the lapels of his jacket even closer, focusing on my breathing until the nausea subsides.

"Salama," he says, and my gaze settles on him. His camera is in his hands and he's fiddling with the buttons and flaps before catching my eye, looking as if he can read my mind. But I know my emotions are displayed on my face for all to see. "Tell me something good."

"Why?"

He gives me a half smile. "Why not?"

He wants to busy my mind with something other than the hospital. This won't end well for my heart, but at this moment, I don't care. He's here beside me and for a while I want to pretend.

I want to believe in Layla's words.

I throw the end of my hijab over my shoulder and look up at the sky, watching the way last night's thick clouds refused to scatter. They look like a healing scab. There are dark gray ridges between the clusters, and slivers of the late-afternoon sun's rays lighten the mass in between.

"I—" I clear my throat. The wind blows against us, and a stray piece of wrinkled paper dances along the road. No one's walking on the pavement. There's an abandoned car at the end of the street that's been burned down to the frame, the flames having scorched the path beside it black.

Kenan is staring at me, but I can't bring myself to look at his gravitational gaze, so I reach down and pick up a twig. It's slightly wet from the touch of winter. I run my fingers over the protrusions and rough edges.

"I used to dream about the color blue," I say, and I feel his surprise. He leans in a bit closer, and I don't think he realizes it. The twig's scars mirror the ones on my hands. No longer able to sustain new life. "Layla had painted a shade so unique, I thought it would bleed into my hands. It was a painting of a quiet sea and gray clouds. I've never seen a color like that before in my life. And the more I looked at it, the more I wanted to see the real thing."

I chew my tongue, focusing on the twig. "Back then, Syria felt too small for me. Homs felt too small. And I wanted to see the world and write about the blue in each country because I'm sure they're special and different in their own way. That not one shade looks like another. I wanted to see Layla's painting in real life."

I shudder in a breath, reopening coffins of dreams I long sealed shut. I give a small laugh, realizing. "The 'something good' doesn't come for free, Kenan. Now it's tainted with sadness. There's no blue here, not one that inspires anyway. Just the one that decays the victims' skin from frostbite and hypothermia. All the colors are muted and dull and there's no life in them."

I grip the twig tightly and turn to him. He's smiling. It's gentle and it makes my heart ache.

"That's still a beautiful dream, Salama," he says. "One that can happen."

I don't mean to, but I snort. "Where? In Germany? I'm not sure I'll see colors there like I used to." And even then, people like me don't deserve to see them. No matter how much I want to.

Kenan stretches each finger, flexes his wrists. "It might be difficult at first. The world might be too loud or too silent. It might be neon bright or pitch black, but slowly, it'll put itself back together. It will resemble something normal. Then you'll see the colors, Salama."

My lips part and a desire awakens in my heart. "Do we even deserve to see them, Kenan?" I whisper after a minute, and from his expression, I know he understands I'm not talking about colors. Survivor's remorse is a second skin we are cursed to wear forever.

He looks away, his lips drawn tight, because this isn't an easy question to answer. Time is the best medicine to turn our bleeding wounds to scars, and our bodies might forget the trauma, our eyes might learn to see colors as they should be seen, but that cure doesn't extend to our souls.

It doesn't. Time doesn't forgive our sins, and it doesn't bring back the dead.

I fidget with the twig. "You don't have to answer that."

He looks at me guiltily. "Salama—"

I shake my head. "Let's sit here for a while, okay? Before the next storm hits."

He cracks his knuckles and nods, stray strands of his hair catching in his eyelashes.

We sit side by side, resting our hands on the pavement, fingers inches away from one another. And I can't remember the last time my mind was so quiet, comfortable in the unspoken words filling the silence.

And it's in this silence I replay the fleeting look in his eyes when he held me.

Longing.

16

"WE'LL DEFINITELY NEED A CHANGE OF CLOTHES," Layla exclaims, rushing through the corridor from the kitchen to the living room to my room and back again.

I'm sitting cross-legged on the couch, counting our money.

Two thousand and thirty dollars.

Five hundred will go to Am at the end of this month along with the gold necklace.

My mind whirs with plan after plan for how we'll survive on foreign soil with so little. Will the man driving us to Munich also demand some sort of payment? Am said it was all inclusive, but you can never know what will happen beyond the sea. Greed is an illness and it won't take pity on the weak and desperate.

It doesn't matter. All that matters is that we get there.

I look up to see Layla standing breathless in front of me, her eyes shining with newfound excitement. Now there's a clear goal in front of her. Something solid to hang on to and invest all her energy in.

"We'll pack two hoodies and three pairs of jeans. Is that enough?"

I nod, thinking. "Nothing heavy, though. Like blankets or something. It'll weigh us down."

She looks at me pointedly. "And it's going to be March when we leave. As in the weather will be *freezing*. You're allowed one thing that keeps you warm."

I sigh. "Fine. A coat, then. And we only get one outfit each to balance the weight!"

She pouts, throwing me a sad look. Layla was a fashion icon. She was a walking piece of art that could have been hung in the Louvre, radiating inspiration. And now she's being forced to give up the identity she forged for herself.

"We'll buy more in Germany," I reassure her, and her eyes light up. "New jeans, blouses. Everything. We'll even have a moolid for Little Salama. A celebration for her."

An astonished joyful smile lights up her face, but it quickly vanishes into guilt. "No, it's fine. We don't have to do . . . especially since Hamza—"

I shake my head. "It's what he would have wanted. You and me celebrating his daughter."

I hold out my hand and she takes it.

"You're my sister and I love you." I squeeze it. "I want us to be happy for Little Salama."

Her smile is gentle. "Happiness starts here, Salama. In this home. In Old Homs. Remember?"

I remember Kenan and the way he sat with me yesterday until my breathing was calm. I remember the longing creased in his eyes.

Longing for me.

I suddenly feel hot under my sweater and scramble for a distraction. "So what else do we need to take with us?"

Layla's lips have turned into a knowing smile, but I stare at her defiantly, daring her to say what's on her mind.

Then she lets it go and says, "Our passports and high school certificates."

I nod. "Those are the essentials. Think, Layla, we're on a boat at sea. We're cold so we have our coats. What else?"

"Panadol," she says, and I feel my veins turn to ice. "If we get headaches or anything. You still have the stash, right?"

"Yeah," I answer immediately, forcing my tone to be casual, and play with the hem of my sweater. Surely I can salvage one strip for Layla and me until we make it to the boat. Hopefully we won't need more than that, and she won't know why I had to trade our supply until we land in Italy. Then she can hate me all she wants. Look at me the same way I look at myself in the mirror.

Murderer.

My stomach lurches and I stand quickly, startling Layla. I run to the bathroom, my sock-clad feet thumping on the carpeted floor, before I reach the sink and heave. My hands clutch the edges tightly, the blood disappearing from the capillaries as I vomit bile.

I haven't eaten anything in two days save for a small piece of dry bread. When I glance up at the bathroom mirror, I fight the urge not to cry out. The sour taste burns my throat. My eyes are bloodshot, my hair sticking to my sweaty forehead in clumps. Black shadows encircle my eyes. I'm deteriorating from guilt.

"Salama!" Layla's voice cuts through the heavy air.

I cup my hands in the water bucket and splash my face.

"*Salama,*" Layla repeats, and she clutches my shoulder, spins me around.

I'm met with worried eyes and instantly put on my *everything's fine* face.

Her grip is firm on me. "What the *hell* happened?"

I give a half-hearted shrug. "I think I ate something bad."

Her eyes narrow. "You didn't eat anything when you came back from the hospital."

The sour taste is pungent in my mouth. "I ate at the hospital," I manage to say in a convincing voice.

Before she can say anything else, I push past her and walk back to the living room, crumpling on the couch. Layla appears a second later, arms folded and lips curled with suspension.

"Are you hiding something from me?"

I groan and reach down, picking up the hoodie and hugging it. It has a musty closet smell. "No, I'm not. Layla, I don't have the energy to keep things from you."

Calendula, I think, remembering the dried flower I taped into my scrapbook with my scribbled notes beside it. *Bright orange petals. Used to heal burns and wounds. It has excellent antibacterial, antiviral, and anti-inflammatory properties.*

Layla tuts but, when I peek at her, she looks concerned.

"I'm fine," I whisper. "I promise."

But I'm not fine.

Samar isn't at the hospital when I arrive the next day, which means Am took her home during the night. My heart expands, glad it won't squeeze painfully at the sight of her heavily bandaged neck. Still, the shame is in my vessels, poisoning my blood.

A patient calls for me, complaining of a pain in his amputated leg, and I run to him, quickly clearing the troublesome thoughts away.

I work like I worked yesterday until my vision blurs, and when I stop running on fumes, I run on remorse. Today brings in a wave of victims from a military plane's bombs that rained on a residential area south of Old Homs. Just on the other side of where our home is. For now, for another day, Layla is safe.

The patients vary from civilians to a couple of the Free Syrian Army's soldiers. With Nour's help, I operate on one whose right arm is hanging on by just a few tendons. His whole face is twisted in pain but no whimper escapes his lips. Instead, through silent tears and a pool of blood, he sings softly.

"How Sweet Is Freedom."

Torn, bloodied muscle curls over the fractured humerus, the tendons pink and stretched like an elastic band. My stomach heaves but I swallow down the nausea. I hold up his arm carefully and when I look at Dr. Ziad, who's operating on the laceration on the soldier's thigh, he shakes his head. The patient has lost too much blood. Not even the manual transfusions would be enough, and it would take too much time and effort that could be spent saving another life. Not to mention the high risk of infection. Our hospital isn't built on preserving limbs, but on preserving life.

The soldier suddenly stops singing and looks at me. "You're going to cut it off, aren't you?"

I nod slowly, my eyes aching with tears. His uniform is shredded, the green turning dark with blood. It leaks into the stitched revolution flag on his chest, coloring the white stripe red. He's not that much older than I am, his dirty blond hair matted and his forest-green eyes glistening with tears. In another life, he wouldn't live with death. The world would be his oyster and, starry-eyed, he'd venture out to find his place in it. He'd have read about wars and revolutions in schoolbooks, where they'd remain confined. Never a reality.

But even with *this* reality, his face betrays no hysteria. I presume it's a combination of shock and the minimal dose of anesthesia we gave him.

"Do it," he grits out.

His arm suddenly feels very real in my hands. Usually patients scream, begging us to save them. All they know is the pain.

"But—but how will you fight?" I ask.

He grins and nods to his left arm. "I still have another one, don't I?"

This time the ache transforms into my own tears that slip down my cheeks. The soldier lays his head back on the hospital bed, casts his eyes to the ceiling, and goes back to singing.

His arm is sent with the rest of the casualties from today to be buried in the cemetery.

I lose track of time as I try to race against it and catch the souls before they rise from their bodies. Only when Dr. Ziad physically intervenes and confiscates my scalpel do I stop.

"Salama," he says, eyes blazing. "Enough. Go home."

My stare drops to my hands, which are sticky with dried blood.

The main atrium's lights are dimmer, the moans of those in pain low, and doctors and families alike are sprawled against the walls and floors, catching their breath. The sun's rays filtering through the windows give the colors a harsh hue. The red vicious, and the gray desolate. These are the shades seen when twilight takes over the world. I've never stayed this late before. During the day, the colors are electric, urging me to work faster before they slip from my fingers into nothing. The red is vibrant, carrying life, and the gray promises the fall of rain.

The atrium suddenly feels like a casket.

"*Okay*," I choke out. "Okay."

I clean my hands and grab my bag. Dr. Ziad gives me a reassuring nod. I stumble through the patients, dragging my feet, until I push the hospital doors wide open. Cool air washes me from head to toe and I take in a deep breath, begging it to launder away the residue of bile and blood from my mouth.

Daisies. Daisies. Daisies.

I'm standing on the brink of sunset, the honey-orange dye taking over the sky and the horizon above me deepening into a rich navy blue. A canvas for the stars.

It looks . . . haunting.

Someone moves and my eyes snap down to see Kenan lying on the hospital's steps, his camera atop his chest. His long legs stretch out in front of him and he glows under the twilight sky. The way stars shine in his eyes and the small upturn of his lips make him look like something out of a story. For a minute, in the day's tail end, he looks as if he's dreaming aloud.

God, he's beautiful.

I watch him for a while, remembering how near he was to me last night when he walked me home. I feel warm all over.

My hands coil tightly into the fabric of my lab coat, frustration about to cleave my heart into two. It's during the quiet times that it raises its head, taunting me about my lost teenage years. We're so young. Too young to be suffering like this. And I know I'm holding myself back from falling for him. But his kindness is addictive, and I've found myself craving it, basking in the image he's constructed of me. In the lie—a selfless girl who saves the wounded regardless of her own safety.

In that *might* life, with his ring glittering on my finger, we'd be going out for dinner on a Thursday night to a fancy restaurant where the street would be filled with laughing people and couples celebrating the end of winter, drinking warm tea. The shops would be open until late, the lights keeping the night at bay, flickering to yellow sunbursts on the century-aged stone walls. We'd be lulled into our own world where everyone else's conversations would be muted and the clock's arrows would blur, defying the laws of time until he'd take me home. And under the flowering lemon trees outside my apartment building with the lunula moon as our witness, he'd cup my cheeks and kiss me.

Without meaning to, I let out a sigh and his chin snaps back down, eyes sparkling when they catch on my silhouette.

"Salama," he says, his voice warm as a summer's day.

"Kenan." I relish his name. It leaves a sweet aftertaste on my tongue.

He jumps to his feet, stretching his arms overhead.

"Let's go?" he asks, and I nod, trying not to look too eager.

He falls into step and I notice he's wearing the same jacket he draped on my shoulders. My fingers tingle, wanting to run along the seam and the collar.

"Did you—" I begin.

"How are—" he says.

He looks away, blushing, and I do the same. Is this a symptom of falling in love? Or a crush? I'm hyperaware of each breath he takes in and lets out.

"Sorry. You go first," he murmurs.

I clutch the strap of my bag and take a deep breath. If this is an ailment, then there must be a cure. "I wanted to ask if you recorded today?"

He nods. "I got good footage. Two people I talked to are from Hama. It was good hearing stories about my mom's hometown. About what's happening there too. I'm thinking of compiling everything into a documentary and posting it on YouTube. Not too long, though. Just straight to the point."

I give him a small smile. "That's great."

He scratches the back of his head and then says, "I, uh, also brought the money."

I start. I didn't see Am all day and I know he wouldn't miss the chance at collecting his money. But his daughter is still in a critical condition, even if she can't stay at the hospital.

"The man you were talking to yesterday. He's the one who gets the boats, right?" Kenan asks.

I nod. "I don't think he came in today."

"Me neither. I walked through the whole hospital recording but he wasn't anywhere."

"I'm sure he'll be there tomorrow." And after a heart-beat, I add, "Do Lama and Yusuf know you're not coming with them?"

A shadow falls on his face, and he grips his camera. "Yes. They . . . weren't happy. Lama threw a fit and Yusuf . . . he went straight to bed and hasn't even looked at me since."

The sky is now an iris hue, and we begin to pass people walking in groups, all carrying handmade signs. A few have the Syrian Revolution flag draped over their necks. A nightly protest. I recognize one young woman I stitched up after she tried to escape from the guns at another demonstration. She grins when she sees me and mouths a "hello" before hurry-ing after the others.

"Kenan," I begin and feel the aura around him twist with apprehension. "You can still come with us."

Nervous energy evaporates off him and he lets go of the camera. It swings down, hitting his side. He averts his gaze, gluing it ahead. Is he too ashamed to tell me he wants to leave? I see the similarities between us so clearly. But as Layla is my weakness, his siblings are his.

"I can't," he whispers. "I won't forgive myself."

"And you think I will? This isn't an easy choice, but it's not wrong."

He stops walking and stares at me for a few seconds before pulling out his phone. He opens it, presses the screen, and then holds it in front of me. It's the comments section on a YouTube video. "Look at the comments, Salama."

I squint. There are about fifty, all of them praying for Syria's safety and liberation. A few users talk about how the channel has been covering what's happening better than any news outlet.

"This is my video. My channel," Kenan says. "I'm making a difference. I'm adding English subtitles and explaining what's going on so the world can know. Arabs know, but the rest of the world doesn't. They don't know it's a revolution. They have no idea we've been living in a dictatorship for fifty years. The news shows the military killing people. They don't know who the Free Syrian Army is. Who the military is. Syria is just a word to them. But to us, she's our life. I can't leave her."

My heart hammers painfully.

He puts his phone back in his pocket. "I talked to my uncle yesterday. Once we know when the boat leaves, we'll tell him, and he'll come to Syracuse. He'll pick up Lama and Yusuf."

I don't like this. I don't like how he's not including himself. "Kenan—"

"So there's no need for them to go by car to Munich. My uncle will also help you, of course. I told him. He'll make sure you and Layla are safe."

"*Kenan.*"

He stops talking, stops walking, but there's a wild desperation in his eyes. Like he's swallowing down the words and wants threatening to spill from his lips. He's clinging to duty like a burning coal. I ignore the stab of remorse at having a hand in this and focus on how it could save him.

"The journey to Syracuse is long," I say. "We're going by *boat*. Do you understand that? It's not a luxurious ship with a five-course meal. You've seen pictures of them on the internet. We all have. The boats are old and weak, and some... some don't even make it. They're overcrowded. Out there in the Mediterranean, there are no laws. Everyone's mindset will be to survive regardless of who gets hurt in the process. And people *will* get hurt. Lama and Yusuf are perfect candidates."

His shoulders sag as if the world and all seven skies rest upon him. He's tired and I don't know him well enough to be sure if my nagging is doing more damage than good. So I decide to take a page out of Layla's book. Remind him of the happiness. Or at least of the past, so he knows this pain isn't eternal.

"I remember your mother," I say, making my voice gentle, and he looks at me with surprise. He stands in front of a building charred black from a fire. I have to tilt my chin up to look him in the eyes. Those beautiful, hurting eyes of his.

I silently scold myself. I can't think of him like this. He might be holding on to a burning coal but he has no intention of letting go. He's been holding on to it ever since he was born. In a month's time, I'll be sailing away and he'll be stuck onshore, growing more distant by the second. He'll be a daydream I visit when I'm alone in Germany, mourning the loss of my *might* life and obsessively checking his YouTube account for any updates, wondering if he's still alive and free.

I grip the loose end of my hijab and squeeze with frustration. This isn't *fair*.

"She was at my brother and Layla's wedding," I continue. "I remember seeing her. You—you have her eyes."

Those same eyes soften, and he takes a step closer.

"You know, my mom told me about you that night."

My stomach flips.

He laughs lightly, all traces of agony disappearing. How we can skip from one emotion to the other like a well-coordinated dance, I'll never know. "Yeah, she came back home talking about this girl who's a bubble of life. Whose confidence and joy infected everyone around her."

Heat envelops me whole.

I miss that girl.

"She was absolutely determined to have us meet." He runs a hand through his hair, and it gets messier. "Said you and I were like two peas in a pod. I was curious, but your mama wanted you to focus on your studies before we met. Honestly, I thought you'd be more stuck-up."

I splutter and he grins. *"Excuse me?"*

He laughs again and it sounds heavenly, full of life. Not like Khawf's laugh.

"Sorry. I judged you by your appearance. Freshman at pharmacy school, a good family name, a brother who's a doctor, the only daughter, the youngest in your family. I mean, all the factors pointed toward it. I didn't think some-one like me would meet your standards."

I blink.

He cracks his knuckles, looking guilty. "I was wrong, obviously." He gives me a shy smile. "I'm sorry."

"How do you know I didn't become less stuck-up after

everything that happened to me?" I ask, needing to know the answer but worried just the same.

He shakes his head. "I don't think so. You've always been this way, I'm sure. I was feeling awkward about being set up, so I kept making silly excuses like that."

"For the record," I say, not believing the words I'm about to utter, "I would have thought *I* wouldn't meet *your* standards."

He tilts his head to the side, puzzled.

"The eldest child, all the responsibility on your shoulders. And instead of taking the safe route of studying medicine, which you could have, you followed your heart and studied what you love. Even after everything you've been through, there's light in your eyes. You still laugh. So I can only imagine how you were before. I'd have felt self-conscious about how free-spirited you are. How you see the world in all its colors and shades of beauty. I'd have worried I couldn't keep up." I stop talking because the way he's staring at me is making butterflies flap their wings in my stomach.

"Well," he says after a while. "Our fears had no basis, then."

"I—I guess so," I whisper and shudder in a breath. "It's . . . it's a shame, Kenan."

"What is?" His voice is hushed, and I know he knows what I'm about to say.

"That we never had the chance to find out if we're each other's Pazu and Sheeta."

When he doesn't say anything, I step so close I can count the freckles on his neck. His breath hitches in his throat and his gaze drops to my lips.

"I wish we had that time," I whisper. "I really do. I wish—"

I stop.

He glances at my lips and reads the words I'm too shy to speak.

I wish you'd come with me.

I wish we could fall in love.

17

KHAWF ISN'T PLEASED ABOUT MY CONVERSATION
with Kenan, but I refuse to speak to him, instead lying on
my bed and facing the wall, thinking about Kenan's eyes
and our interaction today.

"Aren't you concerned you didn't see Am today?" he
goes on, standing in front of me, so I twist to the other side.
He appears there too, and I groan loudly. "What if he's run
away with your money?"

"Run away where? The only way he makes money is by
taking people to the boats, and with the way food prices are,
the money I gave him won't last forever. I'll see him tomorrow. His daughter was injured, remember? He won't be
missing the chance at more medicine."

Khawf purses his lips, his eyes gleaming like icicles in
the dark room. "Fine," he finally says. "Kenan isn't changing
your mind, is he?"

I blow out a puff of air. "No. I will always choose Layla.
Over anyone."

He smiles, satisfied. "But are you choosing yourself as well?"

I frown.

He gestures at me. "You haven't eaten anything all day."

I clench my jaw. How annoying it is for my brain to have me in its clutches like this.

Earlier I whipped up a dinner of canned tuna immersed in olive oil and salt, which I took one bite of before my stomach threatened to expel everything. I don't feel hungry anymore. Not with what I did to Samar. Layla didn't eat either, and when I asked her if she'd eaten anything, she said she wasn't hungry. She wants to save as much food as she can for the journey.

Khawf's voice is as deadly as nightshade. "If you're not careful, Salama, you might become the instrument of your destruction."

"I already changed my mind about leaving," I grumble. "So why are you tormenting me?"

His lips curl into a slow smile. "You did. But a lot can happen between now and the boat's departure. I can't have that. You're not in control, Salama. I am. Remember: If you're arrested, then I'm not going anywhere. I'll be showing you all sorts of terrible things. Kenan beaten to within an inch of his life. Hamza, a husk." He leans forward and I stand my ground, refusing to let my lips tremble. "What's interesting, Salama, is that you'll be the one coming up with all these scenarios. I'm a part of your mind. You *need* all these horrible hallucinations. You need me."

I scowl. "I know this is my brain trying to protect Layla and me. You made that clear. But it doesn't mean I have to like it!"

He snaps his fingers and Layla is sprawled on the floor beside my bed. Blood seeps onto the floorboards, and she twitches.

My heart lodges in my throat and I tear my eyes back to Khawf. He's studying my reaction.

"It's not her," I say, my voice barely a rasp.

"Never forget who's in control here."

I close my eyes, whispering "daisies" to myself, and when I open them, hallucination Layla is gone. But she still lives in my mind.

To my utter relief, Am is at the hospital the next day. His eyes are dull, and his beard is patchy. He looks as miserable as I feel.

He stops when he sees me, eyes narrowing as I extend the hand that has the Panadol tablet in it.

"Here."

Am chews his cheek and opens his palm.

"Kenan is coming in later. He'll have your money."

He grunts.

"I want to ask you what we should pack. What do we need for the journey?"

He massages his forehead. "Important documents. Food. Your own water. Something to fight the seasickness. Nothing too heavy."

My head spins. "Okay. Okay."

"Is that all?"

I fiddle with the end of my hijab. "How's—how's Samar?"

His stare is filled with dislike. "Fine."

"Her stitches?"

"I said she's fine," he snaps. "Look, this is a business transaction, all right? You give me money and I give you a boat. We don't have to get all personal."

My throat is dry, so I nod.

He moves past me but halts for a second. "Don't think about asking for forgiveness," he says and walks away.

My stomach churns with the buildup of gastric acid and I scuttle to the medicine stockroom. I slide against the wall, my breaths irregular and a dull ache pounding behind my eyes.

"Forget him," Khawf says, and I start.

He stands a few feet away from me, examining a red box of aripiprazole. "Forget what he said, Salama. He's not the bigger picture. Germany is. Your new life with Layla and her baby."

Hawthorn. Red berries that can be used to lower blood pressure. Have excellent antioxidant properties and strengthen the cardiac muscle. Hawthorn. Hawthorn. Hawthorn.

I stay in the stockroom a bit longer until I can see those white hawthorn petals behind my closed eyelids. Then I walk outside to face whatever fresh hell barges through the doors.

This time when the victims from a sniper shooting are rolled in around noon, I stand strong, pushing down my terror to make up for what I've done. Amid the bodies and the screaming, I see Kenan standing to the side, his camera covering half his face.

And no matter how much I try to beat death, he still

wins. I close five pairs of eyes today. Three children, one young woman, and one young man. Their faces smeared with blood, their mouths hanging open, an expression of betrayal forever etched on their faces.

I recite Al-Fatiha for their souls and feel Kenan standing beside me.

"Everything okay?" he murmurs.

I shake my head, not taking my eyes off the corpses.

"Salama," Kenan says gently. "Let's go. Take me to Am."

I don't move.

His fingers tentatively brush the cuff of my sleeve and I inhale sharply. "You did everything you could. This isn't your fault."

My lips quiver and I swallow my cries.

"Yalla," he says, and I allow myself to turn away.

The main atrium is filled with new and old faces. We find Am standing beside the back door, where the martyrs are transported to the cemetery.

I don't even hear what Am and Kenan talk about, my thoughts becoming too dark and twisted, blaming me that I was too slow, too pathetic to save lives.

"Salama." Kenan's voice cuts through the air and I look up at him.

He looks stricken, and Am is watching me curiously. I glance down and see I've been digging my nails into my palms while shaking all over.

"I'm fine," I say in a hollow voice.

Am makes a disgruntled sound, and before Kenan can say anything, he says, "We'll provide you with the life jackets, but that's it. Carry little. Everything but your lives can be replaced."

"I have to go," I say suddenly, and Kenan turns to me.

"Okay." He moves toward me. "Let me get—"

I shake my head, holding up a hand. "It's fine."

I twist around, hurrying away and out of the hospital as my heart thunders in my ears. I can't take it anymore. I can't take another dead body. I can't take this guilt. I'm tired and my stomach is ripping itself to shreds with hunger. My palms are red from my nails, my scars horrendous. I need to breathe in something that isn't blood and bile and guts. I need to hold Layla and remind myself she's alive.

I want to scream.

I want Mama.

By the time I reach my home, I'm out of breath and wheezing.

"Layla!" I call out, slamming the door behind me.

"Salama?" Her surprised voice answers from the living room. She appears a second later, hair tumbling over her shoulders. Her washed-out mustard dress stretches over her bulging stomach, and I throw myself in her arms, hugging her.

"Hey, is everything all right?" She holds me closer. "Oh my God, did something happen? Is Kenan okay?"

"N-no," I stammer. "I'm fine. Everything's fine. I just needed to see you."

She holds me back, eyes searching me. "The circles under your eyes are darker." She grips my arm. "Your face is thinner. Something's happened. Salama?"

"I'm fine," I repeat weakly.

She doesn't believe me. "It's nearly four o'clock. Your shift isn't over until five."

I tear myself from her and plod toward the couch, where I all but collapse. I shrug my lab coat off and remove my hijab, throwing it over the couch's arm. "I'm tired. Please, can you play with my hair?"

She exhales and sits down, and I lay my head in her lap. Her touch is gentle as she untangles the knots in my tresses. I feel the blood moving in the vessels in my scalp and sigh with relief.

I close my eyes and whisper, "Thank you."

"Anything for you, silly."

We stay silent for a while and I remember how dramatic I used to get if a pimple popped up unbidden on my face. My bookshelf was stacked with homemade concoctions I'd whipped up from all the herbs and flowers I'd gathered, neatly arranged beside one another alphabetically. Jam jars filled with sprigs of tea tree, buds of witch hazel, dried rose petals. I would make pastes out of them.

"Dab it under your eyes," I remember saying once to Layla, who would always volunteer as my guinea pig. She was perched on my bed, drinking coffee from a huge blue mug. She put it down on my desk and opened the jar.

"Mmm." She smeared the pink cream on her cheekbones and under her eyes. "It smells so good. What is it?"

"Arabian jasmine, daisies, and a dash of almond oil." I went through the jars' labels. "It's supposed to make your skin smoother and erase your dark circles."

Layla huffed, feigning offense. "Are you saying I don't take care of my skin?"

I laughed. "Layla, you owe half your beauty to me."

She flicked her hair to the side. "I won't comment on that."

Now, my skin is dry and flaky, my lips chapped, and the dark circles under my eyes have become permanent. The old Salama wouldn't recognize me.

"Salama," Layla says, and I crack my eyes half open. "Talk to me."

I sort through the problems, trying to decide which will distract me enough from my pain and won't be a burden on Layla.

"I think," I whisper, "I might like Kenan."

Her fingers still and I brace myself for her inevitable shrieks of joy, but she doesn't do that. I glance up to see a sad smile on her lips.

"What are you going to do?" she asks.

"Cry?" I joke weakly even though I'm trying my best to stifle the tears in my ducts. Now that the words are out in the open, they refuse to be ignored any longer. It seems I'll be leaving Syria hurt in every possible way.

"I'm sorry," she says.

"I thought you'd be screaming and jumping up and down."

She shakes her head lightly. "I know I've been excited for the day you fall in love but I never thought it would be like this."

"Is it okay that I hate him a little because he wants to stay here?"

She lets out a small laugh. "Yes, it's perfectly fine."

I groan, rubbing at my wet eyelashes. "I know we'll be apart in a month, but Layla, I don't want to stop meeting him. I'm thinking…anything is better than nothing. I know it'll hurt so much in Germany. I know I'll spend days and nights praying he's safe. I know that and still I can't— *don't want to*—stop."

Layla stares at me for some time. "That's okay too, Salama. I know what you mean. Anything *is* better than nothing. I told you to find bits of happiness in Homs. Kenan is a happy moment."

I swallow thickly.

A knock on our front door startles us and we exchange a glance. I stand, wrapping my hijab around my head before tiptoeing slowly to the door. Through the eyepiece, I see Kenan. He's staring at the ground, hands in his pocket.

"Who is it?" Layla asks in a hushed voice.

"*Kenan,*" I mouth.

Her mouth drops with astonishment and she silently claps her hands, looking giddy. "*Open the door,*" she mouths back, miming the action.

I exhale deeply, commanding myself to stay calm and open the door, wearing—what I hope is—a casual smile that feels weird on my face.

"Kenan," I say, and he looks up. "Hello."

His expression is stunned but he recovers quickly. "You—um—I'm sorry to come over like this, but—you left the hospital pretty quickly and I wanted to make sure you were all right."

I play with the hem of my sweater, feeling all warm at his concern. "Yes. I'm fine. It was—I'm fine, I promise."

"I'm glad."

He scratches the back of his head, and the movement presses his sweater against his body.

He steels himself, rocking on his heels, and he cracks his knuckles. "I was wondering if you'd go with me somewhere."

Oh.

Oh!

Layla gasps from the living room and I try to remember how to breathe.

Kenan panics when he sees me staring at him dumbfounded. "If—it's all right if you don't want to."

"No," I say too quickly. I blush, hugging myself. "I—yes."

He looks relieved, his chest expanding with air, and a smile lights up his face. It's as if I'm gazing at the sun.

"Just a second." I hurry to the living room, where Layla is still crouched on the sofa, her mouth dropped open, and she quickly takes my hands in hers.

"*Oh my God,*" she exclaims, shaking me. This feels like a hint of our old life seeping through the pain. It almost makes me dizzy with nostalgia.

Anxious thoughts take over. "Is this a bad idea? Will this hurt my heart? Should I pretend I'm suddenly sick?"

She laughs. "No, dummy. It's *still* happiness. And you deserve to be happy."

Samar sprawled on the hospital bed flashes in front of my eyes.

"You deserve it," Layla repeats firmly. "Now go."

I nod and she lets go. "I won't be late."

She smiles. "I know."

I glance at the sea painting, taking strength from the

feeling it gives me, and walk back toward the door. I pass my reflection in the mirror hanging in the corridor and sigh. In my *might* life, I'd be dressed in my favorite dark blue jeans, a soft rose-colored blouse with a matching fleece coat, and ankle boots. My hijab would be ironed and spilling across my shoulders like a waterfall. A casual outfit Layla and I had ready in case a spontaneous date ever happened.

But in the mirror stares back a girl wearing an old pair of washed-out jeans and a black sweater with fraying edges. She's sad and skeleton-like, her eyes dim with despair and hunger.

I look away and walk out of the house, closing the door behind me.

Kenan is leaning against the wall, looking up at the sky, his jawline more pronounced. "Let's go?" he asks.

"Where to?"

He pushes himself off the wall, eyes gleaming with a secret. The clouds have parted, allowing the sun's last tangerine rays to peek through the holes in the hollowed buildings of my apocalyptic city.

"It's a surprise," he says, and walks in the opposite direction of the hospital.

I hurry after him. "Surprise?"

He smiles. "You don't like surprises?"

"I . . . I don't know."

He stops for a second, giving me a confused look. "You don't know?"

I shrug. "I used to like them. Now they make me anxious, I guess."

He nods solemnly. "That's fair. This will be a good

one. I hope." Then he adds, "But...if you want, I can tell you."

My heart glows. "No, that's okay."

We pass by a mosque still standing strong after everything that's happened. A huge corner is missing from a blast, the green carpet inside muddied. *DOWN WITH THE GOVERNMENT!* is spray-painted across one of the walls.

Puddles of murky rainwater are everywhere. A couple of children zoom past us, their shoes worn and their cheeks thin. I want to call after them to put on something warmer because it's still February.

Some men stand in front of a supermarket on the other side of the street, deep in conversation, while other people walk about, carrying groceries or in a hurry to be somewhere. I know this area, and if we take the upcoming right, my home—my old home—would be a five-minute walk away. I've only been back once, when I tried to salvage what I could from the rubble.

But Kenan doesn't turn right. He walks straight ahead and then takes a left turn into a narrow alleyway. The road is uneven here; one building's floors have collapsed on top of each other like upset dominoes.

"Here!" he finally says, and ducks inside a building. Its dusty red doors have been torn from their hinges and lie cracked on the floor. I hesitate for a second before following. He's climbing a set of ceramic stairs. His legs are longer than mine, and he's at least five steps ahead of me.

"Yalla!" he calls, an entire level above me. "To the roof!"

I glance upward and can estimate there's more than five floors to go.

197

"I'm trying!" I shout back.

After what feels like decades, I make it to the roof, where Kenan's already standing outside. Despite the cold, I'm sweating and out of breath. I stumble out the doorway, feeling my heart pumping against my throat.

"What's this place?" I manage to huff out.

Kenan smiles. He doesn't look the least bit bothered by climbing eight flights of stairs. "This is my old home. I used to come to the roof after school and do my homework."

I look around. It's a simple, standard building roof, and the floor is bare save for three broken satellites swept to the side. The view is Old Homs and the sunset. There are no other buildings obscuring it, and I'm able to witness the sun begin her descent on the horizon.

Kenan swings his legs over the edge and I stifle a cry of warning. Slowly, I come up beside him and gingerly near the edge but don't swing my legs over.

He turns toward me, his smile serene. "When was the last time you saw the sunset, Salama? Properly saw it."

I frown. "I don't remember."

"With all the destruction happening down there, it's easy to forget the beauty that's up here. The sky is so beautiful after rainfall."

The most beautiful sunsets are always the ones that come after a rain, I had said to Layla once when we were at her family's summer house in the countryside. We'd been stuck inside all day, watching a storm rage against the windows, unable to go swimming in the river beside the gardens. Layla played with my hair while we watched *Castle in the Sky* from Baba's laptop. It was the perfect comfort movie when the clouds were gray and the raindrops chased each other on the windows.

And I was right.

The sky is now a burst of purple and pink fragmenting through the tangerine orange, the clouds taking on a lavender tinge.

"You asked me if you could see colors again, Salama. If we deserve to see them," Kenan says quietly. "I think we do. I think you can. There's too little of it in death. In pain. But that's not the only thing in the world. That's not all that Syria has. Syria was once the center of the world. Inventions and discoveries were made here; they built the world. Our history is in the Al-Zahrawi Palace, in our mosques, in our earth."

He points to the ground below and I peek over the ledge, my nerves electrified with the fear of falling. I squint and see two little boys and three girls laughing, playing some sort of game.

"Look at them," Kenan says. "Look how even the agony hasn't stripped their innocence."

Then he points to a tree situated at the street's side. Its three thick trunks twist through each other, the branches brittle-looking, a hint of green leaves surfacing through its pores. "That lemon tree's been here forever. I used to climb it all the time when I was younger. I think there's a picture Baba took of me sitting atop it, with Yusuf hanging to my side."

I stay silent and glance at him. His tone is full of melancholy, his eyes capturing the golden light.

He sighs, shaking away the memories, and looks at me, smiling. "There's still beauty, Salama. Still life and strength in Homs." He nods toward the sun. "There's *color*."

199

Slowly, I dangle my legs over the brink, keeping a few inches between us. It gives me a rush of adrenaline, being balanced between something solid and air. A sweet breeze tickles my nose and I close my eyes, inhaling it deeply.

When I open them, I'm taken aback by the magic unfolding in front of me. A few stars twinkle through the wisps of cloud. Decorating them like sapphires, precious gifts for those who would gaze upward. Eight levels above the ground brings a unique kind of peace. A quiet that accompanies a late winter night. It's as if we're floating in the cosmos, detached from everything weighing us down.

It's a Studio Ghibli movie.

"Do you see the colors, Salama?" Kenan whispers.

The sunset is gorgeous, but it pales in comparison to him. He's drenched in the dying day's glow, a kaleidoscope of shades dancing on his face. Pink, orange, yellow, purple, red. Finally settling into an azure blue. It reminds me of Layla's painting. A color so stark it would stain my fingers were I to touch it.

As the sun sinks, in those few precious moments when the world is caught between day and night, something shifts between Kenan and me.

"Yes," I breathe. *"Yes."*

IN A HISTORIC CITY PLAGUED BY BOMBS, LIFE HAS persisted. I see it in the green vines waking up from their winter slumber, squirming through the rubble. Daffodils blooming, their petals opening bashfully. I see it in Layla, who smiles more, now that I do. When I see these subtle signs of life on my way to the hospital, my heart expands.

But there are times where it takes everything in me not to fall into despair. Inside I'm still broken, haunted by a little girl I threatened to kill.

Still, Am and I have fallen into a routine: I give him one Panadol tablet; he reassures me with updates about the boat. Though the updates never change, I cling to hope.

Kenan, however, has been losing one thread of life after another as he spends more time at the hospital. His hands shake when he holds his camera, and his eyes are always filled with tears. I'll never forget how he looked when he saw a seven-month-old baby who had been caught in a fire from a bomb's blast.

He's shown me more of the comments he's gotten on his YouTube videos. Everyone is in awe, sending prayers for us and praising him for risking his life to document what's happening. During those moments, there's a certain glow on his face. A serenity I don't see at other times. Like all of this is worth it. But it only exists in these brief moments and disappears entirely when death takes his hold on the hospital once more.

It hurts to know I've caused this breakdown in his fighting spirit when the words he spoke to me three weeks ago atop his old home have been reviving me. Our days together are numbered and I can't stop myself from getting to know him. It hasn't taken long for him to become a source of happiness and comfort for me. And I wonder if I'll ever be able to tell him about Khawf. I wonder what he'd do.

When I walk out of the hospital after today's shift, the evening sky is a dark blue canvas and Kenan is looking up at it.

"Hey," I say, and he beams at me.

Outside the hospital and away from the harrowing realities he documents daily, Kenan usually manages to collect himself. Even though I see the cracks he's trying to cover. During our walks, we either stay silent, untangling the trauma that has woven another knot in our brains or, if it's been a really bad day and we need a distraction, we discuss other things. He's told me about his drawing software and how he has a half-completed graphic novel saved on his laptop he wishes he could finish. I told him about my scrapbooks and flower-filled jars, and the way he looked at me with such awe made me ache for that *might* life. Wishing I could have shown them to him personally in my room, where he'd then press me against him, lips on mine.

A thought occurs to me as we walk back home now, and before I can rethink it, I blurt, "Imagine if you and I wrote a book together."

He stops, gazing at me so intently, I feel its touch on my skin.

"You write?" he finally asks.

I nod, fidgeting with my sleeves. "I mean I want to. I have a couple of ideas for a children's book. I was thinking you'd illustrate, and I'd write."

He looks at me with wonder. "Tell me one of your stories."

I glance away. "I've . . . never told anyone about them."

He nods, and then smiles serenely. "All right. Then let's make up a new one."

My heart somersaults, grateful he isn't trying to wheedle them out of me. "I have a setting."

He grins and we walk. "Go on."

"An ocean, but instead of water it's gigantic trees that touch the clouds."

His grin widens. "I can absolutely draw that. Leaves that are blue instead of green? The trunks a coral pink?"

My bashfulness ebbs away slowly. "The higher you go, the bigger the leaves are. Oh! Fish that fly through air currents instead of water!"

"Yes!" he says excitedly. "A story about a girl who longs to see the water-filled oceans!"

"They're a myth in her world but they have something she needs," I add, nearly skipping with enthusiasm.

And we go on like this, one chaotic thought spilling after the other, unaware that we've long since reached my home. We stand in front of the door talking for twenty extra minutes before a distant rumble of a plane shatters our day-dream. We return to reality with trembling hands and nervous eyes cast upward.

And when I look at him, I see that pain. He and I will never be able to write a book together.

And I wonder if this ache in my heart will ever fade away. Or if it'll only grow stronger.

The next day, Am finally has new information regarding the boat.

"It will be here in ten days. Twenty-fifth of March. We meet by Khalid Mosque at ten a.m. Do you know where that is?"

I nod. Baba and Hamza prayed Juma'a prayer there every Friday. It's a ten-minute walk from Layla's home.

"Good. Bring the money or there's no boat."

I grind my teeth. "I know." But before I can ask about Samar, he shakes his head and walks away. My stomach feels queasy, and I hide out in my medication stockroom until Dr. Ziad needs me.

My mind wanders to the boat, and an anticipation builds in me, my fingers tingling with the promise of safety. For Layla to finally be able to sleep in a bedroom that doesn't remind her of her incarcerated husband. Where Baby Salama would take her first steps in a house filled with flowers and the aroma of freshly baked fatayer.

My daydreams scatter with a quick knock on the stockroom door.

Kenan smiles. "Hey."

"Hey."

"Dr. Ziad is looking for you."

I jump to my feet. Dr. Ziad is in his office and when I walk in, he stands.

"Salama." His face is white, his expression twisted with a silent pain.

Immediately I'm on edge. "What?"

Dr. Ziad looks at Kenan. "Can you give us a moment?"

Kenan glances at me before nodding slowly and closing the door behind him.

Dr. Ziad rests his hands on the desk. "I'm not going to sugarcoat this, Salama, because it's not fair to you, and you have the right to know." He takes a deep breath and I begin trembling. "One of the Free Syrian Army soldiers was here with information concerning detainees in the military's detention facilities. The ones who are alive. Your brother is on the list."

The wind has been knocked out of me.

Dr. Ziad massages his forehead, his eyes shining with tears. "He's alive, but your father passed away."

I'm detached from my body, my mouth uttering in a voice I don't recognize, "Where is he?"

Dr. Ziad's eyes don't meet mine. "Sednaya Prison."

The floor is falling apart, and I sway before catching the door's handle. Sednaya Prison is one of the most brutal detention facilities in Syria. Located near Damascus—a two-hour drive from Homs. The place is worse than a death sentence. Its prisoners are stacked atop one another in cells too small to breathe in.

"I'm sorry, Salama," he whispers. "I'm so sorry. Please, take care—"

"I need to leave," I interrupt, flinging the door open and rushing out. My feet pick up the pace until I'm outside and I collapse over the hospital's steps. My breaths heave in and out.

"Salama!" a voice calls, and I look back to see Kenan standing at the top of the steps. "My God, you're shaking."

He shrugs off his jacket and drapes it across my shoulders before sitting beside me. I close my eyes, breathing in the lemon scent of it, praying it's enough to put the darkness back in its place. Minutes or hours pass, I don't know, but he stays beside me on the broken steps, waiting.

He doesn't ask but I need to form the words. I *need* to tell someone. The words need to spill out before they drown me.

"My brother," I begin hoarsely. "Hamza. When he was arrested with Baba . . . Layla and I—we thought they'd both died. We wanted to believe that. But Hamza is still alive."

I hear Kenan's sharp intake of breath.

Hamza is alive right this second being tortured while I'm outside, planning on running away from Syria. My hands shake and I clutch my head, trying to calm down.

"Jasmine," I murmur. "A tea made from its leaves eases body aches and helps with anxiety. Jasmine. Jasmine. Jasmine."

In my heart of hearts, I know we still must leave or Layla and I will face a fate like Hamza's. I know that. I *know*. Yet . . .

My chin snaps up. Layla. This is too big of a secret for me to hold in my heart. I can't stack it atop my tower of lies.

Khawf materializes on the pathway leading up to the hospital stairs and watches me with an impassive expression. There's a calculating look in his eyes and he's gauging my reaction.

"I need to go home," I choke out, and stand, catching Kenan's jacket before it falls. I don't want to give it back yet; I need the feeling of security it's giving me to last a bit longer.

"I'm so sorry," Kenan whispers.

When I look at him, his pained eyes are still on me, and a thought awakens in my brain. My grief can be used to persuade him. Khawf smiles.

"Don't you see the reality, Kenan?" I keep my voice from trembling. "Torture. Death. This is happening. It *will* happen to you if you don't leave."

"Salama—" he begins, standing.

"No!" I shout, balling my hands into fists instead of shaking him. "Why isn't this getting through your head? Your siblings will *never* heal. You will die for a cause no one outside Syria cares about. Those YouTube comments are great, but no one is helping us. You'll rot in jail and be tortured for the rest of your life with no one to save you. Are you seriously leaving your siblings to the wolves? Do you even realize what's happening to the refugees in Europe?"

He clears his throat roughly. "I've . . . heard."

Tears blur my vision, and he shudders in a breath.

"Kenan, you think you're being selfless." My voice breaks this time. "But you're not. Imagine Lama and Yusuf have reached Syracuse and something happens and I'm separated from them. They never find your uncle. I can't guarantee their safety. I don't even know what *I'm* doing. They could so easily be kidnapped and sold. Imagine that happens and you're here, stuck in a detention facility, your life sliced away from you piece by piece." My nails dig into my sleeves. "Is this what you want?"

"No, of course not!" he says loudly, and he breaks his gaze to rub an arm over his watery eyes.

"The boat leaves March twenty-fifth," I say, praying the seeds of doubt are working their way into his mind. That they'll grow like cress. "Think about whose lives you're risking here."

My brain's synaptic signals are malfunctioning, and I can't focus on anything except getting back to Layla. I want to be far away from people and scream and cry and mourn.

"I'm going home," I say.

He nods. "I have your bag."

Before I can say anything, he walks down the steps. I'm lost in my own agony, relying on muscle memory to take me home as tears stream down my cheeks. Tremors run up and down my skeletal system, fissuring my bones. A war rages inside me and it seems I'm the only casualty.

"We're here," he says, and I nearly slam into his back.

"Thank you," I say quietly, offering him his jacket back, and a part of me considers asking if I can keep it for a day. My shock at that thought eases some of the sadness I'm feeling. He takes it and hands me my bag.

He notes the tear tracks on my face, a realization unclouding in his eyes. "Salama," he says softly, and my eyelashes flutter. The way he says my name, pronouncing each vowel and consonant, even now makes me feel like flowers are growing in my veins.

"Yes?" I say, matching his tone.

He bites his lip. "Please take care of yourself."

I wrap my arms around my middle. "I am."

He smiles sadly. "Are you?"

His gaze dips from my sharp cheekbones to my bony wrists. I may have started seeing the colors, believing in Layla's and Kenan's words, but that has no power over my guilt. It's as if I'm being slowly poisoned. Finding happiness is merely treating the symptoms and not the cause of the disease that grows stronger by the minute. My stomach can't hold food down long enough, and I spend my nights either tossing helplessly to the nightmares or suffering from insomnia. The result is a frail body holding a brittle mind, waiting for a whisper of a catastrophe to fall apart.

Kenan takes a step closer, crossing whatever chasm of intimacy lies between us, and, as the laws of physics go, the pressure increases. A halo, courtesy of the afternoon sun, rests on his chestnut hair. He's saturated in gold, and I feel my breath catch.

"There are enough people hurting you," he whispers. "Don't be one of them."

He raises his hand, and his fingers skim my sleeve. His breaths are low, he's closer than ever before, and I glance up at him. Longing drips from his gaze and I have one foot over the edge of a cliff.

"See you tomorrow?" he asks, his voice a mix of hope and anxiety.

"Yes," I say breathlessly, and the next second his back is to me as he walks away.

My heart is still pounding dangerously when I close the front door and slide against it. In the few seconds of quiet before Layla discovers me, the shock transforms to reality.

I sob big fat tears. I sob like the tears have been building up behind my eyes for months, waiting for one more drop to flood out. Frustration cleaves my heart.

A thudding of footsteps rushes down the corridor, and Layla skids to a halt in front of me.

"Salama!" she exclaims. "What happened?"

I can't speak, covering my face with my hands, drawing my knees to my chest. She sits beside me, immediately pulling me to her warmth.

She holds me close, hugging my head to her chest. "Tell me what happened."

Through a blubber of tears, I gasp out each word. I can't look at her. Her arms go slack around me and she stiffens. For a long time she doesn't say anything. Muffled voices from outside filter through the door. I don't dare look at her, lost in the burning feeling inside my chest.

"Should we stay?" I say between hiccups.

"Salama." Her voice is quiet, defeated. "Look at me."

Reluctantly, I drag my eyes to hers and see them, ocean blue, leaking tears down her cheeks.

"We're leaving," she says in a strange voice.

"But—"

"*Please.* We have to leave. He would want this." Her voice is fractured with the pain she's trying to hold back.

I bang my head against the door. Yes, he would. I *promised* him.

"If we die here, it'll destroy him even more," she says. "Salama, we hoped he was dead. But it was just a wish. A part of us always suspected he wasn't."

I clear my throat.

She shakes her head. "I can't . . . I can't think about that now, Salama. If I do——" Her voice breaks. "I don't think I can convince myself to be okay." She takes hold of my hands. "Let's talk about something else."

There's desperation in her face; she's wildly looking for something to distract her before she succumbs to the grief.

"Tell me about Germany," I breathe. "Tell me what we'll do in Munich."

She closes her eyes briefly and inhales deeply, and her grasp tightens. "I was thinking we should have our own restaurant there."

The surprise freezes my tears. "What?"

She nods, gaining strength from that dream. "Our food is delicious, and I read once on Facebook about a Syrian restaurant in Germany that was successful with the locals. We can make money for your university, an apartment, and stuff the baby needs. It's also a way to spread the word about what's happening here."

I'm astounded, taken aback by her endless optimism. "And finding happiness?" I smile weakly.

She doesn't return the smile but kisses my knuckles. "Finding happiness."

Her eyes are bloodshot but she stares right back at me and I don't want this moment to end. "But you know I'll be the one to make the knafeh, right?"

A short laugh escapes her lips. "Of course. You don't have the approval of every Syrian grandmother because of your charm."

The smiles come easier now. "You know I think that's why Kenan——" I stop.

Layla's brows furrow. "What?"

"I . . . remember Mama asking me repeatedly to make it when they were coming over," I say slowly, snippets of my old life floating out of reach around me. "She was asking if I had all the ingredients. Being so insistent." I let out a disbelieving laugh. "I didn't even . . . Wow! Takes a war and one whole year for me to realize: I think Kenan *really* likes knafeh!"

She squeezes my hands. "He really missed out."

The thought makes me sad. *Yeah, he did.*

Layla goes to sleep early, wanting to be alone, and I tuck the blanket around her firmly. She turns away from me and collapses in on herself; I watch her for a minute before going to my room.

Khawf stands in the middle of it. Since Kenan showed me the sunset, it's become easier for me to deal with Khawf. The visions he shows me feel less all-encompassing now, and we spend most of the time talking, working through worst-case scenarios. The talks have helped with my guilt, giving my heart the motivation it needs to leave.

"Don't worry," I say tiredly, slumping down on my bed and shaking out my hair. "I'm still leaving."

He taps his fingers over an elbow, looking almost sympathetic. "Good. You might not get your money back. Not to mention that if you're—"

"Caught," I interrupt, falling over the bedspread. "Waterboarded. Electrocuted. Raped. Layla's baby ripped from her uterus and left to die. Yes, I know the horrors. We've been over them."

He watches me silently. "A shame that could happen to the boy you love."

My fingers curl around the paper-thin covers and I twist to the side, finally surrendering to the fear that has proliferated in my body. Will I be able to appreciate all the colors in Germany without him? Will I want to? With whatever is left of my heart, I love Kenan and the hope he's given me, and I'm not ready to let go of him.

I hug my pillow to my chest, focusing my thoughts on his easy smile and kind eyes. On his words.

On him.

Because if I don't, if I think about Hamza, I won't be able to breathe. I won't be able to live.

WHEN I SEE KENAN THE NEXT DAY, I NEARLY DROP the bag of haloperidol pills I'm carrying. He's standing by a patient's bed. A little boy about six who has one side of his head heavily bandaged, covering his right eye. Kenan crouches, talking animatedly, and the little boy's face is entranced. As if he's forgotten what's happened to him. Kenan's hands move like a maestro, weaving stories to life between his fingers.

I place the bag in a cupboard and step closer to Kenan, absentmindedly touching my ring finger. I scold myself. I may be in love with him, but is it real, or just my longing for an escape from this horror? If he were just a boy and I were just a girl, living ordinary lives, and we'd met anywhere else, would we still have fallen for each other?

Besides, even if this is real, none of it matters as long as he's determined to become a sacrificial lamb. The pain is nothing compared to knowing what Hamza is going through.

This morning I decided I'm angry with Kenan. He has my heart and he's breaking it. Along with Lama's and Yusuf's. If this past month has done nothing more than scratch his armor, how much more time is needed for it to disintegrate entirely? What will be his undoing?

"And then the boy and girl were rescued by pirates," Kenan says. The little boy still can't take his eyes off him. "They sailed all seven seas and battled monsters together."

"Then what?" the boy asks.

Kenan leans in a bit closer, his voice hushed, and I take another step forward. "Well, the girl wanted to keep the diamond her mother gave her safe. And the boy wanted to find his grandfather. The pirates had the answers to both these things, and so——" He stops and turns around, catching the look of awe on my face. "Salama. Good morning."

"M-morning."

If he's still thinking about how I shouted at him yesterday, he doesn't show it. "How are you?"

I play with the ends of my hijab. "Alhamdulillah."

He looks at me softly. "Is there anything you need?"

You. I need you to leave with me. "No," I reply instead.

He smiles and stands, taking something out of his pocket. He holds out his hand. It's a neatly folded piece of paper. "Open it."

I do and softly gasp. He's drawn the ocean forest. Colossal trees surrounding a little girl, leaves fluttering in the wind. At her side is a small fish with stripes along its body.

"That's a flame angelfish," Kenan points out. "I thought she'd have a friend the color of flames. Could light the way when it gets dark."

My pulse quickens, and I hug the paper to my chest. "Thank you."

He scratches the back of his neck, his cheeks pink. "I wanted to cheer you up after—you know."

"I'm going to treasure this forever." I manage a brave smile.

He returns it and then gestures to the little boy. "Would you like to hear the story with him?"

I laugh. "Yes."

Standing beside the eager little boy, I tuck the drawing in my pocket and watch the way Kenan lights up. He commands the words, injecting each with wonder, and soon enough we're surrounded by people, all huddling closer, wanting to forget their pain and escape into another world. Kenan stands up, his voice getting louder as he conjures ships that fly and magical lemons that revive you from the brink of death. He's captivating, a natural-born storyteller.

But with each word, a heaviness falls on my heart and I slowly back away through the crowd until all I can see is his disheveled hair and broad shoulders. It hurts to see him, a dead man walking, when he has the power to influence the world.

I turn around, but before I make it out of the atrium, Kenan calls my name. The people behind him are talking among themselves and they go back to their beds and families, their eyes shining a little brighter. Two people clap Kenan on the back, and he smiles at them. He walks over to me, his brows furrowed, and I'm rooted to the spot, every cell wanting him near me.

"Is something wrong?" he asks.

There's a dull ache reverberating behind my eyes, threatening to spill the tears.

"What do you think, Kenan?" I whisper. Everything's written freely on my face for him to read.

He closes his eyes for a second, catching on to my thoughts. "Salama," he begins. His tone is low, almost choked. "I—you have to realize this is difficult."

I feel as if I'm standing on shaking ground. "You think it's *easy* for me to leave? My mother is buried here! My father too. My brother—" I stop, covering my face with my hands, forcing myself to take deep breaths.

Please, God, let him die. Let him find that peace.

Kenan is still staring at me with anguish when I look back at him.

"We are stripped from our choices, so we latch onto what will ensure our survival." I push away all my emotion. My voice comes out calculating and cold. "The world is not sweet or kind. The ones outside are waiting to eat us and pick their teeth with our bones. That's what they'll do to your siblings. So we do everything to make sure we and our loved ones survive. Whatever it takes."

Fear breaks out behind his irises, but whatever he's about to say next disappears when his vision trails behind me, his eyes widening with horror.

I turn around to see Yusuf carrying Lama in his skeleton-like arms, and I wonder how he managed to make it all the way from their home. Kenan runs toward them, his terror infecting me. Lama's eyes are half-closed, her dry lips hanging open. Kenan takes her from Yusuf, cradles her head against his shoulder, and looks back at me wildly.

"Bring her here." I gesture to an empty yellow bed, and he sets her down gently, murmuring words of love while brushing her hair back before taking her hands in his and pressing them to his lips, praying. Yusuf stands beside him, his own face white with terror and his lower lip trembling.

"What happened?" Kenan asks Yusuf, who shakes his head, motioning with his hands.

I check the wound on her stomach, but it's mostly healed, the skin pink, with no sign of pus or infection.

"Lama, habibti." I press my stethoscope to her heart. It's hammering against her rib cage. "How are you feeling? Where's the pain?"

She stirs, eyelids fluttering. "I feel . . . sick. And my head hurts."

I lay a hand on her forehead. It's cold. Flushed skin. Chapped lips. Headache. Everything comes together.

"She's dehydrated."

Kenan looks up at me with shock, silent tears running down his cheeks. "What?"

"Give me her hand," I say, and he does. I pinch her nailbed for a few seconds until it's all white and Lama shifts uncomfortably. When I ease the pressure, it takes a while for it to regain its pink color. "Yes. Dehydration."

I run to the medical store, grab one of the IV bags, and race back to hook it into her vein. She doesn't even protest when I nudge the needle's tip into her skin.

"Kenan, go find her a cup of water," I instruct him, and he looks at me, disoriented. "She's going to be fine, insh'Allah. But she needs to drink."

He nods and returns with water shortly, helping her

take small sips. Nour has heard what happened and brings Yusuf a chair to sit on. She pats his back while he looks on. No one should live like this. Worrying if their sister will die from lack of water.

"The IV will replace what she's lost." I bite my lip. "Alhamdulillah it wasn't something worse."

Kenan's jaw is tight, his shoulders shaking silently. He gets up and walks toward the front doors. I blink, taken aback, before following. He hurries down the steps, running his hands in his hair.

"Kenan," I say hesitantly.

He turns around, looking like he's in physical pain.

His voice sounds broken. Defeated. "Yesterday, after you brought up what happens to the refugees in Europe, I went back home and researched more of it." He stops, blowing out a forced breath of air. "People are getting tricked, robbed—left alone in the middle of nowhere. Girls are . . . being trafficked or married off. And boys are forced into child labor."

He sinks to the ground like his legs can't carry him anymore and I rush to him.

"Kenan!" I kneel beside him.

A strangled sound escapes his throat. "You're right. I promised my father I'd take care of them. That I'd carry them in my eyes. I can't guarantee they'll find my uncle when they land in Italy. I can't even guarantee that Lama will survive being dehydrated. But—I also have a duty to my country." He threads his hands through the dirt, and the dull red-brown stains them, smearing itself into his nailbeds and the cracks in his skin. "Salama, you have to at least acknowledge that this isn't *right*."

"Of course it isn't!" I exclaim. "It's not fair and it's not right. But you *can't* abandon Lama and Yusuf."

"One by one, everyone leaves," he whispers, and rubs his eyes, streaking Syria on his forehead, smearing himself with the land of our ancestors. "Soon enough there won't be anyone left to defend Syria."

"Not true. You, more than anyone, can change the world. Do you have any idea what your imagination can do? Didn't you see how the people looked at you in there?" A glimmer shines through his dark green eyes. "The fight *isn't* over, and it's not only here. Syria's entire history has become faded in people's memories. They don't know what a gem she is. They don't know the love this country has. You owe it to them. You owe it to *us*," I say fiercely.

He runs a hand over his face, then clears his throat. "What about the guilt?"

"Your love for Syria will drive you. The guilt is just a side effect." I smile sadly. "Without that love, your stories would lose their meaning."

He blinks a few tears before wiping them with his sleeve.

"I can't believe I'm going to do this," he whispers.

My heart softens, breaks. "Kenan. Syria isn't just what we're standing on. It's Lama growing up, reaching her teens with her two big brothers right there with her. It's Yusuf getting the highest grades and telling everyone about the lemon trees in Homs. It's you, making sure we never forget our reason to fight. It's you and—" I stop, catching myself before I say something stupid. Something about a *might* life.

A small smile finally settles on his lips, and I feel myself blush.

"You're right," he whispers.

I sigh with relief.

We stay kneeling in our soil, rubble digging into our knees, mud smearing our jeans. And in that moment, enclosed by the harsh truths we have to live with, somehow the future doesn't feel so bleak anymore. The colors are vibrant.

"I'll find Am tomorrow," I say. "He left early."

He bites his lip. "What if it's too late? What if all the seats are taken?"

I shake my head. "Money buys everything, Kenan. And if it doesn't, I'll smuggle you on the boat if it's the last thing I do."

He stares at me, and I wonder if I've said too much. If my feelings for him are bared so freely on my face I don't need to say the words.

In his eyes, something changes. He doesn't smooth his expression; he lets me glimpse every thought he's had about me since the day we met. They're in the crease between his eyebrows, in the gentle lift of his lips, in the longing in his eyes.

I clear my throat. "You should go back to Lama."

I thought it would be enough to break the spell over us, but Kenan smiles, leaning closer, and my breath catches, the scent of lemons enveloping my nose. "Is it okay if I skip walking you home today?"

I nod.

"But may I tomorrow?"

"Yes," I breathe.

Satisfied with my answer, he stands and heads toward the hospital, but before he disappears inside, I ask without thinking, "How come you smell like lemons all the time?"

He pauses and turns around slowly, surprised. "It's Baba's cologne."

20

IT'S LAYLA'S IDEA TO USE LEMONS TO FIGHT SEASICK-
ness when we're on the boat.

"Of course," I say. "Why didn't I think of that?"

She laughs, glancing at the three sets of clothes she's
deciding between. "That's because I'm not the one experiencing the blossom of love. Now more than ever, it seems,
with Kenan joining us."

I ignore her and go over the checklist, aware of the
bulkiness in my pocket where Kenan's drawing sits. A heavy
coat. Passport and school certificate. At the beginning of the
uprising, I started carrying my passport everywhere in case
anything happened or we had to flee at the last second.

I count the other necessities. Eight cans of tuna and three
cans of beans. One strip of Panadol. A couple of bandages.
Four water bottles.

"You don't have to say anything for me to know." Layla
flops on the couch after finally settling on a navy-blue dress

and thick wool stockings. "You were never able to hide secrets from me. Perks of knowing you all my life."

My fingers tighten over the snugly rolled dollars as Samar's frail, bloodied body flashes in front of my eyes. I command myself not to vomit, even though I haven't eaten more than five spoonfuls of lentil soup. "Is there anything else we're missing?" I ask, and I focus on the fact that Kenan will be on that boat with me.

She lets out a sigh and nods toward a USB stick sitting beside me on the floor.

I pick it up.

"It has our family photos. We'll have Hamza with us there. And our parents too."

A lump lodges in my throat. "When did you do this?"

She shakes her head. "Hamza did. The first week of the revolution."

I press a hand over my mouth and look away, tears burning my eyes.

What are they doing to you, Hamza?

"He knew this was going to happen," Layla whispers. "Or at the very least, he suspected."

"He was always the smart one," I whisper back.

I glance at Layla. Tears decorate her eyes like sapphires. She holds out her hands and I take them.

"Alhamdulillah," she says. "With whatever happens to us, to him, I will cling to our faith."

I nod, my throat slick with secrets and regrets.

The next morning, as soon as I step inside the hospital, I make a beeline toward Am. He's stationed in the main atrium, looking out the window.

"Am," I say, and his gaze snaps to me.

"Salama."

I pull out one Panadol tablet and drop it in his hand. "I need a place for one more person."

He stares at me with disbelief. "And next week there'll be another one. And another and another."

"No," I force out. "Just this one."

He waves the tablet in front of me. "You only have so much leverage, Salama. The Panadol won't be enough for a discount."

"You're already getting my gold!"

He half shrugs and flicks the cigarette butt to the ground before grinding it under the heel of his boot. "Not enough. What's more important? Gold or a person's life?"

I want to scoff, to strike him across the face for the hypocrisy coating his tongue. Instead, I mutter, "A ring."

He mulls it over. "Fine."

The faraway sound of a crash makes us both start, but the moment passes and outside, a few birds take to the cloud-speckled sky.

Am fiddles with a cigarette. When he looks at me again, it's like he's seeing me for the first time.

"What?" I say defensively, folding my arms.

"Have you always been so"—he gestures at me—"hollow?"

Self-consciously, I fuss with my hijab, tugging it across

my other shoulder. I'm sure it would delight him to know that the guilt of what I've done has turned me into skin and bone. But before I can answer, Dr. Ziad calls my name and I turn around to see him waving me over, a frantic look in his eyes.

I hurry to him, my heart beating wildly in my throat.

"Doctor, what is it?" I ask, and he glances around quickly before leading me to a corner of the atrium.

"Did you hear what happened yesterday in Karam el-Zeitoun?" His voice is hushed, a strangle of pain.

My mouth goes dry and I shake my head.

"The military . . . they mass—" He stops, pain glazing his eyes, and takes a deep breath before continuing. "Women and children with slit throats. None left alive. Not a single gunshot. The children . . . they were—" He loses his composure once more, his eyes glistening, and mine burn with tears. "They were hit with blunt objects, and one girl was severely mutilated. The neighborhoods beside them heard the screams. The Free Syrian Army confirmed it to me just now."

My stomach churns and I manage to whisper, "What . . . we're next, aren't we?"

He runs a hand through his hair and straightens his back, all traces of horror fading from his expression. He's our head doctor—from him we get our strength. If he crumbles, we all fall. "The FSA was able to get vital intel about an attack planned nearby for this morning and they've warned all the hospitals. It's worse than anything we've had."

"Worse than missiles?" I ask, unable to imagine what else they could use.

He nods and I notice the vessels in his eyes are more pronounced—redder.

"Like what?"

He takes a deep breath that gets lost somewhere in his lungs. "Attacks that violate the Geneva Convention."

I frown. "So everything they've done up till now is legal?"

"No, of course not!" he exclaims, rubbing his eyes, and his hands tremble. "But this is taboo." Sweat glistens on his forehead.

"What are you talking about?" My voice comes out strangled.

"It may not happen," he says, but I can hear the lie in his tone.

"Doctor, this is the regime we're talking about. If they want, they could drop a nuke on us." I laugh humorlessly and press a hand to my forehead.

Gardenias. Alleviate depression and anxiety and stress. Gardenias. Gardenias. Gardenias.

His eyes flit from the doors to me and back again. "Salama, I consider you my daughter. So please, don't run away from the hospital if this happens. None of us are prepared to deal with it, but we're going to be *fine*."

"If what happens?" I nearly shout. "What did the Free Syrian Army tell you?"

But he doesn't have to tell me. A scream rips the air, and I turn around, shocked. I've never heard a scream like that in my life. The doors open to a horde of victims swarming in, but I don't see any injuries.

"What's happening?" I shriek, trying to understand.

Dozens of casualties on stretchers or on the ground are convulsing like someone electrocuted them.

Teenagers with their heads stretched back, arms and legs shaking uncontrollably.

Little children with foam at their mouths, looking up, trying to make sense of what's happening to them.

My feet are rooted to the ground. I don't know what's happening. I don't understand.

"Chemical attack," I hear Dr. Ziad say. "They've finally used sarin."

21

My hands fly to my mouth in horror. My mind races through a list of medications, a list of *anything* to combat sarin, but I come up short. No one is *ever* prepared for a chemical attack.

"How—how the *hell* do I treat this?" I ask with nails in my throat.

"Atropine," he yells so the rest of the staff can hear, as they move toward the victims. "Diazepam for convulsions."

He looks back and sees me rooted to the spot.

"*Salama!*" he says sharply. "We need to act now! They'll die within minutes, do you understand? An incredibly small amount of sarin is enough to kill a grown man. These are kids. *Go!*"

My mind activates and all fear shuts down, except that which will motivate my feet to run and my hands to work. Nour drops a handful of atropine syringes into my arms, and I make a break for it. We don't have anything to protect ourselves against the gaseous nerve agents in the patients, so gloves will have to do.

I assess who needs to be taken care of first. The more they inhaled, the less time they have. I spring to a boy lying on the ground, shaking violently, and push his wailing mother to the side. I don't have time to explain anything as I jam the needle in his vein, praying all the while. I don't even check to see if he responds. Time is a luxury we can't afford now. As soon as I get up for another patient, Nour takes my place and administers CPR.

Another girl with tears streaming down her face and foam at her mouth stares at me without looking, and I fear I've lost her. *Intravenous injections work fast*, I keep chanting in my brain. Her pulse is weak, and her eyes are slits. My breath hitches in my throat. I try not to look into her eyes as I grab her elbow and jab the syringe's bevel in her median cubital vein. I move on to the next victim. Little Ahmad's last words ring in my ears the whole time, and I feel his ghost watching me move too slowly to save anyone. His eyes burn like hot coins at the back of my head, impatient with my sluggish hands that don't inject the antidote fast enough.

I'll tell God everything.

I lose count of how many I can't save. Their eyes black, like a starless night, a frozen expression of fear and confusion forever inscribed on their faces. I realize I'm trembling when my hands helplessly clutch at a young woman's frail shoulders, trying to shake the life back into her.

"*No*," I say through gritted teeth. "Please, don't be dead!"

Her breath doesn't fog her breathing mask, and she stares lifelessly at me. The smell of bleach burns my nostrils.

Chlorine.

They didn't just use sarin.

Shit. Shit. Shit.

The next bodies my hands touch are dead. No one's alive. I'm too late. They were right there, and I couldn't get to them in time. I rise slowly to shaking legs and look at the catastrophe all around.

Bodies upon bodies surround me, and I stand in the center, watching them judge me. My hands are raw and red from the gas coating the victims. The same story is repeated with different characters, but the ending is always the same. And yet, despite knowing it, the pain is great. Greater than I can handle.

Everything unrolls in front of me in slow motion.

I watch young children grabbing the sides of their protectors, howling with anguish. I see entire families lying beside one another, holding hands, hoping when they ascend to Heaven they will still be entwined. I walk slowly, training my eyes on the exit door. I need air. I need to breathe something that isn't chlorine.

"Salama!" Nour grabs my arm before I open the front door. "What are you doing?"

"Outside," I rasp. The sarin from treating the patients has finally absorbed into my skin and is beginning to close my throat. *God, it burns.*

"Not without this you're not." She shoves a surgical mask in my hands. "It won't do much, but it'll help."

It won't do anything. But how would we know? We weren't ready for a chemical attack. Are normal doctors even prepared for this?

I collapse on the hospital's steps, shivering from head to toe. Hours have already passed without me noticing and now it's late afternoon. Death steals the seconds away from us. Oxygen slowly creeps back into my lungs, and I finally begin to remember my family.

"Layla!" I spring up, looking in the direction of our home. She's safe. I know she is. Because none of the victims were from our neighborhood, which is a fifteen-minute walk from the hospital. The sarin didn't reach the hospital, which means it didn't reach my home either.

My next thought latches on to Kenan and his siblings. My stomach twists on itself with terror. I have no idea if he came in today. *Oh God, please don't let his neighborhood be affected.*

I take off the mask, fiddle with it, and pace around, trying to summon rational thoughts.

If they were affected, they would have been brought here. But . . . what if they died as soon as they inhaled the gas? Oh God. Oh God!

I breathe in deeply and decide I should leave right now, check on Layla, and then immediately head to Kenan's house to make sure everything's fine.

"Salama!" a voice shouts behind me, and I whirl around to see Kenan standing in front of the hospital doors, holding a makeshift cloth to his face. Alive. He lets out a deep breath I feel inside my soul.

My knees go weak with relief and I collapse on the steps.

"Salama!" he shouts again, hurrying down to me. "Are you all right? Oh my God, please tell me you are."

He crouches beside me, removing the cloth from his mouth, and I fill my eyes with him. His bright green eyes, his beautiful, honest face.

"I'm fine," I whisper. "Are you? Lama? Yusuf?"

He nods quickly, his hands hovering beside my head,

steeling himself before he takes them back. Still, I can feel their warmth, the blood gushing through his veins.

"The attack wasn't . . . it wasn't near where we are, but I had to come here to make sure you're alive," he says, and as if the energy has suddenly been siphoned out of him, he all but collapses beside me. He smells of smoke and remnants of the gas and lemons. My legs shake with weariness, my arms ache, and all I want is to lie here on these chipped steps and sleep forever.

The faint voices of the injured seep through the cracks in the hospital walls and I close my eyes, unable to hold their pain in my heart without folding into myself and crying myself to death. Why? *Why* is no one helping us? Why are we left to die? How can the world be *so* cruel?

I hug my knees, propping my head between my arms. "I'm exhausted," I whisper.

"Me too," Kenan replies.

I shake my head. "No. I'm exhausted from all of this. I'm exhausted we're suffocating and no one gives the slightest bit of a damn. I'm exhausted we're not even an afterthought. I'm exhausted we can't even have basic human rights. I'm *exhausted*, Kenan."

I feel his eyes on me, but when I lift my head, I stare at the sky's horizon peeking through the demolished buildings instead. At the blue and gray.

"I'm also angry," I continue.

And I realize the anger was always there, growing slowly and surely. It began long ago when I was born under the thumb of a dictatorship that kept on applying pressure until my bones fractured. It kindled into a small flame when

Mama and I held hands and prayed as the protestors' throaty voices ricocheted off our kitchen walls. It fused with my bones, its flames licking through my myocardium, leaving decayed cells in its wake, when Baba and Hamza were taken. It built and built and built with each body laid in front of me. And now, it's a roaring fire crackling along my nervous system.

"Tomorrow's the revolution's anniversary," I say, and Kenan shifts. "I want to go."

Those four words fall from my lips, and I wait for the familiar feeling of terror to rip through me, souring my wish. But it doesn't happen. No. Enough is *enough*.

Khawf appears in the corner of my eyes, but I refuse to look in his direction, knowing I won't find support there. This is my choice, not one governed by him. Instead, I glance at Kenan, whose eyes are heavy with emotion.

"Are you sure?" he asks, and I almost smile.

I nod. This decision clears my mind. I want my voice to join my people's. I want to sing my sorrows away. I want to mourn our martyrs. This may be the last time I'll ever feel as if I'm a part of Syria before the boat whisks me away. I don't want this fear anymore.

Kenan stands, looking away, and then he says in a rather rough tone, "You called it a revolution."

I glance at my sneakers. "Well . . . that's what it is."

He fidgets with his jacket's sleeve before turning to me. "Let me take you home."

I look up. "Your siblings?"

"Trust me. I wouldn't be offering if I wasn't sure they're all right," he says. "Insh'Allah."

"Let me get my bag, then." I pick myself up and move toward the doors, but my hand grips the handle tightly, my muscles freezing me. The anger is there, but it hasn't erased the weight the dead leave on my shoulders.

"I'll get it. It's in the stockroom, right?" Kenan says softly. I nod. When he opens the door to slip inside, the coughs and soft cries of the injured make my throat constrict before the door falls shut, muting them.

Our walk back is filled with silence, and I allow myself to stare at him, taking notice of the way his shoulders are slumped. I sense a storm raging in his mind as well. What he's seen today is quickly splintering his resolve to leave. But he must know that in this equation, there's no right answer. Leaving is the lesser of two evils. The outside world isn't safe for his siblings to venture to on their own, and Kenan would be destroyed if anything happened to them. But I need to know—need to *hear* the words once more.

When we reach my front door, he leans his head against the bullet-riddled wall.

"You're still coming with us, right?" I whisper, and he looks at me.

"Yes," he says quietly.

He pushes himself off, runs a hand through his hair. There's a glassy look in his eyes, and he kicks a stray pebble. It bounces away, clattering pathetically against some debris.

"I just—" he begins, blowing out forcefully. "Salama, I feel so helpless. I'm leaving them behind. And after what happened today?" Pain sears in his eyes. "Syria needs me, and I'm abandoning her."

I shake my head. "No you're not. What our people

are doing here—the protests? That's beautiful and much needed, but whose minds are you changing here? You can do *so much* from the outside. You can physically reach the people leaving the comments on your videos. With your talent for weaving stories, we need your voice to amplify those here. That's how *you* fight."

He stares at me, a faint pink blush dusting his cheeks.

"And we *will* come back," I say, my voice wavering. "Insh'Allah, we will come back home. We will plant new lemon trees. We'll rebuild our cities, and we *will* be free."

I turn to look at the dying sunset and then up at the twilight blue eating away the light. Night approaches fast, but I know it's not eternal. This blanket of darkness isn't our forever. Their evil isn't forever. Not as long as we have our faith and Syria's history running in our veins.

"Salama," Kenan whispers.

The way he's looking at me makes the air vanish from my alveoli. It's a look I've only read about in books and seen in movies. Never one I thought I'd experience in real life, and certainly not in these circumstances.

He comes closer, his fingers touching the edge of my lab coat, and everything stills. The dead leaves dancing beside our feet, the cold breeze, the chirping birds. Everything. Even my mind.

My heart migrates from its position in my chest cavity all the way up to my esophagus, and I stare at his long fingers grasping the top of my pocket.

"You're right. We will come back," he whispers, and I dare to glance up. I'm intoxicated by the way he's staring at me. So close, so kind, so beautiful.

A newfound need rises in me to touch his cheeks, to bring him closer and feel his stubble under my hands. To just forget all this pain.

His emerald eyes drop to my lips for a few seconds, and then he looks away.

"Salam," he whispers, and then he's gone.

Life comes back to the world, the leaves rustle. And I'm left yearning for more.

"So you're going?" Layla asks quietly, and I lean my head against her shoulder, my arm linked through hers. We haven't moved from this spot on the couch since I came home, our limbs still slightly shaky from today's terror.

"You think I shouldn't?"

She shakes her head. "Not at all. This is your path in life, Salama. Besides, you're Hamza's sister, I'm not surprised. But what made you decide to go?"

I squeeze her arm, biting my lip. "I've been scared for so long. Of course I hate the regime, but a part of me— a cowardly part—thought that maybe if I didn't go to the protests and, God forbid, the military won before we got on the boat, I wouldn't be tortured. That they'd let Baba and Hamza out. But now . . . Baba is dead and Hamza . . ." I stop. "A part of me wanted things to go back to how they were. Back to living in fear. And I *hate* those thoughts." I lift my head up to see the sympathy in Layla's eyes. "I feel like a hypocrite."

"Salama, it's human to feel scared. And you're not a hypocrite."

"I hope so," I whisper. "I would split a vein for Syria. If my blood could save her. If my death would bring our people their justice, I wouldn't . . . there's no question about it."

"I know."

I close my eyes. "This is the closest I'll feel to being—it's my way of asking for forgiveness for leaving."

Layla rests her cheek over my head. "I know."

After a few moments of silence, I say, "I don't know what's going to happen tomorrow. But if I don't . . . if . . . please find Am. Get on that boat. Live for me and Hamza. Raise Baby Salama." I lean back and grab both her hands fiercely. *"Promise me."*

She takes a deep breath, steeling herself. "Only if you promise you'll do everything not to die. You will come back to me, insh'Allah." Her voice turns soft—too soft. "Salama, please. Don't be a martyr. Fight to stay alive."

Her words fall like little stones at the bottom of a lake, and the back of my eyes burn. "I promise."

Her hands loosen in my grip. "Then I promise too."

Khawf waits for me by the window when I close my bedroom door.

"This is a mistake," he says. He looks exasperated with me. "You're so close to leaving. Why would you put yourself at risk?"

I sigh and sit on my bed. "I know you want me to stay out of trouble. But nowhere is safe in Syria. I could be bombed right now."

He stands in front of me, arms folded. "You're a fool if

you think they won't be focusing everything they have on the protests tomorrow."

I nod. "You're right. And you won't give me peace the whole time. So let's make a deal."

He straightens his back. He doesn't exude a terrifying aura, only interest.

I stick my chin out. "Show me the worst-case scenario."

He laughs. "Come again?"

"Show me the worst possible outcome. You've been showing me the past. Show me the future. Show me Layla's pain. If I'm able to handle it, you'll leave me alone the whole night. You won't threaten me."

He tilts his head to the side, his eyes gleaming. "Show you your arrest. Kenan tortured. His siblings murdered. *Everything* to deter you from going tomorrow?"

Cold sweat breaks out on my forehead. "Yes."

He studies me for a minute, then raises his fingers. "Don't blame me if it leaves you destroyed. They might be hallucinations now, Salama." He bends down, bringing his face closer to me. "But they are *very* real possibilities."

My hands tremble and I fold them into fists. "Do it," I say, my voice wavering.

He smirks and snaps his fingers.

22

THE NEXT DAY PASSES IN A WHIR, MY THROAT burning with the taste of bile. I haven't slept a wink, and my head feels like lead after what Khawf did yesterday. I rub my eyes, shutting out the tortured screams still ringing in my mind. My extraocular muscles ache from how much I cried yesterday, but I stand firm.

"Got everything packed?" Am asks me when I hand him his Panadol tablet. "Nothing too heavy. It's a refugee boat, not a cruise ship."

"I know," I bite back. I look at my patients scattered all over; I see their red eyes, hear their rib-racking coughs. "How will we get through the military borders?"

He glances sideways, making sure we're out of earshot. "I know the guards stationed there. Some want to make money. It's no skin off their backs to let you pass for the right price."

Disgust leaves an aftertaste worse than bile on my tongue.

Am shrugs. "It's business, Salama."

I snort. "Call it whatever you want, but don't lie to me."

During my break, I retreat to the stockroom, read the labels on the medications to help me calm down.

"Hey," I hear Kenan say from the doorway.

My heart skips a beat and I banish the image of him beaten, blood pouring from his eye sockets. "Hey."

"May I join you?" He plays with the hem of his sweater. His face is lined, his hair is in disarray, and he looks like he hasn't slept either. The weight of his decision to leave must have taken a toll on him.

"Sure," I say, and I wave my hand to the empty space in front of me. "How's Lama?"

He sits down and leans back against one of the cabinets. "She's *much* better. Alhamdulillah. Her heartbeat is normal—I counted it myself. We're making sure she's drinking lots of water. Yusuf breathes easier now that she is." He stretches his fingers and after a heartbeat says, "About tonight. You need to promise me something."

"What?"

"We'll be together. But if anything were to happen to me, you save yourself. If you see me get dragged away, you run. Understood?"

No. I don't like this. "Kenan—"

His expression is fierce. "Salama, you promise me this." When I don't say anything, he repeats more firmly. *"Salama."*

"Fine," I whisper, hating even thinking about it. "I'll— I'll make sure your siblings find your uncle if . . ." I go quiet. I can't even say it. "And if anything happens to me, please take care of Layla."

"I will." He cracks his knuckles. "I've told Yusuf where Layla lives, in case both of us . . ." And his words die out as well.

"Right."

His eyes study me, and I fight the urge to cover my face. Instead, I clear my throat and grab a medication box.

"What's that?" he asks.

"My favorite," I answer, happy to focus on something other than the way he's staring at me. "Epinephrine. Magic drug of the heart. It saves so many lives."

"How is it given?" he asks, his voice low, and I feel like I might need a shot of it myself.

"Straight to the heart. But it doesn't matter really. It's intravenous and works instantly."

He nods but doesn't stop staring, and I start to wonder if there's something on my face. "Um, is—"

"How do your eyes always shine so brightly?" he interrupts.

"What?" I laugh.

"When I first met you, I thought it was a trick of the light. But that isn't it. This stockroom has horrible lighting, and they still look like melted honey."

My breath catches in my throat. His face turns red, and he breaks the stare, glancing toward the door.

"I'm sorry," he stammers. "I didn't mean to be so forward."

"It's okay," I whisper, fidgeting with the epinephrine box. Me? Beautiful eyes? Haven't heard that one in a while.

Voices drift through the open door. "They killed him. The man with the roses."

"Ghiath Matar?" an old woman says, shocked.

"Yes. All he did was give the military flowers. His wife is pregnant with their son. It's right here on Facebook. He's been tortured to death."

The epinephrine box slips from my fingers and falls to the ground with a thud. Kenan closes his eyes, and his features become pained with grief. When he finally opens them, he stands and stops at the door. "We'll meet at the Al-Ameer bakery, okay?"

I nod and he walks away. My heart goes back to beating normally, but the sadness erupts into tears. I tilt my head back and take a deep breath.

"Thinking of backing out?" Khawf asks, appearing in front of me.

"No," I whisper, and my voice shakes. Not from terror this time. "I hate them."

"I know," Khawf replies kindly. "And I must say, it's a wonderful look on you." He pauses. "What I showed you last night, Salama . . . all of those scenarios could come true."

It hurts to swallow, but my desire to be stronger than the horrors I face far outweighs anything else. It steadies my heart.

"I can't say I'll be thrilled if you go today. So are you absolutely ready to face those consequences?"

I nod slowly. "This is the price of a future with freedom, Khawf. It's a price Hamza pays every day. But I'm Syrian. This is *my* land, and just like the lemon trees that have been growing here for centuries, spilled blood won't stop us. I have my faith in God. He'll protect me. I've been force-fed oppression, but I will no longer swallow its bitter taste. No matter what."

23

THE SMALL HAIRS ON THE BACK OF MY NECK RISE IN anticipation as I make my way through the people rushing toward the scene of today's protest.

Freedom Square.

The moon hovers above, showing our way with his gentle touch. Combined with the feeble handmade battery-powered lamps and flashlights, I'm able to see everything. Young men hurry past me, some carrying large signs painted in red.

The bits of conversation reaching my ears are full of hope and determination; people are full of pride that they're still going strong after a year. I wonder how many more deaths, how much more trauma, until their spirits are truly crushed. Their faith is strong. In both God and the revolution. And now that they've tasted true freedom, they can't go back to the dark days.

The square is supposed to be under the Free Syrian Army's jurisdiction, so we'll be safe for a portion of the night, but the military always comes. I pull my hoodie over my head tightly so no one can see my face. Even though the darkness makes it hard to distinguish anyone's features, it's better to be safe. In the end it doesn't really matter; there are no innocents in the eyes of the military. They'll kill us all, protestors or not. To them, the idea of freedom is infectious, and we need to be put down before it spreads.

I try not to think of Layla and our goodbye. I didn't think she would let go of me. But whatever happens tonight, I won't regret it.

Khawf stands tall by my side, looking like an omen of death.

"Remember our deal," I say, and he rolls his eyes.

"I won't talk to you with the boy here. But he's not as oblivious as you think. He already suspects something."

We've finally reached the square and I can hear the protest beginning. The voices are throaty, coming from deep within bruised souls, each finding its own footing before mingling together, strong and united. Each person knows full well that every word might be their last.

"We don't know that. And even if he does, it's just suspicion," I retort, threading my way carefully between people protesting until I find where Kenan told me to meet him. It's secluded, close to the action, but far enough away if we need to make a run for it. I lean against the wall where a huge chunk of concrete has been obliterated by a shell. Splinters of glass crunch beneath my sneakers.

"Fine. Just make sure your hood covers your face." Khawf glances around. "Let's be safe, not sorry."

I crane my neck and watch the people gather as if they

are one soul, one life running through everybody. I see children on the cusp of their teen years, fear stripped from their expressions. There is no room for that here. Young men, raised in the shadows of their parents' terror, who decided to make this country their own. Old men who grew tired of the dictatorship stepping on them, waiting their whole lives for one spark to light the fire that would burn down this tyranny.

Fear dies here.

A boy about my age or younger walks by. The flashlights gleam over his bare chest. His ribs stick out where skin meets bone. FREEDOM is traced on his chest with charcoal.

"Hey!" I call out in surprise.

He turns my way.

"Aren't you scared?" I ask loudly.

He looks at me for a second before grinning. "Always. But I've got nothing to lose."

He turns around and dives into the crowd, making for the center of the protest. This place operates at a different level from the hospital, where death clings to the tiled floors. Here, life shines so strong it washes away doubt. I feel peace.

My lungs rejoice with a full breath of air. The pressure on my chest lifts, and I feel lighter. My head whirls, and my tongue itches to begin chanting and singing. Khawf lingers beside me but doesn't say a word, watching the masses with interest.

One man in the pulse of the crowd taps on his microphone. His voice booms and people start cheering wildly. His words are half drowned by everyone else, but I can make out the gist; he's recounting what has happened in the last year. It's unreal to think this has been going on for three hundred and sixty-five days. Time moves differently here. Sorrow does that. Each day is a year, and as each one passes we hope tomorrow will be better.

I notice many people taking out their phones and recording. Some slip pieces of paper marked with the date and location from under their jackets, along with a few sentences: *"Go to hell, Assad," "We're coming for you," "We fear no one except God,"* and *"Assad is a murderer."*

One of them stands out to me. In perfect red-studded letters they spell out an old poem.

"Every lemon will bring forth a child and the lemons will never die out."

The lemons are still growing, flowering, nourishing the revolution. I remember the lemonade Mama used to make for me during the summer. I can almost taste its cold, sour-sweet flavor, and my mouth waters at the thought. My heart craves those freshly picked lemons and Mama's loving glance when she handed me the lemonade. I shake my head, banishing that longing away.

Not here.

Now my nerves are jangling like I've injected myself with adrenaline. My hands can't stop shaking, so I rub them together. I take comfort in the solid slab of concrete supporting me, but when I look down, I see hints of red scratched into the gray. I inhale sharply and force myself to look ahead.

The revolution's flag is flying high over our heads, and it makes me dream of a day when we can raise it in our schools, proudly singing the national anthem. When it will represent us worldwide. For now, this flag is our shield against the cold winters, the bombs falling from the sky, and the bullets that tear into our bodies. In death, it's our shroud, our corpses swaddled in it as we return to the soil we vowed to protect.

The individual voices are one and louder than life. "How Sweet Is Freedom" soars into the air, captured by the cameras in low quality to be transmitted to the whole world. I've heard this song more times than I can count. It's everywhere. It's the alphabet of our revolution. Our children will be taught it as soon as they learn to speak. Patients' weary voices rattle the walls of our hospital with it. It's the salve against their wounds. I've had many on my operating table unconsciously humming it to themselves. It's become rooted in their brain cells, and nothing can ever remove it.

I sing softly, my voice a contrast against the deep resounding ones thundering into the skies above us. A prayer in song.

"Salama."

His voice washes over me like sunlight. I turn, trying to suppress a smile. His clothes are identical to mine. Old jeans and a black hoodie. His hair is swept back and streaked with wet droplets as if he's dunked his head in a bowl of water.

"Hey." I nod nonchalantly, remembering the way his eyes searched me in that stockroom and how the words he said have folded themselves between my ribs, cushioning my broken heart. The heart that loves him.

"How are you?" His gaze flits bashfully from me to the ground. He's probably thinking about that moment too.

"Fine," I whisper.

"How's Layla?"

His concern makes my withered heart bloom. "Scared for me, but good." I pause, finding a topic that will bring a drop of serotonin. "How happy were Lama and Yusuf when you told them you're coming?"

He smiles. "Happier than they've been in a long time. Lama burst into tears and Yusuf wouldn't let go of me."

"Yusuf still doesn't—I mean he's—" I don't know how to say the words without sounding insensitive.

"No," he says sorrowfully. "He still doesn't talk."

In some ways, Yusuf reminds me of myself. I wonder if there are hurricanes in his mind that he doesn't know how to articulate. Khawf is a burden I don't know how to share with anyone. I desperately want to. The loneliness makes my throat close up and tears prick in my eyes. It's a pressure that builds and builds until it fissures through my skin and bones.

"We'll find help for him in Germany," I assure Kenan.

He scratches the back of his head. "We?"

My ears feel hot and I take a deep breath. Why are we dancing around this? I know exactly how I feel about him, and his expressions tell no lies. I know he feels the same. "We won't be separated there, right?"

He turns fully toward me and his hand slips into his pocket. He looks hopeful. "Salama, I don't ever want to—" he begins softly.

Suddenly a cheer resounds in the crowd and we jump, blushing furiously. The man holding the microphone begins a new song in his deep, somber voice. I notice Kenan didn't bring his camera.

We stand in silence, watching emotions sizzle in the crowd. Between songs, we send prayers for the souls of the martyrs, and for the ones suffering in imprisonment. I brush a tear from my eye. How lonely Hamza must be.

After a while, Kenan asks, "Do you see the colors?"

My lips turn into a sad smile. "Yeah." I glance at the trees lining one side of the street. Leaves pattern the trunks, spiraling around in circles to the top. "There's life in the smallest, simplest of things. I see why this is happening. Freedom was never an easy price; it's paid with—"

"Blood. More than we ever thought possible," he finishes bitterly.

"Yeah," I croak.

"But you knew that all along." He stares ahead. "Do you think it's worth it?"

Five more verses of the song float up.

I remember the blond Free Syrian Army soldier who was at peace with his right arm being amputated. *I still have another one, don't I?*

"I don't know. I *want* it to be worth it. I want to know the grass growing over the martyrs' graves will give life to a generation who can be whoever they want to be. But we don't know when that will happen. It could be tomorrow or decades from now."

"That's why we have our faith, Salama. It's our duty to fight, live, and pave the way."

I admire the way he says it confidently.

"Which is your favorite song?" he asks suddenly.

I'm taken off guard. "Um . . . 'How Sweet Is Freedom.' "

"Me too."

"It's what Baba used to sing all the time before they took him. He had this look about him every time he sang it, and it didn't hurt that his voice was like a canary."

"Ibrahim Qashoush was pretty smart to come up with it."

"All his songs are amazing."

Ibrahim Qashoush was one of the roots of our revolution. A simple man from Hama who penned most of the popular songs that give us the strength to fight on.

Kenan's voice is quiet. "May God rest his soul."

My heart mourns for his loss as if I've just received the news. The military caught him. They cut his voice box from his throat so violently his whole head was nearly decapitated. Then he was thrown in the Orontes River for us to discover.

"Ameen," I whisper.

"We want freedom! We want freedom! We want freedom!"

The crowd starts chanting each word with the force they've been cultivating for fifty years. Kenan joins them, singing in a steady, strong voice, holding an iPhone high to capture each second. I lean closer to him, spellbound by his beautiful voice.

In the corner of my eye, I see Khawf with his arms folded. He notices me staring and winks.

I grimace.

"This is going on longer than I thought it would," I say to Kenan. He pauses his recording and leans down to hear me. "When are we supposed to run for our lives? How long until they come?"

"We're under the Free Syrian Army's jurisdiction. If the military comes, the FSA will be their first line of attack, and trust me, we'll know if that happens."

I nod, but my ears are straining to catch the planes' death frequencies. I can't lie to myself and pretend I'm confident I'll make it to see tomorrow's sunrise.

I raise my hand to my throat, feeling the way the muscles contract when I swallow. The act makes me feel alive and more aware of my surroundings. I could hear a butterfly's wings if I wanted to.

"You okay?" Kenan's voice echoes everywhere.

I nod. Thankfully he doesn't press the matter.

"This is inspiring," I say before he has time to expose my white lie. "I honestly didn't expect myself to feel so encouraged."

"Yeah, every time I post footage of a protest on YouTube and read all the comments, I feel like I'm part of a huge change. I'm not a big-shot politician or a well-known activist or anything. If I die, I doubt anyone in the world would know. I'd just be a number, but still, I feel like I'm changing people's thoughts. Making them see the truth. Even if it's one view. Does that make sense?" He glances shyly at me.

"It does." I smile. "Every time I stitch a person and ease their pain—even if it's temporary—I feel like I did something. That these people *aren't* numbers. They have lives and loved ones, and *maybe* I helped them in the right direction. If there's one thing people are scared of, it's being forgotten. It's an irrational fear, don't you think?"

He scratches the back of his head and breaks into a half smile that could inspire books, and my stomach flips. When his eyes slip to my scarred hands, I don't cover them with my sleeves. I haven't thought of them in weeks. Before, I hated how they were a reminder of what I lost, but now they're a testament to my strength.

I take a deep breath, relishing the fact that the air isn't stained with blood. A cleansing breeze blows past us, and I catch a glimpse of the world Kenan sees. I see and love it. Truly. But it's like loving the ocean. It's unpredictable, the blue sparkling water turning from heavenly to horrifying in a second.

"I think—" I begin, but I don't have the chance to finish my sentence. I feel the warning before my ears register the noise. Death has a unique tone.

"We need to—" I try again, but I can't even finish my words.

24

First, a bomb falls two blocks from where we're standing, and the ground rumbles and breaks.

Second, the singing stops, as if someone shut off a TV, and panic ensues.

Third, memories rush past my eyes as my body refuses to believe I'm reliving last year. Even though I was expecting it, my body doesn't care.

I shake my head quickly. I can't shut down or I'll die. Hesitation is my death sentence.

"We have to get out of here now!" I hear Kenan yelling, but so many shapes are rushing past my eyes, they begin to blur. A hand latches on to my arm and drags me in the opposite direction from where the bomb fell. I stumble after Kenan, praying he doesn't let go. Bodies swarm past us, trying to push us apart in their urgency, but his grip doesn't weaken. I try my best not to trip over my feet as urgency turns into desperation.

"Salama!" Kenan's voice rises above the din of chaos. He can't turn his head in my direction or we'll both stumble.

"Keep going!" I yell before he stops.

"I have to get out of here," one man keeps screaming, moving against the current. "I have to go, *please*. The bomb fell on my home!"

I keep pressing forward despite the hysteria choking me.

Another one falls, lighting up the sky. Closer this time. Screams rip the night apart, and my knees buckle.

"Salama!" Kenan's hand tightens around my wrist, and he stops in the middle of a stampede to help me up. People curve around us now, running. Kenan grabs me by my shoulders and hoists me up. His eyes burn determination into mine.

"Salama," Kenan says eerily calmly. "Don't panic, and don't let go of my hand."

I nod. His hand slides into mine, and we make a run for it with the crowd once again. I hear guns going off and another bomb falling. It must be an all-out clash with the Free Syrian Army now. Kenan turns right, separating us from the mob, and ducks into alleyways. The shouting doesn't stop, and it's not only coming from the protest. Buildings have crumbled onto sleeping children, and mothers are crying desperately for someone to pull their babies out. Guilt tears my gut for not turning back and helping, but I know I'd be as good as dead if I did.

I know where we are. Layla is still a bit far from here, but there's another place we can seek refuge.

"Wait!" I shout, and Kenan pauses for a second. I dash in

front of him, taking his other hand, and run. "I know where to go."

"Where?" he shouts over the din.

"My old home."

"We need to run faster. The FSA might have lost their ground here."

"Snipers." A pit drops in my stomach.

"Or the military."

I glance back. "You need to get rid of your phone."

God forbid if we're caught and they find the videos on his phone. They'd skin him.

His hand flexes in mine. Our footsteps echo against the broken pavement. "Can't do that."

"But—"

"Don't worry. If we're caught, I won't let them hurt you."

I bite down a retort. He's just saying that to make himself feel better. There are no innocents in the eyes of evil. Luckily we encounter no one on the streets, but I can feel the bombs closing in. I pull him faster and my lungs protest. Every intake of breath feels like fire. I bite my lip to ground myself and push on harder.

People have started spilling out of buildings, their eyes wide with fear. The roads are beyond saving, but there's nowhere for the people to go. I hear children crying and people praying for mercy. A man carries an infant in his arms as his wife rushes out with him. They part for us, and I don't look back to see what they're doing. I pray they have the sense to flee.

"God, *please*, save us!" I whisper.

A shell falls nearer; its blast sends glass shards that just about grazes our clothes and skin as we run past. They sting enough to make us hiss, but we've dealt with worse pain.

The bomb has blown up a neighborhood I used to go to for knafeh. I stumble again, coughing from the debris, and Kenan lifts me up, his hands strong and steady. I pull him again and we run. I try not to think of the people who were breathing just fifteen minutes ago. How fifteen minutes can make all the difference in the world. I block out the sounds of a crying baby I know are a figment of my imagination.

We're finally far enough away to slow down and catch our breath. I reluctantly let go of Kenan's hand and he falls into step with me. Our breaths are harsh, ribs creaking as our anemic blood tries to supply oxygen. I'm both shivering and sweating and try to focus on steadying my breath.

Kenan doesn't say anything, and I don't find solace in speaking either. We hear the bombs in the distance, and each stabs a new hole in my heart. I don't want to see the expression on his face. I don't want to know if it's sadness or anger or desperation. Whatever it is, it's going to scare or break me, and I don't want either. His back is hunched, and every time a scream reaches us, he constricts even more.

We walk through my old neighborhood, where my apartment building stood eons ago. Local shops stacked beside each other are faded, the signs almost impossible to read. There's no one here trying to salvage their family's business. Not a soul wanders the streets, and it brings chills to my body. This place is haunted by the ghosts of those who lived here, screaming for a justice that's not been delivered. The shops have been ransacked, equipment thrown around, windows broken. The pharmacy I interned at has been bled dry.

My old building is around the next right corner, and my heart thuds the closer we get.

I haven't been here since July.

My footsteps are engraved all over this place. My ten-year-old self flashes past me giggling, climbing out of the school bus with her friends, running home, backpack swaying with every step. Fifteen-year-old me stumbles past, eyes glued to the book she's reading, late for her study sessions. Seventeen-year-old Salama walks hand in hand with Layla, Shahed, and Rawan. Happy with today's shopping spree, each carrying the delicious shawarma from the restaurant a few feet away. All these lives rush in front of me. I can see the light bouncing off my hopeful, healthy face. I can see my confident strides and clear eyes. The whole street comes to life, flowers blooming at the sides of the pavement, traders singing their wares, and iris petals dancing in the wind, carrying the smell of yasmine elsham.

"*Salama!*" A voice cuts through my daydream like cold water.

I blink as the darkness replaces my hallucination and I inhale sharply.

"Salama," Kenan says again, and I turn to him. "Everything all right?"

He's worried; soot covers his clothes. There are nicks lining his arms and cuts on his face. He looks nervous, glancing around to see what I was looking at.

"Yes," I say, and my voices catches. Clearing my throat, I

try again. "I'm okay. It's just overwhelming being here. Back home."

He hesitates before smiling sympathetically. "I can't imagine how difficult it is."

Of course he can imagine, but his selflessness overshines anything else.

"Let's go." I walk past him.

I feel Khawf walking beside me and he murmurs, "This place is imbued with your trauma. Do you see why you need to leave, Salama?"

I give a quick nod, carefully hiding my tears as I try not to think that only a few steps from here is where Mama's body lay mangled.

25

I SEE MY BUILDING'S RUINS IN FRONT OF ME AND wonder at the irony. Taking refuge in the place that killed Mama. I try not to stumble on the debris and boulders strewn carelessly on the ground. I can't help but step on broken furniture and the memories of the people who lived here with me. There's no safe place to tread.

"Right here." I point at the top of a small hill of concrete and brick. Kenan climbs in and I follow him, feeling the sharp edges of stones digging into my sneakers. I push through the pain to reach him, trying not to cut myself on the glass lying everywhere. Down and concealed from view is our hiding spot. A huge closet obscures it. It's like the eye of the storm, a center surviving the catastrophe. As if the whole building, with its memories of the generations who once lived in it, decided to make a home for us tonight.

We jump, landing heavily.

The moon shines down, a blessing, so we know where to sit without something poking us in the sides. Kenan sweeps the ground a bit with his shoe and sits down, leaning against a broken wall, his breath ragged. I could kick myself. I was so absorbed with my own problems I didn't stop to think how he might be doing. Sweat pools on his forehead, and he rests his head against the stone, eyes closed.

"Hey," I say tentatively. "Everything okay?"

He wipes a hand across his face and manages a smile that doesn't look as bright as usual.

"Yeah," he murmurs. "Don't worry about it. Just catching my breath."

I move over to him. "Can I have your phone?"

He nods, handing it over, and I open its light and shine it on his face.

"What?" he asks.

"Making sure you're all right."

He nods and stares straight into the light. His pupils constrict, assuring me there's no cellular death taking place in his brain.

"Everything looks good," I say after a few seconds. My gaze slides from his eyes to his lips and back again just as fast. He does the same, though he lingers far longer than I did, and my heart thunders in my ears.

Salama, I don't ever want to—

I wonder how his sentence was going to end.

He shifts a bit, raising his hand, and it's centimeters away from my cheek before it falls beside him.

"Sorry," he whispers. "I didn't mean to—"

"It's okay," I whisper back, giving him the phone. I move to sit on his other side.

Kenan rests his head against the slab once again. I rub

261

my neck and look up at the sky. If we weren't in such a dire situation, this place would be beautiful. The blackness stretches out in front of us, with the moon casting his silvery glimmer, dimming the light of the stars nearby. It's the same sky other people see in their countries. But while we watch it here, hiding, not knowing if our next breath is our last, others sleep safely in their beds, bidding the moon a peaceful good night.

Khawf emerges from the shadows.

He smiles. "Just here to watch." He mimics a key locking his lips and leans against the wall. "Though the silence is boring."

I take a deep breath and turn to Kenan. "I want to believe it's worth it," I say. "The revolution, I mean. But I'm scared."

"I think it will be." Kenan smiles softly. "Empires have collapsed throughout history. They rise, they build, and they fall. Nothing lasts forever. Not even our pain."

"Now that's a silver lining," I whisper.

He looks away, and I see shyness in his features.

"So you're still uploading videos to YouTube?"

"Yes." He opens his phone; the harsh light illuminates half his face.

"I thought," I begin, treading carefully. "Now that you've decided to leave, you'd play it a bit safer and maybe not record the protests anymore?"

Khawf grimaces. "Straight to the point, huh, Salama?"

Kenan sets his phone down and looks at me. "What?"

"I mean—"

"Salama, I've already made the decision to leave. Can't I at least have something that'll make me feel less guilty until then?"

"Not if it's going to increase the chances of your arrest."

"Why can't you support me in this one thing?" he asks, exasperated.

"Because it's not just about you. You're dragging your siblings into this. You're being selfish."

"I don't think it's any of your business." His voice grows colder by the second.

"Well, it's a free country now, isn't it, Kenan? I can say whatever the hell I like!" I snap.

He groans and his eyes flash with annoyance. "Why do you care? This is my life, my family, and my business, Salama. Why don't you commend the fact I'm trying to make a difference, even if it's a small one?"

I stare at him, shock trickling down my spine like icy water.

"Your life," I repeat quietly. I want to strangle him. "*Your* life?"

I stand, my hands shivering. I ball them against my chest, and the shock melts into a fiery frustration. I've had *enough* of this. Everyone I love is either dead, being tortured, or on their way to one of these situations.

"Salama," he begins warily.

I want to laugh. "*Your. Life.*"

I drag a hand down my face, walking in a circle, letting the words build up in my throat before turning toward him.

"How *dare* you?" I whisper, now shaking with anger. "Are you *seriously* going to sit there and pretend if anything happened to you it wouldn't affect me?"

His lips part. "The military won't trace my actions back to—"

I let out a short laugh. "You think *that's* what I care about?"

He looks bewildered, frightened even.

"You *can't* do this." The words spill out of me like a broken dam, each one tripping over the other. "You can't record the protests anymore because I swear to God, Kenan, if you get arrested—if you die, I will *never* forgive you!"

His eyes brim with tears. "Don't say that."

I fall to my knees in front of him. I breathe in gasps, my desperation hindering my lungs. "I *won't* forgive you, Kenan. You can't come into my life and show me the colors and tell me about your dreams and just risk it all when we're *six* days from leaving!"

"Because I might be arrested?" His voice breaks.

"Because you made me fall in love with you!" I retort, my heart beating harshly.

My eyes burn with tears that streak down my overheated cheeks. His overflow as well, like two rivers dripping from his chin, and he covers them with his arm, his lower lip trembling.

I refuse to look away, to have any answer from him that isn't what I need to hear.

I whisper, "You can't do this to me. My heart won't take it."

He lowers his arm, eyes shining. "I love you too."

His voice comes out soft and quiet, but it's all I hear. Even if there were a hurricane ripping through Homs, he'd be all I hear. Every taut muscle and nerve cell in me unwinds and I sink lower in the soil, feeling the little grass blades nudging me.

"Then do this for me," I plead. "*Please*. Do this for me."

I want to reach for him—to hold him—but I won't. There's no ring on my finger and we aren't promised to each other.

He doesn't reach for me either, even though it's clear from his expression he wants nothing more. But he does lean forward until there's no space for a flower stem to fall between us.

"Salama," he breathes, and my heart trips, picks itself up, and trips again. Under the silvery moonlight, he looks magical—magnified by his kindness and beautiful soul. He doesn't deserve the cruelty this world has to offer. "I won't record."

I clasp a hand over my mouth and brush away the relieved tears. "Thank you."

He smiles. "Don't cry."

"You're crying too!"

A laugh escapes from him and I manage to beam, my facial muscles stretching stiffly. But the moment passes quickly when I look to Khawf to make sure he's keeping his promise. He looks amused.

"Well, that worked out," he chuckles.

Kenan's gaze drops to my restless fingers. "Salama, may I ask you something?"

I wince slightly, anxious. "Sure."

"I've noticed how jumpy you are sometimes," he begins slowly. "Your eyes dart everywhere, as if you're looking for someone. There was also, uh, what happened earlier. Are . . . you all right?"

There it is. It was going to happen eventually. I bite my tongue and Khawf laughs this time.

"Will you tell him, Salama?" he says. "Or are you scared he won't love you anymore?"

I shudder and a sinking weight settles on my ribs, concaving them. My stomach is hollow with nerves. How do I tell him about Khawf? I want to. That want started when he first showed me the sunset. Like a whisper at the back of my head.

I stare at the scars on my hands, tracing the silvery slashes.

"Salama?" Kenan says. Concern is wrapped in every syllable.

I look up at him and try to keep my breathing steady. I'm not ashamed of who I am and the struggles I go through. Khawf is an integral part of my life who has shaped so much of who I have become these past months. I won't deny that it would feel like a punch to the gut if Kenan flinched away from me after I tell him. But if we're to have our version of a real life together, I don't want to start it with a lie.

"I, uh . . . ," I begin, then clear my throat. "No. I'm not all right."

"What are you saying?" His tone is fearful. For me.

I sit back against my spot and reach for a little plant growing between the cracked concrete, twirl it between my fingers. I say the words quickly, like ripping off a Band-Aid, exposing my secret. "Since last July, I've been having . . . visions. Hallucinations, I guess."

I pause, staring at the plant's baby leaves, but the only sound I hear is Khawf's slow clapping. He looks impressed and there's a glint of pride in his eyes.

I peek at Kenan under my eyelashes and catch the surprise in his expression.

"Visions?" he asks, and he glances a few feet from where Khawf stands. "You mean you're seeing things that . . ." He falters.

"Aren't real," I finish for him. "Mostly I see one person."

Khawf straightens his back and dusts off his suit. "Oh my God, are you going to introduce me?"

I ignore Khawf and continue. "Khawf. He's been in my life since Mama died. I fell pretty hard on my head that day and, I don't know, maybe a head injury coupled with my PTSD has affected the relationship between my brain's frontal lobe and sensory cortex, but I won't be sure until I can get checked."

Kenan looks stunned. "Khawf?"

I nod, throwing the plant away, and force my tone to stay calm. "He shows me memories. My regrets." I leave out the degree of trauma I feel after each one. He doesn't have to know all the details. I take a deep breath. "I've learned to live with it." I exhale. "Now you know."

I hug my knees to my chest, burying my head in my arms to hide my teary eyes, my heart shivering with what he'll say. It's taken me a long time to accept Khawf, and I have no idea if Kenan will be able to come to terms with it. If he'll see *me* and not someone haunted by her mistakes.

Kenan doesn't say anything for a while, and I let him have that. He needs to unravel the words I've just said, understand what they mean for him. For me. For us.

"Salama, look at me," Kenan finally coaxes gently.

Reluctantly, I peer through the folds of my sleeves.

"I'm not going anywhere." He smiles. "You're my Sheeta."

Joy reclaims my heart and I feel foolish, but I say it anyway: "You're my Pazu."

Kenan looks away, a shadow falling over his cheeks, and he presses a hand to his forehead. Then he twists toward me.

He looks nervous, but a different kind of nervous. "Salama, I want to do this right. Even if we don't have our families fussing over us, chaperoning our dates and whatnot. Even if Khawf is around. And I don't want to wait until we're in Munich to do this. I don't want to do it on a boat. I want to do it *here*. In our home."

My internal temperature rises. "Do *what*?" I stutter.

He swallows hard and slips his hand into his pocket. When he opens his palm, a ring sparkles on it. "I want to marry you. If you'll have me."

"*What?*" Khawf snaps.

"*What?*" I exclaim, the air vanishing from my lungs.

He fights a grin. "Is that a good what or a bad what?"

My mouth falls open. "I—I didn't think you'd do that *here*!"

"Proposing on the revolution's anniversary?" His eyes twinkle. "I've been planning this for a week."

"You're impossible," I breathe, pressing my hands to my cheeks.

Kenan bites his lip and says, "I thought you'd say something like that. Salama, you and I live our lives second by second. We might live to ride that boat to Syracuse. We might settle in Munich. We might learn German, paint our apartment in vibrant shades of color we haven't seen in Homs in a long time, and build a life. An *amazing* life. You'd become a pharmacist all the hospitals would trip over themselves to hire, and I'd draw our stories. We'd have our own adventures." He looks away bashfully, stumbling on his words. "We'd write a book. Together. But . . . we also might not survive these six days. We might be buried here. *Anything* can happen, and I don't want to wait anymore. No one knows the future. But I know how *I* feel. I know how *you* feel. So let's find our happiness here in Homs. Let's get married in *our* country. Let's make a home here before we make one somewhere else."

His words illustrate a universe of *what ifs, mights,* and *maybes* that feel possible. I want this universe so badly I feel its fire burning through me.

He holds the ring up and with hesitant eyes and blushing cheeks asks, "Salama, will you marry me?"

I stare at him. With every other situation in my life, I dissect all outcomes to the bone before deciding. But with this? The decision is as easy as breathing. It feels like how peace probably does.

But even breathing can be painful sometimes, and if I say yes, Kenan and his siblings will be a part of my heart forever.

It will become real.

I stare at the ring and find that I don't care about whatever uncertainties lie in our future. All I know is that I love him and that even in the darkness surrounding us, he's been my joy. In the midst of all the death, he made me want to live.

The answer slips easily from my lips.

"Yes," I whisper, wiping my tears away, feeling my heart glow. *"Yes."*

26

THE SUN'S RAYS ON MY FACE JOLT ME AWAKE AND IT takes me a second to realize I'm not at home. A bird flies above me, its silhouette streaking through the pale blue sky. My gaze follows it.

That's right. I am home.

Beside me, Kenan stirs in his sleep, and I glance at him. His chest rises and falls steadily, comforting me. He winces and I hope it's because the ground is unkind to his back and not due to nightmares. His hair is longer than when I met him, and his scruff is more pronounced. I wonder how it would feel to run my fingers through his hair.

My nerves spark when I remember last night. I take the ring out of my pocket and hold it high, admiring it in the light. I didn't want to wear it in the darkness where I couldn't see how it glitters on my finger. It's rose gold, encrusted in the middle with a line of white gold, perfectly modeled to resemble tiny diamonds. It's beautiful and simple and what I'd have picked out if I had been in the shop.

"It was my mother's," Kenan says, and I jump.

He sits up as well. His eyes are bright and a morning blush blooms on his cheeks.

The ring suddenly feels heavy in my palm. "It's so beautiful," I whisper. "I . . . I don't know what else to say."

He smiles sadly. "You don't have to say anything."

I shake my head. "I'm so sorry about your parents. I—I would love to have known your mother."

He fiddles with his fingers. "She never really understood why I decided to become an animator instead of studying medicine, but she supported me anyway. And even then, she knew me so well. Just from seeing you at your brother's wedding, she knew we'd be perfect for each other." His eyes gloss over for a second, then he shakes his head. "She would have loved for you to have her ring."

"I'm honored to wear it." I try to slip it on my finger, hoping it will fit. But it doesn't. My fingers are made of skin and bone, and it hangs loosely.

"Too big?"

"Yeah." I sigh and then remember my necklace. I pull it from under my collar. "I have this. My parents gave it to me when I graduated."

He peers at it. "Fits perfectly with the ring."

I thread the chain through the ring and it glitters prettily. "What do you think?"

"Beautiful." But he isn't looking at the necklace.

I blush and tuck it away under my sweater.

He scratches the back of his neck. "We have a week left and I know I said I wanted to get married in Syria, but I didn't ask if you—"

"I want...," I cut in. "I want one of my last actions in Syria to be this. Something good."

He beams.

"What's the saying? 'Make haste with good deeds'?" I smile. My head feels a bit light with the excitement of a decision I didn't think twice about but leaned on my feelings for. "Let's get married today."

He laughs and stands. "Why don't you check on Layla first?"

I gasp, scrambling to my feet. "Oh my God. She must be worried out of her mind!"

He nods. "Let's go."

I can't hear anything apart from our breathing, which hopefully means there's nothing dangerous outside my home's ruins. I move to climb up the rubble and Kenan stretches a hand out, stopping me.

"Let me," he says. "Please."

I nod. Kenan hoists himself over the wreckage. As he looks from side to side, he moves slowly out of my view. Then I hear him drop to his feet on the other side with a grunt of pain. A few minutes pass with no sound except the birds.

"Okay, it's safe," Kenan calls, and a few seconds later I jump down beside him.

In the day, more of last night's catastrophe comes into view: from the faint smoke spiraling to the sky to the grave-yard silence that has taken over. We grimace as we trudge forward, reality scratching through our shield of bliss.

I look back at my long-ago home, feeling my heart tighten. I wonder whether I'll be back or if it's the last time I'll see it.

When we reach Layla's home, Kenan insists he'll be fine walking back to his place on his own.

"I have to check on my siblings. Lama is still recovering."

I chew my tongue.

"I'll be fine, Salama," he laughs. "You're marrying me today. I'm *more* than fine."

I duck my head to hide my red face. "Yeah, just—I'll tell Layla the news and then we can work on that."

He winks. "I'll see you at the hospital?"

I nod, then a thought flutters in my mind. "Why don't you bring Yusuf and Lama? I mean, if Lama's feeling up to it. Also, it could distract Yusuf from . . . well, everything. I'm sure they'd want to be there."

Kenan's smile is so warm I feel it all the way to my extremities.

"Yeah," he says softly. "I'll ask them."

I click open the door and shut it behind me to find Layla sitting in the hallway, her legs stretched out in front of her and stomach still bulging. Her head droops to the side, eyelids closed.

I crouch down beside her. "Layla," I whisper, and she starts.

"*Wha*—" she says groggily, blinking rapidly before settling her gaze on me. "Salama! Oh, alhamdulillah!"

I quickly hug her, breathing in her daisy scent.

"What happened yesterday?" she asks.

"I'm going to tell you, but you can't interrupt me till the end."

Her expression turns curious, and I notice she looks a bit worn out. "Fine."

I fill Layla in on everything. To her credit, she doesn't utter a single sound but as soon as I finish, she grabs my arm and lets out an *Oh my God!* I show her the ring and she squeals.

"*When?*" she asks, breathless.

I can't help but grin. "Now."

She collapses into another fit of *Oh my God!* and is able to pause it to say, "I *told* you someone was going to snatch you away from me!"

I laugh. "You'll always be my priority."

She chuckles, although it doesn't sound full of life like it usually does. "Good. Then I give you my blessing. Who's going to marry you?"

I fidget with my hijab. "I was thinking Dr. Ziad. At the hospital. That way there would be witnesses."

She sighs. "Perfect."

I take a deep breath. "I was wondering if Kenan and his siblings could move in with us. I—I don't want him to be so far away from me."

Layla beams. "Of course! It's better we stick together till we leave."

I exhale, a weight slipping off my shoulders. "Well then, you know I want you to be there. Can you come?"

She laughs lightly and brushes her pregnant belly. "I wish! But Baby Salama is being difficult. I'm feeling a bit tired."

I press a palm to her forehead. She's not too warm.

"I'm fine," she says. "Just weary."

"Well, of course you're tired. You slept in the hallway!" I scold and help her onto the couch.

She settles comfortably under the covers before noticing the disappointed look on my face.

"Salama, I really want to come." She squeezes my hand. "I would crawl if I could, but I can't even do that now."

Guilt washes over me. I can't be selfish. "I know. It's just, I didn't think I'd get married without you at the wedding. It's weird."

She grimaces.

"I could ask Kenan to postpone it until we get to Germany. Or tomorrow. I'm okay with that."

She shakes her head. "No. Today. You get married today. You never know——" She stops. "You're not putting off your happiness for me. Besides, we're definitely having a party and another wedding ceremony in Germany. And of course, I'll be the center of attention then, even if you *are* the bride."

I laugh, my sadness lifting at the beautiful image it's creating in my mind. Being this close to leaving is allowing the suppressed dreams to wake up and grow like ivy between the cracks. Layla and I picking our dresses and a matching smaller one for Little Salama, who will have her mother's eyes and her father's hair. Holding her in my arms would make me feel closer to Hamza. Her pudgy hand grabbing my thumb in a tight grip and her little nose breathing in air that isn't polluted with smoke and death.

Her time in Syria would be a dream she dreamed in the womb. One that exists only in the stories her mother and I tell her. Until one day she can come back to her country and grow the lemon trees.

I massage Layla's shoulders for a bit. They're stiff and

bony under my hands and it's an icy bucket of water on my dreams.

"Thank you," she murmurs, eyes half closed. "Now go." When I don't move, she repeats, "Go! I'll be here."

She takes my hand in hers, peering at me through her eyelashes. "I'm so happy for you. So proud. Your parents and Hamza would be too. Look how you've changed."

I give her one last squeeze before grabbing my lab coat. Today, this is my wedding dress, but in Germany, I'll have a real one. With Layla. Safe and sound.

WHEN KENAN ARRIVES AT THE HOSPITAL, HIS SIB-
lings are right beside him. Lama's eyes are wide with wonder, while Yusuf's expression is curious and unclouded by
sadness, giving me a glimpse of how young he truly is.

"Hey," Kenan says, his eyes brightening at the sight
of me.

"Hey." I smile, feeling giddy.

"Hey," Lama says, and I tear my stare away from Kenan
to look at the little girl clutching his side.

She looks stronger, life lifting her features.

"How are you, Lama?" I ask.

"Good," she replies and then glances up at Kenan, who
nods at her. "Thank you for saving my life."

Oh, ya albi. My heart.

I extend my hand and she takes it softly before I pull her
into a hug. "Thank you for being strong."

Her face is pink with shyness and she lets go of me to
hide her face in Kenan's side. He bites back a laugh, but there

are stars caught in his irises, and I can't believe the absolute peace I'm experiencing here, at the hospital of all places.

I peek at Yusuf, who's staring at the ground, seemingly determined to ignore me.

"Salam, Yusuf," I say, raising a hand in a wave. He glances at me briefly before looking away, his hands in his pockets and slightly frowning.

I look at Kenan, scared I might have done something wrong, but he shakes his head.

"He's a bit jealous." He sighs. "Thinks things are about to change and you're stealing me away from them." Then in a louder voice he says, "But I told him things are changing for the better; we just have three extra people as family now."

Yusuf shrugs, still not making eye contact.

Kenan sighs again. "He'll come around."

"It's okay. He and I will become best friends soon enough."

I hear Dr. Ziad talking to a patient from the right side of the atrium.

"Let's get married?" Kenan grins.

I blush. "I don't have anything planned for today, so sure."

We walk over to Dr. Ziad, who's just finishing up with the patient. His hair is in disarray, and his shoulders are hunched from exhaustion. But when he turns around and spots me, he smiles.

"Salama!" he says. "Good morning."

"Good morning, Doctor," I reply and glance back at Kenan, who looks as shy as I feel.

Dr. Ziad looks between us. "Is everything all right?"

My palms sweat and nervousness churns in my stomach. "Yes. I—Dr. Ziad, I want to ask you a favor."

He straightens. "Of course. Anything."

"I—I mean—what happened—" I stutter, and Kenan steps in.

"I asked Salama to marry me, and we were wondering if you'd be the one to officiate," he says in a clear voice, but his face and ears are red.

Dr. Ziad glances between us before laughing joyously. The sound turns many heads our way, and I'm afire.

"I—I—" he stutters, caught off guard with happiness. I have never seen Dr. Ziad this way before. He rubs his eyes and laughs again. "This is wonderful news! Salama, when did you two . . . ?"

I fiddle with the ends of my hijab. "It's a long story, but"—I look up at Kenan—"it was fate."

Kenan smiles.

"You want to do this here? Now?" Dr. Ziad asks. His grin is as wide as a crescent moon.

I nod. "Our next moments aren't promised. And you've always been like a father to me."

His exhaustion vanishes and he looks ten years younger. "It would be my honor to officiate."

I can't help the smile that twitches my lips upward. I feel like I'm in a dream. Buds of hope begin to bloom slowly in my heart, petals opening to meet the sun. I wish Layla was here, holding my hand. But I take comfort that Lama and Yusuf are able to attend, watching something other than trauma unfold in this hospital.

A crowd begins to form around us, the pale faces curious

about what's happening. Patients offer their congratulations, and Kenan bows his head. Usually I wouldn't like this invasion of privacy, but seeing anything other than pain and suffering on the people's faces is worth it. I catch Am lurking at the edge of the crowd, his stare judging. I look away.

We stand in front of Dr. Ziad, who has finally composed himself. He begins with a small speech about finding happiness through the hardships, and everyone quiets down. After that, we all read Al-Fatiha together and Kenan recites the marriage vows after Dr. Ziad. I give my consent in a small voice.

And then we're married.

I get married in my lab coat, a sweater three sizes too big, with dust on my hijab and dirt marks on my jeans. We don't have cake, a proper wedding dress, or even clean clothes. But it doesn't matter. It feels like the whole thing happens in snapshots. I try to memorize each word said, every action and look, but I'm having a hard time keeping up. Kenan looks dazed, like he's walking through a daydream. We glance shyly at each other.

Nothing will ruin this moment for me. It's mine to enjoy, to love, to be happy in.

Everyone claps and some even cheer. Lama's face looks like the moon on a full night, and she's bouncing on her feet, while Yusuf gives a small smile as if he just can't help himself.

Nour squeezes herself through the crowds, grasping my hands and kissing my cheeks, her eyes shining bright.

Little by little, the crowd dissipates and Dr. Ziad calls for all the staff to begin work, but the energy powering the

hospital is different now. The hope I've so carefully cultivated is no longer only in my heart.

"My office is empty," Dr. Ziad says to Kenan and me in
a low voice. "I'm sure you two have things to talk about in
private."

"Th-thank you, Doctor," I stammer from shyness.

"You deserve all the happiness in the world, Salama." He
smiles warmly at me, and it reminds me of Baba. "Congratulations to the both of you, and may God fill your lives with
joy and blessings."

He shakes Kenan's hand before hurrying off to his duties.

"I'll look after the kids for a little while," Nour says.
She smiles at Lama and Yusuf, and Lama returns the smile.
Yusuf slumps down on one of the plastic chairs, but he looks
less tense than when he walked in.

Thankfully, everyone's busying themselves too much to
notice us slipping into Dr. Ziad's office. Kenan closes the
door softly, disturbing the dust particles.

I feel warm in my sweater. *Should I say something? Where
do my arms go?* I swing them awkwardly for a few seconds,
then stop.

"Salama?" he says, and I turn around slowly. He takes a
few steps toward me, and suddenly he's closer than he's ever
been.

I look up at him, nervous, and am surprised to see that
his expression holds no tension. I can see the specks of hazel
in his eyes, and if I concentrate I can count them. His hair is
tousled from last night and from how many times his hands
have attacked it all morning. I see a faint scar splitting his left
eyebrow in half and wonder how I haven't noticed it before.

It feels like I'm seeing him for the first time. He doesn't say anything, just smiles warmly at me, and before I can speak, he leans forward, hooking his arms under mine, pulling me close. I gasp, and after a few moments of hesitation, I wind my hands around his shoulders. He buries his head in the nook of my hijab, holding me tight. My nerves jingle; a million thoughts race through me, crowding my mind.

Suddenly, a stillness sweeps over us, and every nervous thought and feeling dissipates. I feel at peace. I can breathe, and I breathe him in. He smells like Syria in the old days. A hint of lemon picked from the gardens, mixed with the rubble and soil. He smells like home. He mumbles something I don't hear, his words caught in the fabric of my hijab.

"What?" I whisper.

"Nothing," he says in a louder voice, but there's roughness to it, like he's trying to hold back tears. Then, after a few moments, he says, "I'm sorry I couldn't give you a proper wedding."

I tear myself from his embrace and eye him curiously. "You think I'm upset?"

"I don't know," he says sheepishly, one hand behind his neck. "I know we're down on our luck now, and I can't provide enough for the both of us. But I swear I will. My family has some money saved up, and we have land here as well. I can't use any of that yet, though. *Damn*, I should have given you something. Maybe a dress? You should at least have had a wedding dress. I'm so, so——"

I cut him off when I stand on my tiptoes and clasp his cheeks between my hands. He stares at me.

"I want a marriage. Not a wedding." I smile. "Besides, this is *way* more romantic."

"Really?" he asks uncertainly.

"Oh definitely! A wedding amid a revolution. Isn't this a good premise for a story?"

He smiles back. "It does sound like a wonderful plot."

"Exactly. I'm a pharmacist with experience, Kenan. I can take care of the both of us while you are a stay-at-home dad who draws," I say with a teasing smile.

"Ha ha."

I fall back to my heels, taking my hands with me before they start sweating.

"I was wondering . . . ," I say, playing with the hem of my lab coat. "If you'd like to move in with Layla and me."

There's a second where we hold our breath.

"It's—you have that huge hole in your balcony, and I can't imagine it's very warm," I clarify.

He chuckles and holds my hands, rubbing soft circles on them. "What's the real reason?"

I blush. "That's one of many."

"All right, then." He smiles. "I'll take my siblings home, we'll pack, and meet you at the end of your shift."

"Okay."

Summoning every ounce of bravery in me, I reach up and kiss his cheek. He freezes, breath catching in his throat. He stutters a goodbye and heads toward the door before glancing back at me.

"See you later."

"See you."

Khawf is waiting for me in the stockroom, and I jump when I see him.

"Didn't expect me on this joyous day?" His lips twist in displeasure.

I close the door, sighing. "And why are you upset now? Kenan being my husband gives me more motivation to leave with him."

He nods. "That's true, but it doesn't come without risks."

"How do you mean?"

He steps closer. "If—God forbid, of course—Kenan or his siblings were killed or, worse, arrested. You'd still leave?"

Dread slithers in my stomach.

"A lot could happen in five days," Khawf continues matter-of-factly. "Who will you choose? Layla or Kenan?" His eyes gleam. "Or yourself?"

I clear my throat. "I'm leaving my brother, aren't I?"

He taps his chin. "Right. But will another tragedy make you break your promise? Make you want to die here rather than take a risk at life?"

"No," I answer.

He steps toward me. His breath is cold, but there's worry in his eyes. "I hope for your sake you don't. It would be a shame to bury you here."

28

KHAWF'S WORDS WEIGH HEAVILY ON ME THROUGH-
out the day. My heart is at war, trying to latch on to wisps
of happiness. Hope is a ghost roaming my body.

The occasional person congratulates me as I go on with
my rounds. Glimmers of joy spark briefly, but it's like trying
to hold on to fog. Nour hugs me tightly again, and I try to
absorb her delight.

"I knew he liked you!" Nour exclaims, walking beside me.

"You did?"

"Yes. He always looks at you while you work. Not in a
creepy way . . . I don't know," she says thoughtfully. "Like
you're the only one who exists."

I blush. "Oh. I didn't think anyone saw that."

"It's been a nice distraction from all the patients running
in constantly. I mean it's a miracle we have our wits!"

"You know, in the West and other places where people
have normal lives, the medical staff can get therapy for what
they see while dealing with their patients."

"What a strange word! How do you pronounce it? *The-ra-pee?*" she asks sarcastically.

I crack a genuine smile. "Alhamdulillah our humor is alive and well."

"It'll take more than that to break us." She winks before hurrying over to a crying child.

I watch her go, her words striking a chord. When I look into my heart, I expect to find it in shambles courtesy of Khawf's words and the military's actions, but I don't. Perhaps that was the case at the beginning, but now there's a candle lit in the darkness, illuminating my path. It promises a life.

"Congratulations, Salama," Am says from behind me, and I jump. He's wearing a worn-out brown jacket and there's the shadow of stubble on his face.

"Thank you," I say, but it tastes like sawdust in my mouth.

"Does the happy groom know about your broken moral compass?" His smile is anything but kind.

I go still. "Are you threatening me?"

He raises his hands. "God, no! We have an agreement. But I do think I'm within my rights to scare you after you nearly destroyed my life."

He holds out his hand, and I fish for the Panadol tablet in my pocket, then drop it in his palm. But before he walks away, I find the courage to say, "How's Samar?"

He stops, his back rigid, and pivots toward me. His eyes have gone murky brown with displeasure.

"I thought I told you this was a business—"

"I don't care," I interrupt. Acid roils in my stomach, but

I power through. "I may have done something horrible, but I still have a conscience."

A vein pulses on his forehead, then he answers slowly, "She's fine. Sutures are removed. No infection."

I let out a relieved sigh from deep within my gut, the acid's strength subduing.

"She has a scar," Am says. "That way we'll always remember you and your *conscience*."

He walks away and my stomach resumes digesting itself before I dash to retch into the sink.

Kenan and his siblings are standing in front of the hospital steps when I walk out at the end of my shift. Yusuf has a beat-up Spider-Man backpack and he's pawing the pebbles with his shoe, while Kenan holds Lama's hand, her pink Barbie backpack frayed at the edges. Kenan's bag is black.

My heart expands when I see them, and I hurry down the steps.

"Hey," I say, and Kenan smiles at me. "Long time no see."

I step to his side to brush Lama's light brown hair. "I missed you."

She beams, swinging the hand that's holding Kenan's.

I turn to Yusuf, who's still staring at the ground. "I missed you too, Yusuf."

He refuses to look at me, and another pebble clatters against the steps. I look at Kenan, confused. He'd been in a lighter mood after the ceremony; I had thought he would carry it with him throughout the day.

Kenan shakes his head sadly and in a low voice says,

"He's upset we left our apartment. Too much change happening today."

"Oh."

Kenan reaches over with his free hand and ruffles his brother's hair. Yusuf swats at his hand but there's no mistaking the concealed delight in his eyes—he's happy his older brother is giving him attention.

"You're fine?" he asks, and Yusuf shrugs.

Kenan sighs, turns to me, and picks Lama up. "I can't tell you how much I appreciate this. Our neighborhood has become one of the hardest spots to defend after the chemical attack. I don't think we could have stayed much longer."

I press a hand against my mouth, shocked. My eyes travel to the pale orange skies and I search for the planes. "Let's go."

Lama's chatter fills up the silence as we make our way back; it looks like she has gotten over her shyness. I walk to her side and she looks at me. Despite being a shade darker, her eyes hold the same intensity Kenan's do.

"How old are you?" she suddenly asks.

An amused smile tilts my lips up. "Eighteen."

She frowns, trying to calculate how much older that is than her. "Kenan's nineteen," she finally says.

"I know."

"And you married him," she says in a matter-of-fact tone.

"I did."

"Why? He's always on his laptop. Sometimes I have to yell three times before he hears me."

She says it in such a solemn tone I burst out laughing, and

Kenan's shoulders shake with his own suppressed laughter. Yusuf surges forward and grabs the hem of Kenan's sweater.

"Why are you laughing?" Lama demands.

I reach over and brush her cheek. "I'm sorry. You're just so cute."

Her nose scrunches as she debates with herself whether she should analyze this more or accept the compliment. She decides on the latter.

I look at Yusuf and smile. "I like your backpack. Spider-Man is really cool. Is he your favorite superhero?"

For the first time since I've met him, Yusuf's eyes brighten up and he nods once before pressing his lips together and clutching the straps. He breaks my heart. It's clear he's been forced to grow up so suddenly that he's holding on to anything resembling the innocence he lost. Normally by thirteen he would have thrown away his Spider-Man backpack for video games and meeting his friends for a football match in one of the alleys. His emotional growth is a plant that people forgot to water, so it tries to capture any moisture it can.

A crowd emerges from my neighborhood. Young men, women, and teenagers, all carrying various signs and banners for a protest, and Kenan's eyes trail after them. His jaw clenches and I immediately touch his elbow, trying desperately to tether him back to me. Back to the promise he's made.

The fiery gaze disappears when he looks down at me, and I can breathe again. I press a hand against my ring. His eyes fall on the movement and his gaze traces my scars.

My home looms in the distance and I take out my keys. My nerves suddenly come alive when I unlock the door as I realize that Kenan and I will be living under the same roof.

Together.

Where will he sleep? Layla will let me use her bedroom for Lama and Yusuf. Maybe she'll stay with me in mine, and Kenan can take the couch.

He'll be footsteps away from me. Just one hallway over.

"Layla," I call out when I walk in, banishing the butterflies from my stomach. "I'm home and Kenan and his siblings are here!"

Silence answers me and the hairs at the back of my neck stand on end. She's fine. I'm just a paranoid mess of a person who treats each bout of silence as danger.

"Come in," I say to Kenan. "Layla's probably still sleeping."

They shuffle inside and Kenan closes the door behind them. Everything feels too real. Kenan's height fills the narrow hallway and Yusuf peeks from behind his brother curiously. Kenan sets Lama on her feet and tells them both to take off their shoes while I go look for Layla.

When I walk into the living room, I see her sitting on the couch with a faraway look on her face. She's staring at her sea painting like she's trying to separate each brushstroke. Her hair dangles in waves over her shoulders, one hand resting on her stomach.

"Layla!" I say loudly, and she jumps.

"Salama! You scared me!"

"I was just calling you. Everything okay?"

She smiles but it looks haunting. "I'm good."

I take a step closer. "Are you sure? Why are you looking at me like that?"

She tucks her hair behind her ear. "Nostalgia for the good days. Remember when I painted that?" She nods at the sea painting.

"Of course."

She smiles lightly. "Remember how much I hated it when I was done?"

"The colors are all wrong!" she cried out, navy-blue streaks on her forehead and cheeks. She'd been painting for the last seven hours, not moving from her seat to drink or eat. Her daisy-printed apron was smeared with an assortment of blue and gray shades. She'd called me in a panic, barely able to get two words through the phone. "The shades! Ugh. It's garbage!"

I laughed, looking around the living room. Paint was flecked over the latex put down to protect the floors. The rest of the furniture had been stacked against the wall to make room for Layla's creativity. She stood in the center of the hurricane, tearfully holding up the canvas, her hair tied up in a messy bun.

"Are you kidding me?" I exclaimed, stepping over to her, careful not to kick the opened acrylic paint set. "Look at it!"

"I am!" she wailed. "It took seven *hours of my life, Salama!"*

I grabbed the canvas from her and set it over the mantelpiece. I made her stand in the middle, facing it. "No you're not. Close your eyes."

She did.

"Think of a storm deciding whether it'll rage through the sea. The middle of nowhere. No ship in sight. No human being. Imagine the colors no human would ever see. The storm will bellow and tear across the waves and no one will be there to witness it. Or maybe it won't. Maybe the clouds will break and the sun will shine."

She took a deep breath.

"Now open your eyes."

I smiled. "You captured something no one has ever seen before. Your imagination did that."

She turned to me, beaming. "Thank you."

"Do you remember that?" Layla asks again from the couch, and a strange lump forms in my throat.

"Yes."

"You made it one of my favorite paintings." There's something in her voice I can't decipher. Something melancholy.

"Then why do you look so sad?"

She shakes her head. "I'm not. I want you to know how incredible you are. How you touch people's lives."

"Salama?" Kenan says from behind me, and I immediately jump in front of Layla, hiding her from him. His brows are furrowed, his eyes glued to my face.

"*Kenan!*" I scold. "What are you doing? Layla's not wearing her hijab!"

"Layla?" he echoes.

"Yes!" I wave him away. "Layla, put on a scarf or something."

"I don't have anything," she answers glumly.

"Find something!" I say, exasperated.

Kenan's confusion deepens, and then his lips part. "Salama."

I peek over my shoulder to check if Layla's found a shawl or a tablecloth. She rummages through the cushions, pouting.

"*Salama.*" Kenan's voice comes out firmer, and I look at him.

"What?" I snap. "Why are you still here?"

He hesitates. "I came over because I heard you talking and no one was answering. I thought something had happened."

Now *I'm* confused. "*What?* I'm talking to Layla."

He steps toward me gently as if approaching a wounded deer. "No, you're not."

My arms fall heavily to my sides. "Excuse me?"

Kenan reaches for my hands, enveloping them in his warm ones. "Salama, no one's here. There's no Layla. I can't see her."

29

I LAUGH.

Kenan's expression is a mix of sadness and panic.

"Of course you can't see her," I say. "I'm standing in front of you, silly."

He runs a hand through his hair. "Standing in front of me isn't really hiding the couch."

I whirl around to see Layla perched on said couch, her hands hugging her pregnant belly. Her hair auburn and her eyes ocean blue and I can *see* her. I can smell and touch her.

"Layla?" I say in a panicked voice.

She smiles sadly. "I'm sorry, Salama."

A newfound fear drags my heart through a black abyss and I stumble forward, collapsing to my knees in front of her.

"Kenan," I say in a hollow voice. "I'm *begging* you. Please tell me you see her. Please tell me you see her face and the blue dress she's wearing."

Kenan shifts behind me. "I don't," he says softly. "It's just the couch."

Layla brushes my cheek. "I'm real in your heart."

A strangled sound escapes me. "No. *No*, you're not."

She bites her lip, tears trickling. "Remember the shooting in October?"

I am hollow. A burnt-out tree.

As she continues, each word she says pulls a thread, and another and another until I wholly unfurl. "I went to the grocery at the end of the road. There was a sniper. I didn't survive. I was bleeding but I was able to be carried home during my last moments. I died outside the front door."

My hands shake, agony splintering through my skeletal system, and I let out a choked scream.

I was at the hospital when it happened. Layla died without me there to hold her hand. Fragments of my memories come in splashes, seeping through the ones I've fabricated for myself. *I had run back home but it was all over. She was walking back from the supermarket when a military sniper's bullet went through her head. And the other through her uterus. The trail of blood outside on the cracked pavement is hers. It was thick, unwilling to dissolve into the soil. Just like that, she was taken away from me. And my niece was taken away. And I was all alone.*

Layla's burial was hurried, that very same day. Some of my neighbors helped me wash her and wrap her in white, and she was tucked beside her parents.

But I forgot all of that.

I woke up the next day to find her sitting on my bed with her cheeky grin and I . . . forgot.

No. I changed reality.

Layla's hands are on my cheeks and I shiver. I can *feel* her hands. "It wasn't your fault, do you understand me? You *didn't* break your promise to Hamza."

My sobs are dry, heaving painfully through my chest, and I can't form coherent words. I've been living *alone* since October. For five months my mind has been spinning a fiction to keep my agony sealed away.

I gaze at her face, trying to commit her to memory. I needed her in my life. I needed that comfort and safety after I lost my whole world. The small moments of happiness I experienced with her were a lifeline. I know I'm owed so much, so I forged my own *might* life. She let me heal bit by bit. She's as real to me as anything.

Her thumbs stroke my cheeks and she smiles, blue eyes brighter than a star. "You know I'm in Heaven. You know I'm safe and happy. So is Baby Salama." She presses a hand to my chest. "You have your faith *here*. You will live for me, for your parents, and for Hamza. You'll keep your promise to him by saving yourself."

"Don't go," I beg. "Please."

She takes my hands in hers and kisses my knuckles. "You have a family now, Salama. You're not alone."

A heavy, solid hand rests on my shoulder. So different from Layla's touch, which feels more like a cloud whispering along my hands. I blink through tear-stained eyes and turn around and see Kenan's sorrowful stare.

"Salama," he whispers. "It's okay. You're okay."

I look around. The living room is dull and the colors murky. The Arabian rug beside the couch has a thick layer of dust on top. A cold aura hangs in the air; it gives the place an abandoned feel. It reminds me of how it was when Kenan walked me home after Lama's surgery. This does not look like the home that Layla and Hamza put pieces of their souls into. This is not how I've been seeing it these past months. That place was softer and brighter with Layla's touch.

And I realize I haven't said anything for some time. The shock has forced me to retreat to where Layla exists. In my mind.

Kenan draws me to him, and I let him wrap his arms around my shoulders, my back to his chest. He becomes my solid wall to lean on, and my muscles loosen.

"Salama," Layla says softly, and the world becomes brighter again.

She stands in front of me, cradling my cheeks, but her touch is barely there. I can hardly feel it now.

"It's not your fault," she says.

I swallow hard.

"Hamza would never want you to blame yourself. I don't blame you. No one does." Her expression is fierce.

I nod.

Satisfied with my answer, she takes a deep breath, and when I blink, she's gone.

Kenan's hold on me slackens, but I immediately grab his hands before turning into his embrace, hugging him tightly. I bury my face in his sweater, inhaling his lemon scent.

"You're real, right?" I finally whisper. "Please be real."

He lifts my head up and the stars are still in his eyes.

"I'm real," he says firmly. He takes my hand and presses it against his chest. His heartbeat pushes against his ribs and the vibrations jump along my skin. I close my eyes for a few seconds, relishing the feel of it. I don't think I can ever let him go.

I nod and press my lips together to stop myself from crying when I see Lama and Yusuf peeking from behind the wall.

Kenan notices them as well and his face changes. He beckons them over before crouching to his knees to hug them. All the while he doesn't let go of my hand, which makes for an awkward hug, but he's determined not to let go.

"Where's Layla?" Lama asks, looking around with a curiosity that turns to apprehension when she sees my red eyes.

Kenan grimaces and he looks at me. I nod once.

"Layla's in Heaven," Kenan says gently.

Lama frowns. "But you said we will live with Salama *and* Layla."

Kenan looks away, not knowing how to find the exact words to explain it to her. But Yusuf's eyes suddenly widen with the realization and his gaze darts to me. Emotions flicker on his face.

In the quiet space between us, he sees me. Not as the girl with nerves of steel who saved his sister. Or the girl who fell for his brother and took him away. He sees himself in me as I saw myself in him.

Kenan finds the words carefully and Lama listens, but I don't.

I'm looking at the window where the curtains flutter with a light breeze and a single ray of sunlight passes through, dropping on the Arabian rug.

30

I LAY ON THE COUCH, IN LAYLA'S SPOT, FOR MOST of the evening. Kenan asked if I wanted privacy, but I don't. Not now. I've been alone for the past five months and the thought of it makes the hairs on the back of my neck stand with horror. Alone. I talked to thin air. I laughed with thin air. I cried with thin air. Now I fill up my eyes and ears with real, breathing people.

Lama and Yusuf have a simple dinner of canned tuna, and I almost smack myself at my naivete. Layla never ate with me; I always assumed she ate when I was at the hospital. That should have tipped me off. All her touches, her mannerisms, were echoes of ones in my strongest memories of her. Everything about her was my memories magnified until she became solid.

My heart is at ease, knowing she's in Heaven. My regret is that I wasn't there in her final moments.

I remember the last day I had with her. The real her.

We were sitting on the Arabian rug in the living room

right in front of the couch, and she was laughing herself silly about the time our car got stuck in the sand in the suburbs.

"You thought Hamza would kill you for ruining his car," she giggled, clutching her stomach. She was three months into her pregnancy and her bump was small.

I grinned. "I overestimated the sand's depth."

Layla and I wanted to be spontaneous and drive out of the city toward my grandparents' summer house. I thought I'd take a shortcut, but we ended up stuck in a ditch with the evening fast approaching.

Her eyes twinkled. "I loved that day. Sure we had to endure Hamza yelling at us for half an hour before he pulled the car out, but remember how the stars looked?"

They were hanging from the dark sky like lemons, ripe for the taking and so near. "I do."

"I hope we can see them like that again." Layla patted her stomach over the blanket I'd tucked around her. "If not in Syria, then somewhere else."

She wanted to leave but was too afraid to form the words. I rub my forehead exhaustedly and sink into the pillow that somehow still has her daisy scent. My hijab hangs loosely from my head, wrapped around my neck. I'm too shy to take it off just yet. But I do pull my necklace out and run my wedding ring up and down the chain.

"Hey," Kenan says in a low voice. He's standing at the living room door.

"Hey."

"Lama and Yusuf are asleep on your bed." He looks flustered, which in turn makes me flustered. He's been inside my room, and I can't for the life of me recall whether I left it in disarray. I hope not.

He kneels in front of me and I instinctively clutch the blankets closer. "I'm so sorry about Layla," he whispers.

A lump forms in my throat and I extend my hand. He immediately holds it, and I press his hand against my cheek, relishing its solid feel. His fingers are calloused, proof of a hard life, but they're warm with the blood running in his veins. "I'm okay. Maybe it's shock, but . . . I think it's acceptance. She's all right, and that's all I ever wanted for her."

He brushes my cheek, smiling lightly, and I melt into his touch. But a thought has struck me.

"Why am I leaving now?" I whisper, and he pauses. "My whole reason was to honor Hamza's wishes. And now . . . I've lost Mama and Layla. I didn't keep my promise."

Kenan threads his fingers through mine, brings my hands to his lips, and kisses them. "Salama, you can't stay."

His eyes are full of terror.

"You knew you were hallucinating Khawf; but you thought Layla was alive," he murmurs. "I'm worried for you. Staying here, in the place where she died, it'll only make it worse. You won't be able to help anyone if you don't help yourself first."

I close my eyes for a few seconds, remembering my hallucination beside the wreckage of my home. When my brain reconstructed my neighborhood back to life.

"I'm not leaving Syria without you," Kenan continues. "You said it yourself, the fight isn't just here. You are needed outside just as much as I am. And I can't sit back and watch you be in pain like this and not know how to help."

His tone is beseeching, his expression desperate. Mirroring mine when I asked him to stop recording. I can't do this to him. Staying wouldn't benefit any of us. It would mean I'd continue breaking my promise to Hamza. I'm still alive and he'd want me to stay that way.

"Okay," I whisper.

His face sags with relief. But there's a look in his eyes that makes me believe he has more to say. I wait, but instead he fishes something from his pocket and hands me a folded piece of paper. "I drew you something else."

My heart soars but I don't open it. An uneasy feeling pricks my nerves and my stomach flips. Kenan had been more than understanding about Khawf, never wavering. But I had warned him about Khawf. Layla is another story.

"Kenan, what are you thinking?" I ask quietly. My palms sweat.

He glances at me and his Adam's apple dips. "What you went through with Layla, I get it. I've wished every day to be able to see my parents again. And I've seen what PTSD has done to me, to Lama, and especially to Yusuf. I can deal with what I know, and I've taught myself how to help. Lama's wounds, Yusuf's shock, my nightmares. But Salama, I'm scared of what I *don't* know." He lets out a shaky breath. "I don't know how to fix this. I don't know what to say or do to help you. I've reached the limit of what I can *do*."

I brush his hair back and his eyelashes flutter. He's so young and stretched so thin between three people and an entire country. "You being here is enough." I smile. "I promise. You ground me."

He smiles back. Tentatively at first, and then it becomes genuine. "When we get to Germany, we'll find help."

He again thinks it could happen. And it might. So I nod.

"Let me see what you drew," I say, and I open it to see a sketch of . . . me. He drew me as Sheeta with her yellow blouse and pink trousers. My hijab is a pale pink and I'm sitting atop an airplane's wing. And beside me . . .

"Oh my God, is this you?" I exclaim.

He smiles shyly. "Yeah. As Pazu."

He takes out another piece of paper. "This is another sketch for our story. I detailed the house our protagonist would live in. I was thinking the community would build them on trees. Like a whole village suspended in the air."

"Growing crops and flowers on the tree's branches. So the tree would supply its own nutrients to the growing plants!"

He beams. "That's an amazing idea."

We spend the rest of the evening slowly building up our story, adding elements.

Kenan drifts off before me, his head nodding, until I get off the couch so he can stretch out properly. He protests for a bit, but ultimately sleep weighs his eyelids down. I tuck the blanket around him, and the nostalgia of having done that for Layla when she was alive—and in my hallucinations—makes tears prick my eyes.

He looks peaceful in his sleep, the worry lines around his eyes smoothed. His eyelashes are so impossibly long that they brush his cheekbones.

I stare at him for a few more minutes, my heart expanding with love for him.

"We'll be okay," I whisper, letting the night capture my wish. We're owed that at least. A life of not scanning rooftops, of not being relieved the ceiling didn't cave in on us during the night.

He and I are owed a love story that doesn't end in tragedy.

With my bed and the couch both occupied, the only place left is Layla and Hamza's room. I pause in front of the door, my fingers over the handle. I take in a deep breath and open it with a click.

A rush of cold air greets me. The room still has hints of Layla's daisy scent and Hamza's cologne. Or maybe it's a hallucination.

I don't turn on the lights, instead letting my corneas and lenses adapt to the darkness. I run a finger over the forgotten furniture. A thick layer of dust lines the bedspread, commode, closet, and nightstand. I haven't set foot inside in five months. The room has become a relic, belonging to memories, never wanting to be revived. Or probably it's impossible to revive. Just like Layla. Like Hamza.

I sit on their bed, feeling oddly comforted. As if echoes of them are here. I close my eyes for a brief second and I know that when I open them he'll be standing in front of me.

And he is.

The red dots on Khawf's shoulders look like poppies in their shade and shape, and his eyes are blue ice chips gleaming in the darkness. He gives me a lopsided smirk.

"You knew," I whisper. There's no shock in me. My head

scar and everything it represents—my grief, my PTSD—
has created layers in my subconscious that I never thought
were possible.

He shrugs. "It was quite amusing to see the degree of
your delusions."

I don't say anything; I look at the window on the side. The
curtains aren't drawn tight, which allows a bit of the moon's
light to filter through. Soon enough we'll be safe. And I won't
have to look out the windows and pretend the world isn't
on fire.

Khawf takes a step toward me, and I tear my gaze back
to him.

"What do you believe in, Salama?" he asks quietly. A
shadow flits across his face, a secret smile dancing on his lips.

My mouth goes dry. "What do you mean?"

He takes out a cigarette. The white tube flickers,
becoming almost translucent before going back to opaque.
"You believe in your faith. You believe in yourself. In Kenan.
In Layla, when she was alive. You believe this revolution will
be a success with the people sacrificing their hearts."

"Yes."

He takes a drag. "Did you believe in Layla the *hallucination*?"

I nod.

"Do you believe in me?" His smile widens.

My brows furrow. "You're right in front of me. Of
course I do."

He taps the cigarette, ash falling, but it disappears mid-
way. His gaze is far away. He looks at me, but it feels like he's
seeing beyond me. "I am. But I won't always be."

I straighten up. I know he won't always be in my life. But hearing him say it both saddens and elates me. "How?" I ask.

He flicks the cigarette away and moves toward the window. "Fear and dread run high in Syria. They're enhanced in you, which is why you see me. It's safe to presume you won't have these same horrors in Germany. So why would I follow you there?"

I stand, putting the pieces together. "You mean . . . when I get on that boat—when I leave—"

"*I* leave," he finishes for me. He turns around and we stare at each other for a few minutes.

In this moment, he looks so solid, as if he were cut from the night and made into flesh and bones.

"Where would you go?" I find myself asking the silliest of questions, but Khawf doesn't laugh. His face is solemn, his eyes ancient.

He closes the gap between us, and I raise my chin to look at him.

"Everywhere," he answers and then disappears when I blink.

31

KENAN TAKES ME TO THE HOSPITAL THE NEXT morning. Lama and Yusuf remain at home. I made sure Lama had a water bottle beside her to stay hydrated. Kenan stays by my side, talking to the patients and helping the doctors when needed. We're still recovering from the chemical attack and lost some patients in the middle of the night, but it makes me breathe easier to have Kenan near me.

My mind goes on autopilot for some time as I replay the conversation I had with Khawf last night. In less than a week, I'll be free of him. In two weeks I'll be in Europe, in a new city, surrounded by people who don't speak my language. Homs will feel light-years away from me. But I'll feel every wound inflicted here, every bomb falling, every life lost. I will feel Hamza's agony, never knowing if he died. It will continue to slice away at me until I'm bone. And when it reaches the bone, it will scrape away the endosteum, burrowing into the medullary cavity and reaching the marrow.

And yet, the fight here continues.

The protests have spread far and wide throughout several Syrian cities. Hama, Douma, Ghouta, Deir ez-Zour. Every one of them is outraged at the escalating bombings we in Homs are facing. Kafranbel has the most beautiful, creative signs. I wonder how the outside world fares, how they sleep at night knowing we're being butchered in our sleep. How they allow this to happen.

Kenan's hand slides into mine when we walk back home, and I empty my mind of everything save for him. I furtively steal glances at him. He hasn't seen my hair yet and we're properly married. He hasn't asked me to, and we never talked about what degree of physical affection we'd feel comfortable showing each other here. Our love story may be unconventional given the circumstances, but why can't we grab at the small moments of happiness? I want to make a home and find joy in Homs before we leave. My last memories don't have to be full of anguish and loss.

We're all sitting, having a simple dinner together in the kitchen and going over the list of what we'll be bringing, when Kenan looks at me like he's just remembered something.

"Salama, you were going to pay Am for Layla's seat on the boat, right?"

My spoon clatters into the tuna I've been shoving around my plate for the past five minutes. "Right. I don't have to do that anymore."

That's five hundred dollars added to my savings. I doubt Am would want it over the more valuable gold ring I promised him for Kenan's seat. I stare wistfully at the table, wishing I could hug Layla now.

Kenan clears his throat. "What else are we missing?"

I'm grateful for the distraction. "Something to fight the seasickness. Layla suggested we use lemons."

"That sounds like a great idea," Kenan says gently. "I'll pass by the grocery tomorrow and see if there's any. The weather is still pretty cold, so they'll last until we leave."

After dinner, we all pray Isha together. Lama and Yusuf stay up for a bit before going to bed, and I slip to the bathroom to wash my face.

In the mirror I try to find the girl Kenan sees, the one with the beautiful eyes, but all I see are my sunken cheeks and pointed chin. I *used* to be beautiful. My olive-toned skin, glowing with life, was soft. My brown hair, deeper than a wild tree's bark, matched my eyes, and it was something I was rather proud of. I tug on my hijab. It drapes against my neck and my hair unknots from its bun. The brown shade has faded; it looks washed-out as it falls across my shoulders.

In that *might* life, I would be winking at myself, admiring the way the blue eyeliner contrasted with my chocolate-brown eyes and how my sharp collarbones peeked through my off-shoulder dress. Kenan would blush when he saw me, unable to look away.

Well, at least this is my favorite sweater, I think glumly. A soft maroon. Sighing deeply, I tug my necklace out so the gold ring rests brightly against the cotton material and steel myself to walk out, leaving my hijab behind.

Flickering lights seep out of the living room and into the hallway, shadows dancing on the floor. Kenan must have lit the candles, and I peer from behind the wall, suddenly feeling self-conscious.

Kenan sits on the couch, one elbow propped against the arm, gazing at the sea painting. The candlelight illuminates his face in a magical way, washing him in gold. Suddenly my sweater is too hot.

He feels me standing there and turns my way, his face breaking into a smile.

"What are you doing?" he says, a hint of teasing in his voice. The night and feeble candlelight hide me from his eyes. "Are you *staring* at me?"

"Maybe." I grip the wall's edges.

He grins. "I have to tell you, I'm a married man now. My wife won't like it if random girls ogle me."

The heat on my face spreads up to my hair's roots. *Wife.*

"But if you insist on doing so, how about you do it up close?" He pats the seat beside him.

I clear my throat, tucking my hair behind my ear, and slowly step out.

His grin slips, replaced with a sharp intake of breath, and his mouth falls open.

Our quiet breaths fill the silence. I find it hard to look at him, so I stare at the rug, following its whorls. A full minute passes before he says, "Salama."

His voice is breathless, and it sends shivers along my spine. I hug myself, and he stands, crossing over to me until he's a whisper away. His lemon scent takes over the tiny space and he lifts my chin to stare into my eyes. My heart is hotter than the sun, its fiery tendrils spreading along my vascular system.

"Beautiful," he murmurs. There's reverence and awe in his tone. In his touch. In his eyes. "So beautiful."

I let out a nervous laugh. "You don't have to humor me."

He looks confused. "I'm not." He reaches up to thread his fingers through my curls, and my eyelashes flutter. "I wish you could see yourself the way I see you."

He holds up a lock of my hair. "Your hair is beautiful."

His fingers skim my cheeks. "Your face is beautiful."

He presses a hand against my chest, over my wedding ring. "Your heart is beautiful."

My knees tremble and I stumble back until my spine hits the wall. He moves with me, holding my waist.

"But I can get specific if you want," he whispers.

"I don't mind," I stutter.

Amusement glitters in his jade-green eyes and he presses a kiss to my forehead. "I like your forehead."

That makes me laugh and it eases the nerves crackling through me.

"I like your laugh." He grins. "No, scratch that. I *love* your laugh."

With a soft sigh, I absently clasp my hands on his shoulders, pulling him closer. Pleased, he kisses my nose. "I love your nose." Then my cheeks. "I love your cheeks." Then atop the pulse in my throat. "I love your neck."

My lips tingle when he hovers over them, and I count down the seconds until they touch, but he stills.

"What else do you love?" I finally whisper, my eyes half closed.

Kenan smiles. "Your lips."

And he kisses me. It's a soft, tentative kiss that coaxes a kaleidoscope of colors to twirl behind my eyelids. I cup his face and his stubble pricks my palms, but I hardly feel it with the heady effect his kiss has on me. I exist in this canopy where time stands still and washes away all my worries.

All but one.

Regret snatches me away from the moment and I push my hands against his chest.

Kenan stops, letting go immediately, concern clouding his eyes. He holds up hands. "I'm sorry. I took it too far."

I shake my head, heartbeat thundering. "You didn't." I shudder in a shaky breath, trying to regulate my pulmonary activity. I can't keep the secret about Samar inside me for one more second. It'll continue to creep up on every happy moment.

"I have to tell you something," I say and move to sit on the couch.

He sits beside me, cracking his knuckles nervously.

"You said I'm strong. That I have a beautiful heart." I focus on my hands, which were pressed against his skin seconds ago. "But I'm not. I did . . . something. It was a rash decision, and I regret it so much."

Kenan draws closer. "What?"

I take another deep breath and tell him everything. From how I couldn't afford the boat to endangering Samar's life for it. I don't leave out any detail. By the end, my eyes are closed, hot tears pricking the edges.

"If I could take it back, I would," I whisper.

Kenan's hand finds mine and he squeezes it tightly, prompting me to look at him. There's hurt in his eyes, but there's also understanding.

"Is this why you've lost so much weight? And all the times you've vomited?" he asks.

A lump forms in my throat. Of course he'd notice that. "Yes," I say, breathless.

He tugs me to him, and I fall against his chest. "You've paid your debts," he whispers, wrapping his arm around me, and he kisses my forehead. "Samar is alive, you've made sure of it, and that's all that matters."

"But—"

He shakes his head fiercely. "We're human, Salama. Pushed into a corner, we're forced to make decisions we wouldn't normally make. You were thinking of Layla when you did that. I'm not saying it was right, but you've suffered enough for it. You saved her life and you saved many, *many* after her."

I swallow a sob and bury my face in the worn material of his sweater, breathing him in deeply.

He lifts my head up, brushing my hair back, and his touch awakens butterflies in my stomach. He looks solemn. "It's okay."

I press my forehead against his chest and a relieved sigh escapes me.

"I love you," I murmur.

32

"I'M TALKING TO MY UNCLE TODAY TO SEE WHEN he's coming to Syracuse," Kenan says as I shrug on my lab coat. "I'll check the grocery at the end of the street, and if they don't have any lemons, I'll go to the one by the hospital."

"Okay. Be careful." I stifle a yawn. We dozed off on the couch in the early hours of the morning when our sleep-deprived bodies couldn't run on fumes anymore. But I was able to stomach the small tuna sandwich Kenan made me for breakfast. That alone has given me a boost of energy.

He kisses my cheek. "I'll see you after your shift."

When I get to the hospital, Dr. Ziad has me check on some of the patients whose respiratory systems have taken a major hit from the sarin. A few more passed during the night, most of them children, their faces still frozen in petrified expressions. I swallow down the breakfast threatening to come up. I hand out water and administer antibiotics and anesthetics until noon.

When I finally stumble into the main atrium, I find Dr. Ziad alone, and it strikes me as strange.

"Doctor, is everything all right?" I ask. I haven't told him I'm leaving, not knowing how to put it into words, and guilt twists in my soul.

He grimaces. "The chemical attack has weakened the FSA's defenses greatly. They're finding it difficult to hold up against the military's tanks."

Air vanishes from my lungs. "What does that mean?"

"It means we need to pray. The FSA is doing everything they can, but we have no one but God now."

I close my eyes, my lips mouthing a supplication.

Dr. Ziad smiles sadly. "If we die, Salama, at least we die doing the right thing. We die as martyrs."

And I'll see Layla, Baby Salama, Mama, and Baba again. Hopefully Hamza as well.

"Death doesn't scare me, Doctor," I whisper. "It's being taken alive."

He shudders, nodding. "Insh'Allah it doesn't come to that."

A patient calls for him and he walks away, leaving me stewing in my thoughts. It's clear Dr. Ziad thinks we have but days, if not moments, of fragile safety before the walls come crashing down.

I have to find Am. I search all the patients' rooms before locating him at the back door, chewing on a toothpick.

"Am," I say, and he straightens.

"What?"

I let out a breath. "Have you heard what the people are saying?"

He must have. People talk. Members of the Free Syrian Army live among us. He gives me a half shrug. "I've heard enough."

"What if the military breaches before the twenty-fifth?" I ask in a low voice lest I invoke the breach myself.

He sighs. "Salama, I'm the person who gets the boat. I'm not a military man or someone with influence. I stand to lose more than money if that were to happen, but some things are outside my control. This is one of them."

"Can't we leave earlier?" I ask. "Like today?"

He shakes his head. "I know the guards stationed at the borders. I know their timing and shifts. The ones letting us through will be there on the twenty-fifth. We risk all our lives if we gamble with guards I don't know. There are ones who'll take you *and* your money. No law holds them accountable." Flashes of the horror Khawf showed me the day before the protest appear before my eyes and I stifle a terrified gasp.

Am steps toward me, and it surprises me to see his face full of pity. "Salama, you've done everything. The rest is up to God. To fate. If you're meant to be in Munich, you will be, even if the whole military rips this place apart. And if you're not, then not even a private plane landing in the middle of Freedom Square to whisk you away will do that."

I'm taken aback. These are words I believe to my core, as does every Muslim. Fate has his strings, but we're the ones who twist them together with our actions. My belief in what's meant to be doesn't make me a passive player. No. I fight and fight and fight for my life. Layla fought for hers. Kenan fights for his. And whatever happens, we accept the outcome, knowing we did everything. I haven't heard these words in a while and it jerks something awake in me to hear them from Am of all people.

"Thank you," I whisper. I consider telling him it'll just be four people on that boat, but somehow the words can't make it past the haze of grief.

"Khalid Mosque, ten a.m.," he reminds me. "It's just three more days."

I nod, feeling my resolve strengthen. Am's words sustain me for the rest of the day until exhaustion wobbles my knees.

When the sky becomes a bright orange, I sit on the broken steps of the hospital, letting my thoughts find one another. There's a serenity in this silence. Thankfully, there have been no victims from bombs or military attacks today. It unnerves me for a few seconds; we've never had a pause on the attacks before. A horrible thought whispers to me that the military might be planning something, but I banish it away when I see Kenan walking out of the hospital.

He lights up when he sees me, and I can't stop the smile on my face. He sits beside me, stretching his long legs in front of him, and I lean my head against his shoulder.

"Long day?" he asks.

"Yeah."

He links his fingers in mine and raises my hand to his lips. His breath is warm against it, and he kisses my scars.

"Thank you for your hard work. Thank you for saving lives," he whispers, and my eyes sting with tears. I've had people thank me before, but it's always when terror was running high, and I've never had the capacity to absorb their words. No one's ever said it to me during the quiet moments. No one who knows the horrors I go through, the fight I put up every single day, has truly seen me and said those words.

My soul expands with love for him.

He notices the tears and becomes alarmed. "What happened? Did I say something wrong?"

I shake my head, rubbing my eyes. "No. I'm fine."

He still looks worried, so I throw my arms around his shoulders and hug him. "I really am fine. But you've made me think of something."

"What?" he replies, his voice muffled in my shoulder.

"I think I want to stay at the hospital these last three days. Help as many people as I can before I leave."

He leans back. "You mean stay here at night?"

I nod. "You don't have to stay with me. Lama and Yusuf will need you."

He cracks his fingers. "You know the military is closing in. If they're able to get into our part of the city, they'll come here straight away and . . ." His words collapse on top of each other, and he goes silent.

I smile, touching his cheek and think back to what Dr. Ziad told me this morning. "Kenan, they'll also go to each house, break down the door, steal, destroy, rape, and kill. Or they'll arrest us. You know this. So, if we might die, I want to die at the hospital doing something to help. Not hiding in my house."

I know Layla would be proud of me. I wish I could tell her.

Kenan looks away and his eyelashes flutter. I know he's holding back tears from the tightness of his lips.

"All right," he finally says and takes both my hands in his. "But we don't split up. I'll bring Lama and Yusuf here and we stay together until the boat arrives."

And I fall for him even more. I was too shy to ask him to stay with me. I didn't want him to choose between me and his siblings. His siblings are a part of him. They're his responsibility and I'm a newcomer in his world, trying to find a space to fit in. But he's made more than enough room for me.

"We stay together," I agree.

He presses a quick kiss to my forehead before jumping to his feet. "I'll be back within the hour."

I grab his hand and squeeze it. "Be safe."

He smiles. I miss his hand as soon as it leaves mine, and I watch him until he crosses the gates and turns around to wave at me before disappearing behind the wreckage.

I sigh. I look at the sky and send a quick prayer for him.

"Layla," I murmur, watching the first stars begin to twinkle. "Mama. Baba. I hope Hamza is with you. I imagine you're all sitting beside one another laughing and eating and drinking. I love you and miss you so much. But . . . I don't want to join you just yet. I want you to meet Kenan later. When he and I have grown old and had a lifetime together. I still have more in me. I can still go on. I know I can. Because I know that's what you'd want me to do."

I take in a deep breath and feel serenity settle in my heart. Being a hair away from death fills me with calmness I never knew could be possible. I've done my part. I will continue to fight for what I'm owed and whatever happens, I'm okay with that.

The breeze rustles through the budding leaves on the trees, and I feel Khawf sitting beside me.

He doesn't say anything, and neither do I.

After a few minutes, I get up and walk back into the hospital.

33

LAMA AND YUSUF PROTESTED AT HAVING TO MOVE again until Kenan promised them all the candy they want when we get to Germany. Now they're settling in one of the rooms that's been put aside for the children whose family members are at the hospital recovering.

The children there are already sleeping, a couple of them crying out occasionally and others restlessly kicking their legs. Kenan finds a space in a corner for Lama and Yusuf. Lama falls asleep as soon as Kenan sets her on the blanket. Yusuf lies beside her, his eyes as huge as an owl's.

He glances at me and I smile. He looks away, and even in the dim light filtering through the opened door I can see his blush.

Kenan makes sure they're both covered and warm before closing the door behind him.

"Aren't you sleepy?" I ask, glancing at the hallway clock. It's nearly ten p.m.

He shakes his head. "I can't sleep while my wife works."

There's that word again. *Wife.*

He notices my flustered expression and grins. "Wife," he repeats.

I stop, covering my face with my hands, unable to look at him without bursting into flames. He holds my wrists, dragging them away.

"Look at me," he whispers.

"If I do, my heart might stop," I reply, staring at the floor, and then looking over his shoulder and around us. "We can't do this here. Anyone could walk by."

He responds by taking my hand and walking us through the hallway. I feel like I'm supposed to feel in a *might* life. A teen sneaking away with the boy she loves, her heart racing. We reach the stockroom and he closes the door behind us, backing me against it.

He doesn't touch me, doesn't raise my chin, but he's a breath away from me.

"Would you look at me now?" he asks. His voice is low and throaty, dancing over my skin. I look up at him and catch the amusement in his eyes. A peek of who he is when the revolution isn't forcing him to build a shield and hide pieces of himself. The realization makes me laugh and he raises his eyebrows. "That wasn't the response I was expecting."

"You're a flirt, aren't you?" I chuckle.

He shakes his head, laughing. "You're just realizing this now?"

I give him a curious look.

"Salama, I've been flirting with you ever since we met," he says. "I guess it was a bit too subtle."

"Well, what else do you have up your sleeve?" I ask,

feeling emboldened in the privacy of this room. This tiny place exists outside reality. As do all our times together.

A secretive smile plays on his lips, and he lowers his head. I instinctively close my eyes, waiting for his lips to touch mine, but he doesn't kiss me. Instead, he lays his forehead against the door right beside my ear and his body is flush against mine.

Somehow this feels more intimate.

It's too hot under my sweater and I press myself firmly against the door until I'm sure I'm about to fuse with it.

"I've thought so much about the time stolen from us," he whispers, and I nearly sigh. His voice is so close. "If things weren't like they are, we'd be long married. I would take you all over Syria on a road trip. We'd visit every city and village. See the history that lives in our country. I'd kiss you on the beaches of Latakia, pick flowers for you in Deir ez-Zour, take you to my family home in Hama, have a picnic under the ruins of Palmyra. People would look at us and they'd think how they've never seen two people more in love."

I can't move. I can't breathe. I hope he never stops talking.

"I wanted so many things," he says and rests his forehead on my shoulder. Melancholy drips from his tone. "But meeting you, loving you . . . you made me realize how life can be salvaged. That we deserve to have happiness in this long night."

Finally, he leans back and gazes at me so tenderly I might actually start weeping.

"Thank you for being my light," he whispers.

And this time, I don't wait for him to kiss me.

I link my arms around his neck, pulling him in. The kiss is sweet, and it fills me with hope for a future where I'll wake up in his arms, no nightmares dragging us down. Just us in a house we made into a home with a flowering garden and half-filled sketchbooks.

He tilts my chin up, staring deeply into my eyes, and says, "We'll be okay."

"Insh'Allah," I whisper.

We pass by Dr. Ziad when we go into the atrium holding hands. He doesn't say anything, just smiles at us and rushes to check on a patient. I guess seeing me leaning on someone for support is putting him at ease.

That night, Kenan becomes an assistant, helping me around the hospital. He's a quick learner, and after showing him how to change bandages without wasting gauze, he's able to do it on his own.

We sneak glances at each other, smiling foolishly before looking back at our work, and it's the strangest feeling.

When the rhythm at the hospital slows, Kenan and I sit on the floor against one of the walls, exhaustion finally overcoming us. All the beds are taken, so he gestures for me to lay my head on his lap, and I do, too bone-tired to feel flustered. I fall into a state of dissociation from reality, not quite asleep and not awake. Somewhere in between. It's as if my mind and body aren't able to fully rest.

Around the early hours of the morning a loud crash not far away jolts us all. Like shrapnel falling. Like a tank's rifle puncturing a building. I clamber to my feet, heart in my throat, and Kenan wakes with a gasp.

"What's happening?" he asks wildly.

"I don't know."

Another crash. This time closer, and the patients who can move scramble, fleeing to the walls and deeper into the hospital's hallways. Children cry and panicked voices echo against the ceiling.

"Kenan, get up," I say in a hollow voice. Urgency swells in my heart. "Now! We have to get Lama and Yusuf."

Whatever is happening outside, it's coming here, and when it does it'll leave the hospital in ruins.

KENAN GRABS MY HAND, BUT BEFORE WE'RE ABLE
to take a step, the hospital doors burst open and five soldiers walk in. Their green military uniforms reek of murder, their rifles hanging across chests that are bare of the
Free Syrian Army's flag. One takes out a handgun and
shoots a patient execution style. A little girl with an eye-
patch and two mismatched hair ties.

I stop dead in my tracks and grab Kenan's arm. We stare
as the little girl slumps over, a pool of blood swallowing her
small body, staining her short black hair.

A woman screams, and the sound of it tears into my gut.
She falls to her knees beside the girl and hugs her close, all
the while begging her to be alive.

"Te'eburenee!" she wails.

Another shot and the girl's body slumps back with a low
thud to the floor as her mother joins her.

"Anyone else want to say something?" the soldier shouts.

The terrified wailing is instantly muted, and muffled

whimpers fill the space. I can barely focus over the thundering of my heart and force myself to think. Where's the rest of his group? The military would never send only five soldiers into FSA territory. Are they right behind them?

The soldiers fan out, strutting between patients, whacking the occasional one across the face or digging the butts of their rifles into their injuries.

"Does that hurt?" they mock. I pray the FSA gets here before the rest of the military joins them.

Kenan's arm tenses under my hand and I know he's thinking of Lama and Yusuf. They're just down the hall and will have definitely woken up with the other children.

He slowly pulls me closer. "Take off your lab coat," he whispers so quietly I barely catch the words.

Terror freezes my blood. Being a girl and a pharmacist makes me a special kind of target. I'll be accused of helping and healing rebels. I'll be tortured with the very tools I use to save people. I'll be raped.

Kenan shifts deliberately until I'm behind him, his back covering me. I grasp at my sleeves and pull them down ever so slightly.

But as I do so, my eyes catch on a little girl of about seven cowering against the wall as one of the soldiers advances on her. Her arm is in a sling, a set of old bandages wrapped around her head, and her eyes are bulging with fear. In her face I see Ahmad. I see Samar. I see how this will happen to Lama and Yusuf. I see a girl whose last minuscule shred of innocence is about to be torn to pieces.

And without thinking, I move.

I grab a discarded basin and fling it at the soldier's back.

It promptly hits him and clatters to the floor. Silence settles over the atrium, broken only by the soldier's grunt of pain. My arm shakes as the soldier turns slowly.

Better me than the little girl.

His gaze rolls over me and the trembling spreads all over my body.

"Did *you* just throw that?" he barks.

At his tone, Kenan immediately clamps his hand in mine and pulls me back, but the soldier is faster. He grabs my other arm, yanking me out of Kenan's grasp, and I turn to glimpse the shock and terror in Kenan's eyes as I'm suddenly slammed against the wall.

The soldier's forearm presses against my throat, holding me tightly in place, a squeeze away from being strangled.

"You think you're real brave, huh?" he says, spitting the words.

From the corners of my eyes I see Kenan restrained by two soldiers. His face contorts with fury, curses spilling from his mouth. One of them slams the butt of his gun against Kenan's face, and blood spurts from his cheek. I try to get to him, but the soldier shoves me back against the wall. Hard enough that I can't breathe for a bit.

"You work here? You're healing these rebels? All these traitors?" he sneers.

"Get off me," I snarl, not knowing where the courage is coming from. But I don't fear death. Khawf has shown me the worst outcomes. And what stands before me is no man, only an animal in human skin.

The soldier laughs and lets go of me. Before I fully comprehend what's happening, a sharp pain shoots through the side of my head and I'm slammed against the wall again. I groan, eyes closed, trying to get my bearings through the hammering in my brain. It takes me a few seconds to realize he's hit me with the metallic part of his rifle. I wipe my arm over my lips and find them coated with blood. It hurts to breathe, the air coming in and out in wheezes. It hurts even more to look at Kenan and see pure fear in his eyes.

"You don't tell me what to do," I hear the soldier snap.

"I'll *kill* you!" Kenan bellows, blood dripping to the floor.

The soldier turns toward him, raises his gun right at Kenan's temple, and I scream.

"*No!*"

He stops, the gun still pressed against Kenan's forehead. Kenan's face betrays no fear. Not for himself. Only for me. The soldier glances at me. "No?"

I stare at him with hate-filled eyes that are dripping with tears.

"Then how about this?" His gaze gleams. "I let your boyfriend live so he can watch this, huh?"

Anger chokes my throat.

"We don't have time for this," his friend says in a low voice, yanking Kenan back as he struggles. Kenan swears and the soldier hits him in the face. "The rebels could be near. The military won't make it here. We need to buy time until they—"

"We have time," the soldier interrupts, and he grabs at me. My mind snaps as soon as he touches me, and I twist against him, kicking.

The patients behind us watch the macabre spectacle

329

unfold with terrified eyes, not one of them daring to move. To say anything. And I don't blame them.

He shoves the barrel of the rifle under my chin. It smells of blood and smoke. I cough.

"*Go to hell*," I snarl, refusing to give him the satisfaction of seeing me tremble.

He smiles, inching the rifle's mouth deeper, until it nearly punctures my skin.

Before I can blink, the rifle clatters to the floor, and he seizes my arms in a death grip. He's bigger and well fed, while I'm surviving on fumes. He pushes me against an empty bed and I scream, clawing at his face. He grasps both of my wrists in one hand, immobilizing me, half leaning on top of my body, facing me. He reeks of stale cigarettes and sweat.

"Let her go!" Kenan yells despite the gun being pointed at his head. A second soldier comes up behind him and slams his rifle against Kenan's back.

I spit in the soldier's face. My saliva is reddish as it trails down his cheek, and it only makes him laugh, wiping it away while his other hand tightens around my wrists.

"Hit him again," he says, and Kenan lurches forward with the force of another blow, a gasp wrenched from his aching lungs.

"Don't give up, Salama." Khawf's voice cuts into my mind. I can't see him, but his tone is sharp, prompting a shot of adrenaline to clear away the hazy panic. "*Don't.*"

"It's been a while since someone put up a fight. I like it," the soldier sneers. He runs his free hand along my body. Revulsion sours my blood and I jerk my knee up between us, but he anticipates it, pressing his own down on my thigh until stars burst in my eyes from the pain. My thigh blisters with agony and I'm sure the skin is bruised.

I hear the clink of metal along a belt, a zipper pulling down, and reality begins to set in. I twist in place, screaming until my throat is raw. He ignores me, his eyes full of malicious glee and his mouth hitched, and he sticks his hand under my sweater, touching my bare skin. I swallow a scream and, reacting on instinct, slam my head against his. There's no room for shock to paralyze my limbs when anger is burning through me. Fueling me. Safety is *two* days away. I've lost Mama, Baba, Hamza, Layla, and Baby Salama. I've learned to see the colors and I've found my own version of happiness. I'm *owed* myself.

I'll either die or get to Germany, but I will *not* be touched by this animal.

He stumbles back, howling with pain and clutching his forehead while I collapse on the bed, my head swimming. Is it enough? Hazy thoughts trickle like honey, thick and disoriented. My blood thunders against my skull, pounding against the bones. Every ounce of energy forsakes me. I can't think or move, and I'm too scared Kenan will be shot if I try anything. Kenan's shouts and the soldiers' yells dim and my vision blurs.

But once it steadies, I see the soldier is seething, all hints of his humor gone. An angry welt swells on his forehead. I almost laugh. He takes out a blade from his holster and jerks me by the shoulders before pressing its sharp edge under the pulse on my neck.

"You should be put down like a *bitch*," he snarls and drags it along my throat.

Time slows. It comes apart at the seams one red thread at a time. And with each strand, I remember Karam el-Zeitoun. How just days ago, children were butchered in this exact way. How they must have begged and screamed for their lives. Mere children.

I think of Baba and Hamza and how they'd rather die a thousand deaths than see me tortured like this.

I think of Mama and her soft hands brushing my hair back, calling me her eyes and heart.

I think of Layla and her larger-than-life laugh, her ocean eyes.

And I think, *This is it. This is how I die.*

I'll finally smell the daisies.

But his hands loosen and I fall once more against the bed. Everything goes black.

I wake up with a jolt, something heavy on my throat, and I frantically scrape at it.

"Whoa!" a voice says, alarmed, and someone grabs my arms. "Careful, Salama!"

I squint, my surroundings sharpening in front of me. Kenan's worried face comes into view.

"You're all right, sweetheart," he murmurs. "You're all right."

I gasp in a breath; there's a rough fabric around my throat. It's gauze. My stomach lurches when I remember how easily the soldier's blade sliced against my skin. Cutting me open. I shake my head, willing the image to disappear.

My hands fly to my bare head, shock coursing through me.

"My hijab," I gasp, shaking.

Kenan hesitates before gently taking my hands in his. "Dr. Ziad bandaged your cut. It needed small stitches. You're in his office and it's just us, don't worry. No one's coming in." He exhales loudly. "Alhamdulillah you're fine."

My breaths steady. I turn my head slowly as I examine the room, which is empty save for Kenan and me. Dr. Ziad's desk, still cluttered with yellow papers and a few syringes, is pushed against the wall, and the bed I'm lying on is in the middle of the floor. The door is closed and so are the blinds. It's nighttime.

Kenan sits back on the plastic chair beside me, relief and exhaustion in his features. His left eye socket is a deep scarlet. He has a cut on his lower lip that's been stitched and a mottle of budding bruises is scattered carelessly across his face. His eyes are glassy with the residue of the adrenaline, and he's wearing a forest-green sweater free of any blood.

"What happened?" I whisper, scared to speak any louder. I can't stop staring at his face. They hurt him. "Are—you're hurt."

He shifts in his seat. "Dr. Ziad checked me. I have a minor concussion, but that's all."

His voice is casual; he's trying to lighten what he's saying.

"*Minor?*" I repeat loudly. "They hit your back. Your chest. Are you okay?"

He doesn't reply, instead taking in a deep breath. I notice that his hands are shaking. "Are you thirsty?" he asks.

I cough, suddenly aware of how parched I am. I nod.

He stands and gingerly fetches a water bottle from Dr. Ziad's desk, then helps me drink.

"You've been asleep nearly the whole day." He holds the bottle. "After that soldier—There was blood everywhere. I thought . . . I thought you died. But Dr. Ziad burst in at that moment with about ten Free Syrian Army soldiers. He had slipped through the back door and contacted them. Three surrendered, but the one who hurt you and another didn't. But they were outnumbered." A cold, satisfied tone takes over his voice. "They're dead."

He reaches over and squeezes my fingers. "Dr. Ziad rushed to you and was able to stop the bleeding. You woke up then, do you remember?" I don't answer, so he continues. "Dr. Ziad gave you something to sleep. Your cut isn't deep. It didn't sever an artery, alhamdulillah, but you needed blood. One of the Free Syrian soldiers was able to give you his."

I shudder. I was a whisper away from being six feet underground. "Why were they here?"

"They were able to find a way through a weakened spot at the borders with the Free Syrian Army. Go on an easy murder spree at the hospital before the rest of the military joined them."

"So the fight is getting closer?" I ask.

He nods sadly. "The FSA have high hopes. Their faith is strong and they have their weapons, but . . . I worry."

"Me too." Then I gasp. "Lama? Yusuf?"

He puts a hand on my shoulder, calming me. "They're okay. The soldiers didn't make it to their room. They're sleeping now and—" He stops, his voice breaking, tears trickling down his cheeks.

"What?" I say, panicked, my mind jumping to the worst of conclusions.

He sits on the edge of my bed and hooks his arms under my back before pulling me to his chest.

"I almost lost you." The words come out choked, dry sobs shaking his shoulders. "God, I felt *so* helpless. When he cut you, I . . . I can't bury you, Salama. I can't."

He tightens his hold, and I sink into him, eyes brimming with tears. "We made it."

He presses a kiss to my cheeks, my forehead, and a soft one to my lips.

"Bury me before I bury you," he whispers in prayer. "Please."

I clasp his face between my hands, brushing away the teardrops. "I—"

"I love you," he says before I can. I smile. It only takes a few words from him to untangle the vines gripping my heart. Kenan is magical that way. I'll be fine. *We'll* be fine. I need to believe that. I need to look at the colors instead of closing my eyes to beauty and hope.

Even when it's hard to do so.

"Tell me something good," I whisper and scoot over to make room for him. He slowly lies down on his side and I face him, our legs tangled.

He threads his fingers through mine and kisses my knuckles. "I've wanted to draw you even before I met you."

"What do you mean?"

"My uncle lives in Berlin. I remember seeing pictures of it on Google a few years ago. The architecture is breathtaking. They have this monument called the Brandenburg Gate. I always fantasized about taking my wife there. Have her sit right in the middle while I drew her. As if the whole place was built just for her."

In this eye of the storm, his words come alive in my mind. I see us strolling around Berlin, hand in hand, while he balances his art supplies on his shoulder. I'd pick carnations from the local florist and fashion them into a crown. On certain days, when the sun shines through the clouds, rays scattering over the fields, it would remind us of Homs. Of home.

"I'd like that," I murmur.

Kenan lets go of my hand to twirl a lock of my hair around his finger. "I feel like I've known you all my life, Salama."

I smile. "Everyone knows everyone in Homs. Odds are we must have met before."

"As children? I spent most of my time in the playground, playing football and making a mess in the sandpit."

"Oh, then we didn't meet. See, I was either on our balcony gardening or playing Barbies with Layla."

He smiles. "It might sound cheesy, but I'm sure our souls met way before they found their way into our bodies. I think that's where we know each other from."

Heat rushes to my face. What he's saying is part of our faith. Souls existing beyond mortal bodies. Yet hearing him say that makes my ears and face burn.

He chuckles. "Tell me something good, then."

I pick at the cuff of his sleeve, appreciating how he distracts me from feeling flustered. "Studio Ghibli inspired me to write," I begin, and he looks at me with awe. "After watching *Spirited Away* when I was ten, my mind became hyperactive. One day I thought, why not write my stories down?"

"Did you?"

I shake my head. "Never a full story, no. School happened. But I never forgot them. Especially when I fell in love with botany."

He nestles closer. "Would you tell me one of them? It's all right if you don't want to."

My blood must have recovered somewhat because it rushes to my face.

My heart pulls. "It's silly."

He looks offended. "Silly? How dare you call my wife's stories silly?"

I bite back a laugh. I know this moment of happiness will trickle by like sand in an hourglass, but I want to make each second count. I want to keep the pain at bay for a bit more.

"Fine."

35

THE BIRDS ARE CHIRPING WHEN I WAKE SUDDENLY, tucked against Kenan's chest, his arm wrapped around my shoulder protectively. Dread slithers along my skin, unwelcome and unbidden, and my heart races.

A nightmare?

I sit up and untangle myself from Kenan, praying he doesn't stir. He mumbles something unintelligible in his sleep.

I can't remember if my dreams were troubled, but my anxiousness hasn't dissolved. If anything, it's escalating. The cut on my neck burns a bit when I twist my head. I stand, looking for my lab coat, and find it draped over Dr. Ziad's chair. I wet a corner of it and rub the spot on my stomach that the soldier touched. I frantically press harder, trying to shed the cells, until it burns and my skin protests.

"Morning," someone murmurs from the corner of the room. My eyes adjust to the scarce early light leaking through the blinds, and I make out Khawf's silhouette.

"Morning," I whisper, letting my lab coat fall to the floor.

He steps out of the shadows, his dark suit rippling like the sea on a moonless night.

That explains the dread.

Khawf looks wary. "Does it?"

"What do you mean?"

He glances around Dr. Ziad's office and suddenly advances toward me. His voice is urgent, very different from his usual drawl. "If five soldiers from the military were able to breach the Free Syrian Army's defenses, what does that say?"

Fear is a cruel thing. The way it distorts thoughts, transforming them from molehills into mountains.

"Listen to me very carefully," Khawf continues. If I didn't know better, I'd say he sounds anxious. "It means this hospital isn't safe anymore. The hospital will be the first place they attack. Either with foot soldiers or bombs. You know hospitals are always targeted, and the clock has run out on yours."

The veins and capillaries in my hands constrict.

"It means you need to leave right *now* or else—" He pauses, sussing out my reaction, but I don't move. My heart is racing as I try to understand why he's acting like this. Something about him, about his tone and the way he's looking at me, feels different. It's almost as if I'm talking to someone whose soul isn't extracted from mine.

He groans, his jaw twitching. "You never learn. Fine."

And he snaps his fingers.

Dr. Ziad's office shifts, morphing into a graveyard. In

front of me are four cracked slab stones crowning four hast-ily made graves. Mine, Kenan's, Lama's, and Yusuf's. The backdrop is my hospital, flattened.

The scenery changes sharply before I can comprehend. I'm standing on the shore, with a gray sky lining the horizon, watching a boat filled to the brim with refugees sail away. Waves crash over the sand, soaking my sneakers, and the salty sea air burns my nose. Behind me the sound of falling missiles thunders against my eardrums, and the sky glows a lustrous orange-red, swallowing the dreariness. Trees catch fire and the cries of the injured rise with the smoke.

My future is on the sea, disappearing.

"*Wait!*" I scream at the boat, lunging forward through the winter-cold water. The iciness of it makes me hiss.

A bomb falls, and the force of it obliterates everything in its path, creating a hot current of wind that pushes me to my hands and knees, drenched in the Mediterranean Sea. Trem-bling, I glance over my shoulder to see the outline of another missile dropping.

It's seconds away. I open my mouth to scream again and—

I stumble, my back hitting the wall of Dr. Ziad's office, and I slide to the floor, sobbing quietly into my sleeve. I bite into the fabric as my chest heaves. Khawf crouches in front of me.

"Death will take over this hospital," he whispers. "Do you remember what the soldier said? Think, Salama! Think!"

The military won't make it here. We need to buy time until they—

My heart is about to burst—I know it will. Khawf's face breaks out with a relieved smile and he nods. There are hidden words in his eyes he refuses to say but expects me to know.

When I blink, he's gone. I clamber to my feet and grab my hijab.

"Kenan, wake up," I say, my voice raspy. I can still taste the acidity of the smoke in my throat.

He sits up, eyes wild. "Wha—what happened?"

"Nothing." I pull my lab coat firmly over me. "We need to get out of the hospital."

He rubs his eyes. "What?"

I hoist my backpack on. "No time to explain. Get Lama and Yusuf and meet me outside. We need to leave now."

I open the door and see the doctors and patients starting their day. I hurry to look for Dr. Ziad. Thankfully Kenan doesn't argue and follows me.

My heart beats painfully and with each passing second I'm sure we're closer to our deaths. After frantically searching through a couple of rooms and the atrium, I find him in the stockroom.

"Doctor!" I gasp. "We need to evacuate the hospital."

He starts. "Salama! Are you all right? How are you—"

I zoom past him and snatch Panadol and amoxicillin packs from the shelves, then shove them into my pocket. "Doctor! Grab whatever medications you can carry and let's leave!"

His confusion deepens.

My desperation is making it hard for me to string my thoughts into a coherent sentence. "We must—there's probably going to be—all the other hospitals—"

He raises his hands in an attempt to calm me. "Salama, slow down."

I inhale deeply, holding it in my lungs, and in a forced calm voice say, "If the military was able to get into the hospital, it means they're already at our doorstep. One of the soldiers yesterday said something about buying time until the military did—*I don't know what*. It might be a bomb. It might be something else. But we need to leave. . . ."

I can't explain it. Something's about to happen. Khawf is right.

Where would you go?

Everywhere.

Dr. Ziad's face is stricken, but he doesn't move. We don't have *time*.

"I haven't been able to contact the FSA for the past three hours," he says.

My stomach falls. "We have to go."

He nods, grabbing a stray cardboard box and shoveling the medications inside. "Salama, tell everyone to evacuate right now."

I don't waste another second and run through the hallways to the atrium.

"*Everyone!*" I yell, and all the faces turn toward me, recognition flickering in some. "Leave the hospital *now*! It's not safe!"

For a few precious seconds, they glance at one another with unease.

Frustration builds inside me. It's because I'm a teenager. They're more reluctant to listen. It's not easy for some of them to move, because they're missing limbs, and others are hooked to IVs. Many are children and elderly.

"The military is going to bomb the hospital! We have to leave!"

Kenan screeches to a halt behind me, holding Lama's and Yusuf's hands. He is horrified.

"Bomb?" he says, out of breath. With the lighting, I can finally see that his left eye is swollen, barely open, and the bruise has turned darker in the daylight.

"Where's Dr. Ziad?" one patient moans from their bed. "He'll know—"

"Dr. Ziad says we have to leave!" I snap. I'm not sitting around waiting for them to listen, so I grab Kenan's arm and start pulling him behind me. Lama and Yusuf trail after in shock.

The action triggers an effect in the rest of the room. The mothers are first to rise; they grab their children and fling the doors open, then run.

Chaos unfolds. The crowds shove against one another. Doctors help the bedridden to their feet. My hold on Kenan tightens. I refuse to let my grip waver.

As soon as we're by the door, I hear Dr. Ziad's voice booming over the masses. "Leave now!"

His tone sparks another urgent rush, and footsteps rumble along the floors. We all run down the stairs and out of the hospital's gates. My eyes dart to the skies and I search the blue for planes as we cross the street. The mob pushes against me, and their panicked force nearly makes my grasp on Kenan's sweater slip. Pins and needles prick through my arm, but I don't care. Out of the corner of my eye, I see Am, pushing his way through, and I feel a surge of relief. After we pass the first building, I yank Kenan to the side, moving against the current to take refuge behind a torn-down wall, and let him go.

Our breaths are ragged as we stare at each other. The sun is out today, the rays hot on my hijab. Lama and Yusuf are confused and scared, their eyes glued to Kenan. He gives them a reassuring smile.

I glance back toward the hospital, and my heart starts thundering when I can't spot Dr. Ziad among the people hemorrhaging out. And then the realization hits me.

The babies in the incubators are still inside.

My stomach drops and I hold the wall for support. I need to go back. I need to save the babies. But my legs are heavy with fear, half of me screaming to stay put—to stay safe. The other replays Samar's ashen, bloodless face as I held her life hostage.

I grit my teeth, pushing away the fear, and before I can rethink my decision, I fling myself from behind the wall and run toward the hospital.

"*Salama!*" Kenan shouts.

I dash across the road, pushing through the swarms, through the courtyard, and back up the steps.

The atrium is empty, a sight I never thought I'd see. Linens are strewn on the floor, some of the beds overturned in the panic. Two figures emerge from the hallway. Dr Ziad balances a huge cardboard box under one arm and cradles two small shapes with the other. Nour's white hijab flutters as she sprints past me, huddling two babies close to her.

Dr. Ziad stops short and hands me the babies. They're wrapped in thin white blankets, each the size of a small loaf of bread. Their skin is red, their mouths tiny, and their fingers barely visible.

"There's a third in here," Dr. Ziad says, panting hard

and putting down the box. The wrinkles around his eyes deepen. I glance inside the box and see a baby resting atop a small pile of medication packets. "Can you carry the box? I need—"

"Give it to me." Kenan stops short beside me, his breaths shallow. He tucks the box under his arm, twists on his heels, and flees. Dr. Ziad turns, heading straight back toward the incubators.

"Doctor!" I shriek, rooted to the spot. *"Doctor!"*

He doesn't look back.

"Salama! Come on!" Kenan shouts from the front.

Tears erupt from my eyes, and I sob as I hug the babies closer and run after him.

As soon as we cross the road, we hear it.

The plane.

We reach the wall where Kenan's siblings are peering out, scared out of their wits.

"No," I choke, whirling around to face the hospital and hugging the babies closer to me. *"Please* come out!"

Patients, rescuers, and staff are still spilling out the front doors. At the very last second, I see him. He nearly stumbles, supporting two more babies as he runs. His lab coat is half torn and the distance feels impossibly great.

"Yalla," I beg. "God, please!"

The piercing sound of the bomb slices through the air as it falls.

"No!" I scream, my arms trembling. *"Doctor, quickly!"*

Kenan grabs me, ducking my head down as the bomb shatters the one place in Homs that held hope. The earth rumbles and cracks as if an earthquake hit. My eardrums ring from the force and debris-filled smoke blinds and chokes me. My limbs shake and I hunch over, trying to protect the infants.

After a few heartbeats where the only sound is the crash of the hospital's columns collapsing, howls of mourning shake the dust-filled skies. Heart-wrenching cries and prayers rattle my core.

"Are you okay?" I direct at Kenan. The dust settles just enough for me to make out his shape.

"Yes," he says, coughing hoarsely, and he winces. He turns to his siblings, making sure they're all right.

"Kenan, take the babies," I order. "I need to find Dr. Ziad."

He shakes his head fiercely. "I—"

"Salama, give them to me," Nour says, and I glance up at her, my heart soaring for a brief moment. She's unharmed. "They can't stay here. They need fresh air. Some are already struggling without their incubators." Two volunteers stand behind her, and I hand the babies over to one of them while the other picks up the cardboard box.

"If you find Dr. Ziad—" Nour stops, her voice shaking. "Tell him—tell him we'll be at his house."

I nod and stand despite my wobbly knees. The wreckage throws me into another whirl of despair. The hospital I spent all my days in is gone.

It's a graveyard.

The building has been reduced to rocks. The volunteers are scattered over the remains, desperately trying to remove the debris. When I get closer, I hear the faint screaming of those still trapped inside. It tears my heart in half. Their agony makes me forget the reason I'm leaving.

From the smoke, Khawf emerges, his eyebrows raised, not a wisp of the destruction touching him.

"Salama, there's nothing you can do," he says coldly. "Don't you dare rethink your decision. The hospital is gone. Your workplace destroyed. There's nothing left for you here. Your family is dead or arrested. I *know* you don't want to be next."

I look away from him, tears streaming down my face, and trudge forward despite my limbs shaking from fear.

"Dr. Ziad!" I call over the moaning. "Doctor!"

Slowly, the dust settles. The sun's rays poke holes through the plumes of smoke. The ringing in my ears lessens, and when I scream his name for the fourth time, I hear a faint response.

"Salama!"

I look around wildly, tumbling in the direction of the main gates, to find Dr. Ziad sitting on the curb. There's a cut on his forehead, blood trickling down his cheek. His face is ashy gray, the tips of his hair and lab coat singed.

"Doctor!" I exclaim, falling to my knees in front of him. "Are you hurt?"

He shudders in a breath, slowly extending his arms to reveal two babies tucked in the crooks. "I had to choose." He falls quiet, his face white and his eyes void of emotion. "I ran with the ones I chose. But . . . I can't hear their heartbeats."

It hurts to swallow.

"I tried to save them," he whispers. Tears roll down his

cheeks. "I had to *choose*. The rest are still inside. They killed *babies*."

I wipe my eyes. "They're in Heaven, Doctor. They're not suffering anymore."

He raises them, pressing a kiss to each of their foreheads. "Forgive us," he whispers to them. "Forgive us for our shortcomings."

I sit there with him, mourning. They were premature and their chances of surviving without their incubators were slim. Still . . . *still*.

After a few minutes, I say, "Nour took the other babies to your house. I think they're alive."

He glances up. "Thank you."

I shake my head. "We're doing what's right. We don't do it to be thanked."

He hands me one baby. It's a girl, swaddled in a pink blanket. I hold her closer. Would Baby Salama have been this small? I shudder and we manage to stand carefully. The baby's face is still, and if I close my eyes, I can pretend she's sleeping.

"Salama," Dr. Ziad says, and I look at him. He extends one arm and I gently hand the baby back to him.

"You saved a lot of people today," he says after a beat of silence. "Without your quick thinking—your gut feeling—I wouldn't be in front of you now." He exhales. "I should have known something wasn't right when my calls to the FSA weren't going through, but my mind was muddled after yesterday's attack."

"We're only human. No one can expect you to anticipate everything."

His smile turns sad. "If only my guilty conscience could agree."

"What are you going to do?" I gesture at the hospital. "Where will the people go?"

His back is hunched, the years catching up to him, and in his eyes I see devastation. He looks around at the destroyed hospital, taking it all in.

"We'll build a new one," he whispers. Then he straightens his back and determination burns away the sorrow. "Other cities, like Ghouta, are setting up underground hospitals. We'll build tunnels and mazes deep in the ground. They can bomb us all they want—we'll never bow down."

His resilience humbles me.

"May God keep you safe," I murmur. I feel I shouldn't leave Syria without telling him. He'd be worried sick if I just never showed up again. "Doctor, I'm leaving. Tomorrow."

Surprise flits to sorrow, but there's no judgment in his eyes. "It was an honor and privilege working with you, Salama. May God keep you alive and well. Please don't forget us in your prayers."

The backs of my eyes burn, and I manage to nod. He walks away, still carrying the two bodies as if they were his own children.

Layla's home is haunting. It's as if it knows I'm leaving tomorrow.

Kenan limps to the couch as soon as we walk in. We left the hospital site only when we could no longer stand. Kenan hauled debris until his arms shook. He was already weak from the beating he took yesterday, and he suppressed the pain until exhaustion claimed him.

Lama and Yusuf crowd beside him, their faces fearful. I quickly light the candles.

"I'm okay," Kenan says, closing his eyes and breathing in quick puffs. "I just need a minute."

"Can someone please get a glass of water?" I open my backpack and rummage through the contents for the Panadol. There's a strip somewhere.

Yusuf rushes to the kitchen, where he scoops water from the rain bucket into a mug, and hurries back.

"Here," he whispers, and we all freeze.

Kenan reacts first, shock easing the tension in his expression. With a shaking hand, he sets the mug on the table in front of him before holding his hand out. Yusuf takes it. Kenan pulls him closer, not even flinching from the pain, and hugs his brother tightly. Lama bursts into tears and I shed a few happy ones too.

Then Lama jumps on Yusuf and holds him close as her sobs muffle on his shoulder.

"Kenan, take your Panadol," I whisper, handing him the tablet, and he swallows it with the water.

Lama and Yusuf move out of the way, but not too far from Kenan as I help him lie down. Kenan holds his brother's hand in his, grinning. "Maybe I should get hurt more often."

Yusuf blushes, and Kenan launches into an exaggerated tale of the ridiculous ways he'll get injured as they giggle. I recognize the effort in his words and the forced easiness in his tone. He's trying to distract them from the devastation they witnessed today. Of a refuge reduced to ash.

"Or maybe I'll let a whale snap me up!" he says.

Lama titters and Yusuf can't fight the smile on his lips.

"Too unrealistic?" Kenan says thoughtfully. "Then I'll slip on a banana like in those cartoons! What would you say to that?"

Yusuf lightly punches his arm. "You're weird."

Kenan's eyes shine with joy. "I like weird."

They stay like that for a while before Kenan finally convinces his siblings to try and sleep. With a newfound hope in their eyes, they skip to my room. I help, tugging the covers over their small frames, making sure the cold doesn't seep through the cracks. I kiss Lama's cheek and smile at Yusuf. He hesitates for a second before smiling back. My heart swells, and I whisper, "Good night. Sleep well; tomorrow's a big day."

I close the door gently, tiptoe down the hallway, and stop when I get to Layla and Hamza's room. My fingers dance over the brass handle. I don't need to go in. Once was more than enough.

I lay my head against the door and whisper, "Goodbye."

I grab the two bags I packed with Layla and make my way to the living room. Kenan's eyes are closed but they blink open as I walk in and sit on the rug in front of the couch. I slip off my hijab, run my fingers through my hair, and wince from the ache in my scalp. The cut on my throat stings, but I don't dare touch it under the bandages.

"How are you?" he whispers.

"Surviving," I whisper back. "Are you in pain?"

He shifts slowly. "The Panadol is helping."

"Good news is we're meeting Am early."

"When I talked to my uncle a few days ago, he said he's flying to Syracuse today," he says. "He'll meet us at the shore. Worst-case scenario, we call him."

Safety is so close I can almost taste it. I take out the USB stick from Layla's bag and run my thumb over its metallic shell, smiling.

Thank you, Hamza.

"As agreed, we'll only pay him five hundred dollars and the gold necklace now that Layla—" I stop, breathing deeply.

Kenan trails his fingers over my cheek and I look up. His touch is comforting.

I give him a watery smile before rummaging through Layla's bag and taking out the gold. I stash it in my bag's inner pocket and pull the zipper tight. I count the contents inside one more time. Eight cans of tuna, three cans of beans, one Panadol box, my high school certificate and passport, socks, one set of clothes.

"I got the lemons," Kenan says. He nods toward the kitchen. "They're in the fridge."

"Thank you." I jump to my feet and rush to get them.

"Where's your camera?" I ask as I put the lemons in the bag.

He cringes. "I destroyed it the night of the chemical attack."

My mouth drops open.

"It's okay," he whispers. "I uploaded all the videos to YouTube first."

I hold his hand tightly. "Oh, Kenan."

His smile is sad. "It's just a camera."

"I'll get you a new one."

He laughs lightly and kisses my knuckles. When he brushes my cheek, my eyelashes flutter.

"I'm sorry," he murmurs, guilt saturating his voice.

"What for?" I frown.

His jaw strains. "For what happened at the hospital when you were . . . when that happened."

I shake my head. That little girl's terror reminded me of Samar. Of my sin. "I couldn't let him . . . get to that little girl."

"I know," Kenan whispers. "It's okay. You did what you had to do. I'm just glad you're safe." His fingers brush over the bandage on my throat. "It may scar."

I nod, fussing with my sleeves, needing the comfort, so I ask, "Would you be okay with that?"

He lets out an incredulous laugh. "My wife has a battle scar. She's a badass."

I shake my head, smiling. "It's not the only scar I have."

He raises his eyebrows. "You mean the ones on your hands. I love those."

My smile deepens.

"Here." I take his hand and place it at the base of my skull, under my hair. "Do you feel it?"

"Yeah." He traces the ridges lightly, his touch gentle. His eyes are wide with wonder. "Does it hurt?"

"No. I got it when that bomb killed Mama. When I started seeing Khawf."

I frown. When Khawf warned me about the hospital getting bombed, it felt like a blindfold I didn't know I was wearing dropped from my eyes. Now, I can see clearer than before, but I don't know what it is I'm seeing.

"Are you okay?" Kenan asks and I blink. His fingers slip down, and he loops one through my wedding ring.

"Yeah." I smile and it dispels the concern on his face.

"Are you okay with *this*?" He points at his busted lips. "It might scar. I know you fell for my pretty face."

I laugh and delicately run my thumb along the stitches on the edge of his lower lip. His eyelashes flutter. "I guess I'll make do." His expression then turns serious and he sits up and reaches for my hands. "Whatever happens tomorrow, we'll be okay. Even if . . ." He takes in a deep breath and presses his forehead against mine. "Know that even in death, you're my life."

My heart skips a beat. Then another. I have no words to fashion into an everlasting promise that defies the world. So I press a quiet kiss to his lips.

He sighs and after a few seconds says, "Tell me something good, Sheeta."

I blush. "Are you trying to distract me from today?"

He smiles. "And me."

I sigh. "You'll like this one. The day you were supposed to come over, I was going to prepare a whole knafeh."

He jerks back, a different glimmer growing in his eyes, until I swear the candlelight is trapped in them. "You know how to make *knafeh*?"

"From the semolina dough to the cheese to the drizzled orange blossom water over the pistachios and almonds," I murmur and tap my forehead. "It's all saved here."

There's genuine happiness in his expression, all traces of pain gone. "You're perfect," he declares.

I laugh, lacing my fingers through his. "You're not so bad yourself."

And in those final hours of our time in Homs, my bruised heart quietly heals. Cell by cell.

36

USUALLY MY NEIGHBORHOOD EXISTS IN A REPETI-
tive limbo. The wind carries the children's tentative
laughter and cries through the despondent ruins. Hope
colors the conversations of the protestors passing by my
door, their footsteps echoing over the gravel. A father con-
soles his daughter, passing his share of food to her. Jasmine
flowers unfold their petals toward the sun. They bloom on
soil soaked with martyrs' blood. For a while, we live.

Then, when the planes roar through the clouds, the pebbles on the sidewalk tremble. And we stop living and start
surviving.

Today is no different. But today I say goodbye to myself.
My old self.

Kenan and his siblings are already by the front door,
their faces grave. We're meeting Am in thirty minutes. As
I stand in my bedroom's doorway, a rush of nostalgia runs
through me. Miserable and empty as it looks, this was my
home. For a while.

It won't stay empty for long. A family who has lost their own home might take refuge in it or, if the military finally invades Old Homs, they'll ransack the place. I try not to think of that.

I trail through to the living room and hover in the entrance, casting one last long look at Layla's painting. Suspended in the shade, the waves look alive, licking the frame's edges, and a story awakens in my mind.

"Let's go," I say, turning on my heel before my courage fails me.

We shuffle out, backpacks filled with all we own in the world, and I close the door behind me.

"Goodbye," I whisper and press a kiss to the blue wood.

Kenan's hand slides into mine. "We'll come back."

I nod.

Lama is between Yusuf and Kenan, and together we walk, the birds singing a sweet farewell melody.

Khalid Mosque is ten minutes away. We take the second fork in the road that leads away from the hospital, and while we walk, I try to memorize each flowering tree and abandoned building we pass. Every now and then I glimpse the revolution's flag spray-painted over the metallic columns of a garage or wall. The quiet of these last fragile moments is only broken by the crowds standing outside the grocery and the Free Syrian Army soldiers walking about. Their presence calms me, and I send a quick prayer for their hands not to waver, for their love for this land and her people to haul them to victory.

Khalid Mosque is in the middle of a wide clearing of half-collapsed apartment buildings. We step carefully over cracked asphalt and loose, dead electrical wires. Up close, the mosque's walls are scratched and the dusty windows splintered, as are the steps leading up to the front door. It's slightly open, revealing debris coating the dark green rug upon which a few men are in various positions of prayer.

"What's the time?" Kenan asks. Yusuf and Lama sit with their legs hanging over the steps. Yusuf whispers something to her and she leans closer to hear before nodding.

"Fifteen more minutes," I reply, my nerves tingling, and I focus on Kenan's face, counting the bruises decorating his skin. There are about seven in total, and his contused eye has taken on a plum shade. His shoulders are slumped but his gaze is flitting everywhere, committing the sky's blue to his memory.

"Kenan." I take his hand, drawing him closer.

He looks forlorn, heartbreak written all over his face. I haven't the slightest idea what to say to ease his sorrow. It's the same grief tearing through me, so I wrap an arm around him and tuck my head under his chin.

"Syria lives in our hearts," I whisper. "She always will."

He hugs me, pressing a kiss to the top of my hijab.

We stay like this, swaying and staring at our city. The fifteen minutes trickle by. People walk in and out of the mosque and with each extra minute my anxiety rises. What if Am doesn't show up? What if something's happened to him?

If he doesn't come, all four of us might as well dig our own graves right here.

But my paranoia subsides when I hear the faint sound of a car approaching along the road. It's an old gray Toyota, its sides streaked with mud and the windshield in need of a wash. Even from this distance, I can see it's Am sitting behind the wheel. He skids in front of us, stopping short.

"Get in." A cigarette hangs from his lips. "We're on a tight schedule, and we're five minutes late."

"You mean *you're* five minutes late," I retort, folding my arms.

He glares. "Do you want to chat, or do you want to leave? Get in the back and—" He stops, counting us, and frowns. "Where's Layla?"

My eyes burn and I fight the hollowness in my stomach, looking away. Am's expression turns grave.

"So that's one less payment," he says, and even though his tone isn't the slightest bit malicious, the urge to punch him rises in me.

Kenan's hand weighs on my shoulder and he nods at me. I open the door tentatively and Yusuf slides in first, then Lama and Kenan. I get in and Lama shifts to sit on Kenan's lap. We leave the front seat empty, wanting to be close to one another.

Am reverses the car, his eyes reflected in the rearview mirror. He drives onto the road, and as I glance out the window, my body begins to tremble with anticipation and sadness. We pass through narrow streets, edging nearer to the Free Syrian Army's borders.

"You get those bruises when the military breached the hospital?" Am asks Kenan, eyeing him in the mirror.

"Yes," Kenan answers. His voice is still stricken with guilt.

"Are they going to be a problem for us?" I ask, wrapping my hand around his, anchoring him to me.

Am steers with one hand, the other tapping out ash from his cigarette. "It would have been better if he didn't have them, but the guards won't cause us any problems as long as I give them the money. First border coming up in a few minutes."

My muscles clench, my heart hammering fast, and I glance at Kenan and see the same fear in his eyes. Even if Am has never been stopped before, it doesn't mean that won't happen today. Minds and hearts can change. The soldiers he's struck a deal with might have gotten bored of their arrangement.

We finally make it out of Old Homs, passing a tank along the way that's decorated with the revolution flag.

Just a bit ahead, the military border comes into view. I recognize it by the swarming soldiers and the line of cars packed right behind one another. The closer we get, the louder the voices become, and I hear shouting. I turn my head slowly to see, scared the very motion will alert them to us. Am swerves to the far end, and from my window I see three soldiers kicking a man sprawled on the ground. Each blow makes me jump, and Kenan's hand tightens around mine.

"Don't look," he whispers, and I tear my eyes away, drilling holes into my knees. I can still hear the man howling in pain and my throat closes up.

God, please. If we don't make it through, then don't let them take us, I pray hard. *Please let them kill us.*

Am stops in front of a soldier wearing a pair of dark-tinted army glasses. His black hair is slicked back and he looks bored. Am rolls down the window and says, "Morning. How's it going?"

"All right," the soldier replies before tilting his head to the side to inspect us in the back.

I feel the touch of his stare and glue my eyes back to my knees. I'm too scared to glance at Kenan and his siblings to see if they're doing the same.

"Roll down the back window," the soldier says, and Am laughs nervously.

"Is that necessary? We—"

"Roll it," the soldier snaps. The window protests as Am slides it down.

My heart's in my throat. The soldier rests both his arms on the window's edge. I'm aware of his rifle tapping against the car's roof, and the cut on my neck begins to burn.

"Where are you headed?" he asks, and we all freeze.

I clear my throat, and before I can say anything, he says, "Look at me when I'm talking to you."

His voice is quiet, but there's no mistaking the lethality in it. I turn toward him heavily.

"Tartus," I say, and my voice breaks.

His mouth quirks upward, amused. "Tartus? What will you be doing there?"

He's toying with me like a cat playing with a mouse. He studies the bead of sweat making a path down my cheek.

"Visiting family," I lie, hoping he can't hear it in my voice.

He grins, all teeth and no warmth. "Family."

He says it teasingly as if he and I are in on a secret. His eyes bore into mine and he waits for me to squirm. But I resist. At long last, he nods at Kenan and asks, "What happened to you?"

I close my eyes briefly. *Please let them kill us.*

Kenan tilts his head, trying to muster any ounce of pride. I squeeze his hand, begging him silently to let this slide. "I was jumped," he replies in a forced polite tone.

"They got you good, didn't they?" the soldier asks.

Kenan's jaw flexes. "Yes."

"You sure it wasn't because you were protesting and got what you deserved?" the soldier says offhandedly, and horror almost stops my heart. Yusuf and Lama become statues. Even Am jolts upright before twisting in his seat.

"I wouldn't have criminals in my car," he says as if the very idea offends him.

Kenan's face betrays nothing, but I can feel how tense he is. "Yes."

"How about I search through your things to make sure none of you are a threat to this country?" the soldier asks.

We're carrying nothing that would incriminate us, but it won't matter to him. If he wanted, he could pass the lemons off as bombs. Claim the USB stick containing my family photos is filled with classified information.

But I know what the soldier is doing. Torture isn't only physical.

My hands tremble as I hold up my bag, and I resign myself to this fate.

I'll never see the Mediterranean Sea.

He snatches it and unzips it, then shakes it out violently, everything inside crashing and rolling away. Thankfully my passport, school certificate, and gold are hidden in the small pocket. He makes no comment on the strangeness of what I've packed for visiting family. He knows where we're actually headed.

"All clear," he says lazily, dropping the bag on the ground. "Get your shit."

I throw Kenan a glance before opening the door and bending down to collect my discarded belongings.

Humiliation burns through me. My jeans are smeared with dirt and sharp pebbles prick my hands. One lemon has tumbled under the car. After grabbing it, I straighten up, pushing down the hatred in my eyes. The soldier rests one arm over the open door, his eyes roaming me from head to toe. Revulsion threatens to choke me.

I tentatively sit back down and he slams the door so forcefully we all jump.

"Give me the money," he says to Am, and Am needn't be told twice.

The soldier counts the bills, satisfied, and tucks them in his breast pocket. He reaches through my opened window and lightly tugs at the end of my hijab. It slips a bit, my bangs falling out.

"You'd be prettier without it." He smiles, cocking his head to the side, expecting an answer. And from the way

Kenan moves, I know he's at his boiling point—about to do something reckless—and I have to intervene.

"Thank you," I manage, wanting nothing more than to claw the guard's eyes out.

"Have fun with your . . . *family*," the soldier says and slaps the back of the car.

Am steps on the gas and the tires screech, dust billowing behind as we race off.

Once we're far enough away, we let out a collective breath and I shudder, tucking my bangs in.

"Are you okay?" Kenan immediately asks me, and I nod, eyes closed, before resting my head on his shoulder and linking my arm through his.

"I'm fine," I whisper. "Nothing matters as long as we get out."

"That was a close one." Am fumbles in his pocket, takes out another crumpled cigarette.

"How many borders are left?" I ask, breathing in Kenan's lemon scent.

"Fifteen to twenty."

Kenan takes in a sharp breath and I groan.

"Don't worry. That one is usually the toughest because it's the first after leaving Homs. The rest are closer to one another and they're a . . . bit more lenient."

I almost snort at the unconvincing tone he's used and roll the window up, not wanting to risk a cold.

"How come you've never tried to get out?" I ask Am bluntly.

"None of your business."

I glare at him in the small mirror, and he glares back.

"I make good money here, okay? The refugee business is booming."

I give him a disgusted look.

"Whatever," he mutters, knowing exactly what's going through my mind. "You can call me whatever you want, but it's the truth."

The more borders we pass, the more anxious we get. At one, we're made to wait for two hours. At another, Am gets patted down and I'm harassed. Later, Kenan gets mocked and insulted. And at the last one, a soldier heavily implies that he's going to take Lama away. Only her.

"She's pretty for a girl so young." The soldier leers and Kenan's face turns as white as a sheet.

Lama wedges herself against Kenan, her thin arms shivering.

Am manages to distract the soldier with a few questions about the Syrian economy. Eventually he lets us go and Am peers at Lama from the rearview mirror.

"You all right?" he asks her. Lama curls into Kenan's lap to hug him. Tremors run along him as he holds her like his life depends on it. There's pity in Am's eyes. Lama is about the same age as Samar.

After that last checkpoint, it takes us an hour of driving nonstop to finally reach Tartus. With the front window cracked a bit, we smell the sea before we see it.

The Mediterranean Sea.

Just on the other side, safety—not freedom. I'm leaving freedom behind, and I can feel the earth's grief when I get out of the car. The tired weeds try to encircle my ankles, begging me to stay. They murmur stories about my ancestors. The ones who stood right where I stand. The ones whose discoveries and civilization encompassed the whole world. The ones whose blood runs through my veins. My footprints sink deep into the soil where theirs have long since been washed away. They plead with me: *It's your country.* This earth belongs to me and my children.

I take a few steps toward the sea, breathing in its salty cold air, feeling it cleanse me.

The Mediterranean is angry today. A storm brews under his restless waves. I see him rumble and twist within himself. I hear the remnants of those before me walking along the sand, throwing stones into his depth, trying to make sense of what has been happening for more than fifty years.

"The boat is right over there," Am calls out, and I look. If I'd had any expectations, I might have fallen over right then and there.

Calling it a boat would be generous. Once upon a time it must have been white. Now it's dirty and battered, with rusty brown scratches hiding its true color. It floats innocently a bit beyond the shore. I'm not an expert, but I already see at least ten red flags. The huge number of people already on it being one. A baby starts crying, and another joins in. *One wrong move,* I imagine, *and it'll tip over.*

"Made it just in time too!" Am opens the trunk of his car and takes out four life jackets identical to the ones the people on the boat are wearing. Orange, so we can be seen. He tosses them to the kids.

"What the hell is this, Am?" I ask when I find my voice. Kenan stands very still, his eyes never leaving the boat.

"What?" He straps Lama securely into her life jacket.

"What do you mean *what?*" I spit out. "This is a goddamn fishing boat, isn't it?"

"Yeah?"

"I'm pretty sure fishing boats can't carry a small village! There're way more people than there should be."

"You expected a cruise ship?" He whips around and throws my life jacket at me. I catch it deftly. "I'm sorry we couldn't get one to your standards, Your Highness."

"You know exactly what I mean. That boat is a ticking time bomb!"

"You'll make it," he says firmly. "You're not the first boat we've sent off. That one has made the trip countless times."

I look at Kenan helplessly. *What do we do?*

Behind him, the mountains of Tartus stand strong. And behind them? Hell. And, I realize, death.

"If we stay, we die," Kenan says in a low tone. "And if we leave, we *might* die."

We can't stay. There's no guarantee we'd even make it back to Homs.

I'd rather drown.

"The boat will leave without you," Am says.

I take one look at my life jacket before strapping it on, and then help Kenan adjust his. He presses his forehead against mine, his hand on the back of my neck.

"Have faith, my love," he whispers.

I clasp his wrist, nodding. Kenan's eyes fill up with tears as he casts them to Tartus's mountains.

"We're ready." I turn to Am, sniffing loudly.

"The money and gold," he says. I take them out and drop them in his hand.

He counts the money in a low voice, examines the necklace and ring, then tucks the money into his wallet and the gold in his pockets.

"All right, go." He shoos us toward the boat.

"We just get on it?" I ask.

"Yeah." He climbs into his car and starts the engine. "The captain of the ship saw me, and you're not going back with me, so he knows you paid. Go!"

I try not to show how nervous I feel. This seems too . . . easy?

When we don't move, Am sighs loudly and murmurs a prayer to God to give him patience. "Salama, trust me. I promise you on my daughter's life this boat will take you to Europe. Go!"

If there's anything I'll trust coming from Am, it's that he loves his daughter.

"Of course there wouldn't have been a daughter to swear on if you'd let her die. God forbid they let you work again," he mumbles, but I hear him. I close my eyes, taking in a deep breath.

I whirl around, marching right up to him. He pauses.

"I know I nearly destroyed your life with what I did," I say. "But you demanded I bleed myself dry. You're not a saint. And neither am I. But at least I feel remorse."

I walk away, not wanting to hear his reply. After a second, the engine starts and he drives away.

"Let's go," I say to Kenan, Yusuf, and Lama. Kenan

brushes a hand over his eyes, turning away from the mountains. Away from Layla's grave. From Mama and Baba. From Hamza.

I take Lama's hand and Kenan takes Yusuf's. We wade through the waves that crash against our knees trying to push us back—warning us. But we don't listen. We refuse to listen.

37

THE NEARER WE GET TO THE BOAT, THE MORE IT seems that people are spilling from its edges. The person in charge—the captain, I presume—greets us gruffly and helps Yusuf and Lama get on. The faces that greet us as we clumsily make our way onboard and try to find room to sit are starved, cold, empty. They huff in annoyance at more people crowding the already overfull boat.

We find a small, empty space and quickly sit down and lean against the boat's side. My limbs sag with relief, my teeth chattering as I huddle closer to Kenan. He wraps his arm around my shoulders and hugs me closer. Our jeans and coats are wet up to our knees. Lama clings to Yusuf, her body shivering. Her own coat won't dry anytime soon, so I take out a sweater and throw it to Yusuf, praying we don't die from hypothermia.

"Put it around her. It's not much, but it'll do something."

"Thank you," Yusuf whispers.

The sky is gray, matching the sea, and if it wasn't such a

dire situation, I'd have enjoyed this weather. I wouldn't be malnourished; instead I'd be covered in coats and scarves with a piping cup of tea in my hands.

My eyes wander to the other people traveling with us. There are more children than adults. My heart jolts when I spot a pregnant woman, and I look away before she catches me staring. Kenan groans quietly, and I for one sick moment am happy for the distraction.

"What's wrong?" I ask, twisting to look at him.

"I'm fine." He closes his eyes, breathing in deeply. I hope the concussion is letting go of its hold on him. "Can—can you give me Panadol?"

"Yes!" I quickly go through my bag and take out one tablet, pass it to him discreetly. He immediately pops it in his mouth, swallowing with no water. The exhaustion from moving the heavy debris after being kicked and beaten and not having enough sleep is catching up to him. Not to mention our wet clothes aren't helping.

Kenan catches my worried expression and smiles, pulling me against him and our shivering lessens. "I'm fine. Don't worry. Dr. Ziad checked me." He gestures at his face, which is still swollen and bruised. "They're just annoying bruises."

"Do you feel nauseous? A headache?" I take out my phone and shine the light in his eyes. They react normally.

"No, Dr. Salama," he says like a dutiful patient. "I just want to sit here with my wife." He rubs his hand over my arm. "You're cold."

I relent. He really is just tired.

"A bit," I admit, happy he's holding me. "Do you want me to tell you something good?"

"Yes, please."

"I have a new story idea."

I look up at him and there's a twinkle in his eyes. The tension lessens in his brows. "Tell me."

"It came to me before we left home. When I was looking at Layla's painting."

"It's a beautiful painting."

I pat his cheek, and he leans against my palm. "It's a story about a little girl who stumbles on magical portraits that take her to alternate universes. But to cross through, she has to sacrifice something valuable."

He stays silent for a few seconds and then softly says, "I don't want to illustrate this. I want to animate it."

I smile. "*Another* collaboration?"

"It would be my honor to work with the genius herself again."

"Praise me some more and you have a deal."

He laughs lightly and I'm glad to be able to draw his mind away from the terror of the drive here. "Salama, love of my life. My sky, my sun, my moon, and my stars, would you grant this mortal wish of mine?"

I pretend to think about it while my ears burn. "Okay, fine."

"We're leaving now!" the captain calls, and we fall back to reality. The whispering disappears and, as if in unison, all of us look back at the shore.

The boat starts to rock away gently, the waves lapping against its body, trying to find holes through which to enter. I know how to swim. Baba taught me and Hamza. Kenan told me he and his siblings do too. But I don't want us to test our strengths against the sea's. Not today.

For once the humming in my brain stops, and I don't hear anything but the sea and the mourning of my country. I raise my head to get a good, long look at Syria.

My eyes wander on the shore, desperately trying to memorize its features before it disappears, and just there, I see a girl about eight, laughing, running along the beach, her pink dress looking so out of place. Her curly brown hair falls below her shoulders, and when she looks toward me, she grins. I know that face, and the missing front tooth, because I have photos of me looking like that. Ten years will do a lot to the cheeky twinkle in that girl's eyes. Ten years will teach her how to survive. It'll wedge Syria's soil under her fingernails. Despite being a pharmacist, she'll know some wounds will never heal.

I blink and she disappears.

A song begins. One of the revolution's songs that compares Syria to Heaven. *Heaven.* I listen as if it's the first time I've heard it. I take in the words and tattoo them on my heart. And I realize I'm not hallucinating the song—everyone on the boat is singing. My throat becomes tight as the hoarse voices mingle with the wind, carrying our melody to the heavens. I can hear the tears fall down their cheeks and I can taste them in my mouth. They're as salty as the sea.

Soon enough, my voice joins theirs, and I sing through my own silent sobbing that drips, drips, drips to the boat's floorboards, sinking into the old wood. Even Yusuf sings, his voice bruised from underuse.

By the end of it, we're all craning our necks back toward Syria as she vanishes slowly behind us. Kenan leans on my shoulder, trying to get a better look, and his tears drop on my hand. I look up at him and I realize we really are Syria now. Just like I told him. Our small family is all that's left to remember our country by. I hug him, crying, and he cries too.

We don't blink; we don't look away until we can't see her anymore.

At first i don't notice how cold it has got- ten. I blame it on the adrenaline swimming lazily in my blood, which perks up when Kenan brushes against me or I hear a loud wave crashing over the side. The other passengers are huddled beside one another, their faces wet with tears, each lost in their own agony. They rub their hands to try and conjure up some warmth. I'm relieved to see Lama is fine, despite the bite of the cold. But Kenan worries me. His eyes droop, and his head nods like he's about to fall asleep.

"Hey," I whisper, moving over a bit to create more space. "Sleep on my shoulder."

He glances up and shakes his head, but when I grab the front of his sweater and guide him down he offers no resis- tance. My bony shoulder is not much of a cushion but at least my hijab is soft.

"Salama," he whispers. "I'm fin—"

"Shh. We're one step closer to eating knafeh. Dream about that."

He sighs and it takes him all of three seconds to fall asleep. I pray the Panadol eases his pain.

I look up to the sky, watching it slowly swap its colors for dark gray, signaling the end of my old life and the beginning of an unknown one. I distract myself by watching the clouds take their time dissipating after the sun, like handmaidens following their queen. The moon rises instead, throwing his haunting glow down onto the black water. The waves rock gently against the boat, their vibrations spreading through the metal until they reach my skin.

People have started to drift off one by one. But my mind, despite being more drained than it has ever been, is wide awake. I can't stop watching the stars emerge through the darkness, and I realize that the last time I saw these constellations I was with Kenan in the abandoned ruins of my home. It's hard to believe it happened less than a week ago. It feels like years. Eons.

I focus on the stars, connecting them with imaginary lines until I really see the silvery thread my mind is conjuring.

He's here. I look down to find him sitting on the edge of the boat, dangling his feet in the water, his back to me.

"Quiet night," he remarks, and I shiver. He looks painfully beautiful in the moonlight's shadow. My heart jumps.

"What are you doing here?" I frown. "Didn't you say you're bound to Syria?"

He turns my way, swinging his legs inside. "So eager to get rid of me?"

"I'm sorry; I didn't have time to mourn your absence, what with being terrified out of my mind the whole way here," I snap, even though my being here at all was only made possible by his influence. By my brain taking charge.

He smiles.

"Did you lie to me?" I ask. Will he really keep his promise and leave me alone? I shudder, thinking about waking up one random morning in Germany only to find him hovering at the foot of my bed.

He shakes his head. "We're still in Syrian waters."

I glare at him.

"I won't be with you in Syracuse. I promise," he says with a laugh.

I ponder his words. "That's not true," I whisper. "You're a part of me just as you're a part of everyone here."

He gestures to the darkness. "And all those claimed by the sea. All those who have become bone and dust." He sighs. "It's true. I told you before, when you asked me where I'd go. I'm everywhere. But I won't be there with you physically. Not like in Syria."

I shiver. "Everywhere," I say, tasting the word on my tongue. The answer to his existence was there all along.

I can see history woven between his irises. "Everywhere. Since the beginning of time, I have awoken in people's hearts. I've been given many names in countless languages. In yours, I'm Khawf. In English, Fear. In German, Angst. Humans have listened to my whispers, heeded my council, and tasted my power. I'm everywhere. In the breaths of a king executed by his people. In the last heartbeats of a soldier bleeding out alone. In the tears of a pregnant girl dying at her doorstep."

I look away, wiping an arm over my eyes. Layla. My sister.

Khawf says gently, "It wasn't your fault."

"Then why does it feel like it was?" I whisper, letting my tears trickle down my cheeks. Grief isn't constant. It wavers, tugging and letting go like the waves on the sea.

He smiles sadly. "Because you're human. Because no matter what, you have a heart so soft it easily bruises. Because you *feel*."

A low cry escapes me.

"But it's not your fault," Khawf continues. "Remember what Am said? If you're meant to be in Munich, you'll be there, even if the whole world is against you. Because it's your fate. It wasn't Layla's. It wasn't your parents' or Hamza's either."

Fate. A complex word that holds many doors leading to countless pathways in life, all controlled by our actions. And so, I hold on to my faith—in knowing that both Layla and I went above and beyond to survive. In knowing she's in Heaven—alive with Baby Salama. In knowing I'll see her insh'Allah when it's my time. That I'll see Mama, Baba, and Hamza.

"In my heart, I know it's not my fault," I murmur, glancing up at the pearl-encrusted skies. I'd give anything to hug Layla right now. "But it's going to take a while for my mind to accept that. And it hurts. More than I can bear. I just . . . miss her so much."

"I know."

Khawf suddenly stands up, and my heart jumps to see him balanced on the railing, whispers away from falling. But his posture is straight, perfectly balanced.

"You've grown this past year, Salama. I'm rooting for you, you know. You've overcome so many struggles and I'm humbled by them. You might not consider me a friend, but I think of you as one."

"You're leaving?" I ask, my stomach dropping.

He laughs and looks at me. "You look so crestfallen!"

"I'm not," I murmur, but all the same, a blanket of melancholy engulfs me. Without Khawf, I would be buried somewhere in Homs where no one would remember me. Without Layla's appearing to me, I wouldn't have found the courage to live for Syria. To fight for my country.

He sweeps his hair to the side, his eyes the shade of hydrangea petals. "I've done my job. I got you on the boat. Whatever happens next is up to you. But no matter what it is, I'm proud of you." He stretches one leg behind him, giving me a small bow.

"Goodbye," I whisper, and when I blink, he's gone.

I stare at the place he vanished from, thinking he might appear again, but he doesn't. I raise my hands, glance at them, searching my soul for any difference, and I find it in the way my heart feels a bit lighter. Something in the air has changed as well. Like reality sharpening and settling into place.

Kenan shifts, lifting his head up, his eyelashes fluttering sleepily.

"Hey," I whisper, tilting toward him and pressing a palm on his forehead. Warm, but not too warm. "How are you feeling?"

He grimaces. "Slightly seasick."

Lama and Yusuf are fast asleep, their heads slumped over their backpacks, and I'm glad. If they were awake, they'd also be suffering from the nausea.

"Let me get a lemon." I take one out along with the knife from Kenan's bag, cut it into wedges, and pass him a piece. I nibble on my slice, relishing the sour taste.

I settle back beside Kenan. "How's your back? Chest? Head? I saw what the soldiers did to you."

He bites at the lemon, his expression scrunching from its acidity, and coughs. "They're fine."

"Kenan."

He sighs. "The Panadol helped for a bit, though it still hurts."

One-gram Panadols can only be taken every four hours, or else there's a risk of toxicity. He took one less than two hours ago before he fell asleep.

I decide to distract him instead. "Khawf is gone."

"Forever?"

"More or less."

"Well, good," he says, satisfied. "Because now I can tell you I didn't like him."

I clasp a hand over my mouth, laughing silently. "Were you jealous?"

A faint smile pulls at his lips. "Actually, I wanted to punch him for annoying you, but I didn't want you to think he bothered me. Or to remind you of him when he wasn't there."

"Ah, my hero."

He grins. "I try."

I nestle closer, and we finish up our lemon wedges.

"Tell me something good, Salama," he murmurs, pressing his head against mine.

"For the past year," I begin slowly, "Syria was gray. The destroyed buildings and roads. The ashy faces of the starving.

Sometimes the skies. Our life *literally* became monochrome, alternating with a harsh red. While some were able to see past it, I forgot other colors existed. I forgot happiness was a possibility. But when you showed me that sunset on your roof and I saw pink and purple and blue . . . it felt like . . . like I was seeing color for the first time." I glance at him and see his eyes glittering with emotion.

"Imagine what Germany will be like," I continue. "Imagine painting our apartment blue like Layla's painting. And I was thinking we'd draw a map of Syria on one wall."

"I love it," Kenan says instantly. "I love you."

I smile, and in that moment I know Layla would be beaming, her eyes sparkling with happy tears, if she could see me like this: stranded in the middle of the Mediterranean Sea, the cold water trying to sneak under my clothes, and rather than letting my terror take the reins, I choose to focus on a future where I'm alive. Where I'm safe.

I wake up with a jolt. How long was I asleep? The lemon's effect must have worn off, because my stomach flips and nausea sours my blood.

People's shapes dip in and out of my vision, and their voices are dim in my ears. I rub my eyes, groaning from the cramps, and when I open them again, everything tumbles sharply into place. It must be morning by now but the sun is hidden behind thick clouds. Someone shakes me, and I turn to Kenan.

"What?" I ask groggily. A scream pierces the air, and it wakes me from my stupor.

Kenan grips my shoulder tightly, and in a measured voice I don't recognize, he says, "Salama, the weather is bad."

He suppresses a shiver, and I crane my neck to study the sea. Aided by the wind, the waves are throwing themselves hard against the boat, rocking it and my heart as well.

"There's a lot of people. The boat isn't new. It can't handle all of us. We don't have time," he says calmly, but the terror is more than visible in his words.

I don't understand. This boat has made the trip countless times. Am promised!

Kenan pulls me back. The bruise under his eye looks ink black.

"When the boat goes down, you have to stay as close to me as you can, do you understand?" he says firmly.

Lama is crying, and she isn't the only one. The screaming, pleading, and praying are deafening—I wonder whether the sounds have reached land.

"How far are we from Italy?" I ask.

"The captain is trying to signal them right now," Kenan says. "Even if they come, it'll be hours. We'll already be in the water."

I press my hand against his forehead. Warm.

"The water's freezing. You're exhausted and maybe even feverish. If you go in, I don't know what it'll do to your system." *He'll get hypothermia.* My heart beats painfully against my chest.

He shakes his head. "We don't have a choice."

"Life rafts?"

"Salama, this is a fishing boat. It isn't meant to survive more than a few hours offshore. *There are no life rafts.*"

I must be showing signs of distress because Kenan cups my cheek with one hand and draws me closer to him.

"Have faith," he whispers. "We'll make it. Stay close to me and *have faith*."

I nod, squeezing a few tears out. He straightens up and eyes his siblings, who are so petrified they can't move.

"All right, you guys," he says, and I'm astounded at how calm he is. "I need you to stick together, and once we're in the water, kick your legs just a little to stay up, okay? Your life jackets will do the rest. It's important you don't panic. Take deep breaths, and insh'Allah we'll be fine."

Lama clings to Yusuf and they both nod. I strap my backpack inside my life jacket and my heart sinks—I know that when we go underwater my passport and certificate won't survive. The sky looks near, as if promising to drown us in its dark gray as well.

Most of the people are already standing, so Kenan tells us to do the same. The boat tilts dangerously to the left, and we lose our footing, stumbling to the floor. People scream. One mother is in hysterics, holding her baby to her chest, and I look away. I can't help anyone. My head sways with each motion the boat takes, and the water drenches us whole as the threat of tipping over increases. I grip Kenan's hand, and Lama and Yusuf crowd against him as the boat lurches and other people push against us.

We wait, not knowing what to do. *Should we jump? Or stay on the boat until it goes down? Think, Salama, think!*

Suddenly one voice, cutting like glass, rings in my head, warning me not to jump.

Don't do it, Khawf's voice resounds in my mind. *It's suicidal. You don't know what's waiting for you in the water. The boat is safer. The more people jump, the more likely it won't sink. Don't jump.*

I close my eyes and breathe through my nose, visualizing my daisies. Khawf isn't *here*, but he lives in my head, always making me second-guess *every* decision. But that's no way to survive—no way to live.

"Kenan," I say. Tears begin streaming down my face. *The end is near.* "We need to jump. When the boat goes down, it'll create a current we won't be able to swim against."

He looks at me and nods solemnly. The waves lapping at the sides of the boat promise violence. Perhaps a bomb would have been the better choice.

Suddenly, one man carrying his daughter jumps out of the boat and into the water. She clings to his back, sobbing, and he's using all of his energy to get away. It takes everyone exactly five seconds to follow suit.

Kenan grasps my hand tightly. We both nod.

"Now," he says.

39

THE COLD REMINDS ME OF LAST DECEMBER, WHEN I came back from the hospital dripping with snow and sleet. Layla was on the couch, wearing *all* her clothes. I had huddled up beside my hallucination and fallen asleep, thinking I was warming myself, but the cold just continued to coat my bones, forcing itself inside.

But despite its familiarity, this cold doesn't lull me to sleep. Instead, it sends shock wave after shock wave through my body. I sink under the sea, opening my eyes to the dark blue-black that stretches on for miles.

Fear grapples with me. My heart seizes, my trachea constricts, and my extremities are so cold they burn. Before I can scream, my life jacket shoots me out of the water.

"*Mama*," I cry without thinking. "Mama, *save me!*"

I kick my legs in the water, the fear dissolving into hysteria. It chokes out of me in broken sobs when I remember there are sharks in the Mediterranean.

"Mama," I chant, holding on to that one word and letting

it expand and wash over me. "Mama. *Mama*. Please, *please* save me. *Please*. I can't do this anymore!"

At this moment, I'm half crazed, kicking my legs to keep sharks at bay—as if it would be of any help against their razor teeth and soulless eyes. Every thought disappears. I'm forgetting my name and who I was with. Who I'm supposed to be with. All I can think of is how I'm going to be dragged down.

"Salama!" A voice cuts through the hysteria and I clumsily try to turn around, hot tears streaming down my cheeks. The cold sears right to my ribs. It hurts to breathe.

Blurry figures become sharp and I see a bobbing person with terrified eyes. Yusuf. And just behind him is Lama.

My heart resets. Yes. I can't lose myself. My family is here. Yusuf. Lama. And Kenan.

Kenan.

Where is he?

"Lama! Yusuf!" The pressure of the water must have wrenched my hand out of Kenan's. All around, people are swimming, looking for their loved ones, and familiar screams rise on the frigid wind. My bag is still trapped under my life jacket. "Where's Kenan?"

"I don't know," Lama sobs.

"*Kenan!* Where are you?" I shriek. *God, please let him live. He's had enough.*

I swivel helplessly, my eyes jumping from one body to the next, but I only see strangers.

"We need to get away from the boat," I say. I look back and it's starting to sink. They nod and with effort try to swim after me. We keep looking, calling out for Kenan. I splash around, my life jacket making it impossible to easily move. I strain, searching the boat with my eyes, but there's no one.

"There!" Lama screams, pointing at a floating figure. Both his arms are spread out like he's trying to embrace the sea, and his head droops to the side. I make my way to him and brush his hair out of his face to make sure it's him.

"Oh, thank God," I exclaim, hugging him close. "He's here. It's him!"

Awkwardly, I try to check his pulse. It's weaker than I'd like. The shock of the water must have thrown him unconscious, and he can't stay like that for long. His face is ice cold.

"Is he okay?" Yusuf asks, and I lift Kenan's head. His neck muscles are completely slack.

"He's unconscious," I say, and I hear the boat finally going below, but I can't care about that right now. "Kenan. Wake up!"

After minutes of slapping his face and praying to God, his eyes flutter open, and he mumbles something incoherent.

"Hey," I say gently, grasping his cheeks and then grabbing one hand to see that his fingers have taken on a blue hue.

"Hey," he whispers.

"We're in the water. The boat just went down, and you were unconscious. You can't fall asleep. Do you understand?"

"Yes," he says foggily and grimaces from the cold.

"All right, everyone," I call out, looping my hand under Kenan's life jacket. "We need to head to where the others are and see if the captain made contact with the Italian coast guard."

"I'm cold," Lama sniffs.

"That's the other thing. I need you all to keep moving. Keep the blood flowing. Or else you'll fall asleep, and that's not good."

They mumble a *yes*, and we swim slowly toward the cluster of floating survivors. One man is splashing desperately and screaming for his young son. We paddle beside bodies, either corpses or unconscious, I don't know, and I can't stop to find out.

". . . contact and told them, but I don't know when they're coming," the captain is shouting to the frenzied crowd. "We're far from shore. They'll take a while to reach us. Hours at least."

The small flame of hope in everyone's eyes flickers like a dying candle. No one cares about a bunch of Syrian refugees stranded in the middle of the Mediterranean Sea. We aren't the first or the last people to do this. So what if a hundred or so meet their deaths? It'll make a nice headline to spur a small protest or donation campaign before we're forgotten again like foam on the sea. No one will remember our names. No one will know our story.

"K-Kenan," I falter. "D-d-don't s-sleep!"

He nods his head, but it's taking every ounce of energy he has to stay awake. I pull him close and try to encourage him to kick his legs. The life jacket is the only thing keeping him up, and it's barely doing so. The clouds curdle even more until it feels like we're surrounded by sea and sky. Not a single ray reaches us.

"Lama. Yusuf. Keep on moving," I stutter an order. "Help will come."

"I'm tired," Lama whines, half-heartedly shimmying in the water. Yusuf kicks his legs and arms for a minute before surrendering.

"*No*," I yell, pulling myself closer to them with Kenan's arm encircled in mine. "Keep. *Moving!*"

Yusuf takes a hold of Lama's hands and starts shaking them, sending ripples along the water.

"We'll be fine," I babble, focusing on my words and not the hypothermia slowly shutting down each cell. Slowly killing me. I try not to think of the sharks. *"We'll be fine."*

Some people have already surrendered to the cold, their screaming and crying dying out, and I know without looking that the Mediterranean Sea has claimed them for his own.

"Lama, talk to me." I lick the salt from my lips, and it burns my throat. It burns the cut on my neck.

"I'm okay." Her voice is barely audible.

"Yusuf?"

"Yes," he whispers.

I grab Kenan's shoulders and shake him, and he starts. "Kenan, don't you dare sleep."

"I won't," he says and coughs and kicks his legs for a bit. He brings his free hand behind my soaking hijab, pressing his forehead to mine.

The waves have slowly inched Lama and Yusuf away from us and we move closer again, forming a circle, holding hands.

"Good," I encourage. "Now, k-keep kicking!"

We create little froths on the sea's surface as the blood moves sluggishly in our veins. My clothes stick to my shivering body, my hijab slowly slips, but still, I keep kicking.

"Kenan, look at the colors," I say, and he gazes at the horizon.

There's nothing but gray sky and sea.

Not like the gray in Homs.

Gray like Layla's painting with blue scraped between the streaks.

I try to see the other shades, but the gray seems lodged in my retinal artery's cells. I tear my eyes to my family, memorizing their faces.

"Remember how in Ramadan the streets would be lit up with lanterns," I stutter, and they all look at me. "Don't think about the cold. Remember how warm the bread used to be. Fresh from the bakery."

Kenan joins in. "Lama. Yusuf. Remember when we used to go to the country. To Jedo's farmhouse and pick the apricots. How I'd climb up and toss them to you, Lama. Yusuf, remember when you found that pigeon's nest?"

Yusuf nods, teeth chattering.

"Each summer Layla and I would either stay at her grandparents' country house or mine," I whisper. "We'd swim in the pool. We'd play with the chickens. We even rode horses. Her grandfather took us to a neighbor who raised them."

I remember it so well. Fifteen years old and I'd just begun wearing my hijab. It fluttered in the wind as the horse galloped around the field with Layla on her own horse beside me. Our whoops of joy ringing over the horses' hooves.

Kenan continues to encourage his siblings to move and talk, to remember the past and to hope for the future, where new memories wait for them. He turns to me and raises my hand, and water droplets slip back into the sea.

"Salama, we'll have that knafeh." His cheeks are wet, and I know it's not just from the sea. His lips brush over my scarred knuckles. "If not in Germany, then in Heaven."

I swallow my tears, nodding.

We go back to talking, trying to focus on something that isn't the cold. We reminisce on our old life. Visualizing our Syria and painting a description of one we'll never see.

A Syria we'll never know.

An endless bed of green covers the hills, where the Orontes carries life into the ground, growing daisies along his banks. Trees bear lemons golden as the sun, apples firm and sweet, and plums ripe and glittering like rubies. Their branches are low, coaxing us to pluck the fruit. Birds sing the song of life, their wings fluttering against an azure-blue sky.

The countryside slowly dissolves as pavement replaces grass and the sounds of people bustling around the market drown the occasional bird's chirps. Merchants are selling satin dresses, rich, amethyst-purple Arabian rugs, and precious crystal vases. Restaurants overflow with families and couples taking advantage of a beautiful sunny day, platters of barbecued meat and bowls of tabbouleh laid in front of them. The athan rings loud from the minarets and people gather for prayer in the spacious, intricately designed mosques that have been standing there for centuries. Children run around our ancient ruins, reading the history of their ancestors woven between the limestone. They learn about the empires that once transformed their country into the beating heart of civilization. They visit the graves of our warriors, reciting Al-Fatiha for their souls and remembering their stories.

Keeping them alive in their memories. They take pride in their grandfathers and grandmothers, who laid down their lives so they could grow up in a land where the air is sweet with freedom.

Caught in the haze of hypothermia, I dream of that Syria.

A Syria whose soul isn't chained in iron, held captive by those who love to hurt her and her children. A Syria Hamza fought and bled for. A Syria Kenan dreams about and illustrates. A Syria Layla wanted to raise her daughter in. A Syria I would have found love and life and adventure in. A Syria where, at the end of a long life, I'd return to the ground that raised me. A Syria that's my home.

The day passes and I lose track of time. Darkness finally settles and I have no energy left, and my lips stop moving. The cold has invaded every nerve. I don't know if Kenan has stopped talking as well or if I've lost the ability to hear. It takes everything in me to remember where I am and that I need to breathe.

Somewhere in the distance, a glow of light suddenly appears. I blink, its harshness hurting my pupils. I blink again.

Am I dead?

EPILOGUE

A PALE LILAC BLOOMS ON THE HORIZON AS THE SUN slowly breaks through the darkness. September dawn in Toronto takes on many shades of the spectrum, but nowadays it seems to favor skipping from lilac to a bright blue while the stars quietly disappear.

I'm on the balcony, bathing in the soft glow and gazing at the corner I've transformed into a small garden. Daisies. Honeysuckle. Peonies. Lavender. I've grown them all myself, tending to their tiny roots and petals with care, murmuring words of love.

"You're so beautiful," I coo at a baby daisy shyly splaying out her petals against the scars on my hands. "I'm so proud of you."

A light breeze coaxes me to pull my blanket more tightly around my shoulders. Even though I'm in wool pajamas, the cold of the Mediterranean hasn't melted.

Kenan and I have been in Toronto for four months, and I still haven't gotten used to the chill. It's so different from

Berlin, but both have the same kind of quiet on a Saturday morning: one that's occasionally broken by the faint rumblings of a plane flying above. It took Kenan and me two years not to go sick with fear at those. And sometimes we still forget, the trauma coming back to us in the form of shaking hands and panic-filled eyes.

"There you are," Kenan says, shuffling outside with two mugs of steaming zhoorat tea.

I glance at him, smiling.

He's become more resistant to the cold and is dressed only in simple pajama pants and a white T-shirt. His hair is disheveled from bed and his eyes are still traced with sleep. It took a while and a lot of hard work, but both of us are now a healthy weight. I eye his biceps, feeling my cheeks warm up as he hands me my mug.

"Thank you," I whisper, not wanting to disturb the peace.

He sits beside me. I adjust the blanket so it's wrapped around us both and lay my head against his shoulder.

"You woke up early," he says quietly. "Bad dream?"

There are times when the nightmares trickle through our sleep like belladonna's poison. They startle Kenan awake; he gasps for air, sweat running down his forehead. They fill his head with paranoia, convincing him that Lama and Yusuf are trapped in Homs or drowning in the Mediterranean. Only when he calls his uncle in Germany to talk to them does he calm down. Only when I hold him to me and play with his hair, whispering "something good," does he relax and finally falls back asleep on my chest.

And while Khawf has disappeared from my life like a

fever dream, the nightmares have picked up where he left off. Their poison paralyzes me, and I'm trapped in my mind, screaming. At times, it takes Kenan a while to wake me, to convince me I'm *really* here, but his arms are always there to hold me steady—to bring me back.

Kenan laces his fingers through mine and kisses the side of my head. "We promised we'd talk to each other, Sheeta."

I turn to him, eyes softening. We did. And when we don't know how to find the words, we have others to help us. A quiet room with a sympathetic woman looking at us over her round glasses. She smiles kindly, and the way her eyes twinkle reminds me of Nour. When the conversation becomes difficult, all I need to do to ease the heaviness is remember the way she used to say "ther-a-pee."

As soon as Kenan and I settled in Berlin with his aunt and uncle, the shock of what we went through slowly melted into a pain that became more difficult to talk about with each passing day. Layla, Mama, and Baba are buried in Homs. For a while I forgot how to breathe through the agony over Hamza's life in Syria.

I absently touch the scar on my neck. While the one at the back of my head is covered by my hair, this one isn't easy to ignore. It looks like a choker, and when my thoughts become dark, I can almost feel it tightening around my throat. Kenan looks at it, realization creasing in his eyes.

He sets his mug down before lowering his head to kiss the scar. I link my arms around his shoulders, hugging him close.

"Any plans today?" I murmur.

He breaks away, cheeks pink. "I'm meeting Tariq to

make sure everything's going okay with our university acceptance."

"Of all the futures I envisioned for us, living and attending university in Toronto was not one of them."

He grins. "Not a bad plot twist."

It's all been made possible by one of Hamza's friends. Shortly before the revolution started, one of his close high school friends moved to Canada to study medicine. Now a Canadian citizen, he offered to sponsor our move to Toronto. Help us continue our education, find jobs, and live a good, safe life. We connected after I revived my Facebook account in Berlin, where distant family and friends extended all sorts of help.

When Tariq reached out, Kenan and I sat down and studied it from all angles. We know more English than German. In terms of animation, Canada has more options, and I instantly fell in love with the university's pharmacy program. Yusuf and Lama were adapting well to their German schools and life, their aunt and uncle stepping in like they were their own children. It would just be Kenan and me leaving. For now. We're too young to care for two children. And I know it breaks Kenan's heart every single day to be apart from them. But being a refugee limits our options, and I also know that our situation is far better than so many other Syrian families because we have Kenan's aunt and uncle. Families with no relatives living in diaspora are usually torn apart, scattered over a few countries depending on which accepts them.

Kenan hasn't changed his phone's lock screen from Lama and Yusuf, though the background is him and me. He calls them every single day and has been planning how he'll be able to fly to Germany to see them.

"I can't believe university starts in a week." I shake my head. "I can't believe we're sitting here drinking zhoorat three years later."

"I can't believe you're with me." He kisses the wedding ring on my finger, then kisses along one scar sliced into my wrist. "How did I score someone so out of my league?"

I chuckle. "You seduced me with all your Studio Ghibli facts."

He grins. "Miyazaki doesn't use scripts in his movies. He comes up with the dialogue as he goes along."

I act all flustered, fanning myself. "Oh my God!"

He laughs and we finish up our tea. As soon as the sun's light has engulfed the sky, we go back inside.

It's a small one-bedroom apartment but it's home. A few boxes still clutter the floor. Tariq and his friends furnished the apartment for us, and I had to hide in the bathroom to cry from gratitude for a solid ten minutes before I could face anyone.

Sprawled across the dining table are Kenan's sketch-books, all filled with drawings of our stories. Next to them is a half-empty knafeh pan. The charcoal portrait he drew of me at the Brandenburg Gate is enclosed in a wooden frame, hanging over the couch in the living room. The walls are a canvas for our imagination, and we've splashed the white with different shades of blue. One wall hosts Kenan's ongoing work of a map of Syria, while I etched a Nizar Qabbani poem along the surface of the other because it turns out my calligraphy is better than his. It's one I saw at the revolution's anniversary protest.

كلُّ ليمونةٍ ستنجب طفلاً ومحال أن ينتهي الليمونُ

"Every lemon will bring forth a child, and the lemons will never die out."

We place the mugs in the sink, discussing the various elements of storytelling used in *Princess Mononoke*. I open a cupboard to take out a breakfast bar. Each cupboard is stocked to the brim with bags of rice, freekeh, canned hummus, and kashk. I finish up the whole bar, not even leaving a crumb, before throwing the wrapper in the trash.

Kenan takes a chicken out of the freezer to let it defrost and I find myself marveling at the fact we have a *whole* chicken.

While Hamza doesn't.

Daily, I scour Facebook and Twitter pages that post regular updates on the prisoners in the Syrian detention facilities that have been released, as well as those that have information on prisoners still inside. I look for Hamza's name until my eyes cross, but he never shows up. And in my heart, I pray he's become a martyr. I pray he's with Layla in Heaven, far away from this cruel world.

I glance away and feel Kenan's hand on my cheek.

"Hey," he whispers, knowing what's on my mind. "It's okay."

I shudder in a breath, nodding before walking into the living room. To distract myself, I contemplate whether to read a pharmaceutical book or work on a new video. After arriving in Berlin, Kenan picked up where he left off with his activism and, after a few more videos, he began to garner the world's attention. I practiced my English by joining him, writing articles and making videos about what we faced in Homs. I threaded our stories together, and at first it was difficult. I'd burst into tears five seconds into a monologue, remembering the feel of a corpse's cold body.

Kenan catches my arm, spinning me around, and I fall against his chest, surprised.

"*Whoa!* What are you doing?"

He smiles, holding up his phone. An English song I don't know croons out. "Dancing with my wife."

My eyes burn. We weave distractions between the bouts of agony. Reminding the other we're still here.

He drops the phone on the couch beside his laptop, swaying me with the music.

"I'm in my pajamas," I mumble, pressing my forehead to his collarbone.

He shrugs. "So am I." He twirls a finger through a lock of my hair, now cut short to my chin. "You're beautiful in your pajamas."

"So are you."

He laughs. In the distance, we hear the low rumble of a plane and I don't miss the way Kenan's hand tightens in mine for a fraction of a second.

"What do you think of our new family addition?" I draw him back to me.

He glances at the balcony. "We've had her for two months now and we've barely seen more than a green blade."

I laugh. "Lemons take time, Kenan. We're growing a *tree*. They need patience, just like change does."

He gives me a lopsided smile. "I love it when you talk about change."

I giggle and he rests his forehead on my shoulder, humming to the music.

My eyes wander over his shoulder to the blue ceramic pot perched directly under the sun's rays. Seedlings have emerged through the dirt, fighting against gravity, and it reminds me of Syria. Of her strength and beauty. Of Layla's words and her spirit. Of Mama, Baba, and Hamza.

It reminds me that as long as the lemon trees grow, hope will never die.

AUTHOR'S NOTE

THIS STORY IS ABOUT THE ONES WHO HAVE NO choice but to leave their home.

The idea came to me when I was living in Switzerland, where, when someone found out I'm Syrian, I would be met with "Oh, Syria! What's up with that?" and I realized that people don't really know what's happening there. Syrians have rarely been able to tell their stories. What the world knows are the cold, hard facts reported by the media and relayed in books. The focus is on the political parties at play, reducing Syrians—the casualties, the victims, the orphans, the displaced—to numbers.

This novel delves into the human emotion behind the conflict, because we are not numbers. For years Syrians have been tortured, murdered, and banished from their country at the hands of a tyrannical regime, and we owe it to them to know their stories.

I wanted this story to exist free from the confinements of stereotypes. You see that intent in Salama and Layla—hijabi girls who are free-spirited and live life with every cell in their body. You see it in Kenan, who turns his back on toxic masculinity and carries his family in his eyes. In how all of my characters love who they are and where they come from and are willing to risk everything for freedom. You see it in the halal love story that I wanted to be reminiscent of Jane Austen's classics. Simply put, you see representation that has rarely been shown before.

To shine as bright a light as I could on the reality of *Syria's* story, I had to take some literary liberties with the passage of time in Salama's. The revolution started in March 2011 and though it was met with horrific violence from the military, they didn't start bombing civilians until June 2012. But I have condensed the timeline between these two incidents so that they are contained within the span of Layla's pregnancy. Ghiath Matar was arrested on September 6, 2011, in his hometown, Daraya, and his mutilated body was returned to his family four days later. His son, whom he never met as his wife was pregnant at the time, is named after him. Ghiath Matar was twenty-four years old. And while I allude to the Karam el-Zeitoun Massacre in chapter twenty-one, in reality it didn't take place until March 11, 2012. And it is one of countless massacres the regime has committed on the innocent.

The events themselves, though, are all true. There really was a child who, before he died, said, "I will tell God everything." These stories have happened, and more are unfolding as you read these words.

But, despite the atrocities my characters have to face, I hope you see them as more than their trauma. They represent every Syrian out there with hopes and dreams, and a life to live. We are *owed* that life.

This book was very difficult to write, but I tried to weave one message through every page, every line, and every letter.

That message is hope.

And I *hope* you carry it in your heart.

ACKNOWLEDGMENTS

Reader, there's a reason authors write acknowledgments, and it's because a book is born from a thought and is raised by a family. And "*ohana* means family. Family means no one gets left behind or forgotten" (*Lilo & Stitch*, 2002).

Lemon Trees was just that. A thought. A need to shout from the mountains of an injustice befalling millions. Until she found a home with so many, encouraging her to grow from a whisper to a battle cry.

So, to *Lemon Trees*' family, without you, readers wouldn't be flipping through her pages.

First off, to Batool, my sister, my number one fan. Thank you for reading the entirety of *Lemon Trees* in the form of WhatsApp texts. For telling me to go for it. You believed in me even when I didn't. I became an author because of you.

To my mama, Ola Mohaisen, my best friend and so precious in my heart. No one is more happy for me than you. It was a long journey that brought us to this point and we both learned so much.

When I first began writing this book, my life was moving in slow motion while everyone around me was having life happen to them at twice the speed. Because of this, Mama wanted me to put my writing on hold until I got my German language certificate, until I was safely accepted into graduate studies . . . etc. etc. But I didn't listen. I know a lot of young authors out there sometimes find it scary to write. To try and make it a part of their life. I know I would have wanted to hear encouraging words when I first started. And because of that, I asked Mama to say something to all the parents out there who have their doubts.

"It's probably easy to claim I took on a fully supportive parental role during the period of time Zoulfa decided to set on her avant-garde book-writing journey, but it would not be the truth that I feel obliged to share with all parents out there. It would be easy to assert unwavering trust, blind belief, and unconditional encouragement, but it would not be an accurate depiction of my response to her inclinations during a critical turning point for our family, standing at a crossroads in a new country. I tried to set her priorities for her, acted on the impulse of a mother's first instinct and dismissed, at least temporarily, her languishing desire to write her story. But I was wrong, and I am glad she was right. It would be easy to not say anything at all, but I hope for these words to reassure at least one skeptical parent: plant a seed of trust, nurture it with humility and patience, and if you do so despite your doubts, you may be surprised with trees of lemon; their fragrance is unforgettable and ever so gratifying."

To my baba, Yasser Katouh, who is the reason I speak English. Every word written in my books happened because of you. You believed 110 percent that I would make it. Not 100 percent. 110 percent.

To my brother, Moussab, who supplied me with many chocolate bars and muffins and never forgot to bring me a sheesh tawouk sandwich. You cool, kid.

To the White Helmets, who risk their lives to save others. For embodying the Qur'anic verse *"save one life, and you would have saved all of mankind."* May God protect you for protecting us, may your hands never falter, and your souls never waver.

Alexandra Levick, I think if miracles were a person, they'd be you. Words can't express my gratitude to you and for that moment you clicked the favorite button on my pitch. One click changed my life. Thank you for being my agent—for being my friend. Thank you for making my dreams come true.

To Writers House for truly being the best house a writer can ask for. Thank you for believing in me. For believing in *Lemon Trees* and giving her all your best. A special thank you to Alessandra Birch, Cecilia de la Campa, and Jessica Berger for all that you do for foreign rights. You guys are amazing!

To Ruqayyah Daud, who took a chance on my lemon babies. I still cannot believe that you read it in one night. You lit the spark that started this all. Thank you for not just being my editor but also my friend who I can yell with about BTS. I purple you!

To everyone in Little, Brown, you made a one girl's dream become reality. To Patrick Hulse, Sasha Illingworth, and David Caplan in Design. To Jessica Mercado, Allison Broeils, and Nisha Panchal-Terhune in Marketing Design. To Shanese Mullins, Stefanie Hoffman, Savannah Kennelly, and Emilie Polster in Marketing. To Cheryl Lew, my superhero, rock star publicist. To Hannah Klein and Marisa Russel in Publicity. To Victoria Stapleton and Christie Michel working in School and Library. To Andy Ball, Annie McDonnell, and Caroline Clouse, my amazing copyeditor. To Virginia Lawther and Olivia Davis in Production. To Megan Tingley, Jackie Engel, Alvina Ling, and Tom Guerin in Publishing. To Shawn Foster and Danielle Canterella in Sales. I am eternally grateful to each one of you. Thank you for giving *Lemon Trees* a voice. I don't feel so alone anymore.

To my wonderful editor Hannah Sandford and everyone in Bloomsbury, who put time and love into transforming this book from a Word document to a physical copy. Thank you is a small word to how I feel. Literally, you are the best Bloomsberries in the world! Real talk: Eleven-year-old Zoulfa is shaking in her gym shoes.

To my publishers: Verus, Editorial Casals, Gyldendal, Blossom, Nathan, Dressler, Dioptra, Piemme, Poznanskie, Hayakawa, BookZone, and Laguna, thank you from the bottom of my heart for giving *Lemon Trees* a home in so many places. *Lemon Trees* in other languages was a distant dream I never thought would be possible, but you made it happen.

To Kassie Evashevski, my wonderful film agent, who saw something in my story. I'm still so humbled by all that you said about *Lemon Trees*.

A most heartfelt thank you to Beth Phelan for creating DVpit. You have transformed so many authors' lives out there. Thank you for doing that. Every change starts with one person. And your change has caused beautiful ripples in still waters.

To Author Mentor Match that brought so many writers

together and gave them a light to hold high while trekking through this side of life. To everyone in Writer's Club and the fond memories we made together. A special thanks to Alexa Donne for creating this community that gave me the best friends a writer can ask for.

To Joan F. Smith, I want to write your name in full so the whole world knows it. Joan F. Smith is a legend. Joan F. Smith has a heart bigger than the ocean. Joan F. Smith has the moon jealous of her. Joan F. Smith is my favorite person in the world. Joan F. Smith plucked my book from a sea of stories and said this one. Joan F. Smith saved my writing.

To Leah Jordain, a queen in her own right. I learned to love my characters through your eyes. Your eyes were the first ones aside from my mentor and an IRL friend to have read my words. To love them? I'm still in awe that you do.

To Safa Al Awad, who is more than a friend. Who's like my sister. I miss our long walks in Buhaira, our conversations that never end, and our crying over *Doctor Who* and *Agents of S.H.I.E.L.D.* And Everlark. And all the books! Thank you for loving Salama, Layla, and Kenan enough for the both of us. To Shahed Alsolh, who read the earliest of early drafts of this book. Who read *Lemon Trees* at least three times. Who supported me in every single part of my journey. Who read my messy writing and listened to my very, very long voice notes. You're truly an angel incarnate. I cherish you more than you know. To Rowad Al Awad, who may be a smol but is lorge at heart. I love you, my other half. Your support and your incessant faith in me are everything. I miss the days we spent in your room just talking and laughing. It was a simpler life. To Rawan Shehadeh, whose heart is softer than cotton candy. My best friend. My suster. You knew this book would become something solid when I thought it would always be abstract. To Aya Adel, my buddy. The way you and I share one brain cell. I live for our long talks, our adventures, and those sunset days at the beach where we read poetry and were truly living that aesthetic life. To Judy Albarazi, who loved my lemon babies enough to draw them. You're the angelest angel ever. To Amoon, who is a childhood friend writers write about in their books. I love how even the years couldn't break the string of friendship between us. To Miss Josephine, my favorite English teacher, who saw my love for books and encouraged it. To Tata Naima Hatti Dehbi, who sparked the flame of my reading journey. You are the butterfly effect.

To BBH/The Lemon Squad: Alina, Aliyah, Miranda, Rhea. You girls are my sanity. The English dictionary cannot possibly be able to describe the happiness and belonging I feel with you. I thank God every day for how our funny little group came to be. We were fated to be friends. No one is doing it like us. Literally. I adore you all. And we're so hilarious too? Like, wow, we really do have it all.

To FOG, Emily, Meryn, Page. I mean, what is there to say? We are four halves of the same brain cell, dancing around a flaming trashcan and cackling loudly. We are soups and peg and Yoon-gi's bb and melon. We are the beginning and the end. We are the stars. We are. We.

Emily, I think our brains are made from the same stardust. Thank you for existing. Meryn, your before and after pictures when you'd read *Lemon Trees* are *everything*. Page, you're the Dazai to my Suoh Tamaki.

To Kelly Andrew, who I love more than words can

describe. I'm incredibly lucky to have my favorite author be one of my closest friends. You, Meryn, and I are peanut butter, jelly, and premium bread. The chaos that goes on in our little group brings such serotonin that I can't believe we didn't know each other since forever.

To Brighton Rose, a rose in a field of daisies. You complete me. How beautiful is it that our characters are friends in an alternate universe we conjured up? Our minds! Our power! And the never-ending incorrect quotes we curated for them. To Kalie Holford, I am honored to be your friend and to know you before you take over the world. Your soul is as bright as the sun. To Allison Saft, who read *Lemon Trees* in ONE DAY (like? What?!). I love you and will always be *so* grateful for sliding into your DMs. I want to be your writing style when I grow up. To Chloe Gong, a queen with the kindest, softest heart who I'm incredibly lucky to know. You deserve the world, baby. To Rameela, a star that shines bright in the night sky. Salama, Layla, and Kenan adore you. As do I. To Molly X. Chang, it's a testimony to who we are that it was Kim Tae-hyung who brought us together. What a wonderful foundation for a wonderful friendship. To Braden Goyette, whose stories are going to change the literature landscape. Thanks for letting me be part of the ride! To Jen Elrod, my baby, I love you and our voice notes and our talks and everything that we do. I swear, rarely do I meet someone who just ~gets~ me. To Mallory Jones, an icon Yoon-gi would be proud to know. I cherish you. To the LBYR-H :P Maeeda Khan and Ream Shukairy. Maeeda, you are the sun. A whole galaxy. A universe. Ream, my buddy, my friend. I purple you. We're breaking down doors, baby :")

To Janina and Rae and our heartwarming writing sessions where we laughed more than we wrote. To Sabrina, who welcomed me, a new bébé, into NaNoWriMo and made me feel less alone. To Sebastian, who read the 130k words of pure pain and bad writing but still loved them. To Emma Patricia, Janice Davis, Jenna Miller, and Melody Robinette, you beautiful people are so beautiful. To Elizabeth Unseth, Jess Q. Sutanto, Kate Dylan, Marion Gabillard, Monica Arnaldo, Sarah Mughal, Shana Targosz, S.J. Whitby, Sophie Bianca, Yasmine Jibril, who are *Lemon Trees*' defenders. I deserved all the yelling I got. To Naz Kutub, who literally saved *Lemon Trees*. You really did do that. Without you, this journey would have been very different. A special thank you to Hannah Bahn, who so patiently put up with my questions. Thank you so much, love. Honorable mention goes out to Ayesha Basu. Your mind is as diabolical as mine. We love to see it. When I make it big, I'll ~~maybe~~ pass your contact info to Ji-min.

To Meredith Tate, who was there from the beginning of this journey. A friend I miss every day in the Starbucks we made ours. Switzerland is lonelier without you.

To S.K. Ali for all that you do for us. Thank you, thank you, thank you for Zayneb and Adam. Thank you for all your kind messages about *Lemon Trees*. They mean the world!

To Huda Fahmy, who is one of the most supportive people I have ever met. Thank you for being you and for your comics. I have never felt more seen in my life. My heart is so soft.

To Laura Taylor Namey for reading *Lemon Trees* in record time! Oh my goodness, I was so shook! Thank you for your beautiful words.

To Sabaa Tahir, whose existence makes the world a better place. We're all so blessed to be able to read your stories. Thank you for extending a bèbè like me a helping hand.

To Hafsah Faizal, who welcomed me in her DMs, answering question after question. Thank you for your patience—for all that you do.

To Zeyn Joukhadar, the very first author I crashed into his DMs. My heart was about to flutter out of my chest with pride at seeing a Syrian author writing about Syria. Thank you for giving me the strength to put *Lemon Trees* out there.

To Suzanne Collins for the blueprint that is Katniss Everdeen and Peeta Mellark. Without Everlark, there would be no Lemonblossom.

To David Curtis for giving me the cover of my dreams. Both times! There's a whole story in those covers alone and I thank you for illustrating *Lemon Trees*' soul *so* beautifully.

The most heartfelt and special thanks to Maia (twitter: @maiahee_) and Juliana (twitter/instagram: @joleanart) for bringing my characters to life in their art. I can't tell you how emotional it makes me seeing them. Thank you so much.

Thank you, Taylor Swift, for writing "marjorie." It took hearing it three times for me to realize why it felt so familiar. In those lyrics, I found Salama and Layla. My tears never stop falling every time I hear it. And also for "epiphany," which broke me. I mean . . . it's basically Salama *cries*.

To the Fray's "Run for Your Life." This song came out in 2012 and ten years later a book is published where the lyrics remind readers of two girls' friendship who lived, loved, and lost together.

A huge thank you to Dyathon, who weaves soundtracks made from magic. All of Salama and Kenan's scenes were written to "Wander." It's Lemonblossom's song. To Hans Zimmer, who has the power of transforming melancholy, happiness, sadness, loneliness, love, mourning, and belonging into music. To Marika Takeuchi and your heart-wrenching melody "Horizons." If *Lemon Trees* were a soundtrack, it would be "Horizons." I'm sure I'm responsible for more than half of those Spotify and YouTube streams. To HDSounDI, a gorgeous YouTube channel that elicits all sorts of emotions within me that help me write scenes that make me and readers cry. To BigRicePiano and your sweet melodies that accompanied me many rainy afternoons while I drafted and edited. To Hiroyuki Sawano for the *Attack on Titan* soundtracks. Many of *Lemon Trees'* emotional scenes were a product of me listening to the soundtracks over and over again. To Ólafur Arnalds and the melancholic beauty of your poetic songs.

To Ezgi Kalay and Ioanna Kastanioti and the solidarity friendship we have formed during this pandemic as students. To many more days of us strolling around Zürich, achieving our dreams and just kicking butt.

To Studio Ghibli, who welcomed a wide-eyed nine-year-old girl into their home, showered her with islands that fly, boys who turn into dragons, and the brave girls who save them. Thank you for my life. Your stories made me who I am.

To Kim Nam-joon, Kim Seok-jin, Min Yoon-gi, Jung Ho-seok, Park Ji-min, Kim Tae-hyung, and Jeon Jung-kook. You might not read this book, but I'll keep hoping you do. Nam-joon, it's going to be in two languages you speak, so my luck has gone up a few levels. But if this book does fall into one of your hands, let me just thank you. Thank you for being our purple whale. Your words and songs have comforted me when I was trying to gather myself in the spare moments between editing this book. It's a heavy one, and you reminded me that I never walk alone. You've inspired me, held my hand across continents, and wiped away my tears. Thank you for not giving up. Thank you for being the people in Seoul who understand me. We are bulletproof. 보라해요 and 감사합니다 <3

And thank you to you, dear reader. However you heard of this book, thank you for reading it. If you passed by it in a bookshop, liked the cover and picked it up, heard about it from a friend or Twitter, or saw me crying about it on main—thank you for reading it. Even if you didn't buy it, thank you for reading. All I ask is that you spread the word now that you have an idea of what's happening. Let's change the world together. And welcome to the *Lemon Trees* family.

Lastly, but most importantly, I thank the One Whose Eyes don't sleep for watching over me, guiding me with His Gentle Hand and giving my heart the peace and pride it feels. To You, I owe it all.

ZOULFA KATOUH

is a Syrian Canadian based in Switzerland. She is currently pursuing her master's in Drug Sciences and finds Studio Ghibli inspiration in the mountains, lakes, and stars surrounding her. When she's not talking to herself in the woodland forest, she's drinking iced coffee, baking aesthetic cookies and cakes, and telling everyone who would listen about how BTS paved the way. Her dream is to get Kim Nam-joon to read one of her books. If that happens, she will expire on the spot. *As Long as the Lemon Trees Grow* is her debut novel.